# MORE ACCLAIM FOR BRUCE BETHKE AND HEADCRASH

"A funny satire . . . from the man who coined the word 'cyberpunk'."
**—Denver Post**

"It made me laugh and think, which is about the highest compliment I can offer any book."
**—John Edwards, *CompuServe* magazine**

"Bruce Bethke has a rare gift. . . . His computer-driven, on-line, near-future society, colored with outrageous and decidedly loopy dialogue, is both hilarious and too close for comfort. I wish I had written this."
**—Lincoln Spector, GiggleBytes columnist, *PC World* magazine**

"Imagine if Monty Python had written *Soul of a New Machine* . . ."
**—Chuck Von Rospach, member of the Backbone Cabal (ret.)**

"HEADCRASH happily confirmed my worst fears about the future in general and the virtual world in particular. I couldn't stop laughing even while muttering, 'The horror! The horror!'"
**—George Alec Effinger, author of *When Gravity Fails***

"Watch out, Bruce Sterling, William Gibson, and John Shirley. Here comes Bruce Bethke. And he's got a chainsaw."
**—Joel Rosenberg, author of *The Road Home***

"My good news is that Bruce Bethke's 'meglomerated' PC future is at once enthralling, sexy, and very, very funny. My bad news is that it's all true—and only ten years away."
**—Gene Wolfe, author of *The Book of the Long Sun***

# HEADCRASH

## bruce bethke

**WARNER BOOKS**

A Time Warner Company

WARNER BOOKS EDITION

Copyright © 1995 by Bruce Bethke
All rights reserved.

Warner Books, Inc.
1271 Avenue of the Americas, New York, NY 10020
Visit our Web site at
http://warnerbooks.com

 A Time Warner Company

Printed in the United States of America
First Trade Printing: October 1997
10  9  8  7  6  5  4  3  2  1

Library of Congress Cataloging-in-Publication Data

Bethke, Bruce,
    Headcrash / Bruce Bethke. -- Warner Books ed.
        p.   cm.
    ISBN 0-446-67314-5
    I.  title.
    PS3552.E799H4    1997
    813' .54--dc21                                              97-21387
                                                                  CIP

Cover design by Susan Newman
Cover photograph by Dennis Galant and Sandra Lewis
Book design and text composition by H. Roberts Design

# HEADCRASH

```
C:\DOS
C:\DOS RUN
   RUN, DOS! RUN!
>exec com | type READ_ME.TXT
>BEGIN
>
```

*Jack Burroughs.*

Some say he was the best.

Some say he was a complete dork.

Some call him the coolest cybernetic sidewalk surfer ever to hang-ten on the shoulders of the Great Information Superhighway.

Others call him a total loser, completely lacking in even a rudimentary sense of personal hygiene.

Some have claimed he was a virtual *god:* a being of supreme power and intelligence who only reached his true final potential when he jacked in that ProctoProd™ and spread his personal mindware across twenty gigabytes of high-bandwidth laser dataspace.

Others have claimed that Marsha Vang, that cute little brunette down in Document Coding, actually went out on a date with him once, and he took her back to his room in his mother's basement and played "Weird Al" Yankovic tapes at her for four hours straight.

Some still say, "Jack Burroughs. I knew him when . . ."

Others say, *"Who?"*

This, then, is the definitive answer to that question. For a long time, all that we in the outside world knew of Jack came from his actions on the Net, and the occasional leaked memo from the Federal Information Agency security directorate. Then one day the attached file showed up on a public e-mail bulletin board in Tangiers, encrypted in the old ARGL_BARGL compression format and posted from an ancient twentieth-century hotel reservation system somewhere in the Hawaiian Islands.

Now, at long last, we know the true story of Jack Burroughs. Of his life, and apparent death. Of his incredible, and mostly imaginary, sexcapades. Of his impish, and some might say puerile, wit. Of his final, desperate, battle against the grinding forces of bloody corporate darkness, and his betrayal and abandonment by those he trusted most.

Here, then, for your enlightenment, we now present the complete and unexpurgated file, solely as a matter of public service. Consider it an object lesson in the utter, unchecked, absolute *evil* of the modern multinational corporation-state.


P.S. Inquiries from parties interested in purchasing the film and/or hypermedia rights to this story may be directed to our agent at a_graysn@adg.spedro.com.

# 1

---

# INIT

God, I miss my hypertyper.

I mean, if I still had that thing, I could code this all up in Rich Text Format, lard it down with hotkeys and hyperlinks, and make this sucker *dance*. You want to know how the story begins, you tap the backgrounder button and *zap*, Carl Sagan is in the upper right corner of your screen, saying, "Four and a half *bill*yun years ago, a great cloud of hot gas resembling President Gore's 2004 reelection speech—"

Okay, maybe that's a bit wide-focus. So you tap the closelook icon, and a thirty-second sample of Tom Petty's "Refugee" blasts through the audio channel, while the main data thread goes into an explanation of how Mom met Dad at a Heartbreakers concert at the Civic Center in 1980, resulting in me in '81, my sister in '84, a marriage in '85, and a divorce almost exactly six months to the day later. From there I could link out to the Mitchell Motor Vehicle database and give you a fair guess at the current collector's price for a mint condition 1979 Pontiac Trans-Am, as well as some insight into why Dad is *still* pissed he had to trade his in for something that could carry a stroller and two car seats.

But, no.

No, I'm reduced to working with this stupid, stinking, flat-file editor, banging out a simple linear text file—a *sequential* text file, for God's sake—so I have to pick an absolute rock-solid point of *beginning*, follow the thread through the middle . . .

And call me a Clipper-burned paranoid, but I have the strangest feeling that someone else is going to be writing the ending.

So, to begin. Where? If this was desktop video, I'd start with a sweeping, dizzying, panoramic virtual helicopter shot of a traffic jam on the Information Superhighway, or maybe with the audio of that message Gunnar left on my phone the night before it all hit the fan. (*"Meet me at the club tomorrow, 2300 hours. Your life depends on it."*) But why make a big deal out of that? Gunnar was *always* leaving me weird, paranoid messages.

So I guess the thing to do, finally, is just drive a stake in the time/space continuum, pick a point, and begin. **Monday**, **May 15, 2005**. It was a *crummy* day: dark gray clouds scudding by all low and overcast, the wind gusting through in fits and bursts, a hard spring rain beating down in fat, cold, drops. Our Wonderful MDE Corporate Management still hadn't repaired the bomb damage to the west entrance (the PPLF blew us up on April 15; said they really wanted to bomb an IRS building, but ours was more convenient), so I wound up having to park my '95 Toyota Rustcan out in the far reaches of the south lot, pull on my shoe condoms, and slog a quarter-mile through the cold rain and dead worms to the south entrance.

I was almost within sight of the door when Melinda Sharp came blasting by in her shiny new Dodge "Deathmaster," nailed the largest puddle in the entire lot, and left me wearing most of it. Screeched to a stop in her reserved, double-width, executive parking space; bailed out of the car and was sprinting for the door with a *Wall Street Journal* over her big blond hair before I had a chance to flip her off. By the time she was inside the Dodge had shut itself down, dimmed back its lights, retracted its steering wheel, raised and sealed its window armor—

And started threatening the rainstorm. "WARNING! THIS VEHICLE PROTECTED BY ARMED RESPONSE! *BACK OFF*!"

That, at least, broke me out of wondering why Melinda was in so early and let me start the day with a cheap laugh. Three trips back to the dealer and her new car *still* couldn't tell the difference between being broken into and being rained on. If it was following true to form, it was already using its on-board cellular phone to call the cops, and in about five minutes the MDE parking lot was going to be simply crawling with pissed-off police persons in soaking wet body armor.

I'd "accidentally" strayed into the personnel files a few weeks earlier and pulled her cost-of-benefits numbers. Up and coming Executive Tracker or no, sooner or later the company was going to *have* to make Melinda start paying her own false-alarm service charges, else we'd be Chapter 11 by July. Personally I had a lot of history with Melinda and couldn't wait to see her finally take the blame for one of her own messes.

And that was the wicked little thought that kept me warm as I splashed the last fifty yards to the south entrance. Just as I was about to step into the covered outside entryway—and into the full, clear view of the security cameras—I caught a furtive movement from the corner of my eye. Someone was lurking behind one of the pillars!

My reaction was purely reflexive. I had a brown belt in *schwartztortco* Victim Training; in the space of a heartbeat my breathing went fast and shallow, my knee joints locked up and wobbled, and my arms and hands went perfectly limp. My eyes and ears switched into automatic record mode, while my pain sense heightened to an excruciating pitch and an alphabetized list of personal injury attorneys' phone numbers danced before my eyes. My God, if I could just manage to get assaulted on company property, I'd be set for life!

As if in slow motion, the short and swarthy man behind the pillar slid into view. My mind raced. Who was he? An assassin? A corporate spy? Another (albeit strangely thin) PPLF terrorist?

No. He was my boss, Hassan Tabouli. With his head down and his jacket collar up, his thinning black hair and gray-streaked beard plastered down by the rain, water beading the thick lenses of his wire-rimmed glasses; trying to hide from the wind and rain on one hand and the security cameras on the other, and taking a last, desperate, furtive drag on—

Egad, a *cigarette*. The list of attorneys in my mind instantly jumped to those specializing in personal air pollution, before I finally managed to shake myself out of that damned reflexive mode and start acting like a normal human being again. "G'morning, Hassan."

I'd thought he'd seen me. I was wrong. When I spoke, Tabouli jumped like I'd hit him in the butt with an electric cattle prod. He sucked his breath in sharply, palmed the lit cigarette (ouch!), spun around in a blind panic—

"Oh!" He recognized me and relaxed a very slight notch. "Oh, uh," he coughed, and then, realizing the cat was out of the lung, relaxed the rest of the way and exhaled a thick stream of hot, carcinogenic smoke. "Well, hi, Jack. I, uh—" He noticed the cigarette in his left hand and waved it around helplessly. "I, er, suppose you're wondering—like, I just *found* this, uh, this—" He pointed off in a vague direction. "In the bushes, over there, and I—was just about to, y'know, report it. To Connie. In Environmental Health."

He may have been management, but I *liked* Tabouli, and considered him something fairly close to friendlike. Very deliberately not looking at the cigarette, I said, "Report what, Hassan? I don't see anything."

He screwed his eyebrows together in a puzzled look and shook the ciggy. "This, uh—" It dawned on him. "You don't?"

I shook my head. "Nope."

Hassan broke out into a big, fuzzy, brown-toothed grin. "Well, in *that* case," and he went for that filter tip the way my Mom goes for a long-neck Budweiser. A deep drag; an exhale that turned into a heavy, contented sigh; a satiated smile. He nodded at me. "Keep up the good work, Jack. See you inside." I turned and started for the door.

"Oh," Hassan called out after me, "and thanks for coming in Saturday to finish up the mid-quarter statistical report! The Duffer was impressed!"

Under his breath and mostly to himself he added, "He didn't understand a word of it, but he was impressed."

Tabouli may have said more. I didn't hear the rest of it, because by then I was through the door and into—

Well, first the metal detector grid, to make sure I wasn't carrying any concealed assault rifles. Then the Faraday pulse cage, to make sure I wasn't carrying any hostile software. Then the Olfactory Evaluation Containment Unit, to make sure I wasn't carrying any illegal pharmaceuticals, followed by a quick scan of my Mr. Movies videotape rental card, to make sure I hadn't watched any questionable movies over the weekend. Then I slipped my employee ID badge into the ID card reader with my left hand, laid my right hand on the plate of the palm-print scanner, stared into the laser retinal scanner with both eyes fully open, all the while hopping up and down on my left foot and whistling the first four measures of "Old Man River" . . .

And then the inner airlock door chimed and slid open, and I went toe-to-toe with *Carl*—the last, best line of defense, prototype for the twenty-first-century man, the most heavily implanted rentacop in America—and, I suspect, Employee Number 00000002. Every morning, it was always the same.

Carl would stand there, gaunt and tall and inhumanly erect (thanks to some extra servo motors in his artificial knees and hips), pacemaker and insulin pump throbbing audibly in three-quarter time, skeletal-thin right hand resting on that ancient revolver on his hip while his palsied left hand held the employee ID badge I'd just handed him like it was an annoyed live scorpion or something, squinting at the ID photo through his floaters and cataracts and trying to decide if the picture matched my face, or if maybe he should just shoot me and save himself some work. I had this mental game I'd play while waiting, of trying to make a picture by connecting his liver spots. Usually I came up with a horsie.

And then he'd smile (*nice* dentures), and hand the ID badge back to me, and vosynth, "Good morning, Mr. Burroughs" (lost his larynx to a cigar, they say), and clank aside to let me pass.

Actually, I rather liked that. *Mister* Burroughs. A few people called me "Jack," and for some reason I never understood a lot of people at MDE called me "Pyle," but old Carl always called me *Mister* Burroughs, and treated me like a human being, not some fresh-from-college twenty-three-year-old freak.

This morning, though, there was a change in the routine. I got through the cage and the scanners. Got the hairy eyeball treatment from Carl, followed by the usual cheery "Good morning, Mr. Burroughs." He clanked aside to let me pass, and I clipped my name badge onto my shirt pocket and crossed the lobby. Rounding the corner that led to the elevators—

I got jumped by a whole rabid pack of perky, cheerful, multiculturally balanced and hideously wholesome *spokesmodels*.

"Hi!" the athletic blond female one said. "We're from the EarthNice Foods Division, and we've got a special treat for *you*!" I fought free of her and caromed over to the other side of the corridor.

The elderly black female bodychecked me there. "We

know what it's like," she said. "You're looking for a nice, hot, pick-me-up drink in the morning!"

I feinted right, rolled left, and ran headlong into the young Asian male.

"But as a concerned consumer," he said, "you want to be *sure* you only buy products that help the environment—"

The muscular Native American male blindsided me and tackled me at the knees. "—and contain no harmful additives!" As I went down, I got an elbow free and whacked him in the kidneys. He grunted in pain and lost his grip, and I bounced to my feet.

The spindly boy in the electric wheelchair spun around hard and slammed me against the wall. "That's why EarthNice Foods is excited to be introducing—"

The weight-impaired Downs Syndrome woman clamped a forearm across my throat and pinned me to the wall with all her strength. "—this revolutionary new breakfast beverage!" With her free hand, she lifted a cup of something hot and steamy and pressed it to my face. I twisted my head away and clamped my mouth shut. A few scalding drops splashed on my cheek and trickled down into the inside of my collar.

An armed, uniformed, MDE security guard stepped out of the shadows and leaned in so close I could smell the bacon on his breath. His voice was a low, grating, venomous thing. "Dey wants youse ta try da complimentry product sample—" he stole a glance at my employee ID badge, then spat out, "—*Jack*."

I looked at him. Looked at the spokesmodels. Looked down the corridor in hopes of finding help: no one else there but a cluster of haggard, frightened, cowering wretches—in short, typical MDE employees.

I smiled at the guard. "Be happy to," I gasped out. The spokesmodel relaxed the forearm across my throat and lifted the cup again. I gulped hard, closed my eyes, leaned forward and opened my lips.

I felt the cup touch. I took a small, tentative sip.

"It's caffeine- and sugar-free!" the blond woman said.

"It won't stain your dentures," the black woman added.

"It's one-hundred-percent natural," the Asian man pointed out.

"And uses no rain-forest products," the Native American announced.

"Best of all," the kid in the wheelchair concluded, "it was developed without any animal testing!"

"So what do you think?" the woman who held me by the throat asked.

"Honest opinion now," the guard said, as he scanned my name and employee number into a handheld computer.

They closed in on me. Hanging like vultures. Waiting.

"Can I try another taste?" I finally asked. The guard snarled. The large woman held up the cup again. I took another drink; a large gulp, this time. Rolled it around on my tongue. Listened to what my nose and taste buds were telling me.

"It's hot water," I said at last.

*"NO!"* they screamed in unison. *"IT'S COFFEE CLEAR*™!"

With a disgusted snort, the large woman turned me loose and sent me on my way with a shove. The other spokesmodels drifted back up the corridor to set the trap for the next hapless victim. I wasted a moment looking for my briefcase before remembering I hadn't brought it that day, then pulled myself together and started heading for the elevators.

Oh no, the guard again. I smelled the potent reek of his aftershave before I saw him; heard the anguished cries of those four lost and lonely brain cells searching for each other inside his skull. He stepped out of the shadows, blocking my path. "I don't like youse attitude—" he stole a glance at my employee ID badge "—*Jack*. I t'ink I'm gonna keep an eye on youse."

"Thank you, that's very kind of you." I tried to step around him. He sidestepped and blocked me again.

"What's wit you? You t'ink you're some kinda smart guy—" he stole a glance at my employee ID badge, "—*Jack*? You tryin' to make trouble?"

"No sir, I'd never want to make trouble for you." I tried to go around him on the other side. He blocked me yet again.

"What da hell's your *problem*—" he stole another glance at my employee ID badge, then whipped out a pen and wrote my name on the back of his left hand "—*Jack*? You lookin' to get *hurt*?"

I stepped back and smiled nervously. "Absolutely not, sir."

"*Den why da hell won't you get out of my* way?" I flattened against the wall. He brushed past with a snort and went stomping down the hall in the other direction, a sloping-foreheaded fix to his face that suggested he was looking for branches to swing from and bananas to eat. A couple of really choice smart-ass comments came to mind as I watched him drag his knuckles away.

I wisely decided to keep them to myself.

## BRAIN DUMP * BRAIN DUMP * BRAIN DUMP
### * BRAIN DUMP * BRAIN DUMP * BRAIN DUMP *

**OBJECTIVE:** To clue you in on exactly what kind of cowflop Our Hero is about to stick his foot into.

### MDE = Monolithic Diversified Enterprises

Monolithic Diversified Enterprises is big. Way big. Bigger than the Gross National Product of a lot of countries. In fact, there are in-house rumors that the government of Sumatra is actually just a wholly-owned subsidiary of MDE. (There are out-house rumors, too, but decorum demands that we not discuss them.) MDE has its sticky corporate fingers in a mind-bogglingly broad and totally senseless array of industries; Wall Street analysts continue to claim that there is some fantastically subtle and brilliantly obscure plan behind all this, but they're just lying to protect their jobs. The chain of command, ownership, and reporting within MDE transcends the word "Byzantine" and makes the i786 chip gate diagram look simple and obvious by comparison.

## INH = InterNational Holdings, Ltd.
Moving up the food chain, MDE is in turn wholly owned by INH, an investing consortium put together by a small group of obscenely wealthy PanEuros, Arabs, and Pacific Rimmers. Foremost among these financial demigods is Sir Morton Pinkney Ashcroft St. James Eauxbridge d'Kolaczinski, or "Sir Ed," to his friends. "Sir Ed" reveals himself to us mere mortals exactly once a year, in the form of a direct satellite broadcast from his home on Mount Olympus, which brings us holiday cheer, glad tidings, and a warm cuddly feeling, but no bonuses.

## MKF = Miyoku Kwan Fujitomo
Sir Ed—or at least a portion of his anatomy to which he is deeply attached—is in turn fifty-percent owned by his ex-wife, Miyoku Fujitomo, of the Hokkaido Fujitomos. Little is cared about her.

---

Moving in the other direction, we find that MDE in turn owns a staggering array of businesses, in a staggering array of countries, in a staggering array of buildings, all of which are decorated with exactly the same pale gray modular furniture and large potted split-leaf philodendrons. Of special interest to browsers of this file is Building 305 (B305) in scenic Lake Elmo, Minnesota, because that is where I, Jack Burroughs, work. As far as I can tell, no one in B305 actually *makes* anything. Rather, B305 is the central administrative headquarters for a dozen or so wholly-owned subsidiaries. (The exact number changes from day to day as independent companies are swallowed whole or coughed up, executive careers are built high or toppled to ruin, and employees' lives are squandered senselessly or wasted in dull tedium.) The important subsidiaries are—

## GEF = Global EthniFoods

Along with EarthNice Foods (the less said about which the better), GEF markets a complete line of celebrity-licensed food products, including Spike Lee's Own Barbecue Sauce™, Marilyn Quayle's Family-Valu White Bread™, Russell Mean's Traditional State Fair Walleye-On-A-Stick™, and Boris & Gorby's Old-Fashioned Microwave Piroshki™. Not to mention a long list of high-calorie frozen snack foods sold under the aegis of That Little Purple Guy From Chanhassen™.

All GEF food products are manufactured in a chain of plants in Arkansas, except for the walleye, which is assembled in Mexico from Canadian components.

## DIP = Dynamic Infotainment Products

A recent acquisition, DIP is our cutting-edge effort to avoid actually spending our own money on R&D by devouring smaller companies instead. DIP has created and is marketing a small handful of breakthrough software applications and data services in interactive video, CD-ROM, virtual reality, and on-line service formats. Their greatest success to date has been the *Celebrity Medical Records*™ interactive CD-ROM series, with their all-time best-selling title being *Madonna Guides You Through Her Full Pelvic Exam*, followed closely by *Inside Sylvester Stallone's Prostate Surgery*. Four marketing analysts have already gone stark raving mad trying to figure out the demographic appeal of that last one.

All DIP products are designed and coded in Silicon Gulch, Wyoming, and manufactured in sweatshops in Macao and Hong Kong.

## STS = Sanguinary TechSystems

STS occupies—in the military sense of the word—the first two floors of the west wing of B305. Beyond that everything else is on a need-to-know basis, and I don't. Presumably they make something somewhere, sell it to someone, and make huge profits. Their managers all drive HumVees.

## DTP = Dead Trees Publishing

Besides being the natural mortal enemy of Dynamic Infotainment and the home division of Melinda Sharp, DTP is the parent company of the R. W. Emerson's Print-While-U-Wait™ bookstore chain, the Ostentatiously Expensive™ coffee table art book line, the Excruciatingly Prestigious™ money-losing nonfiction line, and the fantastically profitable Buckets of Bloody Vomit™ horror line (which, they're proud to point out, has the highest book-to-film conversion ratio of any publisher *ever*). What DTP is best loved for, though, is everyone's childhood favorite: *Totally Neutered Young Persons' Tales™*.

I mean, I don't know about you, but I still get choked up when I remember how Mom used to hold me in her lap and read "Vertically-Challenged Scarlet Equine-Exploitation Cloak." Especially that bit at the end where the wolf confronts Scarlet and forces her to admit she's been judging him by humanocentric standards, and that, considered in light of a Lupine-American value system, eating Grandma was not just forgiveable, but in fact morally necessary. And then when the Tree Protector bursts in, and reveals that Grandma and the wolf were in fact old friends, and that Grandma had long ago made the wolf promise to kevork her if her quality of life was deteriorating and she was in danger of becoming a burden to the next generation—

Well, all I can say is, you gotta be pretty tough not to shed a tear or two over *that* scene.

## MIS = **Management & Information Services**

This is where *I* work. MIS is an umbrella organization (though "doormat" might be more accurate) that provides hardware, software, data, and network support to all the other subsidiaries. Which basically means we're gophers (we go fer this, we go fer that) continually on the scamper through the sub-basements, false ceilings, and data conduits of B305, trying to solve everyone else's IOHS (*Insufficient Operator Headspace*) problems. My immediate supervisor is Hassan Tabouli; he in turn answers to Walter L. Duff, the Vice President of Administration & Facilities. Which means—

ready?—I do MIS for MDE in B305 on behalf of
DIP, STS, GEF, and DTP, and report to WLD, the VP
of A&F, whose brain is MIA. Got that? Oh, and
one more thing.—

**CCCP** = ☺

This is the error message all Belarus PCs display,
just before they die of massive motherboard failure.
This is why we don't buy Russian hardware anymore.

# 1A

## AWK

The elevator chimed and said, "Third floor." The doors hissed open. With a certain amount of mooing and bleating, my coworkers jostled out the door and wandered off to their stalls, their cowbells clanking dully in the dewy morning air.

I exaggerate, of course. Our employee nametags didn't actually *clank*—at least, not in audio frequencies. No, MDE was a high-tech company; we were valued and trusted professionals. Management never spied on workers. It was pure coincidence that each employee nametag contained a tiny coded transponder chip, and that the B305 ceilings had transponder pickups the way other buildings have automatic sprinklers. There was absolutely no connection between the nametags we were required to wear at all times and the monthly reports our managers got listing exactly when and for how long we went to the bathroom, what interesting chemicals were in our excretory streams, and who we associated with on our coffee breaks.

By the way, there is also absolutely no connection between releasing an object from your hand and having it fall to the ground. It is a little known fact that the so-called "Law of Gravity" was actually one of Sir Isaac "Shecky" Newton's best practical jokes, and it was such a wonderful knee-slapper that generations of teachers have devoted themselves to keeping the hoax alive. In truth, there is no such thing as "gravity."

Rather, the Great Earth Goddess sucks.

And speaking of things that suck, thanks to the bombed west entrance and the STS occupation of the first two floors, here's how I got to my office: in through the south entrance, down the corridor to the elevators, up three floors to Document Coding, north through global EthniFoods territory to the skyway access, out through a security door and into the skyway tubes, 200 yards along the north face of the building to the west wing, in through yet another security door, *quickly* through "Temporary Purgatory" (all the while looking nervously over my shoulder for the ghosts of contract employees past), then a treacherous short-cut through Dynamic InfoTainment Sales & Marketing territory to the fire door, and down six flights of stairs to the MIS office, which is in the basement of the west wing.

I had high hopes of making it that day. Scott Uberman, before the acquisition DIP's VP of S&M and now Division Manager in Charge of Whatever Scut Work We Give Him In Hopes He'll Quit, was sitting there (as usual) with his wingtips up on his desk, the morning Sports section wide open, and his receding blond hairline just barely visible over the headline: Timberwolves May Move to Rangoon. If I could just tiptoe past his office . . .

My wet galoshes squeaked on the terrazzo floor. Rats.

The newspaper rustled and collapsed. Uberman looked up and caught me. "Say, Pyle? Good thing I found you. The network's down again."

I stopped and simulated the appearance of caring. "Oh?"

Uberman rolled up his newspaper, leaned forward, and swatted his desktop PC like it was a dog that had done something nasty to a nice carpet. "Dead as the proverbial door-knob," he said.

"Can you still work locally?"

His face flushed pink a moment, and he floundered. "Uh, I, er—"

In other words, he hadn't even thought of trying that. What a surprise. "I'll look into it right away, Mr. Uberman." I started moving toward the fire door again.

"I mean." Uberman cleared his throat, adjusted his necktie, and began delivering his morning whine, which is clearly what he'd been intending to do all along. "This is, what? The third network outage this year?"

I stopped. "We're having some problems porting your database to our server, sir." I edged one step closer to the exit.

"I mean," Uberman scowled, "if I can't depend on your network, I'm screwed. Just totally *screwed*, you know?"

*Then how come you're not smiling*? is what I thought, but "We'll have it back up as soon as possible," is what I said.

"I mean," Uberman whacked his PC with his newspaper again, "we never had problems like this *before* MDE acquired us. Dammit, our old Applied Photonics network *never* crashed! Not once!"

"So I've heard." *And heard, and heard, and* heard! *And if you gave me just sixteen users in a one-floor office, I could make* this *network look pretty good, too.*

"I mean," he paused a moment, trying to remember what his point was, then settled for, "know what I mean?"

"Uh-huh." I nodded and started moving again. He unrolled his paper and resumed reading it. I got as far as putting a hand on the latch of the stairwell door.

The papers rustled again. "Say, Pyle?"

I stopped and turned around. "Yes, Mr. Uberman?"

"Did you know you're wearing one brown and one blue sock?"

Actually, no, I hadn't known that, but I wasn't about to let him know that. "It's a fashion statement, Mr. Uberman."

"Oh." He thought it over a bit, then decided to go back to his Sports section. I got the fire door open, made it through, and started down the stairs. Just before the door hissed shut behind me, I heard him add, "Looks pretty stupid, if you ask me."

Clattering down the rough concrete stairwell, I passed the welded-shut fire doors to the STS offices and made it to the basement without further incident. As soon as I popped the door to MIS, though, a strange collage of smells hit my nose: cool, damp air. Wet leaf-mold. Lighter fluid, ozone, and smoke.

Definitely not good things to smell in a computer room.

I threw my dripping coat into my cubicle, hopped and tugged my way out of my galoshes, then grabbed a fire extinguisher and followed my nose to the source of the smell. Rounding a corner, I found—

Hassan Tabouli again. (How the *hell* had he beat me down there?) Standing at the open fire escape door, watching the ducks enjoy the rain in the cattail pond out back of B305, a lit cigarette in one hand and in the other, a little haywire gizmo that was obviously somehow jamming the fire exit alarm sensor.

A flurry of thoughts dashed through my mind. This was so obviously a violation of, well, security policy for starters. Then environmental policy, and health policy, and . . . and . . .

When all else fails, stick to the obvious. "Hassan?"

He turned around, slowly, and looked at me. "Yeah?" Wearily, almost mechanically, he brought the cigarette up to his lips and took a puff.

"Uh, did you know the network is down?"

"Yep." He took another drag and slowly exhaled.

"Well?"

"Direct orders from Walter Duff," he said slowly. "The network was shut down at 0600 this morning."

"The Duffer shut it down? Why?"

Tabouli took a light puff and turned to look out at the rain. "Beats me. I just found out I'm scheduled for a private meeting with him in five minutes. I expect I'll learn then."

I was slow on the uptake. "Private meeting?"

Tabouli's voice was slow, soft, and measured. "You're young, Jack. This is your first real job fresh out of college. You've still got a lot to learn.

"After you've been out in the world a while, you'll realize that corporations have a kind of biological clock, every bit as predictable as the Mayfly hatch or the bluegill spawn." He took another puff, then looked at his watch. "What's today's date, Jack?"

I had to think a second. "May fifteenth?"

"The middle day of the middle month of the second quarter," Tabouli said. "If they're going to make any midyear organizational changes, they're going to make them today."

"Today?"

He took one last, deep drag on his cigarette, then flicked the glowing ciggy butt out the door to land, hissing, in the wet grass. He turned to me. "S'been nice working with you, Jack. Stop letting people call you Pyle, okay?" I was still fumbling for words when he handed me the alarm jammer and started up the concrete stairs.

And that was the last time I ever saw Hassan Tabouli alive.

It took me about ten minutes to figure out how to disconnect the jammer without setting off the alarm. By the time I made it back to my department, the rest of the MIS crew had arrived for the morning, Hassan's office was already stripped to the walls, and the Environmental Health Crisis Management Team was busily shampooing the carpet and vacuuming the ceiling, their white nylon toxic-spill suits rustling with frantic intensity.

Abraham Rubin sat in the cubicle nearest Tabouli's office,

twitching like a cat at a flea circus, muttering softly to himself and up to his bushy eyebrows in a hardcopy source code listing. I knocked on the frame of his cube entrance. He bolted upright and screamed, *"Angel of Death pass by!"* Then he turned around, recognized me, and sighed. "Oh, it's just you, Pyle."

I thumbed at Tabouli's office. "What happened, Bubu?"

He tugged his beard, twitched a little more, then started fiddling with his shawl. "My advice to you," he said at last, as he tapped the splotches of lamb's blood that decorated his cubicle entrance frame, "is to go into your cube, concentrate on your work, and don't *see* anything, don't *hear* anything, don't *think* anything. . . ." He adjusted his yarmulke, then turned back to his source code scroll and resumed muttering, ". . . hashem is his heritage, and may be repose . . ."

Well, that certainly cleared things up. I tried Yuan Huang Dong's cubicle next. "Say, Frank . . .?"

Frank Dong looked up from some bit of busywork, pushed his bifocals back up to the bridge of his nose, and nodded sagely. "Ah, Pyle. Confucius say, when elephants battle, the wise ant keep his nose to the grindstone and his ass covered."

O-kay. *Next*! That would be Charles Murphy, on the other side of the multiplexer junction snakepit. I always felt a little nervous bothering Charles, but . . .

I knocked on the cubicle frame. "'Scuse me. Charles?"

He backed his electric wheelchair out of the interface dock, rotated one hundred and eighty degrees, and fixed me with that bloodshot one-eyed stare. "YES? WHAT DO YOU REQUIRE?" Oh, sweet. He had his vosynth set on Inhuman Monotone again.

That always unnerved me. I mean, I'd been there when Frank and Bubu installed the ROM upgrades. I *knew* Charles' vosynth was capable of a full range of inflection and could sound like anyone from James Earl Jones to Betty Boop. And yet Charles seemed to *enjoy* sounding like a Dalek.

I screwed up my courage. "Yeah, about Hassan. Did you . . .?"

And just that quickly, I realized I was giving Charles yet another opportunity to start shrieking "EXTERMINATE!" Not *again*.

I backed quickly out of the cube. "Never mind. Sorry to bother you." I beat it out of there as quickly as decently possible and went off to hunt up T'shombe Ryder.

I found her in the hardware room, spooning instant coffee crystals into a big, steaming cup of Coffee Clear, leafing through last month's issue of *Bitch!*, and running a diagnostic on one of the file servers. The coffee looked like coal-mine slurry.

"Yo, homechick!"

She swiveled around in her chair and gave me that patented Whoopi Goldberg, heavy-lidded, wryly tolerant stare. "Pyle, do you have any idea how lame you sound when you say that?"

"Sorry." I pulled the door shut behind me, plopped my butt down in the chair next to her, and shrugged. "What can I say? I'm a white guy from the Upper Midwest. My coolness genes have all been repressed since birth."

T'shombe shook her head and let out a small, sad smile. "Face it, Pyle. You're a white *nerd* from the Upper Midwest. You don't *have* any coolness genes."

I thought it over, and finally nodded. "Yeah, well, I suppose you'd know." I gave it one last shrug for show, then nodded in the general direction of the cleanup crew. "So what the hell's going on with Hassan?"

T'shombe tried an experimental sip of her coffee, made a sour face, and went back to spooning in coffee crystals. "First off," she said, "you must realize that MDE is one of the all-time great proponents of the mushroom theory of employee management."

I wrinkled my nose. "Mushroom theory?"

"Keep 'em in the dark and feed 'em horseshit," she clarified. "We will find out *what* the company wants us to know, *when* the company wants us to know it, *if* the company decides we even need to know anything at all. We can presume the company isn't doing a general layoff, since they haven't sent down armed guards to secure the file servers—"

My eyebrows went up.

She nodded. "That's what they did the last time. And we can also presume that our jobs are safe, since we're not getting a firsthand look at the outplacement meeting." She stopped, pursed her lips, and thought it over. "Given that we know that much, and *only* that much, your best option right now is to hang loose and keep on keeping on, until someone else tells you different."

I mulled over what she was telling me, looked down at my mismatched socks, and shook my head. "I don't like that. I mean, I *liked* Hassan. I feel bad about what I think is happening to him. Do you suppose it would be okay, say, this afternoon, to call him at home or something?"

T'shombe shook her head vigorously. "Absolutely not! At least, definitely not from a company phone, and probably not from your personal phone, either. The company *really* doesn't like it when re-org survivors talk to ex-employees, and they can do some downright spooky things with back-tracing and caller ID."

And here I'd thought I was surprised before. "But—"

"Believe it, Pyle." She gave her coffee a stir, tried another sip, and almost spit it out. "Now that Hassan's a nonperson, they could *sue* you for talking to him. In fact, I'll bet that right now, even as we speak, the cops are serving a warrant on Hassan's wife and searching their house for stolen paperclips and ballpoint pens." She forced herself to choke down a gulp of the coffee and watched me narrowly over the rim of the cup.

"But—"

"I couldn't make up anything this ridiculous, Pyle. I've seen it happen."

I was still fluttering. "But—but—they can audit my *home* phone records?"

"Read the fine print on your nondisclosure contract sometime. You'd be amazed what rights you signed away when you joined MDE." She attempted one last gulp of the coffee, fought down a dry heave, then dumped the contents of the cup onto the split-leaf philodendron in the corner, which immediately began shuddering and wilting. "Your e-mail, voice-mail, and working dataspace are all monitored. You knew that, right?"

"Well, yes—"

"And everytime you see a doctor, MDE gets a complete copy of the medical report. You knew that too, right?"

"Well," I shrugged, "of course. 'An unhealthy lifestyle is everyone's problem.'"

T'shombe shook her head and muttered, "Christ. I remember when that was a public service announcement, not a dogma."

I didn't understand the reference. "Excuse me?"

She stopped shaking her head, and looked at me sharply. "Pyle, everytime you renew your car insurance, you have to report the car's mileage. Did you know that your insurance company immediately reports that mileage to MDE?"

That was news to me. "Why?"

"Because MDE has to report it to the EPA Office of Mass-Transit Enforcement." A shrill edge crept into her voice. "Because MDE is under court order to get sixty-percent of its commuters out of their cars and onto light rail!" Her eyes went wide and wild. *"Because the EPA matches your mileage to your exhaust-system test results and counts that against MDE's environmental damage quotient!"* She grabbed me by the front of my shirt and shook me like a rag doll. *"Pyle! Why the hell do you think I spend so much time in this stinking hardware room?"* She didn't stop shaking long enough to let me answer. *"Because this is the only place in the whole goddam building that's SHIELDED!"*

T'shombe caught herself. Stopped shaking me. Slowly released her grip on the front of my shirt and let me slide to the floor. Followed me down.

"Shielded," she whispered. "TEMPEST-certified. Class Triple-A MilSpec. No cameras. No video links. No transponder pickups. No one can watch us."

She leaned closer. Her lips grazed my ear. "Shielded," she said again in a husky, sultry voice. The smell of her sweat and perfume clouded my mind. Her moist, warm breath tickled my ear hairs and made me squirm with anticipation. Oh, my God, if what I thought was about to happen was really *happening* . . . This was *great*! Alone, in a back room, at the office, with an experienced and attractive older woman—I mean, I'd *read* about stuff like this in http://www.penthousemag.com, but I'd never thought, well okay, I'd thought, but never really *believed.* . . .

"Shielded," she whispered, ever more softly. "No audio links." I stole a quick, guilty peek down her ample cleavage and tried to work up the nerve to reach for that straining top button of her blouse. "No one can hear us, Pyle." In a voice just barely audible, she added, "Except the Master."

Something with cold and scaly feet slithered down my spine and made my hand stop right where it was. "The Master, T'shombe?"

"Shhh." She touched a perfectly manicured finger to my lips, then pointed at the split-leaf philodendron in the pot in the corner. "It's listening."

I looked at it. I looked at her. I blinked.

I looked at her again. "That—plant—is the Master?"

She smiled at me and giggled. "Of course not, silly." I

sighed in relief and started to pull back from the brink of panic. Okay, this was all just one of T'shombe's weird jokes. . . .

"It's just a *cutting* from the Master," she completed. "Just one tiny piece of its giant world-wide brain."

*Riiiiight.*

Slowly, delicately, much as I imagine one might tiptoe through a minefield, I began sitting upright and edging away from T'shombe.

She looked hurt. "Don't be frightened," she said gently. Her eyes went far away: for a moment I thought she was hearing voices, then realized she was checking the walls of the hardware room. "It's perfectly harmless in here. Shielded. Isolated. That's why I brought it into this room." Her eyes snapped back onto me. "So I could study it in safety. Learn from it."

I returned her gaze; stared deep into her cocoa-brown eyes. What I saw in there scared the absolute living hell out of me.

T'shombe was utterly mad and totally serious.

"So, uh." I managed to get my hands under me, shift my weight to my arms, and start coiling up for a spring at the door. I took a long, steady look at the plant. *Why the hell had she decorated it with tinsel?* "So this Master, he likes to dress up for Christmas, huh?"

Quiet, catlike, moving on hands and knees, T'shombe slipped around to my left side. "Chaff," she whispered in my left ear. Her soft breath made me shiver involuntarily. "I got it from the guys in STS. Radar chaff. They say it jams the Master's telepathic transmissions."

That got another shudder out of me. "The guys in STS?"

She nodded slowly, seriously. "Oh, yes. They know all about the Master. Even more than I do."

Oh.

Okay. I got to my feet and slowly, carefully, stood up. T'shombe stood with me.

I smiled at her. A big, friendly, totally fraudulent smile.

She seemed to react positively to that.

"Well, uh. Er." I froze a moment, groping for words, much less an idea.

"You won't tell anyone I told you?" she whispered urgently.

I shook my head. "No. No, of course not."

"And you won't mention it outside this room?"

I couldn't decide whether to nod or shake my head, so I sort of did both. "Swear to God. Scout's honor. I won't."

T'shombe nodded seriously. "Good. The Master has cuttings everywhere. Don't let their innocent appearance fool you."

I nodded along with her. "I understand."

"In fact," she whispered, "you should probably go back to your cubicle and pretend you know nothing."

I kept nodding. "Right. Good idea. I'll do that."

T'shombe looked at me and smiled. "Thanks, Pyle." She looked at me again—some mad thought obviously flashed right through her mind—then grabbed me and pinned my arms to my side with an impulsive hug. "I *knew* you'd understand."

"Thank you." *Dear God, get me* out *of this lunatic's arms, get me out, get me OUT*, GET ME OUT!

She relaxed the squeeze, then gave me a nod and a wink and reached for the door handle. "Ready to go back to the battle?"

Not trusting my voice not to scream, I only nodded quickly. She cracked the door.

I didn't stop running until I was back in my cubicle.

Considering the first hour, the rest of the morning was pretty benign. The network was still down, but I could work on local files, so I strapped on my videoshades and datagloves and dove into my working copy of the DIP Marketing Database mess. There's this misconception people like Uberman have, that virtual reality work on relational databases is somehow fun and exciting.

Sorry, kids. Hallucinatory visual metaphors may work for games and student projects, but in the business world, a well-structured database resembles nothing so much as a warehouse full of children's alphabet blocks. And the virtual tools your average MIS staffer gets to play with bear a depressingly strong similarity to heavy construction equipment: front-end loaders, hopper-fed sorters, file compressors; that sort of thing. About the only place where there's any room for fun at all is when you start putting together deep-level user objects, and even then you have to make sure the objects you create will forever remain MIS eyes-only.

For example, my morning project was to create a query agent for that wonderful warm human being, Scott Uberman. For the user side—for what Uberman and any other end-user would see—I took a standard metaphor from the system library and gave the query agent that nice, polite, boot-licking bow-tied little Young Republican toady look.

For the code side, though, in that wonderful realm visible only to we mystic wizards of MIS, I went into our secret library of bootlegged adult cartoon characters and gave him an entirely different aspect: *Pudnose Bobbitt*, the ultimate self-pitying and self-righteous white male dickhead.

Seemed rather fitting, I thought.

Along about noon, I delta'd in my changes, launched a recompile, then shrugged off my gloves and goggles and took a break for lunch. The company cafeteria was in the basement of the south wing. I made it there without incident, caught up with Bubu Rubin and Frank Dong in the serving line, and opted for the daily special. Bubu guessed it was some kind of beef. Frank was a bit short in the wallet department (considering the badge tracking system monitors us everytime we so much as fart, you'd think the company cafeteria would take personal checks, no?), so I wound up fronting him a few bucks.

Then we lucked out and got our usual table by the window, the one that offers the best view of the Cute Babes From Document Coding. We ate; we stole surreptitious glances; we sighed. Bubu made his usual comment ("So many women, so little nerve"). Frank told us once again about how when he was first hired the company cafeteria actually gave out salt. Bubu tried to derail his story by mentioning that T'shombe was brown-bagging it in the hardware room again and asked me if I'd noticed anything odd about her lately. I almost started to answer, then spotted the tinsel-covered split-leaf philodendron lurking in the corner behind him and changed the subject.

# 2

# REBOOT

After lunch we got the call to bring the network back on line. Normally this is a delicate and dangerous operation that requires at least five people, six terminals, and a whole lot of loud shouting and running around—

**Frank "Yuan Huang" Dong** stands before his terminal, hands poised dramatically above the keyboard, like a master concert pianist psyching himself up to tackle a particularly difficult Rachmaninoff piano concerto. A graying, fifty-something, but still handsome, Asian man, he is clearly in command here, and his bespectacled eyes reflect both a deep inner strength and the overhead fluorescent lights.

Reaching the end of his brief meditation, he draws a deep breath, lets it out slowly, then stands on his tiptoes, peers over the cubicle walls, and makes eye contact with the rest of his loyal crew. They are—

- **T'shombe "Babe" Ryder,** the buxom, beautiful, thirty-something female Chief Hardware Engineer, poised at the door of the computer hardware room with a $CO_2$ fire extinguisher in one strong but perfectly manicured hand and a #16 Torx wrench in the other.

- **Charles "Charles" Murphy,** the young, brilliant, but tragically wheelchair-bound Assistant Network Analyst, fully jacked into his interface dock, already deep into virtual reality and beeping and buzzing like an arcade game in attack mode.

- **Abraham "Bubu" Rubin,** the middle-aged, frustrated, and endearingly neurotic Senior Network Analyst, standing between a matched pair of vintage DEC VT-320 terminals, a hand on each keyboard and looking for all the world like a Hassidic Keith Emerson.

- And last but not least, **Jack "Pyle" Burroughs**, the Junior Assistant Software Engineer-in-Training and Guy In the Red Shirt, standing in the middle of the multiplexer junction snakepit, with a hundred feet of coiled EtherNet cable slung over his right shoulder and a complete hardware store dangling from the thick leather tool belt around his waist.

## ACTION

FRANK:      (Surveying his crew.) "All stations ready?"

CREW:       "AYE, SIR!"

FRANK:      "Very well. Commencing Primary Initialization." (Frank turns to his terminal, bites his lower lip nervously, and taps in a short, cryptic, command:)

                        **cat foo ¦ egrep "666"**

(The terminal digests the line. It hums quietly, and spits a few blurry pixels onto the screen.

For perhaps half a minute, nothing seems to be happening. Tension builds in the breathless silence. Then—)

MURPHY: "Frank? I'm picking up an anomalous flutter in the flowgate collectimizer."

FRANK: "Analysis, Mister Murphy?"

MURPHY: "Hard to tell at this time. It could be nothing more than—"

RUBIN: "Uh-oh." (Leans over left keyboard; taps a few keys.)

FRANK: "Abraham?"

RUBIN: "It's—" (Pauses. Taps a few more keys.) "It's the left lateral fibrillation array. I . . . I think—"

MURPHY: "Confirmed. We are experiencing a degradation in the heuristic flowgate stabilizer. I am adjusting delta-V to compensate."

RUBIN: (Worried.) "It's not responding."

MURPHY: "Continuing to adjust delta—"

RUBIN: (Becoming alarmed.) "It's not responding, I tell you!"

FRANK: (To Rubin.) "Get a grip on yourself, man." (To Murphy.) "Can you lock it down and switch to auxiliary?"

MURPHY: "Perhaps. In theory, at least, it is possible to—"

RUBIN: (Gasp.) "My God! The stack pointers have just jumped right off the scale!" (Pounces on left keyboard with both hands; frantically bangs in commands. Terminal responds with ear-splitting string of guttural squawks and high-pitched beeps. Rubin leaps to right keyboard and pounds even faster.)

FRANK: "Abraham?"

RUBIN: "It's breaking up! I can't hold it!" (Right terminal joins in the beeping and squawking.)

MURPHY: "Confirmed. I am projecting catastrophic cache failure in approximately forty-one-point-two-five seconds."

RUBIN: (Backs away from terminal in fear.) "We'll never make it! We've got to abort!"

FRANK: "No! We can do it!" (Leans on intercom button.) "T'shombe! I need more MIPS!"

T'SHOMBE: (For some inexplicable reason in a Scottish accent.) "I'm givin' 'er all I can, Frank. She cannah take much more o' this!"

MURPHY: "Thirty seconds to total cache failure."

RUBIN: "Blowout in the synchronic gilloolystat! We're losing spin control!"

MURPHY: "Twenty-five seconds to total cache failure."

FRANK: (To Rubin and Murphy.) "Steady, lads, steady!" (To the intercom.) "Dammit, T'shombe, I need more MIPS!"

T'SHOMBE: (To sound of $CO_2$ fire extinguisher blasts in background.) "F'r God's sake, mon, I'm still pickin' up th' pieces doon here!"

MURPHY: "Twenty seconds to cache failure."

RUBIN: (Hysterical.) "The dialectical prophylactimizer has failed! We've got zombies and orphans floating all over the pipes!"

FRANK: (To the extra in the red shirt.) "Pyle! Bypass the Number Three Latent Positronic Matrix!"

PYLE: "But sir! That could blow out the entire—"

MURPHY: "Fifteen seconds to cache failure!"

FRANK: "I'll take that risk! Bypass it! That's a *direct order!*"

PYLE: "Aye, sir. Cross-circuiting to B." (Pyle frantically yanks some thick cables out of a rack panel, swaps them around and plugs them into other sockets, then punches the backup M/UX unit into diagnostic mode. The panel lights up like a Christmas tree on amphetamines.)

RUBIN: "The containment buffer is breached!" (Jumps out of his cubicle.) "There's demons respawning *everywhere!*"

FRANK: "Stay at your post, Mister Rubin!" (To intercom.) "T'shombe, I need those MIPS and I need them *now!*"

MURPHY: *"Ten seconds to cache failure!"*

T'SHOMBE: (Grumpily.) "All right, all right. Seems an 'onest civil servant cannah g't 'erself a decent coffee break aroond 'ere—"

MURPHY: "Five seconds to cache failure!"

RUBIN: (Wails.) *"WE'RE ALL GONNA DIE!"* (A long, dramatic pause. Rubin is gnawing on his knuckles. Frank is poised, hands like curved talons, ready to pounce upon his keyboard. Murphy is beeping the last few seconds slowly down. Pyle is—aw, who cares? There comes a blast or two of $CO_2$ from the hardware room. Then . . . )

COMPUTER: (In a voice eerily reminiscent of both Keir Dullea and Barney the Dinosaur.) "Good morning, everybody! I'm happy to be here, and really looking forward to another exciting day at MDE! In fact, I'm so happy, I could sing a little song! Maestro, if you please?" (Music intro. Computer sings.) "Daisy, Daisy, tell me your answer true. *Everybody sing along!* I'm half crazy—"

FRANK: (Shuts off sound. Heaves a tremendous sigh of relief.) "Well." (Looks around, nodding.) "Good job, crew. We made it. Thanks." (Suddenly all business again. Points at Pyle.) "Pyle, go see if you can give T'shombe a hand with damage control."

(After Pyle leaves: quietly, to Rubin.) "Abraham, what the hell happened to you in there?"

RUBIN: "I . . ."

FRANK: "Save it, mister. I want a complete report on my desk by 0700 hours tomorrow, explaining—"

As I said, the normal procedure for bringing up the network is a delicate and dangerous operation. There weren't any managers or marketing people down there to watch us that day, though, so we skipped the normal procedure and instead sent

T'shombe over to the console terminal in the hardware room, to key in the one-word command ("START") that actually starts everything. Then she joined me and Bubu in Frank's cubicle for a few minutes of creative loafing. I believe the topic was early '80s TV sitcoms and why they sucked so badly, but since I was still wearing Huggies during the time frame in question, I adopted my usual posture of hanging around in the doorway and feeling vaguely left out.

The discussion ended abruptly when the network completed its startup procedure, the auto-login routines fired, and every workstation in the department erupted in a fit of frantic beeping and flashing yellow EXTREMELY URGENT! messages.

Frank did an ExecuGlide (that's when you kick off the floor and ride your swivel chair backward across the carpet) over to his terminal and acknowledged the message. A bright red-and-green flashing-bordered message window (known to professionals in the industry as the classic "Christmas at K-Mart" interface) popped open on Frank's screen, an automatic confirmation-of-receipt message was created and transmitted to God-and-Thompson-&-Ritchie-know-where, and six more audible alarms went off.

Bubu yawned with excitement. "Anything important?"

Frank adjusted his bifocals and scanned the message. "Nah. Just the Duffer again, telling us the e-mail system is down and we should bring it back up."

Bubu dug his fingers into his beard and scratched his chin. "I see. The e-mail system was out, so he sent us an e-mail message telling us to fix it."

"That's about the size of it."

Bubu nodded. "I wonder who he calls when his telephone doesn't work?"

T'shombe leaned into the conversation. "I bet he writes his bank personal checks to cover his overdrafts." The three of them chuckled. I wasn't quite sure what was so funny about that last one, but figured I'd better join in the chuckling anyway.

That drew their attention. Frank spoke up. "Say, Pyle? You wanna go do something about—?" He pointed around, in the general direction of all the other beeping workstations that were still waiting for someone to acknowledge the message.

"Sure." I pushed off the cubicle wall and trudged around a circuit of the department, stopping at each workstation to receive and delete all those messages.

The MDE e-mail system, you see, suffered from a classic case of Corporate Vision. Once upon a time, someone high up in the food chain had envisioned that middle managers would only use URGENT messages for matters of extreme life-or-death importance, and even then, only rarely. Therefore, since the contents of URGENT messages were by definition excruciatingly critical, it was decided that the best way to ensure that employees actually *read* the messages was to require them to physically *press a key* in order to acknowledge receipt of delivery.

This was hardwired into the system. No way to bypass it or intercept it in software. Even Charles Murphy had to decouple himself from his interface dock, drag his one functional arm up, and flail away on a QWERTY keyboard until he chanced to hit the Ctrl-V "Verify" key combination.

I hung at the entry to his cubicle and watched him a minute. Poor bastard. I'd worked with him long enough to know how pig-headed he could be about doing physical things himself, but still, I *wanted* to help him, if only I could have figured out some way to do so without insulting him. Life with cerebral palsy must be a real bitch.

But, enough on that fun topic.

The message itself, by the way, was also a prime example of typical MDE corporate style. Walter Duff had sent it, priority URGENT and CARBON COPY ON RECEIPT demanded, to every user account in the entire A&F Division. There would be people in overseas subsidiaries receiving copies of that message. There would be carbon copies of that message echoing back to Walter Duff's workstation for *years* to come, as people accidentally strayed into dormant user accounts and were forced to Ctrl-V out of that message before they could regain control of their workstations. MDE would wind up archiving *thousands* of carbon copies of that message, in gigabytes of otherwise useful data space, and that message would go on to join the *millions* of other idiotically archived e-mail messages which preserve for future generations the urgent details of early twenty-first-century football pools, Girl Scout cookie drives, and off-color jokes-of-the-day.

Forget diamonds, chum. It's e-mail that's forever.

As soon as I acknowledged and deleted the last copy of the message, a new one came through and locked up all the workstations again. This one wasn't quite so idiotic, though: staff meeting in the A&F conference room in thirty minutes. So I ran around the department freeing up the workstations one more time, while Bubu decrypted and launched our LocalNet copy of *Slaughter*. Then we all went back to our respective cubicles, strapped on our videoshades and datagloves, and got down to the deadly serious business of deciding who would stay behind and babysit the file servers while the rest of us got numb butts in the meeting.

For the six or eight people out there who've been living in a yurt in Outer Mongolia lately and have never played *Slaughter*, this is what virtual reality was *really* designed for, and here's how it works:

You, and a handful of your closest buds, jump together into a 3-D virtual reality scenario, like a ruined castle or a state unemployment office or some other similar hellish place. Once there you're supposed to find each other, link up, and along the way explore the scenario, collect treasures and weapons, and survive vicious attacks by zombies, demons, postal clerks, and other depraved and murderous creatures. Then, after you find all the goodies and kill all the baddies, you make your way to the exit and convert all your loot to hit points for the next round.

At least, that's the way it's supposed to work.

The way everyone *really* plays it, of course, is the way that gets Tipper Gore's Secret Service-issue Kevlar pantyhose into a tight Gordian double clove hitch. And that way is, you teleport into the scenario, latch onto the biggest effin' weapon you can lay your mitts on, and then go "hunt up" your friends.

Less splitting of the loot that way, and you get a *lot* more personally involved in the game.

Earphones in, headset mic live, videoshades synced and datagloves engaged: I tapped through the attract scenes and menus, pulled my favorite player/character out of storage, and jumped into the game. Reality melted and ran down the walls. . . .

It was the castle scenario, again. I was standing in the foyer, listening to the rustle and scratch of flea-bitten rats scampering across the dry stone floor at my feet and the squeal of rusty hinges turning as the front door slowly closed behind me. No point in trying to back up; the door was always locked by the time I turned around. I did a quick scan left and right, just to make sure I was alone and that we were only playing at "Level 4: Ankle-Deep In Blood." (Bubu accidentally fired up the game at "Level 5: Brian De Palma On A Bad Day" once, and I got skinned alive by a pack of mutant cannibal Cub Scouts before I'd made it ten feet.)

No company. Good. Ignoring the temptation to grab the flickering torch from the socket on the right wall (doing *that* triggers the trapdoor and makes for a very short game), I slipped into the shadows along the left wall and made my way toward the great hall.

Just before the entrance arch, I paused. Doing the great hall from the foyer could be a little dicey. If the ogre was awake, he'd be just inside the entrance, to the left. Standard procedure with the ogre was to dash into the room, get his attention, then dash back out, hide, and wait for him to lumber past looking for you. And then, of course, to stick the shotgun in the small of his back and splatter his guts all over the opposite wall. The exploding intestines graphic was way cool.

Trouble was, following this course of action required *having* the shotgun, and at the moment, it was still hanging on the wall in the trophy room. If I'd come into the castle through the garden gate or the scullery entrance I'd probably have been okay, but as it was, I was probably hosed.

Which left Plan B: run like hell across the great hall, hope the ogre is asleep when you start your move, and try to get to the secret door behind the tapestry in the gallery before the ogre catches up with you and converts your brains to guacamole. I waffled between plans for a moment.

*Aw, what the hell*, I decided, *it's only a game.* I edged up to the archway, listened a moment for the ogre's heavy footsteps, and heard only the whisper of wind through ancient fluttering miniblinds and the distant screaming of nonplayer characters being dismembered in the dungeon. Taking that as a good sign, I drew a deep breath, punched my hands forward, and lit off into a balls-out sprint across the hall.

It's hard to get the true feel of running when you have to move your POV character by dataglove. I understand Nike now makes a datashoe interface, but you can only use it with the World's Most Boring CD-ROM game, *Jogging Simulator*.

Somewhere behind me, the ogre saw me and roared. (*Nice* stereo spatial imaging.) I heard heavy iron-shod feet thundering across the floor behind me, and the *swish* of an enormous nail-studded Louisville Slugger cutting through the air, not unlike the time Darlene's father caught me and her on the rec room couch in their basement. At least this time I didn't have to pull my pants up while I ran.

Made it across the great hall without getting my brain pulped, grabbed the rotting banner at the archway and used it to take the corner in a slide, cleared the pit of fire-lizards in one huge gravity-defying leap and made a quick right turn in midair to land in the entry to the gallery. Somewhere behind me, I heard the ogre pause a few seconds to club the fire-lizards into submission. Now the tapestry that concealed the secret door was in sight, and if I could just hold on for a few more seconds—

The tapestry rippled, moved, and suddenly this blond Viking *giant* emerged from the secret passage, wearing nothing but a fur jockstrap, rawhide boots, and a pointed iron helmet with horns on it. His broad chest made Schwarzenegger look anorexic; his bulging thews and thighs looked like goddam tree trunks. This guy was definitely *not* one of the standard *Slaughter* menaces, and for that matter, he wasn't a normal player character, either.

I didn't have much time to worry about it. The ogre was thundering up behind me; this geek was standing in front of me, a psychotic smile on his face and a broadsword the size of King Kong's dick in his hands. There was space enough for one small step to my right.

I took that step. The blond giant twirled his sword like a drum majorette's baton and shouted, "Crom!" There was a soggy *whack*! and the ogre's head came sailing over my shoulder, followed shortly by several other large chunks of its body. The blond giant, I decided, was probably on my side.

He surveyed his work on the ogre. Then, apparently satisfied with the results, he turned to me, smiled, and raised his broadsword and started twirling it again. The gleaming steel made a sound like an electric weed-whacker as it described that glittering arc of crimson death. I revised my earlier opinion and tried to back away. He advanced, and for just one moment passed into direct torchlight and I caught a clear glimpse of his face. I had time enough for one shocked gasp of recognition.

*"Murphy?"*

And then the vorpal blade went *snicker-snack*, and my head went bouncing gaily down the hall, and the virtual world started to melt back to reality again—

*Control-Option-E.*

Didn't know about that, did you? There's a debugging mode in *Slaughter* that some sloppy programmer at Perigee Products left user-accessible in release 2.x. Hit the Control-Option-E key combination at just the right time—for example, after you've been toasted, but before the system has cycled back to the startup menu—and you can jump into "audit" mode.

Doing *Slaughter* in audit mode is kind of like—forgive me—being a ghost in the machine. You can move around, you can walk through walls and doors, you can see and hear everything the other players are doing, but they can't see or hear you. You can also move hidden objects, if you're feeling sadistic, but I generally tried to resist the urge to do that. Nobody else in the department seemed to know about the audit mode, and I was in no great hurry to tip them off.

However, I *did* have a real strong desire to find out how Charles Murphy had managed to transform his player character into Conan the O'Brien. So I echoed his movement commands to my player, slaved my point-of-view to follow three steps behind his, and followed him around for a while.

Frank was next on the chopping list.

Charles turned out to have a really extraordinary knowledge of the secret doors and hidden ways. There was a branching passage off the tunnel behind the tapestry; I'd always assumed it to be a dead end, but Charles reached up, poked a brick in the ceiling with the tip of his sword, and a ceiling panel slid open to reveal a ladder up to the next level. He sheathed his sword and caught the bottom rung of the ladder in one pre-posterous leap—I guess there are some advantages to being seven feet tall—then darted up the ladder as the panel slid closed beneath us, to emerge from a trapdoor underneath the table in the library.

Charles was still crouching under the table, hiding, when Frank slipped warily into the room. The library was generally a harmless place, with a small treasure or two sitting in the dark corners and a low-powered revolver hidden inside a hollowed-out book entitled *Mississippi River Law*. But there was also always the possibility of a zombie grad student lurking in the stacks, and the French windows did open out onto a courtyard balcony that was home to half a dozen real horrors, so Frank kept his eyes on the balcony and his back to us as he sidled into the room.

Bad choice.

When Charles made his move, it was with amazing viciousness. I'd been expecting him to leap out, draw his broadsword, and give Frank the Veg-O-Matic treatment. Instead, he waited until Frank was standing in front of the east window, then leaped out and pushed him facefirst through the glass. Sliced to ribbons and bleeding badly, Frank was still screaming with shock and surprise as he landed in the boiling acid fountain.

That death scene was particularly messy, grotesque, and drawn out, so I decoupled myself from Charles and hung around awhile to watch it. Cool.

The internal message for character termination in the acid fountain turns out to be, "It's soup!"

After Frank was done, I went back to haunting Charles, and found him in a footrace with Bubu to see who could get to the trophy room (and the shotgun over the mantelpiece) first. Charles won easily and just about cut Bubu in half with the first blast, but since there were five more shells in the gun I guess he decided it would be a crime not to use them. There were still recognizable chunks of Bubu left when I cut myself loose from Charles and went off to see if maybe I could help T'shombe.

For a few minutes there, it looked like she actually had a fighting chance. She'd skipped the upper levels (smart move, in retrospect), jumped down the shaft into the catacombs, and by the time I caught up with her had already found the BFG-2000 assault pistol. I used my ghostly abilities to arrange for her to find the belt of ammunition around the next corner, but while I was off scouting for the red key that unlocks the door out of the catacombs, she blundered into the wrong tunnel and got jumped from behind by a giant slavering pig-demon.

And thus having scientifically determined that Charles was best qualified to stay behind and attend the meeting by remote telepresence, the rest of us formed up, hit the bathrooms one last time, then trudged off to the A&F conference room.

# 3

## DISASTER STRIKES!

*The meeting.* The A&F conference room was—well, your basic conference room. Large, tastefully decorated in shades of gray, with pale mahogany and brushed-chrome accent bits here and there. Subdued recessed lighting around the perimeter; at least a half-dozen unshielded split-leaf philodendrons sitting brazenly out in plain sight, in ceramic hanging planters along the walls. (These T'shombe eyed suspiciously and gave a wide berth.) The room was designed to seat 100 comfortably; we had about 120 people in there, if you count management as human. Most of the other departmental delegations had arrived before us, so we tried to slip in quietly and fade into the standing-room-only crowd at the back of the room, but the Duffer recognized T'shombe's cleavage as it came in through the door and waved us down to four empty chairs in the front row.

Clearly, this meeting was going to be a Big Deal. Not only were the stacking chairs set out in neat, attentive, church-pew-like rows (as opposed to their usual semirandom distribution). Not only were all six surviving A&F department managers seated at a long, white-draped table at the front of the room, like so many game show contestants. (Bubu leaned over and whispered, "Alex, I'll take Famous Bladder Infections for $500.") Not only was there a portable lectern and microphone set up at the precise corporo-political center of the table.

But the whole panel, lectern, and table affair was set up on top of the portable dais, and getting *that* thing assembled was a union job that took at least eight weeks' advance notice and two rounds of contract renegotiations. Clearly, Hassan had been living with the mark of death upon him for months.

(One might ask: why, with modern multimedia technology, was it necessary to actually herd the whole division together into one room in order to have management speak at them? One may as well ask why telecommuting has been coming Real Soon Now for the last twenty-five years, why companies continue to have bitter and suicidal interdepartmental turf wars, and why business magazines still publish starry-eyed articles about the paperless office of the very near future. The answer, of course, is, "We're not paying you to ask questions. Shut up and get back to work.")

Walter Duff finished chatting up some cute new hire in the document coding group, walked around the back of the table, and stepped up to the lectern. He tapped the microphone a few times, to make sure we were paying attention and coincidentally test the startle reflexes of the poor sods sitting directly under the ceiling speakers. Then he poured himself a glass of water and tried a sip. Composed himself to speak. Took a deep breath. An expectant hush fell over the room.

"Good afternoo—"

*Ping*! An efficient, gender-indeterminate voice came over the paging system. *"Vanessa Schwartz, you have a visitor at the reception desk. Vanessa Schwartz, to the reception desk please."*

The manager of Low Toner & Paper Jams stood up, whipped out her Personal Information Manager, and consulted the microscreen. "Oh, darn!" she said, in a voice just a tad too well-rehearsed. "Was that meeting *today*?"

She turned to the Duffer. "I'm sorry Mr. Duff, but I've been trying to get this vendor in here for weeks. May I—?"

He smiled magnanimously, made a little hand gesture of understanding dismissal, and shot Schwartz's back full of flaming poisoned arrows with his eyes as she left. When the door finished hissing closed behind her, the Duffer turned back to us, took a deep breath, and started again.

"Good afternoon, fellow MDE employees. I'm sure—"

*Beep*! Frederico Singh, the manager of Linear Polymer-Film Adhesives, snatched his pager off his sash and stared at it in horror. His lips moved as he read the message. (Lip-reading is not my strong suit, but I do believe the message was, "Statue of Elvis found on Mars!") Singh went over the message twice again, eyes wide, then he looked to Duff. "Sir, I—"

The Duffer nodded, smiling. "I understand, Frederico. When things need attention, they need attention. I'll fill you in on what happened later."

"Thank you, sir. Thank you." Singh stood, hooked his pager back on his sash and, having learned from Schwartz's example, backed out the door, salaaming.

Butch Kopetsky, manager of Workforce Partnering, saw the opportunity and seized it. "Wait, Frederico!" she called after him. "I can help!" Without even a glance at Duff, she bolted.

Duff's face was still serene and cheerful, but the hands that gripped the lectern had white knuckles. He took a deep breath, gritted his teeth, and tried again. "Good aft—"

*Chirp*! Zeke Jones, head of Positive Attitude Enforcement, flipped his cellphone open, turned his back to the crowd, and answered in a stage whisper just a touch too loud. "Yeah? . . . Honey, I thought I told you never to . . . I'm in a meeting now, and . . . Yes, tonight, I promised . . . yes, your old cheerleader outfit, I'll bring the maraschino cherries . . . No, I . . . No, don't worry, she took the kids to her mother's for the week . . . But . . . No honey, I . . . Honey? Honey, *please* . . ."

Jones snapped the phone shut and turned around. "Sir. It's just come to my attention that—"

Duff scowled and jerked a thumb at the door. Jones dashed out, and Duff laid his baleful glare upon the two remaining departmental managers. He smiled, or perhaps bared his fangs, and telepathically sent them a message that even I could catch.

*Well?*

That's when That Weasel Peabody from Paper Fastening Systems burst into the room, clutching a fistful of still-steaming fax pages. "Mr. Featherstone! We've got a critical shortage of 9023's in—"

Dave Featherstone, head of PFS, stared daggers at Peabody, mouthed the words *Too late, asshole*, and said gently, "Oh, calm down, Peabody, I'm sure it's not that urgent. After all, they're just *staples*." He turned back to Duff, smiled warmly, and said, "You were saying, Walter?"

The Duffer hung there a moment, eyes narrowed suspiciously. Slowly recovering his poise, he smoothed back the hair at his temples, licked his lips, and attempted to begin once more.

"Good afternoon, fellow—"

He stopped short. Glared around, daring someone to interrupt. No one spoke, moved, or for that matter, breathed.

"That's better," Duff muttered. Then another sip of ice water, another smoothing of his white hair, and another try.

"Good afternoon, fellow MDE employees. I am sure by now you've heard many wild rumors and much unfoundered speculation. I have incented this meeting to proactively input you with the straightest possible poop."

He paused to spear the four of us in the front row with a sharp glance. Then he went back to his notes.

"The MIS department has been reorganized," he said in a flat voice. "Hassan Tabouli is no longer with the company. If you have any questions about this decision, outplacement counselors are standing by to transition you to a postemployment state."

The Duffer looked up. "Any questions?"

It was so quiet, you could have heard a mouse dropping.

"I thought not," he said, nodding. Then he stole a quick glance off to his left. Clearly, someone was waiting in the wings.

Duff relaxed visibly, attempted a friendly smile, and switched to his warm and paternal mode. "You'll be pleased to know," he said, "that our search for the *new* MIS manager has led us, once again, to promote from within. In keeping with our long-standing policy of rewarding excellence, we have gone out of our way to find someone whose performance far exceeds—"

(T'shombe leaned in front of me and whispered to Rubin, "Ten bucks says it's Uberman.")

"Someone whose tremendous talents have been underutilized—"

(Bubu relaxed, leaned back at her, and said, "Not a chance. We're due for a minority woman.")

"Someone who shares my personal vision of a greater future for the A&F division—"

(T'shombe touched herself and smiled. *"Moi?"*)

"Someone who has demonstrated, time and again, a can-do willingness to go that extra mile—"

(Bubu shook his head. "Nah, plain black is passé. I'm betting they found us a Haitian lesbian.")

"Someone whom it has been my great pleasure to watch grow, in both a personal and professional capacity—"

("You mean a *disabled* Haitian lesbian.")

"A woman who really understands the meaning of service—"

("I mean a disabled *war veteran* Haitian lesbian, with a prison record and a terminal disease.")

"And so, my fellow MDE employees, it gives me great pleasure to introduce to you—"

("You forgot *practicing snake-handler*.")

"The new manager of Management and Information Services—"

("Reformed *Missouri Synod* snake-handler.")

"My close personal friend: Melinda B. Sharp."

"Oh *shit*," is what I said, loud and clear.

Melinda gave a speech, I think. To be honest, for me the next half-hour was pretty much a blur of cringing, blushing, thinking about updating my resumé", and wishing I could turn invisible or shrink, or both. My face felt hot enough to defrost refrigerators. And every time my blood pressure began to start to edge back down toward normal, Melinda shot me a white-hot glare that left my scalp smoking and my ears bright red. I have some disjointed mental snapshots . . .

(You know, *this* would be the perfect opportunity for hypertext. I mean, if I still had my hypereditor, I could code this all up as a bunch of hotkeys and active links, and then if you're the real dataglut type who needs to know everything about everyone everywhere, you could click on *Melinda Sharp* and get the story of how I first came to MDE as a contract PC engineer, how my first assignment was to spend three months working with Melinda, and how she was having the *damnedest* series of totally unexplainable data failures, right up until the day I caught her sticking a diskette to a filing cabinet with a refrigerator magnet. "But it's so *convenient*," she said in protest.)

(Tell you what. I'm going to screw around with HTML some and see if I can't come up with a way to embed little infonuggets in this document file. And that way, if you're the cut-the-crap Type A sort who just wants to mainline the story, you can read around the nuggets and knock this sucker off in about fifteen minutes.)

Melinda, to us: "First off, I want to assure all of you that my personal relationships had absolutely nothing to do with my getting this promotion. I *am* the best person for this job." She turned her head and looked at Duff. "All the same, I would like to take this opportunity to publicly show my appre-ciation for my mentor and friend, Walter Duff: for the trust, confidence, and personal guidance that he has so patiently given me in many confidential, closed-door, one-on-one meetings."

---
INFONUGGETS

But if you're the real anal datahog type, you can read the info chunks and sort of pretend like they're hot cross-referenced windows.

---

Duff flushed bright red, looked around nervously, and began fiddling with his wed-ding ring.

"Walter," Melinda said brightly, "shall we say, lunch tomorrow? My treat?" I don't think anyone but Duff was supposed to see the way she stuck out her tongue and slowly licked her collagen-enhanced lips. Duff began squirm-ing in his chair as if his pants were suddenly much too tight.

---
PERSONAL RELATIONSHIPS

Bubu, imitating Duff, whisper-ing to T'shombe: "A woman who really knows how to use her head."
"Without using her teeth," T'shombe whispered back.

---

"Sure," he managed to gasp.

Melinda: "Management and Information Services. As I see it, the key word here is *service*. Far too many of you have com-plained to me that MIS can be uncooperative and difficult to work with. I know that *I* certainly have had that experience in the past." She paused to give me another quick blast from her emo-tional flamethrower. The skin on my ears blistered and peeled.

"My objective," she went on, "is to turn MIS into a true *service* organization, dedicated to servicing the needs of you, our internal customers. No more excuses; no more snide remarks when someone has an honest misunderstanding and accidentally reformats a hard disk. From now on MIS will deliver the services you need, when you need them, *without* making you prove to the satisfaction of the network engineers that your needs fit into their unbelievably narrow definition of making 'sense' or being 'possible' . . ."

CLOTHING

Actually, I was sort of blankly staring at Melinda, listening to her talk, when suddenly I realized that her prim pleated skirt, tailored navy blazer, and designer silk blouse represented about a month's worth of my salary—and that was before you started factoring in her jewelry, hair, breast implants, cheekbone augmentations, liposculpting, body piercings, or Cosmetic Surgery Maintenance Organization (CSMO) fees.

*Applause.* I stopped thinking about my resumé and lifted my face out of my pit of despair long enough to realize Melinda's speech was over. People stood; a mob was converging around her, shaking her hand and offering congratulations. "Pathetic bunch of losers," Frank snarled, sotto voce. "The giant sucking sound of a school of hungry remoras, all desperately trying to attach themselves to the new boss and hitch a ride." Frank took advantage of the noise and confusion to make good his

SERVICE

Bubu, whispering to T'shombe: "Check out Duff! He's got a woody! And every time she says the word *service*, he rubs his crotch!"

T'shombe, whispering back: "Don't jump to conclusions. Maybe his penile implant is shorting out again."

escape. Somebody—T'shombe, I think—took my elbow and gently led me out into the hall.

Fifty yards down the corridor, the ambient bozon level tapered off and my head at last began to clear.

"I dunno," Bubu was saying, "I actually think this has some positive aspects, y'know?"

"We are goddam *step-stools*," Frank growled.

> ### BOZON
>
> Akin to photon: a quantum unit of stupidity.

"That woman has *no* business being in charge of MIS. She is just going to walk all over our backs and grind us into the dirt, until the CEO is fooled into thinking she's doing good and gives her *Duff's* job."

"Oh, calm down," Bubu said. "You sound paranoid. I'm sure all that macho butt-kicking talk was just for show. Actually, I've always found female managers to be maternal and patient—"

T'shombe arched an eyebrow, but bit back whatever was on her tongue and instead said, "Why not ask Pyle? He's actually worked for her before."

Frank and Bubu stopped walking, and turned around. T'shombe gave me an encouraging little squeeze on the shoulder. "Go on, Pyle. Tell 'em."

"You—" My voice was barely a hoarse croak. I swallowed hard, and licked my lips, and tried again. "You guys," I said. "Frank? Rubin?

"You have *no* idea what you're in for."

Charles was waiting for us when we got back down to the department. Unusual enough, in that he'd decoupled himself from his interface dock and rolled over to wait by the stairwell, but then he spoke up, and his vosynth was set for John Wayne's voice. "Buckaroos," he said, "you're not gonna believe this."

Emitting a few clicks and a bit of a hiss, he switched himself into playback mode and retrieved a voice-mail message.

The voice was Melinda's. The words were, "This is a broadcast voice-mail message, for Charles Murphy, T'shombe Ryder, Abraham Rubin, Yuan Huang Dong, and—that other guy, oh, what's his real name? You know, Pyle.

"Well kids, I'd really love to meet with you all personally, but I've got commitments this afternoon. So I'm sending you this message to make sure we start off on the right foot together.

"Charles: generally speaking, you're doing a great job, but that *Warning: I Brake for Hallucinations* bumper sticker on the back of your wheelchair has got to go. People might think you're violating the company recreational pharmaceuticals policy."

We all stared and blinked at him. I would have to do a deep record search to confirm it, but so far as I know no one has *ever* criticized Charles. I don't think he even knew how to react. There was some peculiar screwed-up expression on the controllable parts of his face, but it was impossible to read.

Melinda continued. "T'shombe: watch the plunging necklines, lady. What you are wearing today is *not* appropriate workplace attire. Trust me, I know what I'm talking about; I've got a master's degree in Executive Wardrobing, and I expect to see you in *appropriate* business clothing tomorrow."

Our stares all flipped from Charles to T'shombe. Actually, to the top button of her blouse—and then we realized she was fuming mad, and we felt like a bunch of cheap perverts, and we looked away.

"Frank and Abraham," Melinda said. "I've got just one word for you: *mandatory neckties*, starting tomorrow." Frank and Bubu stared at each other and their jaws dropped, but I didn't catch any more of their reaction because—

"And last of all: *Pyle*. Oh kid, kid, I barely know where to start with you—but actually, I do. DTP has an excellent book by a guy named Mallory, the title is *Dress For Conformity*, and the human resources library has fifty copies. Check one out. Tonight. There *will* be a test on it tomorrow."

Melinda paused, clucked her tongue. "Well, that's about it for now, kids. Be good, hold down the fort, lock the door if you throw a party, and—oh yeah, new hours, effective immediately. I'll see you all at seven-thirty sharp tomorrow. Bye."

The message ended. The recording clicked off; the synthetic voice of the VMX system came in with the traditional, "Press *one* to forward this message; *two* to delete this message; *three* to pickle this message in vinegar; *four* to—"

Charles disconnected himself from the phone system. Abraham turned to T'shombe. T'shombe looked at me. I turned to Frank.

"All hands stand by to man lifeboats," Frank said softly. "Women and old Chinese guys first."

# 4

## DISASTER FOULS ONE BACK INTO THE STANDS

Quitting time: at last, thank God. I collected my raincoat and galoshes, wasted some minutes looking for my briefcase before remembering I hadn't brought it that day, and headed for the parking lot.

The weather had cleared sometime after lunch, I guessed. The rain had stopped, the clouds had passed, the sun was out, and the skies were blue and the birds were singing and the lake on the other side of Highway 5 was sparkling in the peachy keen sunlight, and the whole midwestern pastoral tableau was all just so insufferably gosh-darn *nice*, it made me want to puke. The gulls on Lake Elmo were obviously having a swell day, too. I wasted a few minutes in the parking lot watching them soar (after surviving the security exit gauntlet). Gulls screeched; they wheeled. They dove like Stukas to catch fish, and then flew high. Absolutely beautiful.

Up until the moment I realized they weren't so much feeding as refueling for another bomb run on the MDE parking lot. The cars in the far south lot were getting hit particularly hard. Especially a certain blue-and-bondo '95 Toyota in the last row.

What I want to know is, how do they do it with such *pre-*

*cision*? There were plenty of primer-gray surfaces on my car, just begging for a bit of color. But no, every single one of those huge, disgusting, chunky-white splats was on a body panel that still had some original paint.

Of course, I have to admit the real pièce de résistance was the severed head and guts of a bull-head catfish, which some avian artiste left on my car's roof, positioned so that the whiskered face was staring at me as I went to open the driver's side door. Reminded me of a Creole dish I once ordered by accident in a restaurant in New Orleans. After recovering from the shock, I flicked the head away, opened the door, and climbed in. The windshield gasket had leaked again; the inside of the car was like a steambath. She started on the second try, and I eased her out onto Highway 5.

> ## CARS
>
> Melinda's car was gone, of course, but the space where it had been parked showed the clear outline of her car in bird-poop white. Gee, I guess that new Teflon-Kevlar paint really does "shed crap better than Turtle Wax."™

There's one more status thing at MDE. You can tell how someone's career is going by whether they're in the left- or right-turn lane at that intersection. A left turn puts you onto Highway 5 East, which leads to some really nice exburban areas, like Afton, Stillwater, and Marina Del Croix.

I turned right, onto Highway 5 West.

> ## TELECOMMUTING
>
> Like Laetrile, the death of Elvis Presley, and New Democrats, telecommuting was one of the great popular hoaxes of the late twentieth century. The idea the middle managers would actually allow their employees to use a technology that, by definition, makes middle management obsolete, is too ludicrous to bother refuting here.

The geography of East St. Paul is impossible to explain without topographical maps. Suffice to say, they don't call it the land of 10,000 mosquito breeding pits for nothing. Highway 5 snakes across Eastern Heights, and turns into Stillwater Boulevard just west of County Line Road. Stillwater Boulevard in turn becomes a cattail swamp just west of Ferndale, as it was washed out in the '03 flood and never rebuilt, so I turned north on County Line Road with the intent of catching Holloway and taking it across. But the state patrol had set up roadblocks at Granada Lane—the MPOA was planting landmines again and no one was getting through until Channel 5 showed up—so I gritted my teeth, pulled a U-turn, and headed south.

To Third Street.

You don't need to read about Third Street. Every major city has a Third Street, or something like it. Steel bars on all the windows. Concertina wire around the roofs of the few surviving businesses. Burned-out automobile frames like rusting steel skeletons in the glass-

## MPOA

*Maplewood Property Owners Association:* yet another bowling-league-turned-urban-terrorist organization. President Gore has promised that the midnight bowling provisions in his new crime bill will solve this problem, but the legislation remains bottled up in Congress.

strewn vacant lots, desperate unemployed lawyers holding signs saying "Will Litigate For Food" on every street corner, illegal cash-only medical clinics masquerading as legitimate brothels, and mile after mile of gaily colored real estate signs, their strings of addenda flapping like kite tails in the breeze: $0 DOWN. ASSUMABLE. SELLER MOTIVATED. MAKE OFFER. PLEASE. FOR GOD'S SAKE, WE'RE BEGGING.

The reality, of course, is that Third Street looks worse than it is, excluding the time period of 11P.M. to 3A.M. Friday and Saturday, when it is worse than it looks. Which is to say, I survived the trip again, made it to White Bear Avenue, and turned north, smug in the belief I was only twenty blocks from home.

And then, like an idiot, I stopped for the Margaret Street light.

There were some nasty-looking kids hanging out in the bus kiosk to my right. What they were, I couldn't tell at first. Splatterpunks maybe, or shatterpunks, or vegomaticpunks; hell, the punk styles change so fast even *wired* can't keep up with them. What I do know is they were passing around a large bag of Chocolate Frosted Anabolic Steroids™ and giving me the hairy eyeball, so I kept a close watch on them. Their gang colors seemed oddly familiar, though I couldn't place them at the moment. The traffic light wasn't showing any evidence of planning to change anytime soon.

The next sound I heard was the unmistakable rap of a beryllium-plated carbon-fiber hockey stick on my driver's side window. I turned around.

Omigod. *He* was standing there. Six foot four, at least; two hundred and sixty pounds of surgically-enhanced muscle and unusual body piercings. *How does he ever get through airports?* was the first thought that sprang to mind, but that question instantly gave way to the sharp chill of pure terror that scraped through my frozen veins like a nanomolecular Roto-rooter.

*I recognize the gang colors!* My heart pounded as I realized I was surrounded by the worst of the worst, the nastiest of the nasty. Through one stupid detour, I'd fallen afoul of the awful terror that had chased me all the days of my about-to-be-prematurely shortened twenty-three-year life! As the rest of the gang stepped off the curb and surrounded my car, one of them casually turned around, and with a gloating smile over his shoulder, showed me the words written on the back of his gang jacket.

*Mounds Park High School Athletic Department.*

Please, God, anyone but *them*. But no, there was no escaping the awful truth. I knew *exactly* who I was surrounded by.

Letterjocks.

The marginally humanoid monster on my left knocked on my window again and indicated I should roll it down. I did. "Yes?" I said, my voice trembling.

"Good evening, kind sir," he said, his lips barely able to form coherent speech around his mouthguard implant. "We are here on behalf of da Adopt-A-Highway program. We are da disadvantaged youts what have adopted *dis* highway."

His words took a moment to sink in. "You—you're not carjackers?"

One of the other letterjocks snarled an evil laugh. "*That* piece of junk? You got to be kidding."

"Shit," another elucidated, "Coach gave me a better car'n that when I made *junior* varsity." This brought forth a round of vicious laughter from all of them.

The ogre to my left gently but firmly grabbed my lower jaw and steered my attention back to him.

"If you appreciate da effort we are puttin' inta making dis highway clean, safe, and bootyfull, we would appreciate it if you would make a voluntary contribution to da Mounds Park At'letic Assho—Associa—To da team."

Another of the letterjocks leaned in close, and opened his jacket just far enough for me to see the monofilament-laced locker room towel concealed there. "Remember," he said, "da contribution you make today will help keep a disadvantaged yout' from turning to a life of senseless brootality an' crime."

I fumbled for my wallet. "Will six bucks be enough?"

They laughed. It was not a nice laugh.

"That's all the cash I've got," I pleaded, opening my wallet to show them.

"Look like we're gonna hafta teach dis guy a lesson in da meaning of shared sacrifice," one of them said. The guy with the towel drew it and began twirling it up for a lethal snap. My God, I'd *seen* those snaps, you could take a man's *head* off with one of those things! The rest of the gang closed in . . .

"WAIT!" the big ogre with the mouthguard and the hockey stick shouted. He reached across me and pointed at the pile of junk on the passenger seat. "Is dat—is dat a *CD-ROM?*"

I seized the opportunity. "Why, yes it is." I pulled the copy of *Dress For Conformity* I'd gotten from human resources out of my raincoat pocket and let him have a quick flash of it. "I work for MDE. This is a *classified document* my boss has asked me to take home and study tonight—"

"Damn," the ogre said, "I was hoping it was da new Rolling Stones CD. Okay boys. Kill 'im." They all took a step forward.

"WAIT!" I screamed. "Isn't there any way we can bargain?"

The ogre stopped walking, and turned around. "Well, if it's *really* classified." He snatched the CD from my hands before I could react and read the label. I braced myself to die.

His eyes went wide.

"You—your boss, he's really makin' you *read* dis?"

"She," I corrected.

Ogre handed the disc back to me, took a step back, and turned to the

---

### ROLLING STONES

"Mick and the boys are back in top form with their new disc, *Cybergeezers.* By now you're no doubt sick of the hit single, "Keith Richards Unplugged" (reportedly inspired by that incident last year when Mick tripped over Keith's life-support cables and put him in full cardiac arrest onstage), but get the disc anyway. You'll enjoy the masterful new work by anonymous young black session players, the fascinating new algorithms that have been programmed into the CDS-2000 Hendrix Emulator, and above all, producer Tom Scholz' brilliant use of audio sampling and larynx implants to make it sound as if Mick still has a functional voice."

—*Skag Pustule, music critic America OnDrugs*

rest of his gang. "Let 'im go, boys. We'd be doin' him a *favor* if we killed 'im." He pointed to one of them. "Maurice, hit da lights, wouldja?" The one he called Maurice whipped out a remote control and changed the traffic light to green. Ogre turned back to me. "Go on, beat it, get outa here. And don't ever let me catch your stoopid face in dis neighborhood again. We can't *afford* to waste our time robbin' two-bit dipshits like you."

Well, that wasn't exactly the sort of savoir faire I'd been hoping to exhibit, but I took it as a win and went on, beat it, got out of there.

Two stoplights up the road, I got bushwhacked by a gang of Wilderness Girls and relieved of my last six bucks. I did, however, get two really swell candy bars out of the deal.

"Hi, Mom, I'm home!" The aluminum screen door clanged shut behind me. I hung my raincoat on the hook by the door, dropped my galoshes on the empty case of Bud returnables, and picked my way up the back steps, stepping carefully around the bags of flattened beer cans and recyclable bottle glass. Psycho Kitty's litter box was in desperate need of changing again.

"Mom?" She wasn't in the kitchen either, not that

> ## HOME
>
> 1783 Ivy Street, St. Paul. Blt in 1923, ths chrmng stcco bnglw feat. 3 bdrms, 1½ ba., blt-in sntd-gls bufft in dng rm, orig. wdwrk, orig. paint insd & out, rtty shag cpt, lg. spdrs in bsmt, needs TLC, but jst a convnt stggr frm Throbbing Temple Liquors and w/a lit. elbw grs this could be a showcase! If you're the sort of nut who still wants to live in the city.

I've seen her there often. I shut Mr. Coffee off, dumped the left-over breakfast sludge in the sink, and ran some hot water in the pot in hopes the remaining molten tar would go into solution.

I stuck my nose into the dining room. "Mom?"

"I heard you the first two times," her dulcet voice came wafting from the living room, beyond the archway. "Now if you don't mind, they've just turned over the Daily Double and I would like for once to hear the question."

"Yes, Mother." Crossing the dining room, I went over to the built-in buffet and started sorting through the piles of random paper on top of it. Junk, bills, junk . . .

I opened my mouth to ask Mom if there was anything else, then thought better of it, and went back to my informational dig. Bills, junk—

Oh goody, the June issue of *Model Railroader*, which I carefully rolled up and tucked in my back pocket. (Okay, so call me a throwback. I will give up my last hardcopy magazine on the day they come out with a photographic-quality CD-ROM reader

## LATE PAYMENT NOTICE

From: J. Gotti Student
Loan Servicing Center
To:  John F. Burroughs
1783 Ivy Street
St. Paul, MN 55103

Dear Mr. Burroughs,
Your student loan payment is late again. Perhaps you have simply forgotten or mislaid your reminder, but since you do have an outstanding balance of $32,188.56 and a history of late payments, unless we hear from you soon, we will be forced to send Guido and Luigi over to help "refresh" your memory. *Capice*, paisano?

## STUDENT LOANS, ELECTRONIC PAYMENT OF

The federal government has not allowed repayment of student loans by EFT transaction since June 2002, when members of the Caltech graduating class, as part of their senior prank, penetrated the Student Loan Guarantee Agency's computer system and marked every outstanding student loan in the country as paid in full.

## MAIL, THE CHECK IS IN THE

The Official National Lie since 1999, when the U.S. Post Office was pronounced dead and

## Was Your Last Domestic Partner Inflatable?

Let's face it. If the database in which we found your name is an indicator, there are houseplants with more active sex lives than you. Sure, you've got an I.Q. of at least 150, a squeaky-clean medical history, and a decent job in the high-tech industry—but what does that get you on Saturday night? Carpal tunnel syndrome from flogging the dolphin?

If the last entry in your date book was a dentist's appointment four months ago—if you think your telephone might be broken because it hasn't rung in weeks—if you're tired of living alone in your mother's basement, you should know, there is hope for the socially challenged.

### Diminished Expectations
*Dates for the Truly Desperate*™

Our clients aren't much to look at. You'd never give them a second glance if you met them in a bar, which you wouldn't, because you never go to bars anyway. Frankly, if these people were clothes, they'd be marked *Slightly Irregular.*

But then, so would you. So why not call **1-900-867-5309** and join our ever-growing stable of pathetic losers today? Because remember, if you don't stop it soon, you *will* go blind.

that I won't be afraid to take into the bathroom. My first ReadMan™ died from slipping off my knee and hitting a tile floor, and I'm not eager to repeat that expensive learning experience.)

Something happened in the other room, or rather, on TV. A disappointed sort of crowd noise; Mom swore and yelled, "It was Nixon, dummy!" I started for the back steps.

*"Jack?"* Mom shrieked. "Your computer is screwing up my TV picture again!"

I stopped and directed my rolling eyes to the ceiling. "That's not possible, Mom. It's not even turned on."

"Oh? Well, you just come in here and *look* at this mess."

"Okay, Mom." I took a short count of five, sighed, and turned around and headed for the living room.

Gosh. Mom, in all her splendor. Her fading hair

replaced by PostLotto, a fun game in which players buy a $2 ticket that guarantees their mail will be delivered somewhere, sometime, maybe.

## FUNDS, SOURCE OF

NetLore has it the reason the feds were *so* pissed off by the Class of '02's prank was that the funds involved were diverted from a dummy corporation operating in the CIA's black budget, and the theft caused the immediate cessation of a very promising covert war in Bolivia.

## VALUABLE COUPON!

Good for 50-percent off any eye exam at

*Sister Bertrille's*
**Faith Healing & Optical**

Now 4 locations to serve the Lord better!

## VISION, JACK'S

20-15 when tested on a Monday morning, sloping off to 20-40 by Friday afternoon. I hope direct brain feeds get here soon because video monitors really bug the shit out of my eyes.

still dyed a bright, brassy, blond; her ever-larger butt sunk deep into the cat-clawed sofa, which was permanently deformed to fit her shape. A pile of little dead cigarette corpses clustered in and around the Turtle Lake Casino souvenir ashtray on the left arm of the sofa; a matching collection of empty Tab cans scattered on the floor near her feet. (Good. She hadn't switched to beer. Yet.) Left arm in full extension, like a fencer with a remote control instead of a foil, glaring at that 54-inch rear projection screen and thumbing buttons with a speed and dexterity otherwise seen only in twelve-year-olds blessed with Super Mega Nintendo decks.

"See?" she was accusing. "See? That picture is horrible! Your Uncle Dave, he got me such a good deal on this set, and he had the cable working so nice before you started messing with—"

## FAITH HEALING

While it is an established point of law that Native American Healing Centers™ are exempt from the National Health Act, each clinic site being a *de juris* Indian Reservation, the question of whether Christian faith healing is a religious expression protected by the First Amendment or a dodge to get around the National Health Board is still being hotly contested, and promises to keep expensive lawyers in nice cars for many decades to come.

## MOM

Whenever I look at Mom, I'm reminded of that line from that old song:

*Where have you gone, Doc Kevorkian?*
*A nation turns its aging eyes to you.*
*What's that you say, Mrs. Robinson?*
*You've changed your mind, the doc should go away.*
*Hee hee hee. It's too late.*

Simon & Stipe, "Mrs. Robinson" from the soundtrack of the Warner Bros. film, *21st Century Limited*

Oh, Mom. I just shook my head. The TV wasn't hooked to cable, it was hooked to a pirate satellite dish in the attic. And that it worked at all was amazing, because I'd been fighting a five-year war with Hubbard Broadcasting's channel encryption routines.

---

### UNCLE DAVE

Mom's main squeeze when I was about fourteen years old. Of absolutely no biological relation to me, my sister, or anyone else I know.

---

"Okay, Mom, I'll take a look at it. Could you turn it off?"

No, but at least she was kind enough to mute the sound. I rolled the set away from the wall, got

---

### GOOD DEAL, DEFINED

Actually, "Uncle Dave" boosted the TV off the tailgate of a delivery truck in a lonely alley, and I always thought it pretty tacky that he turned around and *sold* it to Mom.

---

down behind it, and checked the connections.

Ah, just as I suspected, Psycho Kitty had been gnawing on the 300-ohm antenna wire again. I broke a thumbnail trying to twist the connector screw, floundered around for a moment wishing I had something metal to pry with, then remembered the alarm jammer I'd had in my pocket since page twenty-one and fished it out. Thirty seconds later, I had the antenna back together.

"How's it working now, Mom?"

"Mmmm," she mmmed. "Still not as good as before."

"Well, that's as good as it's going to get until you let me upgrade it to seventy-five-ohm wiring."

"Oh no!" She would have gotten her back up in an arch, if she could have gotten it out of the sofa cushions. "Your Uncle Dave knew all about TVs! This is the way he set it up, so this is the way it *stays*!"

"Okay, Mom." No use arguing, really. I finished putting everything back together, stood up, and rolled the set back against the wall. "Then this is as much as I can do." She punched the volume back up to twenty.

Psycho Kitty erupted from her hiding place behind the potted philodendron and sank her fangs into my ankle. I staunched the blood flow with a Kleenex and hobbled downstairs to my room in the basement.

Basement, sweet basement: I had it pretty good down there. My own fridge and microwave (brought back from my dorm room at college), my own phone line, my own futon, my own dresser; with drawers for my socks and underwear, and a secret compartment for my *Best of Penthouse* CD-ROM collection. Room enough to set up all my computer gear: it's not like it was a real apartment, but after I got kicked out of grad school—

---

## CABLE TV

In 1998, satisfied that everyone who was going to get cable or a satdish had already done so, the FCC decreed that all televisions sold in the US were henceforth required to have a PAWNSHOP chip. Similar to an EtherNet transponder, this chip transmits the TV's ID code and serial number back up the cable/satlink to the host system whenever the TV set is powered up.

At first pitched to the public as an antitheft device, then as a Nielsen-type survey instrument, PAWNSHOP is now rumored to have latent telnet multimedia capabilities the likes of which make civil libertarians wake up screaming for their mothers.

Fortunately, my Mom's set is a 1997 model.

---

## FLASHBACK * FLASHBACK * FLASHBACK *

*April 22, 2004.* Jack Burroughs emerges from the basement of the University Supercomputer Center after pulling an all-nighter, groggy from lack of sleep and astonished to find the campus mall full of Tree Huggers holding a rally. "It's Earth Day!" he realizes with a start, "and more importantly, some of those Eco-Bunnies are really *cute!*" In a wholesome, long-haired, tie-dyed, blue-jeaned barefoot braless organic granola crystal-clutching New & Improved Age kind of way, if you're into that sort of thing.

"I *could* be," Jack decides as he watches a particularly perky pair of nipples bounce past. Seized by inspiration, he dashes back to his off-campus apartment, changes clothing, and returns to hang out at the fringe of the rally, hoping to attract female attention by the clearly brilliant strategy of wearing a t-shirt that says, "Save a tree. Eat a beaver."

Within minutes, he is surrounded by an angry mob of Rodents' Rights Association members, who tear the shirt from his back and threaten him with reeducation through cranial bone rearrangement. Jack is saved from injury only by the timely intervention of the campus police, who immediately handcuff him, throw him into a squad car, and drag him off to face the Hateful Speech Tribunal. Charged with Insufficient Diversity Appreciation, Advocating Violence Against Semiaquatic Rodent-Americans, and Sarcasm Directed At A Totally Humorless Group, by four o'clock Jack has been expelled from school, ejected from campus, and fired from his graduate research assistantship post. His student loan is transferred to a collection agency, his workfare contract is sold to a cutrate temp agency, and his home county Community Service Board is notified that Jack is now eligible for mandatory volunteer service.

All of which pisses Jack's advising professor, Dr. Avram Mehta, off to no end, as Jack was actually working on an algorithm the professor had already illegally sold to three private-sector firms. Now Dr. Mehta will have to finish out the project with—[shudder]—*undergrads.*

Oh, and did I mention my own ancient analog phone answering machine? There were three messages waiting. One was an ear-splitting beep from someone trying to send a fax to my number by mistake. The second was a computer-generated telemarketing call from a dating service, and it sounded like their machine and my machine really hit it off.

The third was a message from Gunnar. *"Remember, the club. Tonight. 2300 hours. Be there. Aloha."*

I hit the erase button and didn't give it another thought.

---

### ANSWERING MACHINE

No, this is *not* another example of my fascination with retro tech. It's more a matter of my having a mom who's seen *Colossus: The Forbin Project* one too many times, and thus has forbidden me to leave my computer (and its perfectly good voice/fax/data filter) turned on when I'm not home. She's afraid that one day it will sit up and say, "Cogito, ergo I'm going to take over the world."

# 5

## DISASTER SWINGS AND MISSES

*"Wake up, Jack."*

Huh, what? I sat up with a jolt. Oh no, not *again*.

A yawn forced its way out. I blinked a few times, shook my head, and took a bleary-eyed survey of my situation.

Yep. Again. I'd dozed off facedown on the Formica, a cold and greasy quadrant of last Saturday's leftover pizza still clutched tightly in my right hand.

*"Wake up, Jack."*

Just beyond the pizza, a can of (no doubt) flat and warm soda. And a few inches beyond that, the HO scale boxcar I'd been working on when I had my little pang of conscience, popped *Dress For Conformity* into my ReadMan, and by pure coincidence set the boxcar aside to let the glue on the truss rods dry.

*"Wake up, Jack."*

Speaking of my ReadMan, where was it? I let my gaze drift leftward until the ReadMan swam into focus, a few points off the port bow. It was in screen-saver mode: little Klingon warships chased adorable animated Disney characters across the flatscreen and blasted them into smoking, charred skeletons.

*"Wake up, Jack,"* the ReadMan said.

"Shut up," I answered. It shut up. The flatscreen blanked, the drive hummed, and then it displayed "Chapter 7: Dressing To Fool Your Boss Into Thinking You're Normal." I must have spent upwards of thirty nanoseconds evaluating the strength of my desire to continue where I'd dozed off. "Screw it," I said, as I dropped the slab of cold pizza on the table and wiped my greasy fingers on my pants.

"Bad command," the ReadMan answered.

Ah, the wonder of voice control. "Close files," I said as my mouth tried to get out another yawn.

"Bad command," the ReadMan insisted.

The gadget wasn't actually intelligent, of course. It just had rudimentary voice recognition and a rather limited set of verbal commands. I leaned in close to the audio pickup and enunciated very clearly. "Close the motherbiting files."

> ## VOICE CONTROL
>
> Sounds cool, don't it? Now imagine the university library in the week before finals, with 500 undergrads all muttering to their textbooks—and the books are *answering.*

"The motherbiting files are not open," it answered with machine earnestness. "Would you like to review a list of the files now open?"

"No." I gave it a few seconds to make sure it accepted that command, then said, "Close files."

This time it liked the command and buttoned up everything relating to *Dress For Conformity*. When I was satisfied all was going well, I added, "Shut down."

It paused. "Password?"

My own little wrinkle, thank you. Everyone passwords their startup processes. I also password my shutdowns. If you want to know why, ask me sometime about the semester Theta

Chi fraternity had their pledges running through the university library shouting "SHUT DOWN!"

The ReadMan was still waiting for my password.

"Ken sent me."

End of conversation. It beeped politely, ejected the CD, and closed its operational programs. The last thing it said was a sample of Porky Pig: "Th-th-that's all, folks!"

I leaned back in my chair, indulged in a slow stretch and yawn, and happened to catch a glimpse of my bedside alarm clock.

10:47.

*"Shit!"* Whatever sleepiness I had left, it vanished. I bounced out of the chair, ran to my desk, and whipped the dust cover off my computer. I'd had no *idea* it was this late. If I'd gone and slept through the few hours of actual *fun* in my life . . .

A large hairy spider was sitting on the keyboard. I slapped it away and jabbed the power button. The ceiling lights dimmed to brown; twin cooling fans whined to life like an F-21 getting ready for takeoff. *"Warning!"* the computer said. *"Primary CPU boot in fifteen seconds!"* I yanked on my lead apron, dropped into the bucketseat before the console, strapped on my videoshades and pulled on my audio headset. The computer was counting down the last seconds to primary boot. *"Five! Four!"*

Audio on! Video synced! All subsystems go!

*"Two! One!"*

Virtual tires smoking, cooling turbines screaming, the primary CPU boot fired, reality melted and ran down the walls, and I was blasting up out of my mother's basement and onto—

The Information Superhighway.

## \* INFODUMP \* INFODUMP \* INFODUMP \*

Let us take a moment here, while Jack is playing virtual chicken with a virtual UPS truck in the virtual right lane and rapidly running out of virtual merging ramp, to talk about what life on the InfoBahn is *really* like. Sure, you've read about it. Of course, you've seen it depicted in film and video. No doubt, you've even used the Net gateway on your online service to spend a few brief and expensive minutes in one of the virtual Potemkin villages, like VirWorld, or BitBurg.

The reality is a lot messier than that.

First off, you've got to understand that there's this thing called *bandwidth*. No matter how cool the Net architecture is—and trust me, Net architecture is a way cool topic that can put most people to sleep faster than you can say "Transmission Control Protocol with Internet Protocol"—the amount of data that can be pushed through the Net in real time depends on how "wide" the data channel is. To do Net virtual reality in real time you need, at minimum, a bandwidth as wide as a TV channel. That's wide.

Second, you've got to understand that the speed of light is not just a plot complication in a Larry Niven novel: when you get into the Net, it's *real*, and translates to about 11.87 inches per nanosecond. You can actually measure continental drift by tracking the week-to-week changes in your New York-to-London Netpost times. (Try this at home, kids!)

Now, what these two ideas together mean to *you*, Joe Mundane, is that there is no way in low orbit or on earth that your commercial online service can be delivering genuine interactive multiplayer virtual reality across a wide-area network in real time—at least, not at the rates you're paying. Instead, when you pop into BitBurg, what you're actually getting is the base scenario downloaded to your local machine. (Why do you think they put you through that stupid and tedious "red carpet" routine? To keep you distracted while the download is in progress.) Once that's done, all you *really* get in real time is text, primitive sprite movement commands, and telephone-grade audio.

What *I* get is another matter entirely.

But before we explore that, there's one last point to remember about the Information Superhighway: it was built by the government, for the purpose of *furthering commerce*. Which means, just like real-world freeways, the parts of the system connecting suburbs to infomalls and government agencies are clean, well-marked, and well-policed. As long as you're content to stick to the mundane routes and be a good little consumer, the Net holds no surprises.

Go wandering off into the wild parts—the sections that were built before the Feds stepped in—and you are just *begging* to get mugged.

*Meanwhile, on the Virtual Freeway:* some asshole yuppie in a shiny new Tempura was giving more attention to his phone call than his keyboarding, so I waited for a hole in packet traffic and then flipped him the bird as I blew off his doors. Next a quick lane change around a feed-capped redneck in a plodding IBM 4990 loaded with COBOL files; then a heart-stopping stab of the brakes and a sudden swerve right to avoid rear-ending some old balding hippie in a Mac 512. The geezer mouthed obscenities at me as I blew past. I flipped him the bird, too, poured on the electrons, and kept an eye peeled for NetCops.

Another glance at my real-time clock. 10:51. Shit, shit, shit. Gunnar's

---

### INFORMATION SUPERHIGHWAY

As should be obvious, this description is a *visual metaphor* for navigating the Net using virtual reality tools. For those readers who are into 10BaseT, fiberoptic packet switching, and the Motorola Iridium satellite network, I have prepared a separate document entitled, "How I Did It." If you're the sort of wanker who really gets off on a good man page, order your copy today by calling 1-900-GET-A-LIFE.

messages had said to meet him at 11:00, and he was *not* the type to hang around waiting. I was cutting it way too close this time. Maybe . . .

I looked up in time to realize I was heading into the MECCnet interchange, and as usual, there were a bunch of junior-high gremlins dropping bricks from the overpass. (Herein lies the true beauty of doing Net virtual reality the way *I* do it. With wild high-compression algorithms, autonomous scan whiskers, and radical Netspam filtering routines; for lack of a better word I *cheat* my way around the bandwidth limit and see the unseen, hear the inaudible, know the unknowable. Actually, it's rather a lot like doing *Slaughter* in audit mode.)

Which is to say, I spotted the little bastards before they spotted me, and dodged. Checking my rearview scan, I had the momentary pleasure of seeing the old hippie in the Mac get creamed by a rain of virtual cinderblocks and bowling balls, and blasted back to the real world in a flaming, cartwheeling, system crash. That poor, deluded, obsolete fool, trying to brave the superhighway in *that* crate. . . .

*10:52.* I'd made it from the InfoBahn to the University Supercomputer Center in record time. Now the tricky part: I screeched to a stop in the USC online library, morphed into an undergrad, and tunneled into the administrative structure. Down, down—the U opens thousands of undergrad accounts every year, so security is pretty loose—down further, until at last I fell out of virtual reality and was working

---

### SPAM

*Self-Propelled Advertising Material.* Originally used to mean an ad disguised as a legitimate Netmail message, but now taken to mean all of that advertising crap your online service pipes into your computer while you're connected. Filter out the spam, and you can virtually *double* your effective bandwidth.

with plain text and my manual keyboard. Then a quick telnet over to the math department, where I poked around their system until I found an open outbound line, and an immediate telnet back to USC.

And *voila*. Jack Burroughs vanished. Spoofed away. Lost in the switchbacks; totally untraceable. What emerged from the depths of the University Supercomputer Center was something new, something beautiful, something virtually perfect.

Something named MAX_KOOL.

And now, kids, you know who I *really* am.

I walked out of the online library, climbed onto my virtual Harley-Davidson UltraGlide, and gave the starter a kick. She fired up with a sound like testosterone-soaked thunder, then settled down into a low, throbbing idle. I pulled on my black studded datagloves, checked my thick black hair in the handlebar mirror (it was perfect, of course), turned up the collar of my black silk shirt, and tugged back the sleeve of my black leather jacket, to check my (nonblack) virtual Rolex: *10:54*.

Plenty of time.

Sunglasses on; cigarette lit; tilt the bike to the right to get the kickstand up, then I stepped her down to first gear, gave the throttle a sharp twist, and popped the clutch. The back tire *screamed* with smoking delight.

MAX_KOOL was back on the InfoBahn. With places to go, people to meet, and most importantly, an appointment at 11:00, in the Marketplace of Ideas, with an arms dealer named *Gunnar*.


The Marketplace of Ideas is big. *Way* big. The biggest damned thing there is on the InfoBahn, short of BusinessWorld or FedNet itself. You can see it virtual miles away: huge discount price structures sprawling out across the datascape, soaring vertical marketing schemes reaching up to disappear in the haze of high-fashion advertising, and every-

where the banners, billboards, and spam, all trumpeting that
world-famous slogan:

### "Just shut up and shop."

The approach lanes were clogged with mundanes and new-
bies, as usual, all puttering over from CornholeNet or some
such place for a night of online consumption and lowbrow
entertainment. I stepped my nice factor down to zero and took
the Harley right over the top of 'em. Reminded me of kicking
the fence at a turkey farm, the way they all stuck their heads up
and looked around, gobbling to each other, dimly aware that
*something* had happened. I rode into the parking structure and
jumped off: the bike went around the corner by itself, up on the
kickstand by itself, shut the motor off by itself.

Me, I checked my hair again, adjusted my black shades,
and strolled on into Heaven.

That's the name of a virtual nightclub, on the fourth level.
*Heaven.* Most mundanes, they think the Marketplace of Ideas
has only three levels: discount online shopping and "free" stuff
on the first level, expensive online shopping and children's
games on the second level, and weird adult crap like Sexus and
the Ranting Room on the third level. Of course, even the
Marketplace sysops probably still think their infomall is a shin-
ing example of structured code and geometric expansion. I'll
bet it's never even occurred to them that some of the loonies
from *.edu* might sneak
over, pry open one of their
virtual broom closets, and
take a ninety-degree turn
*up* into non-Euclidean
space, to build a private,
outlaw, MUD.

The result being, the

| MUD |
| --- |
| Multi-User Dimension: a chunk of virtual space in which users can meet and interact in real time. |

mundanes can *see* the door to Heaven—just like they're sort of dimly aware that I'm passing them by in the virtual hallways on the lower levels—but they don't know what the door *is*, and they don't know the knock.

I did. I knocked.

A big gorilla—literally, a big cartoon gorilla in a bowler hat; we lifted him out of some old movie—slid open a peephole. "What's da passwoid?"

I tilted my head back, took the cigarette from my mouth, and blew smoke in his face. "Ken sent me."

The gorilla snarled, but opened the door. I stepped through, into the a-grav tube, and ascended.

To *Heaven*.

Heaven was like, totally cool. In the spring of 2005 I believed it was simply *the* place to hang, if you were anything on the Net. To me it was like the best party I ever wasn't invited to, the funkiest nightclub I'd ever chickened out of going into, and the sharpest peer group I ever wished I'd stumbled upon, all rolled into one. Heaven was a dark, crowded, smoky, loud, and *crazy* kind of place: an island of glorious anarchy in a sea of bland consumerism; a monument to dangerous choices in an otherwise safe and boring world.

---

## SMOKE

Actually, that pervasive haze in Heaven is *not* just atmosphere. Given the number of people who can be there, and the fact that they're all moving (some on light-speed delays of .3 seconds or more), the thick and smoky "air" is *critical* to keeping your viewpoint data down to a level that can be transmitted over the Net in real time. The way people seem to "swim into focus" at you is not an affectation; it's an artifact of the way the Net VR routines download more detailed visual data as you approach a person or thing.

However, in Heaven, we do tend to enhance this effect by drinking heavily.

Heaven had the best music, best mind-messing sub-stances, and best bad brains on the entire planet. It was a place where you could go party till you dropped, dance the night away (in Heaven, even *I* could dance), have virtual sex on the baccarat tables, or even cut a deal for some stolen plutonium, if that was your thing.

In retrospect, it probably should have occurred to me to wonder why the NetPolice never closed us down.

Dramatic entrances are for the pathetically insecure. I flooped out of the a-grav tube and strolled into the club, cool and slow, checking it out. Nice crowd, for a Monday. The usual mix: a few elves, a dwarf or two, a cluster of cyborgs sitting up near the front, laughing like tin cans and playing poker for body parts. A couple of insectoid aliens having drinks with a couple of clanking metal battlemechs; a party of old 2-D car-toon characters, one gone so far retro as to be black-and-white, all having a great time bonking each other over the head with big wooden mallets and giggling like an entire troop of Girl Scouts. With a discreet nod here and a small wave there, I established my presence, made eye contact with the regulars.

Like the spectacularly obese Don Luigi Vermicelli, who was holding court at his usual table in the far left corner, flanked by troughs of pasta and meatballs, twitchy young men in expensive suits with slick hair and automatics in shoulder holsters, and a matched pair of overinflated bimbos who appeared to be wearing nothing but jewelry. (I tend to stay away from the Princesses of Mars, myself. Half of them turn out to be guys in drag.)

Or the inhumanly barbaric Jesse Chainsawhands, doing bouncer duty by the dance floor, where a spikey-haired virtual pfunk band was blasting away over the heads of a jam-packed mosh pit and a comfortably loud level of music was leaking through the imaginary transparent soundproof wall. Whoever the real person was behind Jesse, I guessed he was ex-military.

Once again, I threw Jesse a friendly little salute, and once again, he reflexively returned it and nearly decapitated himself.

(I should point out, everyone who makes it into Heaven does so under an assumed name. That's part of the game: keeping your real world identity secret and trying to guess everybody else's. The guy who started that, they say, was DON_MAC.)

And speaking of DON_MAC, there he was, in a dark corner off to Jesse's left: poor, lonely, DON_MAC, last of the werebots. Just sitting there, sulking and rusting, sucking his Pennzoil & Lime and alternating between glaring with red photoelectric eyes at the table to his left—where a foursome of mutant ninjas were waving their katanas wildly and arguing over the bloody remains of a (what I hoped was nonplayer) character—and the table to his right, where a party of characters in burnooses and kaffiyehs sat muttering to themselves and polishing their AK-47s.

DON_MAC could be telepathic, when he wanted to be. I caught his gaze, pointed to the Arabs, then tapped my forehead.

*Yes, Max?* DON_MAC thought.

"The table next to you," I subvoked. "New kids on the Net?"

*Yes, and stay away from them. They're trouble, Max.*

"Oh?"

*From a new node in the WorldNet: Kabul, Afghanistan. Just came online this week. They're teenage mujahadin.*

"What?"

*Khyberpunks.*

Oh. I broke contact with DON_MAC and wandered on.

More elves, more superheroes; a pathetically misplaced pair of teeny-doomer flaming skullheads, dressed like the cover of the latest Offspring album. The usual spillovers from the casino.

(Some advice here. Don't try too hard to visualize this. The basic geometry of Heaven was designed by the legendary "Cowboy Bret" Bollix, and it is *not* Euclidean. That wall in the back that seems to recede into an infinite black void really does, and the pools of lambent light over the tables are just that: pools of monodirectional light, with no source. There are places in Heaven where gravity is purely local; invisible private rooms you can get into only by starting in exactly the right spot and then walking *exactly* the right sequence of steps and turns; there's even a phased-space room, where who you meet and what you see depends on which door you came in. And be careful where you step in the Jobs Memorial Lounge: some of those black floor tiles are actually virtual teleport pads that will deposit you in some really *embarrassing* places in the InfoMall.)

> ## "COWBOY BRET" BOLLIX
>
> One of the legendary personalities on the Net, about whom many legends are told. A recent posting from JPL/Pasadena includes calculations proving that if Cowboy Bret, Captain Crash, and Diana Von Babe actually did everything they are credited with doing, the three of them would have a cumulative age of 640 years.

> ## DON'T PET THE PTERODACTYLS
>
> And whatever you do, *don't pet the pterodactyls*, no matter how tame they may seem. The pterodactyl nest (on top of the Salvador Dali melting grandfather clock) is literally *filled* with severed hands.

I continued to work the room. No sign of Gunnar. That was bad. I made my way over to the island of light that was the main bar and found that Sam was working that night.

Not Sam from Cheers. *Our* Sam was a masterful piece of work: a personality simulator, yes, but created by someone with an absolute pathological love of *Casablanca*. Sam looked up from polishing an imaginary spot on the mahogany bar, nodded at me, and said, "Evening, Mr. Kool. Nice to see you again."

"Evening, Sam." I found an open barstool and sat down.

Sam flipped his towel over his shoulder, picked up an empty glass, and started clinking ice into it. "The usual, Mr. Kool?"

I nodded. "I suppose." Sam put the glass on the bar and poured in two fingers of Kentucky bourbon. (I know, I know, in Heaven I could have had *anything*—since all I was really doing was picking a filter algorithm to skew my virtual perception slightly—but for some reason, I'd settled on virtual bourbon.)

Sam slid the glass across the bar. "I'll just put this on your tab, then. Anything else, Mr. Kool?"

I shook my head. "Nah." Then I reconsidered. "You seen Gunnar in here tonight?"

Sam scratched his chin and simulated thought. "Mr. Gunnar was in here about an hour ago, asking for you."

"Is he in here now?"

Sam shook his head. "I can't rightly say."

I nodded. Knowing Sam, that statement could mean any one of about six different things, all of which resolved to having to find out for myself. "Okay, Sam. Thanks." Someone at the other end of the bar called for Sam, and he left. I tried a sip of the bourbon—it was tasteless, of course. That's how I can smoke and drink in virtual reality. No taste, and no physical effects. In the real world, bourbon makes me puke like in *The Exorcist*.

"Max Kool?" a voice said behind me. I turned around. There was some young geek standing there: orange mohawk hair, mirrored sunglasses grafted onto his cheekbones, implants and chip sockets popping out like acne on his forehead. A whole dimestore's worth of cheap jewelry pierced through his ears and lips, and his mouth reminded me of a walleye I once met on Lake Mille Lacs. I felt a profound desire to put him on a stringer.

"Are you *the* Max Kool?" he asked, a trace of nervous awe in his voice. "The guy who created *Silicon Jungle*?"

I sighed and weighed my response. "Yeah," I said at last. "That's me." *Silicon Jungle* was a MUD I designed as a student project at the U, when I was about eighteen years old.

"I'm Hotwire!" the kid said brightly. Yep, now that he mentioned it, I could see the resemblance. "And I've got to tell you, I have been playing *SJ* since I was twelve years old, and it is just *the* coolest MUD around!" Funny, I'd never pictured Hotwire as a nerd with complexion problems before.

"I'm flattered," I said as I reached for my drink.

"No, really," he said. "I mean, I've hung around *Stardrome* some, and every now and then I go into *Elf Trek* for a few laughs, but *Silicon Jungle* is my life! I'm on the SJ Net Forum, and I've read that official SJ novel by Dafydd ab Hugh, and I've got all the issues of the comic book starting with number one! And now I finally get to meet *you*. It's just so, so—"

I lifted my glass to my lips, took a long drink, and considered the kid as seen over the rim. What should I say? That I never made nickel one from *Silicon Jungle*? That the university owned the copyright, and they sold it to a commercial online service without even telling me? That whatever the hell it was he was playing now, it was the result of five years of expansion and development by game designers I'd never even talked to, and that the one time I tried to pop into the SJ Net Forum, I got laughed out?

Or should I stick to the obvious: that it was pretty damn pathetic for him to build his life around a character in a *game*?

I lowered the glass. "That's wonderful," I said, nodding. "Always nice to meet a fan." I gave him a handshake and a big virtual smile. "I'd love to talk with you more about it, but there's a guy over there," I made a gesture in a vague direction, "that I've been trying to catch up with all weekend." Before the kid could react I hopped off the barstool, disappeared around the corner, and ducked behind a large potted plant. Not a philodendron. Some kind of midget palm tree, I think.

"About damn time you got here," the tree snarled.

I jumped back. *"Gunnar?"*

"Shh." The tree looked around nervously, then morphed into Gunnar. Not that it was a big change: Gunnar's normal aspect was that of a totally camouflaged human commando, all tiger-striped black and green, from the tips of his stubbly green hair to the toes of his mottled green boots.

"I'm field-testing a new aspect," he said in a whisper. "Practicing the art of not being seen."

"Right." Now that the initial shock was wearing off, I was starting to feel peeved. "I got your message. What's up?"

"All in good time, Max. All in good time." Gunnar looked around again, then stepped over to the bar and raised his voice. *"Sam!* A cold Kirin for me, and—what're you drinking, Max?" He looked at my glass. "A bourbon for my friend here!" Every head within earshot turned to stare at us.

"Just picked up a new toy, Max!" Gunnar said, in a voice way too loud. "A pre-'94 Colt H-bar Sporter, in mint condition! Never been fired! Some geek stockbroker bought it fifteen years ago and buried it in his basement, waiting for the end of the world! He cacked from a major coronary a few weeks back, and his widow was all set to turn it in to the Brady Bureau until she found out what she could get for it cash!"

Every head within earshot turned away, the conversations resumed, and I finally figured out what Gunnar was up to. "Oh, Gunnar and Max are talking about *guns* again," I heard a beautiful jewel-skinned reptile woman say.

"The art of not being heard," Gunnar whispered in my ear, as he leaned forward and grabbed his beer off the bar. "Make them not *want* to listen." I felt him press a chip into my hand.

"Some drop-dead gorgeous babe's been blundering around MilNet for the past week, asking if anyone knows how to find MAX_KOOL. This is her card." He leaned back again, took a deep slug of his beer, and belched like a Norse god.

"I got the Dillon on autopilot right now!" he said. "By Saturday we oughta have enough ammo loaded to have some *real* fun! What d'ya say? Wanna come over and bust some caps?"

Sam froze. A hush fell. All eyes were on us again. I caught Gunnar's wink and played along. "Nice try," I said, as I lit a cigarette. "Meet you in real time? You'll tell me your true name if I tell me mine?" I took a deep drag on the ciggy, and blew a stream of blue smoke in his face.

"Don't think *so*, kid."

Gunnar went tight. His fists clenched. His eyes squinted. His jaw muscles bulged.

The truth of the matter, as should be evident by now, is that I *do* know Gunnar in real time. In fact, we'd just had lunch together about two weeks before. But since everyone else in Heaven was there under an assumed name, they didn't need to know that Gunnar and Max Kool both lived in the same city and were friends in real time. Hence our little charade.

The scene broke loose. Gunnar roared and threw a sloppy punch. I ducked it easily and had my monomolecular switchblade out of my sleeve and under his nose before he could recover his stance. He glared down at the gleaming blade a moment, then lowered his hands, and opened his fists, and took a step back.

"One of these days," Gunnar growled. "One of

"GUNNAR SAVAGE"

Real name: Joseph LeMat. Occupation: independent software consultant. Age: approx. 37. Identifying marks: pronounced chip on shoulder, courtesy of ex-wife.

these *days*, Kool." He pantomimed a pistol. "Pow! Right in the kisser!"

I casually folded the switchblade with one thumb and made it disappear. "In your *dreams*, jarhead."

Two hours later: after shooting a few rounds of ØF ball, after ducking behind the bar while the ninjas had a brawl with the khyberpunks (Jesse Chainsawhands won), after bailing out of Heaven and closing down a couple of late-night chat nodes. Me and the Harley were deep into BusinessWorld, cruising slow down an empty backstreet, virtual headlight off.

I hated BusinessWorld.

I mean, like, I *really* hated BusinessWorld. Hated being there in those cold, dark, soulless streets. Hated looking at it, all those miles and miles of huge, gray, windowless corporate data structures. But most of all I hated what it *stood* for.

Which, I guess, is why I liked to go down there every few weeks and plant a couple of virtual stinkbombs.

Weird. I took a scan around for NetCops and saw I was alone, then pulled the bike into a deep shadow and cut the engine. According to the chip Gunnar gave me, the place I was looking for was supposed to be along here. Maybe I'd made a mistake?

I pulled the chip out of the palm of my dataglove, pushed it into the skin of my forehead, and watched the message holo into view again. *For a good time, interface* ♥*AMBER*♥*@ alt.XXX.sex.com.* The message was simple enough.

The medium, however, was *extremely* interesting. Basically, what I saw from the chip was the scrolling text of the message mapped onto the body of an *incredibly* beautiful black-haired woman who was silently dancing to what must have been some really *evil* music. Her long, silky hair was flying, and her slender athletic body was thrashing and gyrating, and her hands were moving like—and her lips like—and her . . . and her . . .

I pulled the chip out of my forehead, took a few deep breaths, and wished I could conjure up a virtual cold shower. Gunnar had said the woman who was wandering around MilNet was drop-dead gorgeous. If the babe in the holo was her, Gunnar was, for once, not exaggerating.

I pushed the chip into the palm of my dataglove again, and checked the datapath. Yup, this was definitely the right domain. But *alt.XXX* was a blank wall. Featureless. Empty. Total empty desolate void. Like Interstate 80 in western Nebraska.

Or *was* it? Maybe I needed to take a closer look.

I put the kickstand down, eased the bike onto it, and dismounted. Took a slow, careful stroll up the sidewalk, my black engineer boots crunching softly on the loose data bits. I stopped in front of the blank wall. Hmm. No visible seams. No obvious handles or entry points. Maybe there was a hidden catch. I reached out with tentative fingers to probe the surface.

My hand vanished.

I jerked back with surprise, and my hand reappeared. A quick finger check: one, two, three . . . I think they were all there.

I screwed up my courage and tried again. Slowly, slowly, I reached forward. Fingers disappeared. Then the wrist. Then halfway up to my elbow.

Ah. Tricky. A *virtual* virtual wall. I took a deep breath and kept pushing forward. Now I was up to my shoulder—

Something clamped onto my upper arm. Something *big*. There wasn't time to react; with a sound like squishing kim chee it pulled me completely *through* the wall and cast me into absolute blackness. No up, no down, no floor, no walls; nothing but the sense of tumbling in the thick, moist, claustrophobic darkness, and the slow, heavy breathing of some vast beast.

Until the eyes opened: two huge, red, glowing coals of eyes that swam up out of the blackness and fixed me like a bug on a pin. When it spoke, its voice was like the rumble of a volcano.

"*Hello, Max,*" it said. "*I've been* looking *for you.*"
I caught my breath long enough to scream: "BUGOUT!"

Fifteen milliseconds later I was back in the real world; Netlinks shut down, switchbacks disabled, bridges blown and circuit breakers engaged. The virtual reality aspect that was MAX_KOOL was a cloud of randomizing electrons in a Netspace databank somewhere, and everything that could even remotely possibly link Jack Burroughs to MAX and what had just happened in BusinessWorld was being erased and deleted faster than I could even think about it.

I *told* you I always password my exits.

Still, that'd been too close. I unstrapped my videoshades, peeled off my headset, and shrugged out of my datagloves. Between shudders of raw fear I had time to wonder: what the hell *was* that, that had grabbed hold of me? My scalp and armpits were drenched with sweat; my bladder was screaming for relief. I staggered up out of my bucketseat, started toward the bathroom, and caught a glimpse of my bedside clock: 1:27 A.M.

Well, whatever that monster was, I was going to have to let the mystery sit until tomorrow.

And hope to God it didn't know some way to follow me home.

# 6

# DISASTER BELTS ONE OUT OF THE PARK

Somehow, even though I was fried so crispy you could have served me through a drive-up window, I managed to be awake, showered, shaved, Dressed For Conformity, and into the office by 7:29. It turned out to be a rather quiet and lonely place.

I was the only one there.

Clearly, the 7:30 department meeting with Melinda wasn't going to happen. But the DIP marketing database mess was still waiting for a solution, and I didn't have anything better to do, so I strapped on my videoshades, pulled on my datagloves, and dove into the files. As a result I missed it when Charles rolled in—sometime around eight, I think. I didn't even think to check the back of his wheelchair for bumper stickers.

T'shombe showed up around 8:20, wearing this absolutely gorgeous batik wrap sort of thing that was tight in all the right places, loose in all the right places, and left absolutely no doubt that she was not wearing any underwear. If Melinda had felt threatened by what T'shombe was wearing on Monday, I figured she was going to have an entire herd of Holsteins when she saw what T'shombe was wearing on Tuesday.

Frank and Bubu strolled in around quarter to nine, seemingly still carrying on the argument they'd checked out with the night before. Frank was wearing a plaid shirt and polyester slacks. Bubu had on a moth-eaten sweater and some kind of jeans. Neither was wearing a tie, I noticed.

Melinda finally came blasting in at about 9:30. It wasn't so much an entrance as a flyby: the stairwell door blew open and Melinda came dashing in, juggling a purse, a briefcase, a Bruegger bagel, and a carry-out coffee in a styrofoam cup while she simultaneously tried to push a brush through her big blond hair and get another coat of red lipstick on her mouth. The cavitation of her passage pulled our heads out into the hallway, but she said not a word to us, opting instead to go straight into Hassan's—sorry, *her*—office, and slam the door. The only sounds that emerged for a long while afterward were the beeping and clacking of Melinda beating hell out of her phone, and an occasional guttural phoneme or two that eluded the building's ambient noise dampening system.

About quarter to eleven, my NEC 1400xm Multi-Modal Desktop Audio Terminal—in other words, my phone—chirped. I glanced at the caller ID readout, saw it was an intercom call from Frank, and tapped the acknowledge button.

"Pyle," he said, "department meeting in Melinda's office in five. And grab T'shombe, would you?" Oh, would I. But no, as always I behaved myself, recognized my impetuous and wild side for the gutless coward it really was, and politely informed Ms. Ryder of the meeting. On the way back to my cubicle I also popped in on Charles and made sure he knew.

Five minutes later we were crowding into Melinda's office with all the enthusiasm of a bunch of death-row convicts fighting over who'd be first to sit in the electric chair.

Astonishing, actually. The facilities people must have pulled an all-nighter; from the looks of Melinda's new office, you'd never have guessed that just twenty-four hours before it was decorated in Middle-Aged Ex-College Jock Moderne. Hassan's office had been a study in functional clutter, with a battered generic black metal desk, a matching four-drawer filing cabinet, a tilt-a-whirl office chair (with one arm missing), several random heaps of books and papers on the floor, a matted and framed 1987 World Series Wheaties box on the wall, and a bunch of old computer parts sharing shelf space with wrestling trophies and photos of Hassan's children and favorite caught fish.

Melinda's office, in contrast, was a model of overbudget *elegance*. With a satin mahogany desk, a worktable with hutch, and a matching two-drawer filing cabinet; a black cultured-marble slab on the desktop that, in a pinch, could have doubled as a heliport; and no fewer than *three* large, potted philodendrons. Her huge, plush, black leather chair looked like it'd been diverted from the CEO's office, and the godawful ugly signed and serialized original lithograph on the wall behind the desk looked like clinical evidence of the artist's final psychotic break. To the right of the desk, an entire wall was filled with plaques and framed certificates that looked very impressive, until I got close enough to realize they were for things like "Most Cheerful Volunteer, Minnetonka Junior League Rummage Sale, 2001." I never knew you could get a diploma for having your colors done.

There were exactly three small objects on top of that vast expanse of desk: a little carved ebony figurine, an ornate brass incense burner, and Melinda's Personal Information Manager.

("Ethiopian fertility goddess," T'shombe explained, pointing to the ebony figure.)

Melinda was on the phone again, with her back to us, listening to the squabbling sound of someone else's voice and nodding vigorously. "No," she said to the phone, "not yet. I'll keep trying." There were two chairs for peons in the room: T'shombe had one, Bubu had the other, Charles didn't need one, and Frank and I wound up standing. A thin plume of smoke was rising from the incense burner.

Rubin sniffed the air. ("What's that smell?" he asked T'shombe. "Are we going to be listening to some Pink Floyd?")

"Right. Bye." Melinda clacked the phone down into its cradle and spun around in her executive chair. "It's burning sage," she said to Bubu. "It dispels evil spirits." Rubin's jaw dropped, but Melinda was already working her Personal Information Manager like a pocket Nintendo and frowning as she read.

At last, she set the PIM down and looked up. "Okay kids," she said, "I'd wanted to make this a real friendly get-acquainted type meeting, but I've got an important offsite meeting in half an hour and a lot to do before then. So if you don't mind, I'll cut right to the chase."

She set the PIM down on her desk. "Charles?" She glanced at him, then quickly looked away. "How's the Sonderson project going?"

Charles clicked, hummed, twitched nervously, and answered, "THERE MAY BE SOME DIFFICULTIES." Oh, wonderful. He'd gone into Dalek mode again.

> PIM
>
> *Personal Information Manager:* A pocketsize electronic device that functions as a combination pager, datebook, phone list, and wireless fax. If you buy one, spend the extra money and get the polarized display. Melinda hadn't, and as a result I could clearly read hers, even though it was upside-down. It said:
>
> 11:30 Meet WLD @ hotel 4 Lnch & ♥!♥! Bring xtra pntyhose, 2thbrsh & brethmnts

Frank jumped in. "What Charles means to say," he cleared his throat, "is that there are some serious problems with—"

Melinda speared Frank with a sharp look. "I'm sure

Charles can speak for himself, Frank." Her smile was polite, but the tone underneath was pure hot oil, talons, and venom.

"NO," Charles said. Melinda tried her glare on him, but he just stared back at her with his bloodshot one good eye, and after a few seconds she blinked. "LET FRANK SPEAK."

Melinda looked back to Frank. "Well?"

"It's pretty technical," Frank said, hoping she'd give up.

"Try me," she said through clenched teeth.

Frank took a deep breath, blew it out, and ran a hand through his thinning black hair. "It's a lot like the Wigman least-squares method," he said at last. "Sonderson clearly evidences a genetic predisposition towards suboptimal cognition, with the resulting directives being—"

Melinda waved a hand to cut him off. "What I'm hearing," she said, "is that you don't think it can be done the way Sonderson wants it done?"

"Well, there is a significant gap between ideation and—"

"I'm not interested in what you *think*," she said in a dead flat voice. "*Find* a way. *Make* it work." Frank tried to sputter something else, but Melinda went back to her PIM and fished up the next topic. "Next. Rubin."

She looked up, set the PIM down, and put her hands together. "Abraham," she said, smiling, her voice all sweetness and light. "Are you *terribly* busy today?"

Bubu shifted nervously in his chair and cleared his throat. "Well, uh, there's the MRP analysis, of course, and, uh—"

"But that *could* wait until tomorrow, couldn't it?"

"Ye-es, I suppose it could. Why? Is there—"

She pursed her lips, and nodded. "Why, yes, there *is*." She darted another glance at Frank, then turned the full force of her glare on Bubu. "I want you to spend the rest of today analyzing every VMX error log for the past month. Clearly there is *something* wrong with the voice-mail system, as you and

Frank obviously did not get the message I left yesterday afternoon."

"But—" Bubu tried to protest.

"*Every* log," she reinforced. "And I expect a full, written report by the time you leave tonight."

"But—"

"*Next,*" she said, biting off the word. She stole a glance at her PIM, fastened her eyes on me, and gave me a long, slow look up and down. I twitched a little, but tried to project an aura of simulated confidence. After all, I'd read the damned book (well, skimmed a few chapters). I *had* the look. Navy slacks, black wingtip shoes, white oxford shirt with button-down collar, and a blue tie with diagonal red stripes.

"Nice try, Pyle," she said at last. "But let me introduce you to a new concept. *Ironing*. And for God's sake, tuck your shirttails in in back." I backed away from the group and tried to discreetly stuff my shirt into my waistband, while Melinda went back to her PIM. "Stick around after the meeting," she said without looking up. "I have a special project for you." *Uh-oh.*

"But first," she sat up straight, put the PIM down firmly on her desk, and glared icy daggers at T'shombe. "I don't know what you think you are trying to pull, lady, but—"

"Pull?" T'shombe said innocently. She smiled, lounged back in her chair, and somehow managed to shift her shoulders and hips so that even more of her cleavage was revealed. "I have *no* idea what you mean."

"Cut the crap. You know exactly—"

"All that I'm doing," T'shombe said sweetly, "is exercising my rights as stated in Section Three, Paragraph Six of the *MDE Multi-Cultural Diversity Guidelines*. Now, I could be wrong, but I do believe that passage says, 'All employees are entitled to wear such articles of clothing and/or jewelry as are consistent with the employees' cultural, religious, ethnic, or affectational orientational heritage, provided such clothing and/or jewelry does not constitute a safety hazard around machinery or an offensive textile/verbal communication directed at another MDE employee, customer, vendor, visitor, or random contact.'"

By the time T'shombe was finished with her recitation, Melinda was red to the roots of her blond hair. *"You—"*

"For example, this outfit," T'shombe lifted her hands and looked at herself, "reflects my ethnic heritage, and is clearly not a safety hazard around the workstations or file servers." T'shombe stood, turned around slowly as if modeling, and somehow managed to arrange to flash leg clear up to her hip. Frank's eyes bugged out. Bubu's mouth dropped. Even Charles started humming and vibrating like an old washing machine with an unbalanced load. I began to suspect that T'shombe could make her astonishingly prominent nipples erect on command.

"And again," T'shombe continued in the same innocent voice, "I could be mistaken, but I don't *think* my coworkers find this clothing offensive." She stopped turning and looked wide-eyed at Frank. "Do you?"

"Oh no," Frank gasped.

"Not in the least," Bubu added.

T'shombe turned and faced Melinda again. "Of course, I have to admit this clothing isn't *quite* culturally correct. Among my Tutsi ancestors, this fabric was worn as a simple skirt, and it was appropriate for women to go completely topless in the summer. Do you think my coworkers would object if I—"

"Not at all," Frank blurted out.

"Don't let us stop you," Bubu added.

Melinda finally lost it and jumped to her feet. *"Enough!"* she shouted. *"Out! Out! All of you, get out!"* We jumped for the door. *"Not you, Pyle!"* I stopped halfway out the door, spared a microsecond to curse my fate, then turned around and shuffled back in.

("Tutsi?" I heard Rubin asking T'shombe as they receded down the hall. "I didn't know you were Tutsi."

("My father was Tutsi," T'shombe answered. "My mother was Watusi. I figure that makes me a Tutsi-Wutsi." Bubu sputtered; Frank snickered. Even Charles emitted an organic sound that seemed a lot like a laugh.)

Melinda was still standing there, a tight scowl on her face and a bit of steam rising from her ears. She was either hyperventilating or counting to a very high number, or both, but in time she managed to get her temper sort of under control.

"Close the door, Pyle." I did.

She plopped into her black leather executive chair module. I figured it was safe to take one of the peon chairs, and sat down. "Jack?" she said. Something in the tone of her voice made me want to start to stand up. "Is it okay if I call you Jack?"

I relaxed a little, and sat down again. "Sure."

"Two things," she said, stealing a quick glance at her PIM. "First off," she kicked off and did an ExecuGlide back to her table, where she laid a hand on the workstation. "What's this?"

A strange question, I thought. I shrugged and said, "A Solaris Systems M-5 Multitronic—"

"I *know* that," she snapped. "What I mean is, what's it doing here in my office?"

I scratched my head. "Well, we figured you being the new manager of MIS and all, you'd want—"

"Never mind what you figured," she interrupted. "I want my Guava 2000 back, is what I want."

That got an arched eyebrow out of me. " *That* old piece of junk? I mean, no offense, Melinda, but that thing's got to be pushing four years old. Now, granted the Solaris isn't exactly state of the art, it's still—"

"I want *you*," she said, as if talking to a particularly dim five-year-old, "to go back to my old office, get my old Guava 2000, and bring it *here*."

I shook my head, a little. "Melinda, believe me, the Solaris really *is* better. If there are any files or apps on the Guava's local drive that you want I'm sure we can—"

"And then," she continued in the same voice, "I want you to take this Solaris workstation, and return it to storage, and never mention it to me again. Is that clear?"

> ## GUAVA 2000
>
> One of the last of the "fruit" computers. After the success of the original Apple™, the market was flooded with products seeking to exploit that concept. Orange™, Banana™, Apricot™, and of course, the sadly misnamed Lemon™: in time all spoiled, leaving only Guava to compete with Apple for the coveted "produce computing" market share.

Yup. I nodded. "Yes," I said.

"And after *that*," she paused, a sweet little smile played across her lips, and for a few moments there I remembered just how delicately beautiful I thought she was, the first time I met her, before I actually got to know her.

She scooted her chair back over to the desk, put her elbows on the desktop and her face in her hands, and leaned forward. "Jack?" she said sweetly.

I leaned forward to match her. "Yes, Melinda?"

"Remember, when you first started here? How we worked so closely together?"

"Yes?"

"Side by side, day after day?"

"Yes?"

"How sometimes our fingers would touch, by accident?"

"Yes?"

"Remember how you used to look at me, when you thought I wasn't looking, and I'd catch you doing it, and you'd try to pretend you weren't looking at me at all?"

*"Yes?"*

"It was kind of cute." She smiled. "You were so shy."

*"Yes?"*

"And then remember that silly business with the diskettes, the filing cabinet, and the refrigerator magnets?"

*"Yes!"*

"And how after that you told everyone in my department what a stupid blond twat I was?"

Oh.

"And how I promised myself that if I ever got the chance, I'd have your testicles for my key chain fob?"

Actually, no, I didn't remember that part at all.

Melinda smiled at me: a sweet, soft, heart-melting smile. Then she dipped a hand into the pocket of her blazer, pulled out a ring of keys, and jingled them gently.

"You've had your chance," she said softly. "You screw up just *once* more, and you're mine. Got that?"

A slow, terrified nod was about all I could manage.

"Good." Her smile flickered off. "Now get your worthless ass out of here and get back to work. I've got to get ready for this meeting." Unconsciously, her left hand drifted up and undid the top button of her blouse. "I expect you to have my Guava 2000 down here and running by the time I get back, which will be about two o'clock." She checked her PIM once more, then glanced at me. "Any questions?"

I shook my head, stood, and backed out the door. "No, sir."

"Good. Close the door on your way out." I did.

I was *definitely* on my way out.

## DIGRESSION * DIGRESSION * DIGRESSION

Now, there are several questions that might seem appropriate to ask at this point in the story, such as, "Egad, was she *really* like that?" And, "My God, boy, why did you *stay* there?" And of course there's always my personal favorite, "What's the matter, you *stupid* or something?"

The answers to #1 and #3 being *yes* and *no*, respectively. The answer to #2 is a little more complicated. It comes down to a mix of factors—like my only having a bachelor's degree, and only having about two years' total private sector work experience, and only having about $32,000 in accumulated tuition loan debt. It also has to do with esoteric things like my having a Community Service Draft Board that was really eager to help me find ways to work off my debt to society (a debt which we are all compounding semiminutely by the very act of being eligible for National Health, even if we never actually get sick). And my having been working at MDE as a contract temp on the one day that my job was posted, and thus getting a chance to see the 299 other people who turned out to queue up in the rain and apply for my job.

In short, I took what Melinda gave me because that's life in the twenty-first century. There just *aren't* jobs for undereducated people under thirty, unless you're the kind of highly motivated entrepreneurial self-starter who can create a vacancy by assassination. As I'm told happens routinely in New York.

Melinda left for her meeting/mating/meating. T'shombe waited until she was gone, and then darted up the steps to STS, saying something about needing more radar chaff for all those potted philodendrons in Melinda's office. Frank and Bubu took off for the cafeteria, but I wasn't feeling hungry, so I hiked up to the security office, signed out a key to the freight elevator, then grabbed my toolkit and an equipment cart and headed for Melinda's old office.

Dead Trees Publishing was headquartered in the east wing of B305 and hindquartered in a row of nice window offices on the third floor. The whole operation was really a lot smaller than you might expect: the bulk of the work in the literary world still takes place in writers' spare bedrooms and editors' favorite restaurants (except for young adult franchise books and television series-spinoff novels, which are slapped together by assembly lines of sullen transients in Third World hellholes like Indiana and Upper Michigan). When you go into DTP territory it's not at all uncommon to see high-ranking executives answering their own phones or big-name authors trying to cadge free drinks, the authors apparently being unaware that MDE's corporate bar is out at MDE's corporate golf course.

Most of the DTP staffers were already out to lunch. Some of them had gone out for food, too. I navigated the equipment cart down narrow aisles between the massive heaps of ancient and as-yet-unread slushpile submissions, put a handkerchief over my mouth and nose to fight off the foul stench of recycled bond paper in the late stages of decaying into cellulose compost, and made it to Melinda's old office.

> ### INFONUGGETS
>
> You know, while these things *are* fun and informative and all that rot, they're also a tremendous pain in the ass to code. So if you don't mind, I'm going to stop doing them.

I was under the desk disconnecting cables when someone walked in. It was—actually, I didn't know who it was. Some blond, crew-cut, baby-faced fat guy who didn't believe in wearing his ID badge, obviously.

"Are you from MIS?" he asked.

I considered my answer. "Yes."

"What are you doing?"

I finished pulling out plugs, crawled out from under the desk, stood up, and remembered to tuck my shirttails in. "Taking this workstation down to MIS. Ms. Sharp wants it in her new office." I leaned over the top of the monitor and started disconnecting things from topside.

"Oh," the fat guy said. "That's okay, then. I was afraid you were a furniture vulture."

I paused a moment and took a closer look at what I was doing. "A what?" Okay, a flathead, not Phillips head, no wonder I couldn't budge that screw.

"A furniture vulture," he repeated. "Y'know, when somebody leaves the company, everything that's not nailed down disappears from their office before their chair is cold? That's the work of furniture vultures."

"Oh." I found the right tool in my toolkit and got back on the connector. It came free with a *twang* and went flying across the room. No sweat. We had hundreds more in the stock room.

"So," he said. "How do you feel about having the Crash Test Dummy for your manager?"

That got my attention. "The *who*?"

"No, The Who was a sixties rock band. I'm ta-ta-talking 'bout M-M-Melinda Sharp."

Whatever that last reference was, it went right over my head. "The Crash Test Dummy?"

"That's what everybody around here calls her. She could bring our whole LocalNet down just by *touching* a computer."

"You're kidding."

"Nope. Luckily, we knew how to reboot it." He shook his head, scratched his chin, and changed the subject. "Also, you might want to take a look inside that thing," he pointed at the Guava 2000, "before you go hooking it up to anything important. She had some really *goofy* crap installed on it."

"Oh?"

The fat guy perked up suddenly, turned around, and leaned out the door. *"Lori? Are you back from lunch?"*

"Yes, Rich!" a female voice answered from off in the distance. "Whadaya want?"

*"C'mere! There's a guy from MIS in Melinda's office!"*

A few seconds later a young woman popped around the

corner and into the office. She was short, kind of tiny and pix-ielike, with straight brown page-boy hair parted down the middle and round eyeglasses about four sizes too big for her face. "C'mon in," the fat guy—Rich—said to her. "This guy doesn't believe me. Tell him *your* favorite Melinda Sharp story."

Lori looked at Rich, then looked at me and flashed a close-mouthed smile that suddenly transformed her into someone who was awful darn cute, in an elfin sort of way. "You know that 'Sad Computer' face you get when you try to boot a Guava 2000 with a nonsystem diskette in the drive?" she asked me.

I nodded. "Yes?"

"Melinda was working late one night, and she forgot she had a diskette in the drive. When she came in the next morning—" Lori stopped, and looked around to see if anyone else was listening.

"Go on," Rich prompted.

She flashed that elfin smile at me again. "Well, what *I* heard was a blood-curdling scream, and then Melinda came running out of her office in an absolute panic. When I asked her what happened she said, *'The face of Satan is on my computer!'*"

Rich broke into a belly laugh then and just about fell down. Lori covered her mouth with one hand and snickered.

"The face of *Satan*?" I asked.

Rich was frantically waving for Lori's attention. "Tell him what you did! Tell him what you did!"

Lori looked around again, then said, "So I went into her office, ejected the diskette, rebooted her computer—"

Rich broke in. "*And told her to burn* sage *to exorcise the evil spirits!*" Rich exploded in another fit of laughter, sagged against the doorframe with tears running down his face, and fought to regain control of his breathing.

Another woman came around the corner. "What's all this then?" She was blond, about six feet two, with ice blue eyes, a strong chin, a faint but visible mustache, and a body sculptor's build. I vaguely recognized her, from my time in DTP as a contract temp. Krya, Kyla, something like that. Kyra, I decided.

The way Lori responded to Kyra's entry, I abandoned all hope. "We were just telling," Lori turned around and checked my ID badge, "Jack here, our favorite Crash Test Dummy stories."

"Oh," said Kyra, nodding. Her voice was strangely deep and reedy. "Well be sure to tell him about the time that lovely black woman from his department—what was her name?"

"T'shombe?" I suggested.

Kyra shook her head. "No, that's not right. Anyway, I may as well tell it. Melinda was having computer problems, and this *delicious* black woman came up from MIS, and when they worked through it together, it turned out Melinda was doing something where she was supposed to answer *yes* if she'd made a backup copy, and she hadn't made the copy but she answered *yes* anyway, and the woman from MIS—oh, what *was* her name?"

"T'shombe," I tried again.

Kyra shook her head even more vigorously. "No, definitely not that. Anyway, this woman from MIS told Melinda that the problem was she'd *lied* to her computer, and it hated her. So forever afterward Melinda talked very sweetly to her computer, and promised it nice things, and told all of our new employees how important it was to never lie to their computers." Kyra let out a little laugh at that point; it came mostly through her nose and sounded like a walrus trying to snort golf balls through a vacuum cleaner hose.

"That's a good one," I said as I pointedly checked my watch. "But if you'll excuse me, I've got to get this thing," I laid a hand on the Guava 2000, "set up in Melinda's office by the time she gets back from lunch, so . . ."

So I got back to work. With an audience. Kyra left, Lori

left following Kyra, Rich staggered out into the open office and wandered up and down the rows of cubicles, laughing like a loon and telling everyone where I was. I must have had ten or twelve more people pop into Melinda's office while I was working there to express sympathy, or tell me a new Melinda story, or (worse) retell one of the stories I'd already heard. It was pretty bad.

Except for the young, peroxide enhanced, Overdressed For Success woman who told me how *lucky* MIS was to get Melinda, and how sorely she would be missed by DTP. I thought the woman was being sarcastic with me, up until the moment she started reading me the sonnet she'd written to mourn Melinda's departure.

It's hard to fake that kind of awful sincerity.

Once I got the Guava 2000 disconnected, locked down for travel, and on the cart, that still wasn't the end of it. I had people following me down the halls, talking about Melinda and telling me their departments were switching to adding machines and typewriters. The last one followed me all the way to the freight elevator.

It was Christiansen, from Dynamic InfoTainment's R&D group. After everyone else wandered away, he slipped an unmarked CD-ROM into my shirt pocket. "A little sympathy present from the gang," he said softly. "A couple of the programmers stayed late last night and made a special game for you. Enjoy it when your new boss is *not* around." The elevator chimed, and the door opened.

When I turned around again, Christiansen had vanished.

Frank, Bubu, and T'shombe were back by the time I got down to the department. Frank and Bubu seemed to think they had some gimmick worked out to deal with the VMX error logs, so working together we yanked the Solaris from Melinda's office, installed the Guava 2000, and did a little exploratory surgery while we were at it. Melinda's old computer *did* have a lot of gibberish files on it, as well as a number of add-on interface ports that seemed to serve no useful purpose, but we just shrugged, closed it up, and put it online. It was ready by one o'clock.

As a result Frank figured we had some time to spare, so I loaned Bubu the CD-ROM Christiansen had given me, made a quick stop in the men's room, and hit Vending Machine Hell for a little triangular shrink-wrapped sandwich and a can of Coke. By the time I got back, Bubu, Frank, Charles, and T'shombe were all deep into virtual reality and clearly doing *something* exciting. I tried to ask Bubu what the game was like, but all he would say was, "Get your goggles on and dive in here, kid! You're gonna *love*—ouch! Where the hell did that—? Frank! Behind you!" Bubu punched out with his left hand, while raising his right hand and squeezing his trigger finger as fast as he could.

Standard gun 'n' run stuff, I figured. I ran back to my cubicle, pulled on my videoshades, audio headset, and datagloves, and dove into the game. Reality melted and ran down the walls, and was replaced by—

*Reality*?

I was wearing my VR gear, sitting in my cubicle, and playing a game in which I was wearing VR gear and sitting in my cubicle?

The phone rang. I answered. It was T'shombe.

"Pyle," she said breathlessly, "I know what you're thinking. This is *not* some kind of initialization failure. Your friends in Dynamic InfoTainment have concocted a virtual reality scen—"

There was gunfire in the background behind T'shombe. I heard Bubu shout, "Hah! *Got* one!"

"Pyle?" T'shombe came back on the phone. "Listen to me: you are *not* in B305, you are in a virtual reality *scenario* of

B305. Now, check your desk—there should be a gun in the top drawer. Grab it, and get the hell out of there! We're holed up in the lunchroom and—"

There was a burst of automatic gunfire in the background, and a voice I didn't recognize screamed.

*"Hurry!"* The phone went dead.

Wow. Either reality had gone nuts, or T'shombe was telling me the truth through a virtual reality simulation of my phone, or that was a VR *simulation* of T'shombe giving me the background story line through a VR phone, or else—

Wow, again. The folks in Dynamic InfoTainment had really outdone themselves this time. This game *definitely* did some serious messing with your head. I dropped the phone, pulled open the top drawer of my desk. There should have been paperclips, Band-Aids, and a half-box of cough drops in there.

Instead, there was a large black automatic pistol. I hesitated a few moments, wondering if I should actually virtually touch it.

And about then is when I heard the characteristic snuffling of a giant pig-demon in the next cubicle. I snatched the gun out of the drawer, bailed out of my chair, and hit the ground running. The pig-demon met me in the hallway.

Only it wasn't a pig-demon. It was a giant *Melinda* demon. A fanged, horned, over-dressed blond *monster*, with eyes like fire and tits the size of torpedo warheads. She advanced on me with a harpy's shriek, fresh blood dripping from her upraised talonlike fingers.

I brought the pistol up and pumped half a clip into her. It seemed to work. I didn't stick around to see if she got back to her feet again—the pig-demons will sometimes do that—but instead turned and ran down the hall in the other direction.

Two zombie security guards emerged from the hardware room. I popped them before they could get their weapons up and grabbed their ammo as I ran past. That's the nice thing about virtual reality; all ammo fits all guns, and you never have to stop to reload. I checked my stats: ammo 42, health 100%, armor 0.

Well, it was dicey, but I'd have to risk it. I turned around, charged through the multiplexer snakepit, and sprinted for the stairs.

Someone was emerging from the stairwell door. I almost blasted him before I realized it was Frank. "Are you for real?" I yelled at him.

"No, *better*!" Frank yelled right back. "I can climb these goddam stairs without stopping to wheeze!" That didn't seem like something a personality simulator would say, so I ran over to join him.

*"LOOK OUT!"* he shouted, as he brought up a shotgun the size of a bazooka and pointed it straight at me. I dove to the side; the shotgun went off with an enormous blast and the Melinda-demon came raining down in large chunks.

"This is the only thing that really stops 'em," Frank said, as he surveyed the bloody wreckage that was the demon and patted the barrel of his shotgun. "We'll have to find you one of these. The pistol just makes 'em mad." He pivoted quickly, popped off another shot, and splattered a zombie security guard against the far wall. "We'd better move." He turned and started back up the stairs. I followed him.

"What's the scoop?" I yelled as we cleared the first floor.

"Bubu and T'shombe have barricaded themselves in the company cafeteria!" Frank answered. "I volunteered to find you and bring you back! We're in deep shit; I think—" Frank crouched low, fired, and the corpse of something that I believe was a mutant marketing manager came tumbling down from the next landing.

"I think Bubu brought us in at Level *Five*!" Frank said. "There's zombie guards everywhere, and more Melinda-demons than you can count!" The door at the second-floor landing burst open, and a trio of green-camouflaged *things* came through. Frank and I shot them to pieces, then he lobbed a plasma grenade through the open door and kicked it shut. The satisfying *whump*! of the grenade explosion was followed by some very convincingly rendered inhuman screams.

We kept climbing.

"Charles manifested here as a small Sherman tank," Frank explained. "He went off alone to scout the east wing and wound up in a running fight with some kind of flesh-eating bookworms. His last report said he'd run into a sort of gelatinous monster that came from the slush pile. We think it got him." Frank stopped, motioned me out of the way, and then fired a few shots down the stairwell behind us. "At least that'll make the bastards keep their heads down," he muttered.

"There was some kind of horrible mutant cross-breed bird/swine thing in the cafeteria!" Frank said as he resumed climbing. "Bubu guessed it was a turkey ham." He stopped at the landing, peered cautiously around the corner with gun ready, then lowered it and continued climbing. "T'shombe manifested on the second floor. She said it was just crawling with giant, writhing, person-eating philodendron vines." We reached the fire door at the top of the stairs.

"There's an Uberman on the other side of this door," Frank whispered. "It basically appears to be an unkillable ogre, but luckily it seems to be sleeping most of the time. The idea is to run like hell and hope it's asleep when you start your move." He checked the load status of his shotgun, then smiled at me. "Ready?" I nodded. Frank kicked open the door.

The Uberman wasn't asleep.

A giant razor-edged 6-Iron chopped Frank's legs off at the knees before he'd made it two steps. I emptied my pistol into the Uberman, but it didn't seem to notice or care. It just bent over Frank's screaming form, clamped its massive hands onto his head, and—oh, yech, I'd seen this before and received it a few times myself, now it was going to crush his brain to a pulp—

No, worse. "Lucky thing I found you," the ogre said in what was clearly the real Scott Uberman's voice, stepped down an octave. "I'm having this problem with my desktop computer—" Dragging Frank by his hair, the ogre started shuffling back towards its office.

"SHOOT ME!" Frank screamed. "For God's sake, *shoot me!*" I clicked my empty gun a few times and shrugged helplessly.

Somehow Frank found the presence of mind to unhook his ammo belt and throw it clear. "Take my shotgun!" he screamed as he vanished through the doorway. "Save Bubu and T'shombe!" The Uberman's office door slammed shut with a sound like the very gates of hell.

I picked up Frank's shotgun, slung the ammo belt over my shoulder, and set off for the cafeteria.

The trip to the cafeteria was pretty grim. I killed quite a few security zombies and mutant marketing managers along the way, picked up another twenty rounds of shotgun ammo and something that looked like an antitank rocket, but nothing to launch it from, and blew away about six Melindas. The trick, I discovered, was to get in close enough to make a one-shot kill, but not so close that they could grab you with their razor-sharp fingernails and fasten their lampreylike mouths on your—never mind where they fastened, just trust me, it drained health points *fast*. I staggered into Vending Machine Hell after one attack and discovered that eating the little triangular sandwiches also cost me health points.

By the time I made it down to the cafeteria, the battle, if there'd been one, was long since over. T'shombe and Bubu were gone; there were corpses stacked about the place like cordwood, but all of them mutilated beyond the point of recog-

112 / Bruce Bethke

nition. I was cautiously checking out the kitchen when I ran into the most frightening monster of all. A huge, foreboding, *presence.* . . .

"Pyle," it said in Melinda's voice. "You are dead meat."

I spun around, shotgun at the ready.

"Can you hear me, Pyle?" From the sound it was clearly off to my right, but—oh no, it was invisible. I *hate* it when they're invisible.

"Take off the stupid VR headset, Pyle." I dove left and fired blindly.

It answered with a soft, metallic, faintly musical sound. The sound was vaguely familiar. It sounded like—*keys*.

I took off the VR headset. Melinda was standing there. The *real* Melinda. She was jingling her key ring.

"Oops," I said.

# 7

## DISASTER SLINKS HOME WITH ITS TAIL BETWEEN ITS LEGS

I'd always wanted a corner office with a door that closed. A window would have been nice, though.

Furniture, too, come to think of it. Instead, all this room had to offer was a video screen mounted in the wall behind a slab of Plexiglas, and a hidden speaker somewhere in the ceiling. There was a training presentation running on the monitor: happy music, cartoony graphics, and a smug, well-polished narration. The title of the presentation was, *So You're Getting Fired*.

Obviously, it was made by the same folks who'd produced all those mindless benefits videos I had to sit through when I first joined the company. I wondered if MDE got a package discount.

"And that," said the narrator brightly, "is the whole job termination story. With your cooperation it can be a smooth and nearly painless process. Better for you, better for us, and the important *first step* on that road to a better tomorrow." The video faded into a jolly pastel rendering of our little animated hero (what was he supposed to be, a dog?) striding confidently into the dawning light of a new day, while the music rose and came to a thematic conclusion.

*Ping*! The screen went back to the title graphic and the narrator's smug voice returned. "If you would like to repeat any part of this program, please say *yes* now."

"Fuck you," I said.

"That is an invalid response," it answered. After a pause, it added, "If you would like to repeat any part of this pro—"

"No," I said.

There was another pause. "In that case, this program is now over. If you have further questions, an outplacement counselor will be with you shortly, and he or she will be happy to answer all of your questions personally. Thank you for taking the time to watch this program, and fuck you, too."

*What*? Did that thing say what I thought—

The room lights faded up, the screen went black, and the electric door latch snicked to unlocked. There came a gentle and polite knock at the door. "Mr. Burroughs?"

Oh, no, Kathé again. The program was wrong in one regard—I didn't rate an outplacement counselor, only an under-assistant outplacement clerk, 2nd class—but it was right to say she would be happy. Kathé was amazingly happy, considering what she did for a living. *Pathologically* happy, even. There was probably a treatment program somewhere that was still looking for her to get her back on her medication.

Another polite knock. "Mr. Burroughs?"

If I only had a bar of soap. I could carve it into the shape of a gun and attempt an escape, if I only had a knife.

She knocked again.

"Come in," I said.

The Under-Assistant Whatever-the-Hell-Her-Title-Was opened the door, stuck her cheerful round curly-brown-haired head into the room, and gave me a sunny smile. "So, Mr. Burroughs. Did this program help you to understand your situation?"

"Unfortunately, yes."

Her perky smile failed not a whit. "Good. You know, if you think you might want to watch it again later, you can check out a CD-ROM copy and take it home." She stepped fully into the room and scanned the electronic clipboard in her hands. "All we would require is a security deposit of—"

"Thank you, no. I'll pass."

She nodded, setting her curls all abounce, and touched a spot on the clipboard. "Okay. In that case, before we go any further, I need to make sure of one thing. You do understand that you are not being fired, right?"

I sighed. "Right."

"MDE does not 'fire' people. Rather, your employment status has been transitioned to Unpaid Administrative Leave, pending a review of your case by the Workforce Issues Mediation Committee."

I nodded. "And when can I expect this review?"

"In four to six weeks. You'll be notified when the review is scheduled and given a chance to present your side of the story."

"And *then* I'll be fired."

Kathé shook her curly head and *tsk-tsked* at me. "That is an unnecessarily negative attitude," she admonished me. "Why, it's entirely possible the committee will decide your supervisor was wrong and reinstate you with back pay."

"Has that ever actually happened?"

It was worth asking. For a few seconds there her perky smile failed, and a look of cloudy confusion drifted across her sunny round face. "Well I'm sure it has," she said at last. "Otherwise the employee handbook wouldn't say it's possible."

Yup. About what I figured.

With that question firmly resolved in her mind, she went back into perky mode. "So, unless you have more questions—"

I shook my head.

"Good. In that case I just need to get a few more answers from you, and then we can finish things up." (And I can have my belt and shoelaces back, please?) "First," she thumbed something on her electronic clipboard and started down a checklist, "do you own any automatic or semiautomatic weapons?"

"No."

"Do you have any military training or access to explosives?"

"No."

"Have you ever been adjudged mentally unstable, committed to a mental institution, or had a restraining order against you?"

"No."

"Have you ever worked for the U.S. Postal Service?"

"No."

She nodded slowly, and smiled. "Very good. Now, you do understand that MDE will continue to make your National Health contribution while you're on leave, that the cost of this contribution will be deducted from any underemployment benefits you may be entitled to receive, and that the remaining surplus," she thumbed a button on her clipboard, "which we estimate to be $3.53 per week, will be direct-deposited to your bank account?"

"Three dollars and fifty-three cents per *week*?"

"Well," she frowned, and thumbed the clipboard until her face brightened. "Oh. It says here you haven't taken advantage of the vasectomy discount program. You know, you could cut your health contribution by fifty-percent if you'd just—"

I shuddered. "Thank you, no."

"It's your choice." She shrugged and thumbed something off on the clipboard. "Finally, I must remind you that pending the review, you are still bound by your noncompete agreement. You understand what this means, of course?"

"Of course." I shrugged again. "It means I can't even *look* for a job until after the Mediation Committee makes a decision."

Kathé shook her head and tsked again. "Such negativity, Mr. Burroughs! You are *perfectly* free to seek employment, in the," she paused, and glanced at her clipboard, "fast food, domestic service, or car-washing industries."

"Oh," I said as sarcastically as possible, "I feel better already." It was wasted on her.

"I'm glad you're finally starting to understand," she said. "This is not a problem. It's an *opportunity*."

There seemed no adequate response to that. I stood there while she thumbed through more stuff on the clipboard, until eventually she stopped with a satisfied sigh. "Well," she said, "that about wraps everything up. So if you'll just come with me," she stepped out of the interrogation cell, and I followed. We walked down the hallway to stop before a large metal fire door. "Step through this door, please." I did.

*Clang!* The door slammed shut behind me, and the electric lock bolts slammed home. I spun around in a blind panic, then spun around again as I realized where I was.

Outside the building. In the east parking lot. Standing before the entire A&F division, all 120 people, neatly assembled in rows, by department. I scanned for Charles, Frank, Bubu, and T'shombe, but if they were there, they were hidden in the back.

Two uniformed, black-armbanded, MDE security guards began to play drum rolls on their black-draped snare drums. Walter Duff came forward, stopping a foot short of my nose. Without a word, he tore my MDE name badge from my shirt, threw it on the ground, and stepped on it. Then one by one, he plucked my pencils from my shirt pocket, held them in front of my face, and snapped them in two. My pocket protector followed; then he pulled my shirttails out of my pants, stepped on my shoes and scuffed them, and in a final gesture, produced an ivory-handled scissors, which he used to snip off my necktie just below the knot.

And then two more security guards came forward, and grabbed me by the elbows, and frogmarched me across the parking lot to the property line, which is where my car had already been towed. The guards watched me narrowly, hands on their holsters, while I unlocked the door and climbed into the Toyota.

She started on the second try. I eased her out onto Highway 5 West, turned right, and headed home.

"Hi, Mom, I'm home." No answer. I picked my way up the back steps—gee, Psycho Kitty's litter box *really* needed changing—and wasted just enough time upstairs to verify that Mom had gone out. Grocery store, possibly, or liquor store, more likely.

Fine. Sounded like a great idea. If I could drink more than two cans of Lite without either falling asleep or throwing up, I'd probably do it myself. I

---

### EXTRA CREDIT

It is 12 miles from B305 to Jack's house, and 1.75 miles from Jack's house to the No Questions Asked pawnshop. The average speed of a car on Highway 5 West is 32 miles per hour, while the average speed of a pharmaceutically impaired person on foot carrying a television set is 3.7 miles per hour. It takes 19 minutes to navigate the Police Department's voicemail system.

If Jack leaves work and heads for home at the same time as a morally challenged person exits Jack's home with his mother's TV, will Jack be able to report this unanticipated redistribution of material wealth before the set is pawned and the junkie is back in detox?

Show your math.

---

### INFONUGGETS

Okay, so I changed my mind. Sue me.

wasted a minute looking for the mail before remembering it was Tuesday (we were on the Monday/Wednesday/Friday route) and before realizing, There Was a Way.

Fifteen minutes later, MAX_KOOL was strolling into Heaven. The crowd was a bit different at this time of day—more EastBloc EuroTrash, and a few diehard Yoshi Yakitori types still out doing *nemawashi* from the night before. (Or was it from tomorrow? I can never keep this international dateline business straight.) But the place was still packed, and the

## NEMAWASHI

The ancient Oriental art of buying your boss a few drinks after work. See *brown nosing*.

## MIDNIGHT

Actually, in Heaven, it's always a quarter to twelve. That's one of the immutable rules of the MUD. Don't ask why.

music still pounding, because after all, Heaven is a virtual nightclub on the World Wide Net, and it's always midnight *somewhere*.

I flooped out of the a-grav tube and made straight for the bar. Some idiot kid with a purple mohawk and a row of IC sockets grafted into his forehead made the mistake of getting between me and the bar and trying to introduce himself. "Howdy, Mr. Kool, I'm Lowjack from Silicon Jung—*awk*!" I gave my knife an extra twist to make sure he was real dead, then pulled the

## EASTBLOC

Once you know what to look for, it's really easy to spot the eastern Euros. Since they all use PAL video, and we Norte Americanos use NTSC, their colors always look a bit washed out and they tend to crackle when they move. (Dropped sync bits in conversion, I'm told.)

blade out of his larynx and kicked his collapsing corpse out of the way.

Sam was already pouring me a double by the time I plunked my ass down on the barstool. "Evening, Mr. Kool." He slid the glass across the bar to me and spared a glance at the body on the floor. "Bad day?"

"You don't know the half of it, Sam." I grabbed the drink, knocked it back in one gulp, and set the empty glass back down. Sam refilled it without being asked.

"You want to talk about it, Mr. Kool?"

I paused, the glass halfway to my lips. "Why, Sam. I didn't know you cared." The drink resumed its course.

He shrugged, picked up a rag, and polished an imaginary spot on the bartop. "Can't rightly say as I do," he said at last. "But I do know Miss Eliza was in here asking for you."

I almost spit my drink out. "*Eliza*? I heard she was dead."

"She got better." Sam stopped polishing the bar and flipped the rag over his shoulder as the bouncer—some obese cyber-sumo clown I didn't know—waddled over.

"What happened here?" the bouncer demanded, as he nudged the corpse with his foot.

"The newbie got in this gentleman's face," Sam said, nodding slowly.

> ELIZA
>
> What, you expect me to spoonfeed you *everything*?

"I expect he won't be making that mistake again."

"I should say not," the bouncer said. "But why is *this*—" he kicked the corpse again "—still here?"

"The kid was a putz," I said, as I put my glass down and turned around to face the bouncer. "I don't know what kind of amateurs you're letting in here tonight, but—"

Maybe I didn't recognize the bouncer, but he certainly recognized me. "Oh! Mr. Kool, I'm sorry, I—look, could you please just make it go away? It's making the other guests *nervous*, if you know what I mean."

I gave the bouncer a good frown, took a deep breath, and let it out in a heavy sigh. "Well, okay. This time." With a casual gesture, I brought my left hand up and snapped my fingers.

The corpse randomized out of existence. Which is what *should* have happened as soon as I killed it, and *would* have happened if the kid behind it had known jack squat about VR.

"Thanks Mr. Kool," the bouncer said as he backed away from me, bowing. I snagged my drink off the bar and winked at Sam.

"You want I should call Miss Eliza over for you?" Sam asked.

"No way," I said. "I gotta go see a man about a horse. But in the meantime, if anyone *but* Eliza shows up looking for me . . ."

"You're here tonight, Mr. Kool?"

"Yup. Reckon I am, Sam." Someone called for service at the other end of the bar, and Sam left. I took another sip of my drink, then wandered down the bar, around the corner, and ducked into the little alcove that held Gunnar's palm tree.

"Gunnar?" I whispered.

"Hi," the tree said in Gunnar's voice.

"I got fired today," I said, with more anger in my voice than I'd thought I had. "Could I borrow your AK-47 and—"

"I'm not here right now," the tree continued, "but if you leave your name and a brief message, I'll get back to you as soon as possible. Bye!"

*Oops*. Gee, I hoped Gunnar had good security on his voice-mail message file.

"Max Kool?" said a male voice behind me.

I scowled and turned around, expecting yet another geek from *Silicon Jungle*. "Now wha—?" There was no one there.

"Max Kool?" the voice said again. There was something odd about the spatial imaging. It took me a few seconds to place it.

I looked down. There was a dwarf standing there. But not one of your usual pseudo-medieval Tolkienoids. This one wore a nicely tailored three-piece suit and a brown fedora. "Are you Max Kool?" he asked.

"Who wants to know?" I answered. I conjured up a cigarette, lit it, and blew a stream of smoke at him.

The dwarf doffed his hat and bowed slightly. "I am Thorvold, son of Orvold, from the Hall of the Mountain King!"

"I don't care if you're a son of a bitch from the Halls of Montezuma," I said between puffs. "What's your problem?"

"Since the days of future passed," the dwarf prattled on, "my people have been emissaries, process servers, and repo agents to potentates and emperors!" He put his hat back on, and reached forward as if to shake my hand. Reflexively, I responded by extending my right.

Got to admit, the little bugger was *fast*. Before I could react he clapped a chip into my hand and jumped back a full yard. "Lucky for *you*," he said, "I'm just a messenger!" He clicked his heels three times quick and vanished in a puff of smoke.

Well, I'd certainly walked square into that one. I looked around to see if anyone important had noticed how easily the dwarf suckered me, and how many people I'd have to kill to save face. But it didn't look like the damage was too severe—no one at the bar was snickering at me—so I figured what the hell, I'd let them live, and touched the chip to my forehead.

My beautiful black-haired dancer shimmered into view again. This time, though, she was standing still, except for a slightly feline grinding of her hips, and she had a soundtrack.

"Hi, Max," she said sweetly. Her voice was all sex and honey and true love and lust. "I'm *Amber*. Sorry my friend alarmed you last night, but I was just *so* eager to meet you." She paused to smile and wink. "I still am, Max. Please come see me tonight. 0300 UTC Standard Time, alt.alt._really_.alt.sex.com. I promise, this time I'll be alone, and I'll leave the lights on."

She smiled again, and blew me a kiss. "I'll be waiting for you, darling. And I promise, tonight, I will make you an offer I *know* you won't want to refuse." She smiled one last time and indulged in a long, slow, lascivious tracing of her lips with her tongue. The image faded out.

I suddenly realized where I was and looked around the bar nervously. Gee, I sure hoped that was a psychic projection into my mind and not a virtual hologram that everyone else could see.

*Relax*, DON_MAC thought, *it wasn't a hologram. But for the benefit of us telepaths, would you kindly take your libido outside? Just* listening *to you makes my prostate ache.*

"Sorry," I subvoked. I pushed the chip into my dataglove, went back to the bar, and resumed serious drinking.

0300 UTC Standard Time, 10:00 local. I rolled my virtual Harley Ultraglide down the back streets of BusinessWorld, scanning for the address ♥AMBER♥ had given me. The weight of the virtual .45 tucked inside my virtual black leather jacket was comforting.

The weight of the matched pair of virtual Fairbairn-Sykes knives tucked into my boots, on the other hand, was a little awkward. And the weight of the virtual M-62 machine gun strapped across my back was downright annoying. But

> ### TIME ZONES
>
> For the benefit of those six wankers out there who are going to check a map and calculate the time zones: did you remember to account for daylight savings time?

I think it was the weight of the virtual TOW missile launcher slung across the handlebars of my bike that was the real pain in the ass.

I didn't feel good about this. Yeah, Amber had me hooked

by the gonads (ouch!) and was reeling me in. But the part of
BusinessWorld her message had led me into was *not* someplace I usually went. Like pretty much every other venue in the
known universe, BusinessWorld had its hierarchies, its polari-
ties. Yin and yang, good and evil, light and dark, sweet and
sour: if the uniform gray corporate blocks from the night
before were the up side of BusinessWorld, then this was the
sowbug-covered downside.

*ToxicTown.*

Here was the dark heart of the wild, old, prefederalization
Net, where nothing went in a straight line, financial card houses
teetered in blatant defiance of fiscal gravity, and massive pyramid
marketing schemes turned out to be supported, at the bottom, by
absolutely nothing at all. It was a place where datastreams jumbled together like a colander full of overcooked spaghetti, incom-
patible systems stood out like lumpy indigestible meatballs, and
the streets all too often ran red with marinara sauce. A place
where life was cheap, and sunlight was expensive, and you could
never tell when the superhighway might suddenly vanish into a
deconstruction zone, to leave you stranded on a narrow old twist-
ed-pair line with the hungry wolves eyeing you suspiciously and
licking their chops, their paws, their genitals, and all the other
parts of themselves that canines like to lick and that therefore
make it very easy to spot werewolves when they're out in public,
such as, say, riding the bus.

Actually, I rather liked ToxicTown. I'd probably have
spent more time there, except my self-appointed mission on the
Net was to make noise and raise a stink, and it's a lot easier to
do that when you're someplace where the stink will be *noticed*.

You wouldn't notice it in ToxicTown. You'd notice the
two-bit hustlers, hanging out on the virtual street corners: the
InfoPimps, the DataWhores, the dollar-a-go RosiCrucians.
You'd notice the virtual graffiti spray-painted on every flat surface: "Kill All The Brutes!" being the current favorite. For this

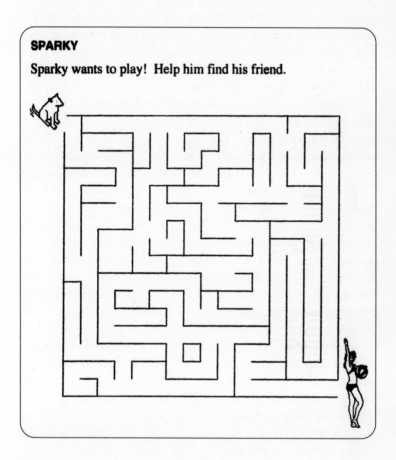

**SPARKY**

**Sparky wants to play! Help him find his friend.**

was a shadowy world of perpetual night, home to shady operators, shady ladies, private detectives, and IRS auditors.

Fittingly enough I found ♥AMBER♥ on a virtual street
corner, leaning against a lamppost, smoking a black Sobranie
cigarette in a long ebony holder, her high cheekbones accentu-
ated by the harsh red glare of the virtual sodium streetlight.

"Hello, sailor," she said as I brought the Harley to a stop. "Is that a gun in your pocket, or are you happy to see me?" I parked the bike and dismounted; she gave me a long look up and down. "Must be a snubnose," she decided.

I hooked my thumbs in my belt loops and gave her my best James Dean. "Heard you been looking for me, lady."

"You heard right." She took another drag on her cigarette, then nodded at a dark, open doorway. "C'mon up to my place, and we'll talk business." She pulled the ciggy out of the holder and flipped it away—it landed on a sleeping newsjunkie, who went up in a ball of orange flame—then hobbled over toward the door, her high spike heels clicking out a seductive Morse code on the pavement in perfect syncopation to the torsion of her athletic gluteal muscles under her incredibly tight knee-length skirt. How she could actually *walk* in that thing, I'll never know.

Amber paused in the doorway and looked over her left shoulder at me. "You can leave all the hardware behind," she winked, "or bring it along, if it makes you feel bigger." She started up the stairs.

I dumped everything but the .45 and ran after her.

Amber's place was on the top level of the data structure, and it was a seduction pit, pure and simple. Nothing but satin and lace and soft lighting, Frank Sinatra at low volume on the virtual Muzak track, and a bed the size of an Olympic swimming pool. She was standing over by the far windows when I came in. After I closed the door, she threw open the curtains and dimmed the lights further to stand silhouetted against the virtual lights of ToxicTown.

Slowly and carefully, with a very clear aware-

---

ROOM DECOR

That, and a row of manacles along one wall, but I didn't feel like asking too closely about *them*.

ness of exactly how much of a tease she was, Amber peeled off her blouse.

"So, Amber," I said between dry gulps. "What's the deal?"

"Penetration, Max," she whispered.

*Oh, boy.*

"Word on the street," she went on, "is that you're the *best*." I couldn't quite see what she did next, but I clearly heard the pop of a button and the rasp of a zipper. Her skirt fell down around her ankles.

*Oooooh, boy!*

"And if you're *half* as good as they say you are," she took a small step, and lightly kicked the skirt away, "then you are *exactly* what the doctor ordered."

*Ohmygodohmygodohmygod!* I threw my leather jacket off and started fighting with all the buckles and zippers and belts and shit on my black jeans. Damn! Why did I have to go for such a complicated retro-techno look? One critical zipper stubbornly refused to budge.

"Max?" Amber sounded puzzled. Then, "Lights!"

The room lights came up to normal. I was standing there with my boots half unlaced and my pants around my knees and my smiley-face boxer shorts snagged on my bullet-proof Kevlar vest.

Amber, somehow, managed to be wearing a black body suit. "Max?" she said, puzzled. Then, *"Ma-ax!"* as it dawned on her. "I said word on the *street*, not word on the bathroom wall! Now if you will kindly curb your raging hormones, I'd like to talk to you about *business*!"

Fortunately, there's no such thing as a data condom, so she had no idea of the true effect of her words.

"It's pretty simple, Max," she said, when I was all dressed and not hyperventilating again. "You have a bad reputation."

"That's too bad."

"No, that's good. I desperately need someone like you."

"That's good."

"No, it's bad. I wish I didn't."

"That's not good."

"Too bad. It's my problem, and I've got to solve it."

"By hiring someone bad?"

"To get the goods. Exactly."

"I'm confused."

"Don't be. It's like this. The word on you is that, given enough time, Max Kool can penetrate any system in BusinessWorld."

"Is that good?"

"Don't get me started. My problem is that my employer—"

"That monster in the shadows last night?"

"You think that was bad, you should see him in the daylight. Anyway, my employer has some critical files that have gotten into the wrong hands. Worse, these are the *only* copies."

"No backups? That's bad."

"Will you *stop* that? The long and short of it is, I want to hire *you* to get them back."

I paused and scratched my chin. I decided I needed to add a virtual five-o'clock shadow to my aspect. "What's in it for me?"

She didn't even blink. "One million dollars, cash. A hundred thousand up front, and the balance on delivery."

I gulped. "Those must be some files."

"Only for my employer and the person who's got them now. To anyone else," she looked at me sharply, "they'd be worthless."

"I'm going to need some time to set this up," I said. It sounded like the sort of thing a guy named Max Kool would say.

"You're going to need more than that," Amber said. "The system you're going to be cracking into has some of the best defenses around. State of the art."

"No military," I said quickly. "I don't do military." Gunnar LeMat spent a lot of time hanging around MilNet, and some of the stories he told about the military systems were enough to make your toe hair curl.

"Not military," Amber reassured me. "But still, you're going to need state-of-the-art tools. We can provide them. Cutting edge stuff: experimental interfaces, radical new things *light years* ahead of what's available on the commercial market. If you agree to do this job for us, we'll supply you with everything you need."

"Hmm," I said pensively. "Sounds a little like you also want me to be a human guinea pig. Busting into this system and grabbing your files is going to be tough enough. Why should I risk my ass on an experimental interface?"

"Because, darling," she said softly as she moved in close and stuck her virtual tongue in my virtual ear, "I'm using this interface right now, and I can assure you, the virtual sex is *fantastic!*"

Somehow, her body suit vanished. Her breasts were small, firm, and fit my cupped hand nicely; her nipples, tight and dark, thrust between my fingers. As she pushed me down onto the bed and covered my mouth with hers, my hands wrapped around the small of her back, and I slowly traced her muscles all the way down to her lithe, athletic, thighs. My God, if the tactile sensation she was transmitting through my datagloves was any indication, this new interface of hers must be . . .

Fade to black.

And fade back to light, very quickly. As if from a dream, a distant voice was calling me. *"Ja-ack!"*

Amber sensed something was wrong. "What is it, darling?"

*"Ja-ack!"* Oh no, it couldn't be. Not her. Not *now*.

I sat up in bed. Amber sat up with me, and nibbled my ear. "What's wrong, Max?"

*"Ja-ack!"*

"I gotta go, babe. No time to explain."

"But—my job. Will you—?"

"I'll get back to you on that." I kissed Amber good-bye, and in a halo of light, exited from virtual reality.

*"Ja-ack! Your computer is screwing up my TV picture again!"*

# 8

## WEDNESDAY MORNING, 7 A.M.

The chirping of my bedside phone woke me. I rolled over, grabbed the handset, put it to my ear, and was rewarded with the ear-splitting squeal of someone trying to send me a fax.

Okay. That worked. I was awake.

But the more I thought about it, the more I wondered, *why*? Why be awake? Why even think about getting out of bed? Why not just crawl back under the covers and wait for the heat death of the universe?

The phone chirped again. I answered again.

Whoever was sending that fax, they were persistent.

I dropped the phone in its cradle, pulled the blankets over my head, and tried to go back to sleep. When that failed, I tried to steer my wandering early-morning imagination into a good erotic fantasy.

After a few minutes, one started to take form. In my mind I saw a woman (always a good start, that) with long, silky black hair and a beautiful, angular face. She had olive skin and a dancer's body: tall and slender, yet lithe and athletic. Her lips were thin and expressive; her eyes, like dark pools of ebony water. Her hips were slim but nicely rounded, and her breasts were small, firm, high, and just the right size to fit my cupped hand—

Omigod. I was wet-dreaming about Amber. And along with that realization came another, which brought me fully awake and sitting bolt upright in bed.

She was *serious*.

The phone chirped again. From idiotic reflex I grabbed it, then winced in anticipation when I'd realized what I'd done.

No ear-splitting beep this time, though. Instead, there were street traffic noises in the background, and after a few seconds, one hesitant, spoken, word. "Pyle?"

It took me a few blinks to recognize the voice. "T'shombe?"

Her relief was audible, and the words came out in a gush. "Oh, Pyle, thank God, I've been so *worried* about you! After what happened yesterday, I feel so bad about that, and then the look on your face as you drove away, I was afraid—"

*"T'shombe?"* I was having just a little trouble believing this was for real, and the thought did flit through my mind to try pressing *Control-Option-E*, just in case it wasn't.

"Yes, Pyle," she said breathlessly, "it's me. And look, I can't talk now—I'm calling from a pay phone in a convenience store parking lot. I don't think the company can backtrace this to me, but all the same I don't want to stay on too long. I just need to know one thing. *Are you okay?*"

I thought it over. "Uh, yeah. I guess so."

"Are you *sure* about that?"

One eyebrow went up; strange thing to ask. "I guess so."

"Good." She paused. In my mind, I could see the way she would bite her lower lip whenever she was trying to work up the nerve to ask a difficult question.

"Pyle," she said, "I want you to promise me two—no, three—promise me three things, okay? Promise me you won't do anything—*reckless*, will you?"

I had absolutely no idea what she meant. "Sure," I said.

"Good," she said. "Now, you know that Mexican restaurant on the corner of Warner Road and Highway 61?" I made an affirmative noise. "Promise you'll meet me there, at seven o'clock tonight?"

That took a second to sink in. "Are you serious?"

"Absolutely. I want you—no, I *need* you, to meet me there at seven o'clock tonight. Promise you'll show up?"

Well, I will be damned. "Yes!" I said, with more enthusiasm than I'd thought possible.

"Good. And finally," she paused, and drew a deep breath, and dropped her voice down to a soft, gentle pitch. "Jack? I know you're going through a rough patch right now. But always remember, no matter what happens, there are people who *love* you, Jack. Promise me you'll remember that?"

I gulped. If T'shombe was trying to tell me what I thought she was trying to tell me. . . .

"Yes, T'shombe," I said in the most sincere, sensitive, masculine yet caring voice I could muster. "I promise, I—"

"Good." She let out a small gasp. "A cop car just pulled in here! I've got to go. Don't call me at home; don't call me at work. But remember, tonight, seven o'clock. You'll be there?"

"Yes, T'shombe, I *will* be—"

"Good. Bye." The line clicked and went dead. I hung up.

Well, well, well. Maybe it was just the afterglow from my fantasy about Amber, and maybe I was misunderstanding T'shombe completely, but thinking back over what she'd said, I didn't think so. *Jack, old boy*, I said to myself, *this day is* definitely *off to a promising start*.

I was still floating on clouds when my phone chirped again. Dreamily, I answered. "Hello?"

"G'morning Jack!" Gunnar barked out. "I got your message! Sorry to hear your bad news, and as for the power tool you asked about borrowing, forget it! But on the positive side, I'd say this means you're free for breakfast today, yes?"

"Yes?" I echoed. I was still trying to absorb "G'morning."

"Right, it's settled then! Get dressed, and get your ass out here! I'll expect you at oh-nine-hundred, and you can tell me all about it when you get here. Got that?"

When Gunnar is in his manic phase, the only thing to do is go along with the flow. "Got it."

"Then, ciao!" He broke the connection; I hung up my phone. But all the while I was shaving and dressing, I stayed near it, wondering who was going to call next on this remarkable morning. Bubu? Amber? Ed McMahon? The pope?

No. Just that dolt who was still trying to send me a fax.

Joseph "Gunnar" LeMat flipped the bacon in the frying pan, then directed his attention to the English muffins in the toaster. "Now, let me get this straight," he said as he tripped the lever by hand and popped the muffins up. "This drop-dead gorgeous babe—"

"Amber," I said.

"—who's been blundering around MilNet for the past week," he plucked the hot muffins out of the toaster with his bare fingers and quickly dropped them onto a plate, "wants to recruit MAX_KOOL to break into a computer and steal some files?"

I took the plate from him and started buttering the muffins. "To *retrieve* some files," I said. "She claims they were stolen from her in the first place." Once the base coat of butter was down, I laid on a thick top coat of Schwartau cherry preserves.

Joseph prodded the bacon one last time, then started lifting it out of the frying pan and spreading it out on a paper towel to drain. "And she's willing to pay you *how* much?"

"One million dollars," I said as I carried the muffins and the coffee pot out to the breakfast table on the sun porch. LeMat's consulting business was doing well—or his ex-wife came from old family money and had him paid a lot to end the marriage, it depended on when you asked him—so LeMat lived in a nice house hidden in twenty wooded acres on the western shore of Lake Minnetonka. The view from the sun porch in the morning was spectacular. "One hundred thou up front, and the rest on delivery." I had to move the carafe of tomato juice and bowl of scrambled eggs to make room on the table, but everything fit.

Joseph shut off the burner, moved the frying pan off to the side, and brought the bacon over to the table. "One million dollars," he said softly as he slowly shook his head and forked some strips of bacon onto my plate. "What do you think, Jack? Is she nuts?"

I poured myself a glass of tomato juice, took a sip, and considered my reply.

"I don't think so," I said at last. "This interface she's talking about is real. I've touched it." And that particular memory sent me off into a wistful, rosy mood that lasted until LeMat cleared his throat.

"But one *million*—?"

I shrugged and helped myself to the scrambled eggs. "My guess is she's some kind of high-powered corporate type who's done some playing around in virtual reality and on the Net. She seems to know her way around BusinessWorld. And she's built herself a pretty kinky little MUD down in ToxicTown."

"Or someone built it for her," Joseph pointed out.

I nodded. "Could be." LeMat was pouring himself a cup of coffee. I held

> MUD
>
> Multi-User Dimension, remember?

out my cup and got a refill. "Mmm," I said, as I savored the bitter, earthy aroma. "Hazelnut?"

Joseph nodded. "We're celebrating the moments of your life," he explained.

I set the cup down and moved an English muffin to my plate. "Anyway, I figure these files got lifted, and they really *are* as valuable as Amber says, so her boss turned to her and said, 'You know the Net. *You* go get them.' And suddenly, it wasn't playing anymore. She had to do this hacking stuff for *real*." I looked at the scrambled eggs a moment, realized something was missing, and reached for the pepper mill. "So she read some literature, cranked up this new interface, and went poking around in parts of the Net she'd never been in before, hoping to find someone who could actually *do* all this magical cyberpunk stuff . . ."

"And that's how she found out about MAX_KOOL," LeMat completed.

"Yeah." I'll confess to a certain smugness at that point.

"But being basically a *naif*," LeMat went on, "it never occurred to her that she was hanging out with a bunch of gamers and posers, and that MAX's reputation was ninety-percent hot air—"

My balloon of smugness popped. *"Hey!"*

"—that the *real* shady operators, computer criminals, and cyberterrorists never waste time with virtual reality—"

*"I beg your pardon!"*

"—and that in any event, she could probably get a couple of college kids to do the job for her for *free*."

My smugness finished its collapse into a black hole and vanished. "Yeah, you're right," I said at last. "I haven't done any serious hacking in over a year. And even when I was doing it, I was only in it for the fun. The whole idea of getting paid to break into someone else's computer—" I shuddered. "I mean, that's a felony or something, isn't it?"

Joseph tried a sip of coffee and leaned back in his chair. "But as you said yourself, you wouldn't actually be *stealing* anything."

"That's *if* Amber is telling me the truth. Big if."

LeMat leaned forward again and took a bite of his English muffin. "Y'know, Jack, I think you're looking at this all wrong. You keep talking about it as doing a break-in. I think you should consider it, oh, freelance security consulting." He bit off another chunk of the muffin, chewed and swallowed it, and chased it with a gulp of coffee. "I think MAX_KOOL should take the job."

I turned and stared at him.

"Furthermore, I think he should cut his old buddy Gunnar in for fifty percent of the action."

My eyes went wide.

"After all, you've been telling me for years that you wish you could break into the consulting racket. Sounds to me like you've found the perfect first client here. A rich chump with an urgent problem and no clear idea of how to go about fixing it; a guaranteed minimum just for saying you'll try and almost airtight deniability if something goes wrong; and no matter what happens, you clear some serious cash, and your client goes away thinking you're a genius."

"But one *million*—?"

"Never argue with someone who wants to overpay you," LeMat said. "If I have learned one thing from consulting, it's that you should *never* underbid a project. If this Amber is convinced that the job should cost her a million—and God knows where she got that number from, a comic book maybe, or a bad made-for-cable miniseries," he shook his head, and took another gulp of coffee, "and you come back and say it's only going to cost ten thousand, she'll assume you're a putz who doesn't know what he's talking about and go find someone who *will* take all of her money."

I could only toy with my fork and shake my head.

"Welcome to the wonderful world of consulting, Jack. I mean, let me give you a clue here. This is *work*, and work *sucks*. That's why we don't call it *fun*."

I looked him in the face, hoping to see some sign that he was joking. A crinkle in the corner of his eye, maybe, or the slight hint of a veiled smirk.

LeMat returned my gaze with level seriousness. "Personally, if someone offered *me* a million dollars, I'd do the job, take the money, and skip the country so fast it'd make your teeth spin. Go someplace where they never even *heard* of quarterly estimated tax returns. The Cayman Islands, maybe."

I cocked an eyebrow at him.

"I'm serious, Jack. Take the job. If the money angle bothers you, then say you're doing it because this Amber babe is practically begging to screw your brains out."

"But—"

"That, *and eat your damned breakfast! What the hell's* wrong *with you? You've been pushing food around your plate for the last ten minutes and you haven't actually* eaten *a single bite! Now your muffin's cold and your eggs are congealed and—*"

And after that outburst, we settled down and had a pleasant breakfast, and a nice conversation after. All the wild talk of skipping the country faded away; LeMat promised to find a role for me in his consulting firm as soon as my noncompete contract with MDE expired. ("I've always felt that J. LeMat and Associates probably should have at least one actual associate.") This led us to a brief tour of his combination dining and computer room, where he showed me some new tricks he'd taught ENIGMA, his personal SuperVAX. (LeMat is the only person I've ever even *heard* of who has his own personal SuperVAX—as well as reinforced floor joists to support it, a liquid nitrogen tank to cool it, and the LeMat Museum of Obsolete DEC Systems occupying most of what other people would consider to be a basement.) At the end of the tour, as usual, we wound up in his walk-in gun safe, where he proudly showed me the latest addition to his assault rifle collection: a

Stoner SR-25. Which I made the appropriate oohing and aahing noises over, even though as far as I can tell these things all fall into three basic categories: the high-tech black ones with plastic stocks, the "normal-looking" brown ones with wooden stocks, and the variations on the AK-47 Terrorist Special.

By the time we were done with fondling guns and a little lunch, LeMat had me just about talked into taking Amber's job. "Now, the first thing we need to do is rent you an office," he was saying as he walked me out to my car. "Set you up with power, blocked phones, an OC1 data line—"

"Whoa." I stopped in my tracks. "Office? I thought we were talking strictly a one-shot deal here."

"You still need an office," LeMat said. He stopped, turned around, and looked at me. "What, you want to try doing this from your mother's basement? I can see it now." LeMat could do a frighteningly good imitation of Mom when he wanted to. *"Jack! Ja-ack! I know you're working on a million-dollar contract, but your computer is screwing up my TV picture again!"*

I resumed walking toward my car. "Okay, agreed. I need an office. What else?"

LeMat ticked off a mental list on his fingers. "Well, phone service, of course. Then high-bandwidth commercial Net access—OC1 at least, OC3 would be better. And a satellite dish probably wouldn't hurt. But before that, we need to set you up with some kind of straw-man financial front."

We reached my car. I pulled the handle, and the driver's door opened with a rusty squeal. "A false front? Why? I thought you said—"

"Uh, Jack?" LeMat's voice dropped to a low, conspiratorial pitch. "Just in case this Amber babe is *not* on the up-and-up, it would probably be a good idea if she didn't know MAX_KOOL's real name, and if there was no way for her to trace the money trail and find out."

I arched an eyebrow and once again reconsidered my involvement in this whole mess.

LeMat threw a disarming smile at me. "Trust me, Jack, this sort of thing happens *all* the time in the consulting business. Clients want to stay anonymous; consultants want to protect their subcontractors and confidential sources. As long as we keep good honest records for the IRS and file our returns on time, there is absolutely *nothing* illegal in what we're doing."

"Well—"

LeMat smiled again and gave my shoulder a squeeze. "Leave the details to me, Jack. I'll make some calls this afternoon and have the groundwork laid out by the time we meet at the club tonight. Say, about seven-ish?"

"Sure—" Oh, wait a minute. *T'shombe*.

Joseph looked at me with sharp eyes. "What's wrong?"

For a change, *I* smiled. "Oh, nothing. It's just—I can't make it. I've got a date tonight."

And finally, at long last, I learned what it took to put an amazed expression on LeMat's face. "You sly dog!" he said with a huge grin as he slapped me on the back and nearly knocked me face first onto his driveway. "So you're gonna do the Wild Thing tonight! Gonna ride the subway tunnel to Paradise! Sail the skin boat to Tuna Town!" He grabbed my right hand and shook it so hard he nearly knocked my wristwatch off.

"Forget the club, kid! You go out and get lucky, and that's an *order*, soldier! I'll take care of business tonight—but I want a full report on your date tomorrow!" He slapped me on the back again and practically pushed me into the car. I started the Toyota up, backed it around, and headed up the driveway. I watched him in the rearview mirror as I drove away; LeMat was still grinning, waving, hooting, and pumping his fist in the air as he disappeared around a bend in the road.

Y'know, I will confess that right up until that moment, I

*was* thinking about my date with T'shombe mostly in terms of whether or not I was going to get into her pants. But somehow, listening to LeMat's macho jocko locker-room banter made me feel, well, *cheap*. And sleazy. And really uncomfortable at the idea that I was somehow being disrespectful to her.

*Which is the kind of prudish attitude you've* always *had about women*, my sarcastic inner voice pointed out. *Which is why in school* you *got clammy handshakes, while the letterjocks were getting* laid. *Which is why, if it weren't for Darlene Franecki, you'd* still *be a virgin. Which is why that arrogant virtual bastard MAX_KOOL has a sex life, and* you *don't. Women lie about it, but they're all secretly* turned-on *by macho creeps who treat them like dirt.*

---

### DARLENE FRANECKI

AKA "The Incredible Human Sperm Bank." Ms. Franecki and I had a steamy relationship during senior year of high school, which began when she failed her algebra mid-term, and ended when she finally realized that mathematical knowledge was *not* transmitted in bodily fluids. Thereafter she took an interest in hockey and made the team—the *entire* team—eventually going on to become president of the Future Welfare Mothers of America, Mounds Park Chapter.

---

Yeah, well, maybe they are, but that isn't me. I told my sarcastic inner voice to stuff a sock in it and started wondering if I had time to get my sportcoat to a dry cleaner.

**Wednesday evening, 7 P.M.:** I stood in the parking lot of the restaurant on the corner of Warner and Highway 61, leaning against the hood of my Toyota, watching the sun sink over the Harriet Island sewage treatment plant and savoring the fertile, earthy smells of a beautiful warm spring evening.

The breeze was from the east, of course.

A flock of migrating Harley-Davidsons passed on southbound Highway 61, their unmuffled exhaust pipes rumbling off into the distance. I moved away from the hood of my car, brushed the dust off the seat of my slacks, and checked my watch again.

7:17.

It was not like T'shombe to be this late. On the other hand, she *had* pulled a lot of practical jokes on me in the time we worked together, and there was at least the possibility that this was some kind of weird, final, insulting gag. . . .

It did not require much imagination to see Frank, Bubu, and T'shombe sitting in the park on the bluff across the river, watching me through binoculars and laughing their damn fool heads off. The idea that T'shombe might stand me up just for a joke actually made me feel a little sick.

I checked my watch again, then straightened my freshly cleaned and pressed sportcoat, adjusted the casually open collar of my neatly ironed dress shirt, and decided to give her just ten more minutes. Fifteen, tops.

A sudden squeal of tires got my attention. My head jerked up like a marionette on a string, and I saw T'shombe's late-model Chevrolet Landbarge come blasting around the corner, up the driveway into the restaurant parking lot, and bouncing over the speed bump without even the slightest hint of slowing. She slammed on the brakes and brought it to a screaming stop just about on the toes of my (freshly polished) wingtips, popped open the passenger side door, and shouted, "Jump in!"

I did. I barely had the door closed before she slapped the car into reverse, lit up the tires going backward, and took us over the speed bump again with a molar-loosening bounce. We flew down the driveway and slammed into both the street and the bottom limit of the suspension; she slewed us around like a carnival ride, speed-shifted into forward gear, and took off down Warner Road like the proverbial bat out of hell. The

Chevy, I couldn't help noticing, moved out with surprising power, authority, and engine noise, but all the fine handling control of a thirty-foot ChrisCraft.

"Sorry I'm late!" T'shombe shouted over the roar of the engine as I dug for the ends of my seat belt like my Mom going for a lit cigarette butt dropped into a crack in the couch. "There was some guy in a white Mazda following me, so I had to take a detour to shake him off!" She threw us into a death-defying slalom around a fully loaded garbage truck, then floored it to squeeze the Chevy through a tiny gap between a pickup truck in the left lane and an oncoming double-bottom semi. I took a quick glance at T'shombe then; I wanted to see her face one last time before I died.

She was hunched over the steering wheel, clutching it tightly with both hands, her bright red lips slightly parted in nervous anticipation. Her dark brown eyes were darting back and forth like chocolate pinballs from the side mirror, to the windshield, to the rearview mirror . . .

Her paranoia was catching, I guess. I finally got my seat belt fastened, and twisted around in my seat to look out the back window. Excluding the garbage truck and the guy in the pickup truck who was making grand and eloquent obscene gestures at us, there was no one back there.

T'shombe took a heart-stopping swerve to the right around a car that was slowing for the Sibley Street light, then floored it to run the Jackson light before the cross-traffic could start moving. "T'shombe!" I yelled. "There's no one behind us!"

*"What?"* she yelled back.

"The white Mazda! You lost him! You can slow down!"

*"I'm not trying to lose anyone!"* She took the corner at Chestnut Street on two wheels and almost got us airborne going over the railroad tracks. *"I'm driving like this 'cause we're late for* church!"

**Thursday morning, 0300 UTC Standard Time**. Gunnar slammed his bottle of Kirin down on the bar and stared at me bug-eyed. *"Church?"*

Max Kool (me) stubbed his cigarette out in the ear of a convenient *Silicon Jungle* groupie, conjured another one out of virtual nothingness, and lit it with a red-eyed glare. "Yeah. That was our hot date. Wednesday vespers."

Gunnar shook his head, took a slug of his beer, and shook his head some more. "I cannot believe it. You have been talking about this woman for months, and I never even *guessed* she might be a Jesus bunny."

"Oh," I sighed, "it's not Jesus. Jesus, I could handle." The bartender—not Sam, he was offline for a code update that night—brought me a bottle of bourbon and an IV line. I pushed the spike and hose back at him and asked for a normal glass.

"Not Jesus?" Gunnar prompted. "Krishna? Mohammed?" He paused. *"Elvis?"*

"Worse," I said. The bartender came back with a whiskey glass and filled it for me. I downed it in one gulp and let him pour another. "My lovely lady friend," I told Gunnar, between deep drags on my virtual cigarette, "is a card-carrying holy-rolling true-believing member of the Church of Vegentology."

"The *who*?"

"No, The Who was a sixties rock band. I'm t-t-talking 'bout a bunch of fruitcakes who believe that since plants were here first, they must be superior. In fact, the core idea seems to be that plants *created* animals in order to have ambulatory servants."

Gunnar took a deep slug of his beer and nodded. "I can see why plants would want to create animals. Especially sheep."

My cigarette was down to a tiny glowing stub. I crushed it out of existence between my fingertips and fought the urge to light another. "Oh, it makes a certain limited kind of sense. If you'd ever met my Aunt Beatrice, you'd believe she was enslaved by African violets.

"But the Vegentologist cosmology gets a *lot* more complicated than that. Eternal wars between good and evil; endless cycles of reseeding and regrowth; life here on Earth as a sort of spiritual R-and-R between the battles on the cosmic fruited plain. The ultimate idea, I guess, is to work through all your past incarnations and find out what kind of plant you were in the Pre-Cambrian."

Gunnar tried another pull on his beer and found it was empty. "Ferns? They all want to be *ferns*?"

A wicked idea occurred to me. "Y'know, Gunnar, if you're really curious about this church, it just so happens I have around thirty pounds of tracts and monographs in my car, and I could be persuaded to loan them to you for a very, *very* long time."

"Spare me." Gunnar broke his empty beer bottle over the head of a convenient dwarf and signaled the bartender to throw him another bottle. I ducked as Gunnar's next beer sailed through the space occupied microseconds before by my head; it came to rest, open and right side up, in Gunnar's waiting hand.

Heaven definitely was a different kind of place on nights when Sam was not working.

"Bet your lady friend really gets off on Arbor Day," Gunnar said.

I sighed. "They had a sunrise service at the Como Park Arboretum this year. They showed videotapes of it during the pot-luck dinner."

*"Dinner?"*

I smiled and shrugged. "Well, the good news is, they're not vegetarians. Dinner was barbecued ribs, teriyaki chicken, and a steak like a slab of two-by-twelve. I made a real pig of myself. Oink." I leaned back in my chair, patted my belly, and sucked down another slurp of bourbon.

Gunnar nodded. "Okay, so that's half of a good evening.

Now, back to your lady friend. Did she give you a chance to, uh, plow the furrow? Spill your seed?" He frowned and scratched his chin. "What would be a good vegentological metaphor?"

I took another pull on my drink and allocated a few seconds to some last-minute polishing of the Lie. *Aw, bugger it*, I decided, *I'll tell the truth.*

"No," I admitted.

Gunnar didn't seem at all surprised.

"We got back to the restaurant parking lot where we'd left my car at about nine. She was driving; she stopped, put it in park, left the engine running. Clearly, she was waiting for me to get out of her car. I screwed my courage up to the sticking point, leaned across the front seat, and kissed her right on the lips."

Gunnar arched one eyebrow. "And that's when she punched your lights out?"

I shook my head. "That would have been better, I think. Instead, she just sort of looked at me with this incredibly blank expression, then said, 'What was *that* for?' I kind of, well, y'know, fumbled around for words—"

"As you do so well," Gunnar noted.

"And then she said, 'Don't take this wrong, Py—, er *Max*. I really am flattered that you feel this way about me. And you know, a roll in the hay with you might even be fun. It's been a long time since I've had a guy who needed training as desperately as you do.

"'But Max, sex without emotional commitment is just tag-team masturbation, and frankly, I'm tired of collecting scalps.'"

Gunnar set his now-empty beer bottle down on the bar. "And that's when she gave you the goodnight handshake?"

I set my empty glass next to Gunnar's empty bottle. "Yep." We both stared at the virtual light refracting through the virtual glass for a while.

"Gunnar?" a voice behind us said. "Max Kool?" In unison, we turned around. One of Don Vermicelli's slick-haired trigger boys was standing there, right hand tucked inside his expensive but tasteless pinstripe suit, looking more like Napoleon in a men's clothing ad than a guy with a pistol in a shoulder holster. "The don will see you now."

Gunnar and I made eye contact with each other, then hopped off our barstools. "How fortunate that we are visible," I said.

"Shut up, Max," Gunnar said. "And for God's sake, let me do the talking. Your attitude right now could get us *both* killed."

# 9

## PARSLEY, SAGE, ROSEMARY & *POLIPO VERACI*

Don Luigi Vermicelli had a private table in the far left corner of Heaven. Most of the tables in Heaven were round. His was crescent-moon shaped, to accommodate his spectacular girth.

I've mentioned before how in virtual reality details fill in as you draw nearer to a person or an object. The don used this effect well. Look at him from across the room, and you might mistake him for a white weather balloon with a hat and arms. But approach his table, and you begin to realize that he's a man—albeit a spectacularly *fat* man—wearing a white linen three-piece suit, a white shirt, a white tie, and a white panama hat. Draw closer still, and you can see that the florid and misshapen lump between the brim of his hat and the collar of his shirt is not a giant mutant tomato, but rather, his head. Then take those last few steps, into the area of the don's supreme influence (not to mention gravitational pull), and you can hear the plaintive mandolin music in the background, see the flickering light of the candles in the chianti bottles, and marvel at how, despite the incredible array of rich food that surrounds him, there is not one grease spot or sauce stain on Don Vermicelli's white suit.

And usually, that's about the point where a few of the don's trigger boys stick their pistols up your nose and ask the don if he wants you dead.

"Boys, boys," Don Vermicelli said, "what's the matter with you? *Relax*." His voice was strangely hoarse and soft, and his accent so thick it would probably be a violation of the Ethnic Humor Elimination Act to attempt to transcribe it, so I won't. "Gunnar and Max are my *friends*."

The trigger boys backed off and let us through.

"C'mere," the don said to us, patting the bench seat that arced around the table to his right. "Sit with me. Let's talk."

I tried to let Gunnar take the seat closest to the don, but he tried to let me, so we did the Alphonse-and-Gaston bit for a few turns until I said to hell with it and took the seat. Gunnar squeezed in next to me.

"So, Max," the don said, "Gunnar tells me you have a little problem, and he thinks maybe I can solve it."

I glanced at Gunnar, who was clearly working up the nerve to say something polite and circumspect, then turned back to the don and decided to go for it. "Yeah. Can you?" Gunnar blanched.

The don considered me for a long, cold moment, then nodded slowly. "Yes, Max. I can solve your little problem for you." Gunnar sighed in relief. "The question is, are you willing to pay my price?"

Gunnar opened his mouth again. I struck first. "How much?"

The don shook his enormous bloated head, and *tched*. "Such an impatient boy! Come, first *mangiamo*. Food is life, Max, and it's bad for the heart to talk business on an empty stomach." With some considerable effort, he got his hands together across the vast expanse of his stomach and clapped once.

Two overinflated blond bimbos jiggled into view, wearing (as far as I could tell) nothing but jewelry, makeup, and high heels. "My friends," Don Vermicelli said, "allow me to introduce the Silicione Sisters: Bambi and Thumper." Bambi was the one on the left, I think, although I really couldn't see any point in differentiating between them. Gunnar, however, clearly could.

"Ah, my lovely *gnocchis*," the don said to them, "my friends are hungry. Bring them some food. Oh," he paused, and stroked his first two chins meditatively, "let's start with a little *polipi veraci all' aglio*, and a *zuppa di cappelletti*. Then maybe some *tagliatelle verdi alla marinara*, some *starne al vino rosso*, and just a touch of *fondi di carciofi trifolati*. And then for the appetizer course, I want—" He stopped, frowned, and waved his hand dismissively. "Oh, no mind, I decide when you come back. Now *andiamo, andiamo!*" He gave Thumper a little swat on the *culo* to hurry her along. The Silicione Sisters giggled and jiggled out of sight.

Don Vermicelli turned back to me and Gunnar. "And now, my friends," he lifted his wineglass, "to business."

About damn time, I figured. "Yeah. Are we talking—?"

Gunnar elbowed me in the ribs and steered my attention to the full wineglass on the table before me. *"He's proposing a toast, Max."* Gunnar lifted his wineglass and joined the don.

"To business!"

Eventually, our food showed up. It was all very interesting to look at, although not much fun to eat because, being virtual, it had no taste and no nutritional value. Bambi and Thumper stayed around to serve and wait on us, which also had no taste and no nutritional value, but became somewhat amusing when Gunnar attempted to illustrate a story about Navy carrier pilots by using Bambi's navel as a wineglass. Thumper then laid down across my part of the table and invited me to attempt the same thing, but by that time I'd figured out the strange tonal quality in her voice was the result of her using a frequency shifter, which is usually a ninety-percent solid giveaway that the person in question is at least very confused about his or her gender.

In the fullness of time, the dishes were cleared away, the Silicione Sisters disappeared, and we were left to sip *vino rosso*, nibble at the remaining *polipi veraci*, and discuss our business with the don.

Gunnar had his virtual mouth full. "This has been a real delight," he told the don. "I mean, I had no idea food could be so fascinating. For example, this," he shook the *polipi* in his left hand, "this—what the hell is it?"

*"Polipi veraci all'aglio,"* the don said.

"No, I mean, what *is* it? What do I ask for the next time I go to Buon Giorno?"

"Octopus," the don said. "Whole octopus, beaten to a pulp to make it tender and then boiled in garlic sauce for two hours."

"Oh." Gunnar waited until the don was momentarily distracted, then set the *polipi* down on the table and covered it with a napkin.

"So!" I said brightly. "I realize this is still early in the evening, but could we spend a minute or two on business? I mean, only to kill time while we're waiting for dessert."

"Dessert?" Don Vermicelli moaned. "So soon? Oh, you children are so impatient—but yes, I can see, the time to dis-

---

### POLIPI VERACI ALL'AGLIO

Take one octopus. Cut out the eyes, mouth, and ink sac, and place on a board and beat with a wooden mallet until tender. Place octopus in earthenware dish and season with olive oil, garlic, bay leaf, and cumin seeds. Cover dish tightly and place over low heat for one to two hours; longer for larger octopus. When tender, season with salt, pepper, rosemary, and parsley, and serve in tureen.

cuss this is now." He nodded, took another sip from his wine-glass, and dabbed at his upper lip with a napkin the size of a bedspread. I was about to ask him to get on with it when he spoke again. "Max? Gunnar has explained your situation to me. You need a—how you say it? A *laundromat*, to make this money clean. I can do this for you."

Well, yeah, that was the general idea.

*"But,"* he raised a finger in the air, "I will not play games with your IRS. For that, they sent poor Alphonse to prison." A sad expression crossed his face—it was a slow journey—and I turned to Gunnar.

("Alphonse?")

("Capone. Sometimes the don gets confused about what century he's in.")

Vermicelli's sad expression finished its voyage. "So this will not be a *perfect* launder. But it will keep your friend Amber from finding out who you really are. Is this enough?"

I looked at Gunnar. He nodded, so I nodded.

The don nodded. "Very good. Then in return, I ask only a small handling fee—a token, really. Hardly anything at all."

He was clearly waiting for a response. "And that is?"

"Ten percent, off the top."

Gunnar almost jumped out of his seat. *"Ten percent?"*

"Hey," Vermicelli shrugged. "Most of the other dons, they charge you fifteen percent. But me, because you're my friends, I only charge you ten percent."

*"That's ridiculous!"*

"Twelve percent."

*"We won't pay it!"*

"Fourteen percent."

I grabbed Gunnar by the front of his camo fatigues, hauled him down into his seat, and turned to smile at the don. "I'm still your friend," I said with an innocent grin, "and I'd be *honored* to have you do it for only ten percent."

Don Vermicelli smiled, nodded, and waved away the trigger boys who had crept up behind Gunnar and were training pistols on the back of his head. "We have a deal, then. You have a way to contact this 'Amber' person?"

I thought it over, and the address of a certain kinky apartment in ToxicTown came to mind. "I know how to find her."

"Very good. Then—" He turned to survey his trigger boys and picked one out of the group. "Bruno. I want you to go with Max." The don turned back to me. "Max, you take my boy Bruno to meet this Amber, and leave him there. He'll tell Amber how to get the money to me."

I looked at Bruno—yet another one of Vermicelli's clones with slick hair and a pinstripe suit—and thought of Amber, and I must confess, my right eyebrow went up slightly.

"Oh, *relax*, Max," Don Vermicelli said. "After all, if you can't trust *la famiglia*, who *can* you trust?"

**Thursday morning, 0530 UTC**. Gunnar left the club with Bambi to either sleep it off or get it off, he wasn't fussy which. I was rolling through the dark, narrow, labyrinthine streets of ToxicTown on my virtual Harley Ultraglide, with Vermicelli's boy Bruno sitting on the p-pad behind me, his arms wrapped tightly around my ribs. The weight of the virtual Desert Eagle pistol tucked into his waistband may have been a comfort to him, but it was a major pain in the left kidney to me.

Finding Amber's place wasn't all that hard. True, a couple of my major landmarks had disappeared since my last trip down here, slightly over twenty-six hours ago—that's not unusual in ToxicTown; the place has all the topographical stability of an ice-cream sculpture on a hot day in July—but enough URL points remained to guide me into the right general domain, and from there I was able to follow the datapath down to the node intersection where I'd last found her.

The damned dwarf was standing there, leaning against the

lamppost, flipping a coin and catching it with almost mechanical precision. I parked the bike, and Bruno and I dismounted.

"Thorvold?" I called out as we walked over. "Son of Orvold, from the Hall of the Mountain King?"

The dwarf caught the coin, palmed it, and stepped away from the lamppost. "Hi, Max," he said. "Amber is tied up in

> ## TIED UP
>
> At the words "tied up" I immediately thought of the row of manacles on Amber's bedroom wall, but decided this was not the time or place for a smartass comment. What a waste of a perfectly good opportunity.

real time and couldn't make it tonight, so she put me here to watch for you."

Thorvold gave Bruno a long look up and down, and said to me, "So, Max. Who's your friend?"

Vermicelli's boy didn't wait for an introduction. "Bruno, son of Rocko, from the family Tattaglia." He stepped forward and offered the dwarf a handshake. The dwarf took his hand, and shook it, and returned it, and the two of them smiled at each other like long-lost friends.

> ## INFONUGGETS
>
> Honestly, that was *really* the last one.

I decided to interject myself. "You two know each other?"

Bruno looked at Thorvold, and Thorvold looked at Bruno, and some sort of unspoken communication passed between them. "More like we're distant cousins," Bruno said.

"Nice suit," Thorvold said, fingering Bruno's lapels and ignoring me. "Primus Softwear?"

"Corvo Novus," Bruno answered. The dwarf nodded knowingly.

I cleared my throat and interjected myself once more.

"Well, I hate to break up your family reunion, but don't we have some important business to discuss?"

Thorvold looked at Bruno. There was that almost-visible flash of unsaid words between them again.

"Not really," Bruno said.

The dwarf nodded. "You came here, and you brought Bruno. So obviously you're taking the job, and everything's going to be piped through Don Vermicelli. That about the size of it?"

"Yes," Bruno said. They both turned to me.

"So thank you, and goodnight, and Amber will be in touch with you within twenty-four hours. You may go now." Actually, I couldn't even tell which one of them said that.

But clearly, there was nothing more I could do there. I walked back to my Harley, mounted up, and kicked the engine into life. Then a tilt to get the kickstand up, and I stepped her down into first gear, popped the clutch, gave the throttle a good hard twist, and blasted off in a cloud of roaring exhaust and a squeal of burning rubber and a hearty Hi-yo Silver.

Damnedest thing. Just before I disappeared around the corner, I glanced in my rearview mirror, and it looked like Thorvold and Bruno were *melting into* one another. But by the time I turned my head to look, I'd gone around the corner, and there was nothing back there to be seen.

I wrote it off to fatigue and headed for my exit point.

## PUBLIC SERVICE ANNOUNCEMENT *

A natural question occurs here: why bother riding the Net to the end of the line? We've already seen Max demonstrate that he can bail out with a single word, or even quit via the stone-ax primitive method of taking off his VR headset and switching off his computer. After all, no matter what happens in virtual reality, *it's just data*, and throughout everything the *real* Jack

Burroughs remains safely ensconced in his mother's basement, immune to all dangers except possibly that of having his gluteal muscles atrophy from sitting in one place too long. (Those readers who believe that Jack's consciousness can somehow be electronically extracted from his cerebrum and functionally reassembled somewhere else independent of Jack's organic brain are advised to drop all their computer science courses *right now* and instead enroll in Fundamentals of Voodoo 101.)

So, to repeat the question: why bother navigating the Net to a virtual exit point?

'Cause it's *neater*, that's why. It's both stylistically better, and you don't go around leaving orphan processes and bits and ends of trash files floating all over the place. After all, no one wants to be a cyberslob. Give a hoot. Don't pollute.

I cleared the worst part of ToxicTown without trouble, found a spur of *.edu* that was still in pretty good shape, and opened up the throttle, heading for the InfoBahn. The spur lifted up above the local tangle and became a virtual viaduct; the towering form of the UNISYS corporate datablock was just coming into view when suddenly the road before me erupted in a line of orange fireballs and a roaring geyser of brilliant blue flame.

Oh, bugger. I recognized that weapons signature. *Plasma cannon.* I slammed on the rear brake, threw the Harley into a long slide, and fought to bring her out of the slide and into a screaming U-turn. I succeeded.

A line of minigun fire ripped up the pavement to my right. The road that had been behind me exploded in a matching gout of fireballs and flame geysers.

And suddenly, that was it. I was trapped on a hundred-yard section of free-floating virtual viaduct, the road blasted into smoking ruin at both ends, with no way out but to jump. I rolled the bike over to the nearest rail and looked down. A flock of pterodactyls flew by far below me, chasing a squadron of tiny single-engine fighter aircraft. It was a good one-mile drop back down to ToxicTown, if it was an inch—and clearly, given that I was sticking to the roadway, but the roadway was floating in the air with no visible means of support, there was something very screwy about the local gravity.

I pulled my virtual .45 automatic out of my jacket and checked the load status. Seven rounds. Well, it wouldn't be much of a fight against someone who could pack a plasma cannon, but dammit, I wanted to *see* my attacker before I got my ass kicked back to real time.

Whoever my attacker was, he/she obliged. I was still scouting for a defensive position when the air over by the far rail shimmered, a heavy-duty cloaking field got shut down, and a really evil-looking giant battlemech fractaled into visibility. I popped off a few shots at it, just in case they might do some good. The virtual bullets pinged harmlessly off the battlemech's shiny chrome hull.

It waited until I was done shooting and had lowered my gun, then put up its plasma cannon, retracted its smoking minigun, and morphed into—

*Eliza.*

I wanted the battlemech back.

"Hello, Max," she said as she came strolling across the smoking, fractured, bullet-scarred virtual pavement. "It's been a while."

"Not long enough," I said. I considered the two rounds left in my .45 and wondered if I could bring it up and get them off before she morphed back into the battlemech, or something worse. She stopped about six feet away from me and studied me with the sort of expression usually reserved for examining disgusting insects impaled on pins.

I returned the favor. Eliza was in her Aryan Princess mode again: a slight, slender, elfin, waif like—aw, hell, a positively *gaunt* body, about five feet two, with a figure that'd look bad on a ten-year-old boy and a color scheme that'd pass for albino if it wasn't for her ice-blue eyes. Her white hair was shorter than ever before, a half-inch long at best, and spiked out in a way that suggested a giant pollen grain.

On a scale of one to ten, she was a negative number.

I broke the silence. "I heard you were dead."

"I got better." This led to another minute of silent standoff.

"I was in Heaven last night," she said. "Looking for you. Didn't Sam tell you?"

"He did. I had other plans."

Eliza vanished.

"I know you did," she said behind me. I spun around. She wasn't there—or at least, she wasn't visible. "I followed you." Behind me again! I spun once more.

Slowly, Eliza faded back into visibility. If she'd followed me, then at the very least she knew I'd been with Amber. And if she was able to intercept me *here*, then she'd probably followed me all the way to Amber's place last night and spent some time peeking through the keyhole and listening at the door. I started to figure out just exactly where all her anger was coming from.

All the same, MAX_KOOL had an image to maintain. "So. You happier now?"

She bit her lower lip, narrowed her icy blue eyes, and balled up her right hand into a bony fist. Then slowly, with visible effort, she opened the fist and took a deep breath.

"You are scum, Max. You and Amber deserve each other." Eliza's lips went tight, and raw hatred flashed through her eyes. "But—" Slowly, a bit of a thaw forced its way in. "But because there once was a time when I was in love with you, I am going to ignore everything that's in my heart and warn you.

"Max, you have no idea who you're really dealing with. This 'Amber' bitch is *way* out of your league."

Eliza seemed to think that statement was self-explanatory. She crossed her arms, snorted, and just stood there, waiting for me to respond.

I—rather, Max—did. "Is this a chick thing? Are you jealous?"

*"Rrrrrr!"* I don't know what Eliza started morphing into, but whatever it was had some pretty scary fangs and claws before she got control of herself and morphed back. "You *bastard*!" she spat, when her aspect was stabilized again. "I was a newbie! You were my first virtual lover! I *trusted* you!"

"Hey," I shrugged, "all's fair in love and virtual reality."

*"You—!"* She vanished again, this time going up in a pillar of flame. The flame became smoke, the smoke a cloud, and the cloud settled out as a gentle fall of dusty snow. "You are such an asshole, Max Kool," the snow hissed softly, as it fell. "I am going to tell you this because I promised myself I would tell you this, but I really hope you don't listen.

"Amber is a *user*, Max. She's going to use you up, and suck you dry, and then she's going to rip your heart out and feed it to the crows. She is *evil*, Max. And far more powerful than she's letting you believe. For your own good, Max, *stay away from her*." The snow stopped falling. A cold wind rose, and swept the icy crystals back into the air.

"Why are you telling me this?" I shouted at the wind. "I fucked you and I dumped you! You hate me! Why should I believe you?"

A freak of the wind formed a swirling cloud of snow dust, which for just a moment took on the nebulous form of a woman.

"Because *she* fucked me and dumped me, too," the cold wind whispered, "and I hate her even *more*." The snow woman flew apart then, and became a snow cyclone, which lifted away into the virtual sky. The wind faded. The virtual sunlight returned.

Interesting. Definitely interesting. For someone who was a green-hide newbie on the Net just two years before, Eliza had definitely developed some pretty impressive morphing skills. I shook my head in admiration, then went back to the problem of figuring out how to get off of this floating piece of virtual bridge. I turned to look at my Harley.

It was gone. In its place there was a pile of deconstructed mechanical rubble, and a message written in bullet holes in the virtual asphalt.

"HAVE A NICE WALK HOME, MAX."

# 10

## LIKE A BRIDGE OVER STAGNANT WATER

**Thursday, local time:** I got three phone calls that morning. The first was the damned fax again. The second was from Kathé in the MDE Outplacement Office, who reminded me I still had a company-owned copy of *Dress For Conformity* checked out and my paperwork was going to be held up until I returned it. The third was from Joseph "Gunnar" LeMat, who wanted me to meet him for lunch at a Lebanese restaurant in Lowertown.

I opted for Door Number 3. Lunch with LeMat.

Lowertown is not to be confused with ToxicTown, although there are some similarities. Lowertown exists in real space, and most of the time in real time, except for the service in a few restaurants and the lines in some civil service offices. In ToxicTown's favor, on the other hand, is the fact that the St. Paul city government has never tried to "revitalize" it.

Lowertown has suffered that fate. Repeatedly.

The area called Lowertown is actually the old lower east side of St. Paul's downtown business district. Its history dates back to the early 1800s, when Harriet Island was still an island, the Mississippi River was still the border between the Objibwa

(Chippewa) and Lakota (Sioux) nations, and a rather disreputable and hygienically repulsive man named Pig's Eye Parrant came up the river, looking for a quiet place to set up a trading post and pursue a life of selling shoddy trade goods and illegal whiskey to the Native Americans.

Now, if you look at a topographical map of the area, you'll see that the Mississippi River makes an enormous S-shaped bend right through the heart of the Minneapolis/St. Paul metroplex, and this bend resembles nothing so much as a giant U-trap, not unlike the one you'll find on your main bathroom drain pipe. This bend in the river functions about the same as a U-trap, too, in that all the crap, detritus, and garbage floating down the Mississippi naturally comes to rest on the north shore of the second loop, right about where the clean-out port would be if this was a union plumbing job. The smell, on long hot days in late summer, is remarkable.

So of course it was on this spot that Pig's Eye Parrant chose to build his trading post, and thereby found the settlement that would eventually become the city of St. Paul. Later settlers, having more discerning noses than Parrant, as well as an appreciation of the dangers of building on flood plains and an awareness of the workings of real estate marketing, wisely chose to expand the city on the bluffs above Lowertown and rename it after the first missionary church built in the area.

But the fact remains, Lowertown *is* the original commercial core of the city of St. Paul, and given the preponderance of historic buildings down there and the frequency of road repairs, Lowertown today still looks much the same as it did back in the early nineteenth century, in the days of fur trappers, keel boats, and horse-drawn wagons.

On long, hot, summer days, it smells about the same, too.

The coffee was thick, sweet, and almost undrinkable. I set

my cup down, picked up my fork, and toyed with my falafel. LeMat tried his urgent, nervous smile on me again.

I decided to make him sweat some more. "The *Hill* Building?"

"Just try to keep an open mind, Jack."

I narrowed my eyes and looked at him. "That mausoleum has got to be at least a hundred and fifty years old."

"Yeah!" he said brightly. "Solid construction! They just don't build 'em like that anymore."

"I got news for you, buddy. They haven't built 'em like that since the *Maine* sank."

LeMat plunged into a funk, then found something buoyant to bring him back to the surface. "Well, what does it matter anyway? You're going to be in virtual reality most of the time."

"Yes," I nodded, "I shall. I will bring my marvelous Babbage Engine up to a full head of steam, and if the situation requires more computational power, I have but to open the gas valve another quarter-turn! Ah, the wonders of science!"

"Jack," LeMat hissed. "People are looking at us, Jack."

"Artists," I announced loudly to everyone else near us. "We are conceptual artists and will be performing a gallery opening this June in—" With remarkable speed, everyone nearby either called for their checks or leapt into intense, animated, and loud conversations.

"The art of not being heard," I whispered to LeMat.

"The art of not being an asshole," he whispered back.

I tried another sip of my coffee and found it more palatable this time. "Seriously, though," I resumed in a far softer voice. "At the very least, we have some *major* power requirements. Does this dump have the wiring to support us?"

"It was completely modernized in the late eighties. *1980*s."

I nodded. "Okay. What about Net access?"

"Wired for that in 2003. Federal grant. You remember

President Gore's plan to revitalize the inner cities by putting everyone on the Internet? St. Paul put their share of the grant money into wiring Lowertown."

I nodded again. "So we'll basically be on an empty spur. Good. Any chance of a satdish?"

LeMat smiled. "We'd be getting a top-floor office. The landlord says we can put anything we want on the roof, including a dovecote."

"That could come in handy." I paused, to think through everything that LeMat had told me so far, and try to find room for that one last forkful of baklava.

"Question," I said at last. "I thought the whole point in looking for an office down here was to find someplace cheap we could rent on short notice, with no money down and no questions asked. If this place is so nice, how come the landlord is willing to meet our terms?"

LeMat spooned more sugar into his coffee, gave it a slow stir, and then looked up at me. "Because the building is ninety-percent vacant. No one in their right mind wants to live or work in Lowertown."

I figured as much. "Because of the senseless, random, violent street crime?"

LeMat shook his head. "Because there's no place to park."

After lunch we walked over to the Hill Building and met the landlord, a short, fat, and balding guy named Jerry, and he gave us a tour of our prospective office. The space he showed us was basically the entire eighth floor of the building, and it was huge, empty, and more suggestive of an old warehouse loft than an MDE corporate office—which, the more I thought about it, the more it appealed to me. We explained to Jerry that we would probably be working late often and might want to partition some space off for a bedroom or two; he explained to us that it would be a serious violation of building codes for anyone to actually live in the office, then showed us where the kitchen and bathroom facilities were and pointed out how the CPA on the fourth floor had done some really nice things in converting her space. We found a broken window on the north side of the building, which explained the feathers and pigeon shit all over the place. Jerry promised to fix that immediately, then showed us the freight elevator and took us down to the Basement Where Office Furniture Goes To Die. It seemed a number of his previous tenants had bugged out leaving their furniture as collateral for back rent, and he was willing to let us use anything we felt like lugging up to the eighth floor. By pure accident we bumped into Inge Andersson, the CPA who officed on the fourth floor and the building's only other tenant, on the stairs: she was another one of those short, stocky, totally humorless middle-aged strawberry blondes that Minnesota seems to produce in such abundance, and she was wearing the traditional uniform of frumpy dress, hair in a bun, and white tennis shoes. Ms. Andersson, however, did achieve something remarkable in that she did *not* get a testosterone fluctuation out of LeMat. I'd always figured if it was bipedal, female, and not on a coroner's slab, he'd make a play for it.

We ended up our tour back on the eighth floor, listening to the pigeons coo in the rafters. Jerry rubbed his hands together and looked at me. "So, what d'ya think?"

I shrugged and looked at LeMat.

A passing pigeon flew between us.

"Um, about these birds," LeMat said.

"I called City Hall," Jerry said, "and the animal control office told me they're urban masonry doves. That makes 'em protected by the Migratory Songbird Act." He looked at me, then leaned in next to LeMat and lowered his voice to a con-spiratorial tone. "But personally, I think they're fucking rats with wings, and I wouldn't cry if any of them met an untimely end." He leaned back and smiled. "Of course, I didn't say that."

"Of course," LeMat said, nodding. "Snares? Poison?"

Jerry shrugged. "You can use 'em for fucking indoor skeet practice, for all I care."

LeMat broke into a big smile. Oh no, I knew that smile. It meant *guns*, is what it meant. LeMat only smiled like that when he thought he'd get a chance to shoot one of his guns.

He turned to me, that idiotic grin all over his face. "I like it, Jack. What do you think?"

I sighed, wondering once again what I'd gotten myself into. "I guess we'll take it," I told Jerry.

We split up after that. LeMat had parked his urban assault vehicle in a secured ramp near the restaurant, while I'd parked my Toyota on a side street near Mears Park. Doing that always involved a certain amount of risk. Even though it was broad daylight on a weekday, and even though the park was theoretically police patrolled, there always seemed to be a few new junkies who staggered out of the bus station, got confused, and wandered down Otto Street into Mears Park, instead of going up Otto Street to Enablement Row, where they would be welcomed with open arms and immediately registered as voting Democrats.

At first my car seemed to be okay. Then, as I got nearer, I saw that the passenger side door was ajar, and picked up the pace. I practically ran the last few yards as it became obvious that someone had broken into my car.

When I found a new radio sitting on the passenger seat, and the note in shaky handwriting explaining that the guy had broken into my car and then realized I needed a radio worse than he did, I just shrugged and drove home.

LeMat showed up on my Mom's doorstep that night, not thirty seconds after the pizza delivery driver. "Okay, it's all set," he said, as we carried the Pepperoni Pig-Out special past Psycho Kitty's really overripe litter box on our way down to the basement and a couple of frosty cans of root beer. "I've opened a DBA account at Midwest Federal, with both our names on the signature card. You'll have to sign it later, of course."

I bit off a slab of hot, greasy pizza and wolfed it down. "What name did you wind up using?"

LeMat looked at me as if wondering how he could get away with changing the subject. "CompuTech," he said at last.

"I hate it," I said.

"I know." He separated another piece from the mass of molten mozzarella and navigated it toward his open mouth.

"It's a nothing name," I continued. "A company called CompuTech could be almost anything."

He choked down a huge mouthful of pizza, and followed it with a slosh of root beer. "Exactly the point, Jack."

"Now 2Kool Enterprises, *that* would have been a good name."

"It would have been a *dumb* name," LeMat snapped back. "The whole point of a DBA account is to give Don Vermicelli something to make deposits to without knowing our names. We *want* a bland company name that'll just disappear into the background clutter."

"I still hate it."

"Well, tough." The toppings on his slice started to slide off of their own accord. LeMat folded his pizza and took another bite. "That's the name I put on the account, and that's the name I gave Don Vermicelli."

I swallowed hard. "You've seen him already?"

"Even better, he's got the money from Amber already. It'll be credited to our account tomorrow."

I was impressed. "That's fast."

"You think that's fast? Amber's new interface hardware is already en route. We should get delivery around noon tomorrow."

Something bothered me about that. I took another bite of pizza, ruminated and masticated. "Excuse me," I finally said. "What's the point of all this financial Mickey Mouse if we had to go and give Amber our *address*?"

LeMat grinned: a rather disgusting cheesy-and-tomato-saucy sight. "No, what we gave Amber was a mail-drop. She sent the hardware there; one of the Don's boys picked it up and relayed it to us. For Amber to trace the package she'd have to get UPS and Federal Express to cooperate with each other, and she'd have an easier time getting the Mossad and PLO to double-date."

I finished my slice of pizza, licked the sauce off my fingers, and wiped my hands on my pants. "So," I said at last. "This is really happening, isn't it?"

LeMat put down his can of root beer and belched from the bottom of his heart. "Damn right it is!"

I looked at him, sighed, and finally decided to drop all pretense and go for it. "I'm scared, man. Are you scared?"

He belched again. "Damn right I am!"

"I mean, this could all go up in our faces and land us neck-deep in dinosaur shit. That ever occur to you?"

LeMat had run out of gas. "Yeah. It's a sure cure for narcolepsy. I had absolutely no trouble staying awake or sweating bullets last night."

I nodded. "Thought so." We both went silent. Another thought crept in edgewise in that vulnerable moment and sent all the little vestigial hairs on the back of my neck leaping to ice-cold attention.

"Say, Gunnar. You met Don Vermicelli in Heaven, right?" LeMat nodded. "Uh, while you were there, you didn't happen to, er, spot *Eliza* hanging around the place, did you?"

LeMat went white. "Eliza? I thought she was dead."

"She got better."

LeMat dropped the slab of pizza he'd been working on,

put his chin in his greasy palm, and looked at me like a deer trying to outstare the oncoming headlights. "Is *she* mixed up in this?"

I nodded.

LeMat sagged in his seat like a sack of old potatoes. "Oh, Lordy." He sighed. "Momma always told me my sinful ways would catch up with me."

The original plan had been to move some of my furniture to the office after supper. The news of Eliza's resurrection got LeMat so upset, though, that we decided to put off moving until the next morning. LeMat went home to chug shots of Maalox. I looked at my computer—which was disassembled for moving—decided I didn't feel like putting it back together for one night, and went upstairs to spend a pleasant evening with Mom.

When that proved impossible, I went back to the basement, popped *Dress For Conformity* into my ReadMan, and jumped to—

## Chapter 9: The Cyberpunk Modality

The origins of the word *cyberpunk* can be traced back to at least 1980, if not further. As it is now the year 2005, it is perhaps time to admit that cyberpunk is no longer a radical vision of the future, but rather a marketing label, and more importantly, a *fashion modality*, every bit as strict in its own way as the blue-suit-and-wingtip look of IBM or the propellor-beanie-and-Rockport style of Hewlett-Apple.

With that understood, it becomes easy to distill the parameters of the cyberpunk style. To wit:

1. *social nonconformity*, as expressed through unusual hairstyles

2. *technological awareness*, as expressed through body piercings and prosthetic implants

3. *sullen stupidity*, as evidenced by the renewed popularity of psychedelic drugs

4. *in-your-face outrage*, as expressed through popular music and personal audio

Ignoring for the moment the obvious dangers of Item #3 (as has been proven repeatedly, drugs *cannot* make you smarter or sexier, they can only make you stupider and poorer) as well as the complete failure of Item #4 (it's hard to believe in music as an expression of social outrage when the Butthole Surfers' "Goofy's Concern" is the theme music for a major Nike television ad campaign), the obvious place to start is with Items #1 and #2.

Granted, an unusual hairstyle is roughly equivalent to tattooing the word "geek" on your forehead. But most people nowadays are too polite to point and laugh, so what the Hell, go for it.

As for body piercings, the medical dangers of poking holes in your skin have long been known. Fortunately, a wide array of clip-on "piercings" and self-adhesive "implants" are now on the market for those who want to fit in with a hi-tech trendoid culture at work and still retain a modicum of sanity for evenings and weekends. If you do opt for actual body piercings, though, and you live in one of the northern states that sees severe static electricity conditions in the winter, please be advised that shuffling across a wool carpet and then accidentally contacting ground through your eyebrow ring is an experience you will not soon forget.

**CAUTION:** If you choose to accessorize the cyber-punk fashion statement with items from other modalities, be *very* careful. Nipple piercings and chain mail shirts, for example, are widely reported to be a *disastrous* combination.

# 11

## JACK GETS
## REALLY WIRED

My 7 A.M. wake-up call from the fax machine was right on time. LeMat showed up around eight with his truck and a bag of bagels, and by eleven o'clock we had the first load of stuff carted over to CompuTech World Headquarters and had successfully completed our first spelunking expedition into the Basement That Time Forgot, which netted us three matching blue plastic chairs, a worktable, a desk, and a talking coffeepot that sang "Volare" when the brew cycle was done. The floor on the east end of our office, which we'd both assumed to be terrazzo yesterday, turned out to be several years' accretion of pigeon guano when seen in direct sunlight. We decided we had space enough to work around that, but the discovery did bring LeMat's 5mm air pistol out of hiding, and he wasted the next half-hour blasting holes in the ceiling tiles every time he thought he heard a *coo*.

Around 11:30 we took a break, and went down to street level and over to the deli in the next block to grab some sandwiches. On the way back we ran into Inge Andersson, the CPA from the fourth floor, again. She was out for a  power walk in her skirt, nylons, and white tennis shoes, and pretended not to recognize us.

As promised, the courier carrying Amber's new interface hardware showed up promptly on the dot of noon. The box was large enough to hold my microwave oven, but apparently quite lightweight, considering the way the courier was tossing it around. We managed to keep ourselves under control until she left the building, then—

*"It's Christmas Time!"* LeMat shouted. We tore into that box like a couple of eight-year-olds. "Look! Look!" LeMat pulled something out of the styrofoam ghost farts and waved it in the air. "New featherweight high-definition video goggles!"

I plunged my arms into the box and came up with the next thing. "Look! Look! New skintight elbow-length piezoelectric datagloves!"

LeMat brushed a shower of styro noodles on the floor, and grabbed the corner of a clear plastic bag that appeared. "Look! Look!" He paused and took a closer squint at it. "A complete EKG harness and an array of scalp electrodes!"

"Look," I said, as I pulled out something that turned out to be connected daisy-chain fashion to about four other things. "A stereo headset with six-axis mercury head-positioning sensors and multiplex short-range wireless network link?"

"Look." LeMat held up the next item at arm's length, between two fingers. "Knee-length skin-tight piezoelectric data *socks*." The socks were connected to more fabric. "Oo, and matching data *underwear*, too. Thank you, it's just what I've always wanted."

"Oh, look," I said dully as I fished a large, heavy, cylindrical object out from where it'd settled into the bottom of the box. "It's a—a—What the hell is it?"

"Look Jack," LeMat asked, "did you see anything that even vaguely resembled instructions?"

I jerked a thumb at the thick brown envelope labeled "Read

Me First" that was sitting right where I'd tossed it, in the garbage can. "Sorry. Reflex."

LeMat retrieved the envelope and tore it open. And with that, we settled down and set everything down, then sat down to the serious job of figuring out just what exactly it was we had.

"Hmm," LeMat said as he leaned back in his plastic chair, looked up from the documentation, and stroked his chin. "Did you know this thing came out of MDE's biomedical division?"

"I didn't even know MDE *had* a biomedical division." I gave up trying to figure out the three interface cards I'd found in bubble wrap in the bottom of the box, set them on the floor—not an easy maneuver, as I was sitting in a plastic chair with my feet up on the table—and turned my attention to the CD media.

"But the kicker is," LeMat went back to what he was reading and underscored a line with his finger, "the interface has clearly *not* passed any FDA tests. Hasn't even been submitted for trials, as far as I can tell."

I spun the CD on my finger and watched the way the sunlight prismed off the surface. Of course, I'd have learned a lot more about the software if LeMat had let me pop it into my computer and scan it, but he'd absolutely forbidden me to get the disk anywhere near my computer until after he'd finished reading the manuals. I tried to tell him I had the best virus traps and scanning utilities talent could bootleg, but *no-o*—

"What this means to us," LeMat went on, since I hadn't asked, "is that this interface is doubly illegal. Not only is it stolen—I'm convinced of that now—but even if it wasn't, the maker couldn't legally *let* humans use it. It's not safe."

I slipped the CD back into its case, looked at LeMat, and shrugged. "So? Are we going to let a little thing like that stop us now?"

LeMat closed the manual, thought it over a minute, and sat up straight in his plastic chair. "Nope." He pointed at the pile of bubble wrap on the floor. "Hand me those interface cards, would you?"

It took us the rest of the afternoon to get the interface cards installed in my computer, run the software through my virus filters, and get everything installed and configured. After that we spent another hour or so running the configured software through every kind of destruction test we could think of, just to see if there were any logic bombs or hostile behaviors hidden deep within the working code. Only after we were satisfied that everything was working correctly did we start messing around with the biological side of the interface. That, of course, entailed a five-minute argument about who got to try it first, but we eventually settled that by employing a binary metallic decision device. In other words, we flipped a coin. I won.

The piezoelectric datagloves turned out to be made of some sort of really interesting material. Black, lightweight, feeling kind of like a cross between Spandex and 200-grit sandpaper, they went up over the elbows, clung and conformed to the skin, and after a few minutes of wear I didn't even notice that I had them on, except that my skin was now glittering and black. As a test, LeMat dropped a dime on the floor. I had absolutely no trouble picking it up.

LeMat laughed. "Quite a far cry from the old data hockey gauntlets, huh?"

I smiled back at him. "Have some more money you want to drop? Maybe a twenty this time? Just as a test, of course."

"Of course." He laughed, but kept his wallet in his pants.

Next, I doffed my red high-top tennies and white sweat socks, and tried on the datasocks. Like the gloves, they went up over my knees, and after a few minutes seemed more like a second skin than a piece of clothing.

LeMat put down the manual he was flipping through. "There doesn't seem to be any reason to *not* put your shoes back on," he said. "It shouldn't affect anything."

I shook my head. "No. Don't want to. I can't explain it, but these things feel—really *good*. Shoes would ruin it."

LeMat nodded. "I know what you mean. I felt the same way the first time I tried support hose."

I took a few tentative hops and skips around the wooden floor. The datasocks seemed to give me really good traction, if nothing else. "Okay, what's next?"

LeMat sorted through the pile of stuff on the table and selected another poly bag full of black fabric. "Take off your shirt." He ripped the plastic open.

"Oh, goody." I pulled my t-shirt tails out of my pants and hauled the shirt up and over my head. "Is it a data hair-shirt?"

"No, more like—" His voice stopped.

"Gunnar?" I finished getting my t-shirt off and threw it on the table. "Gunnar, what's wrong?"

"Jack?" he said softly. "You'd better come have a look at this." I skipped over beside him and looked at the glittering black thing he'd taken out of the bag. It wasn't a datashirt.

It was more like a data *bra*.

"You know," I said, "I think you're right. You *are* the older and more experienced partner. I think *you* should try it, first."

LeMat shook his head. "Nonsense, Jack. You won the toss fair and square. I wouldn't want to take the thrill of this experience away from you." He handed the black bra to me.

I smiled my disarming best. "But as my friend, I would be *honored* if you would accept this small token of my appreciation for all our years of friendship. Please, you deserve it more than I do." I tried to push the bra back into his hands.

LeMat resolutely crossed his arms and refused to take it. "Well, you can be honored until the cows come home," he said, "but I am *not* gonna wear that. So either you put it on, or you call Amber right now and tell her the deal's off."

I looked at him. He was serious. I looked at the data bra. It seemed more like something out of the Victoria's Secret catalog than a piece of computer hardware. I looked out the east window at the darkened windows of the offices on the eighth floor of the Lumber Exchange building across the street. Well, it was 6:30 on a Friday, after all.

"Okay," I said. "But lock the door. And promise me, tomorrow we put curtains on those windows."

LeMat nodded solemnly. "I promise."

He did more than promise. He had to help me with the hooks. I'd only taken these things *off* before, never had to put one *on*. "Thank you," I said when it was all adjusted and everything. "I just want you to know, it takes a true friend to inflict humiliation like this, and I only hope that someday I will be able to repay the favor. Now, what's left?" I hopped over to the table where we'd piled everything and started strapping on parts. LeMat picked up the manual and flipped to a checklist.

"Audio headset?" he asked.

"Check."

"Cranial positional sensors?"

"Check."

"Gross motion sensors?"

"Check."

"Video goggles?"

"Check."

"Dorsal fiberoptic harness?"

"Hold it." I was still fiddling with the video goggles. They were featherweight, yes, but when I had them on, I couldn't see a damned thing. I heard LeMat riffling through pages.

"There's a transparency control," he said. "Right side, just forward of your temple. Down is clear."

I found the control and slid the button down. "Got it." I could see again.

"Okay." LeMat went back to the manual and found the checklist again. "Uh, dorsal fiberoptic harness?"

I felt my elbows, ribs, knees, and behind my ears. The components of the interface were all hooked together with whisker-thin optical fibers that really didn't seem to be strong enough but apparently worked. "Check."

"Network transceiver belt?"

"Check."

"Datashorts?"

*"What?"*

LeMat lowered the checklist, peered over the top of it at me, and then did the back-and-forth glances bit a few times. "Oh dear," he said. "We missed a piece." He shuffled over to the shipping box on the floor, rooted around in the styrofoam noodles until he found another poly bag, and threw it to me. "Here. Drop your pants and put these on."

I tore the plastic bag open, although I really didn't need to do that to see what was in it: a black, sparkling, bikini thong. "Oh, the things I go through for my career," I muttered as I turned my back to LeMat, dropped my jeans and boxer shorts, and struggled into the thong. Amazingly, the fabric *did* stretch enough to keep me decent. I also discovered that the datasocks had sags in them; I gave them another tug, and this time they came up to mid-thigh. After I'd reconnected the optic fibers to the transceiver belt, I turned around. "Well? How do I look?"

LeMat managed to keep a straight face for almost ten whole seconds. *"Like the most high-tech drag queen on the planet!"* He sputtered once, snickered twice, dropped the manual, and just about collapsed on the floor, laughing so hard the tears flowed like rain gutters and his face turned a deep apoplectic red.

"Thank you very much," I said as I minced over to where he lay laughing on the floor and fought the urge to kick him in the ribs. "I just want you to know that if this is a heart attack, you *are* going to die."

LeMat wiped the tears from his eyes, fought for control of himself, then caught another glimpse of me and collapsed in sputters and snickers again. "Sorry, Jack," he said when he'd just about laughed himself out. "But now I understand why Amber—*snort*!—thought she'd have to pay you a million. You should've held out for two!"

I waited until he'd gotten it all out of his system, then helped him back to his feet. "Okay, so what's left?"

"Some *darling* red stilletto heels. You'll—"

*"What?"*

"Just kidding." LeMat picked up the EKG harness. "Next, we hook you up with this and the scalp electrodes. It's not really part of the data interface. It'll just let me monitor your vital signs, in case there are any problems."

I thought the implications of that through for a bit, then looked LeMat straight in the eyes. "Level with me, Gunnar. You've read all the manuals. Is there a chance this thing will get me killed?"

*"Only if you wear it out in public!"* He started to laugh again, then saw the murderous look in my eyes and stopped.

"Seriously," I said calmly, albeit through clenched teeth. "Isn't there a risk here of, like, some security program frying my brain, or something? Y'know, lethal feedback?"

"Actually, Jack," LeMat said equally calmly, "ignoring for the moment the fact that the final link between the desktop unit and you is wireless and therefore about as dangerous as the remote control on your mom's TV, the makers *did* envision the possibility of lethal voltage. To guard against it, they've installed a fascinating little in-line surge protection device. Perhaps you've even heard of it. It's called, a *fuse*."

What he said soaked in. I blinked. I took a breath and sighed. "Oh."

"And now if you're done being ignorant," LeMat said as he picked up the EKG harness and a tube of conductance gel, "we should probably get on with this."

I raised my arms and presented myself. "Lick 'em and stick 'em, doc."

Fifteen minutes later my scalp and chest were plastered with electrodes, the monitor wires were patched into a spare channel on the transceiver belt, and my cardiac and brain-wave traces were displaying cleanly in a window on my desktop computer. "See, Jack?" LeMat said as he pointed to the traces. "I'll have an eye on your biotelemetry at all times. I've also taken the liberty of adding a panic button: if anything looks the least bit out of whack, I just punch *this* key," he pointed to F12, "the program goes kerflooey, and you're back in reality."

I nodded. "What about my emergency parachute?"

"You mean BUGOUT? Yeah, that works, too. The important thing to remember is to shout it *real loud*. I've changed it so it doesn't trip unless it's one hundred and three decibels or louder. You're just lucky no one else ever discovered they could virtually kill Max Kool just by saying that word."

Actually, I'd never thought of it in quite those terms, but I had to admit LeMat was right. I didn't have to admit it out loud, though.

I leaned forward and tapped another window on the monitor. "What's that?"

"Echoed video feed. I'll see what you see."

"And that?"

"Net traffic status. Just in case this puppy," he slapped the transceiver on my back, "is programmed to do something tricksy, like broadcast a homing signal."

I nodded again, and noticed the pen-sized micro TV camera velcroed onto the left side of the monitor, pointed at where LeMat would be sitting. "I'll be able to see you?"

"There should be a pull-down window in the upper right corner of your field of view. You can overlay this," LeMat tapped the microcamera, "into any scene." LeMat picked up an audio headset and strapped it on. "You'll be able to hear me, too, though I don't know if the audio will be encrypted."

"So watch out for telepaths?"

"Exactly."

I took one last look at what was on the screen, then turned to LeMat. "Well, I suppose it's time, then."

LeMat shook his head. "Not quite. There's one last piece to connect." He smiled at me in the smug and infuriating way that meant he'd been holding something back all along, and then with a flourish, produced—

"Okay, it's the cylinder-thingie again. Did you ever figure out what it was?"

*"Yes!"* LeMat said proudly. "This, Jack, is the one piece that makes this a truly *radical* user interface! Everything else you've seen so far is just an incremental improvement over stuff you've already used, but *this*, my boy, is *unique!*"

I stood there with my hands on my naked hips, staring at it. "Yeah, so? What is it?"

"Jack Burroughs?" LeMat said dramatically, "allow me to present," he twisted a little something, and it became apparent that the cylinder was just some kind of packing case, "the *Sacroiliac Neural Induction Device!*" He whipped it out of the case and waved it in my face.

"It looks like a cucumber," I said, as I backed away from it. "A big *pink* cucumber, with the spines and vine attached."

"Ah!" LeMat said. "I will admit that it looks a little, er,

phallic. But this device was developed over a two-year period under a multimillion-dollar NEA grant! No longer will you have to be content with merely seeing and hearing virtual reality. This device uses neural induction technology to enable you to feel, taste, and *smell* virtual reality!"

"Okay," I said. "What's your point?"

"My point, Jack, is that this is *not* just another VR point-and-shoot device. With the Sacroiliac Neural Induction Device," he waved it in my face again, and I brushed it aside, "we have the first fully realized *interpretive dance* interface!"

Oh. "Sounds swell," I said. "I'm sure it'll be a big hit on the club scene. Bigger than amyl nitrate."

LeMat shook his head, but fortunately didn't say "Oh, ye of little vision." "Jack, Jack. I guess the only way to convince you is to hook it up and let you try it out. Turn around." When I didn't move fast enough, he made little circular motions with his left hand. "Turn *around*, Jack." I did, and he started futzing with the wireless transceiver belt on my back.

"The 'vine,' as you called it, connects right *here*, and the induction device simply mounts right—right—" He put the pink cucumber in my right hand. "Here, hold this a minute, would you?" He darted over to the worktable and started flipping through the pile of manuals. "Ah!" I heard him say.

This was followed a short time later by, "Oh."

Another minute or so passed, and then, "Ohhhhh." I turned around. LeMat was staring wide-eyed at the manual and rubbing his forehead as if he had a spectacular headache.

"Excuse me?" I asked.

LeMat looked up. "Er, yes, Jack?" He tried a grin. It looked sickly.

"Care to tell me what's going on?"

He glanced down at the manual in his hands, gulped, and grinned again. "Well, yes Jack, it seems I, er, uh—"

"You *what*?"

"Well, I kind of missed one teensy little point here."

My patience was wearing thin. It was probably a predictable side effect of being dressed like a cybernetic transvestite and holding a thirteen-inch pink electronic cucumber. "And that is?"

"You know how I told you it was developed on an NEA grant?"

"Yes?"

"I, uh, didn't immediately recognize the name of the dance troupe that *got* the grant."

I'd run out of words. I started tapping my foot.

"I should have. They were very famous at the time."

*Tap. Tap. Tap.*

"Rather, *notorious*. And given that, the way the neural induction device works shouldn't be a surprise."

*Tap. Tap. Tap.*

"Really, I should have guessed when I saw that it came out of the MDE biomedical *internal* prosthetics department."

*TAP. TAP. TAP.*

"It's all here." LeMat waved the manual nervously. "The note from MDE Trademarks and Legal. They decided Sacroiliac Neural Induction Device was too much of a mouthful, and SNID was a stupid acronym." He tried another weak grin.

*TAP. TAP. TAP.*

"So they decided to find a new name. Convened focus groups, the whole bit. And they finally came up with one they liked."

*TAP. TAP. TAP.*

"They call it the ProctoProd™, Jack."

My foot froze in mid-air. "The *what*?"

"That's how it works." LeMat gulped, took a deep breath, took a good long stare at it, and then looked me straight in the eye and nodded.

"You stick it up your ass and dance, Jack."

Like a frozen, horrified, clockwork figure, I slowly turned to look at that—that pink *thing* in my right hand.

"I may be your best friend, Jack," LeMat said, "but you're going to have to deal with *this* by yourself."

# 12

## UP THE LOOKING GLASS

Decisions, decisions. One million dollars. The interface. One million dollars. The interface.

I went for it. Slathered the ProctoProd with conductance gel, bent over forward and grabbed my right ankle with my left hand, and then—I don't want to think about it, and I don't want to talk about it.

LeMat's face was white when we made eye contact again. "Are you, uh—?"

"Ready," I snapped. "Let's go."

He turned to the computer (with a certain sense of relief, I thought) and launched the initialization routine. "Interface enabled," he said. "Video synced. Audio online. Datagloves— er, data under—er, softwear engaged. Switching over to line feeds." He plugged his audio headset into the A/V jack on the computer. I fumbled for the transparency control on my video goggles and flipped them to opaque.

"Virtual reality boot on my mark," LeMat said. "Three, two, one . . ."

I was *someplace*.

Actually, I was still in our big empty office space on the

eighth floor of the Hill Building, of course, standing about twenty feet away from LeMat. But that's not what my senses were telling me. According to my eyes and ears, I was standing in a large, cube-shaped, virtual space, about a hundred meters on a side. The walls, floor, and ceiling were empty and black, save for a white one-meter grid pattern on the walls and floor and a jumbled pile of polyhedral objects in the far left corner.

Oh. And I was wearing a ProctoProd. Don't imagine for a minute that my senses stopped telling me *that*.

*"Jack?"* LeMat whispered in my ear, via the headset.

"There is no Dana, only Zul," I rumbled at him.

*"Huh?"*

"Max," I said. "I'm *Max Kool* now, remember? *Gunnar*?"

"Oh. Oh, yeah. Sorry." Gunnar was silent a few seconds. "So, uh, Max. This looks like our test reality, no?"

"Yes."

"How's it calibrate?"

I looked down at the floor, then over to the right-hand wall. "Seems to calibrate okay. The one-meter grids look to be about one meter. Up, down, left, and right all seem to be in the right directions."

"Watch the fast head movements. You're making me seasick."

I thought about suggesting that we trade places, but settled for, "Suffer."

"You're right," Gunnar said. "Sorry for complaining. Okay, next series. What's your aspect look like?"

I took a long minute to study my arms and legs, rotate my hands, run my fingers through my hair, and just generally do everything I could do without a mirror. It all seemed to be there: black jacket, black shirt, black jeans, black boots, greasy pompadour, big sideburns. "I'm Max Kool, all right," I said at last, "but my hands and my head are the only parts of me that seem to be real. Everything else is cartoonish. Thin. I mean, insubstantial. Lacking texture and solidity."

"Well, we can fix that later," Gunnar said. "But now, let's go for the big one. Try walking."

I took a step. It calibrated nicely; one meter forward.

*"Whoa!"* Gunnar shouted in my head.

I stopped. "What's wrong?"

"You're really moving. I mean out here, in reality."

"Am I going to trip over something?"

"Not right now. But you've only got about twenty feet before you walk into the south wall. We're going to be in deep shit if all your virtual movements have to map to real space."

"What do you suggest?"

Gunnar hmmmed, and cleared his throat. "Try pantomime."

It took some trying, but eventually I figured out how to walk in VR while staying in one real place. I made about twenty meters, out to the center of our virtual room. "How's that?"

"Aside from the fact that you look like Marcel Marceau in drag, not bad. Try walking into the wind."

"Huh?"

"Or bicycling. Or better yet, try this: pretend you're trapped inside a big glass box and you're feeling your way along the walls."

"Gunnar?"

"Yes, Max?"

"Shut up, Gunnar. Just, shut up."

I took a few minutes to stroll around the place, do some bends and twists, and just generally get the hang of moving my virtual body. In time the ProctoProd stopped being an obsessive misery and became just a nagging discomfort. When my confidence had increased to a sufficient level, I oriented myself toward the virtual wall furthest from where I was standing at that moment and moved to the next stage of our test plan.

"Okay Gunnar, I'm going to try running in place now." I took a deep breath, shifted my weight onto the balls of my feet, and started into a gentle jog.

*BAM*! I slammed into the far wall with a violence that would have knocked me silly if it was real. As it was, all I felt was a gentle thump through the, uh, the thoracic, uh—

"Wow!" Gunnar said. "Watch the velocity, kid! Did you get any kind of kinetic feedback out of the bra?"

"Yeah." I really wished we could find a better name for that thing. "And by the way, that was just jogging. Any chance you could get a time on my next run?"

"Give me a minute." I heard Gunnar start pounding on the keyboard. "Okay, the timer is set. Hundred meter sprint?"

"Yup. This one's for the record. Whenever you're ready."

"Stand by. On my mark . . . *GO!*"

Had the far wall been made of something less substantial than the absolute edge of the virtual universe—say, six feet of tempered steel—I would have put one hell of a dent in it.

*"Holy Moley!"* Gunnar gasped. "Point-two-five-one-seven—Max, you just went supersonic!" He paused. "Max?"

"I'm okay. It's just—I got some negative feedback when I hit the wall, but not nearly as strong as I expected. There must be some dandy kinetic transient dampers in the system."

"Either that," Gunnar pointed out, "or else this version of Max Kool has more hit points than Gamera."

"Could be." I finished inspecting my virtual self for damage—none found, my hair wasn't even mussed—and decided to move on. "Okay, I'm going to try the polyhedrons now." I carefully strolled across the virtual room, got to the base of the pile of polyhedrons, and allocated a few moments to looking it over and wondering where to begin.

The polyhedron test was kind of an afterthought. We wanted to see how the new interface handled manipulating objects, so we slapped together a few hundred polyhedrons ranging in size from baseballs to Volkswagens and piled them in one corner of our virtual test chamber. Then at the last minute we also decided to see just how subtle the tactile feedback was, so we grabbed a dozen or so surface textures at random out of our library and mapped them onto as many objects as we could easily reach.

As a result, I now stood before a jumbled heap of knotty pine cubes, polished marble tetrahedrons, snakeskin soccerballs, and at least one dodecahedron of raw steak. We'd also assigned density and mass factors pretty much at random; that little chrome pyramid by my left foot, for example, was so heavy it should have bent the fabric of space/time around it.

I kicked the pyramid. It went sailing about thirty feet.

"Max?" Gunnar asked in my ear. "Was that the—?"

"It was." I stooped over, picked up a granite sphere about the size of a bowling ball, and lobbed it the 100-meter length of the room. It shattered against the far wall. "Either something is *way* out of calibration here, or I don't know what." I climbed up on top of a large raccoon fur cube and started touching all the different surfaces I could reach. "The tactile feedback is very clear. I can feel the subtle differences in all these surface textures." Something registered in my mind then, and I took an extra moment to wiggle my toes in the fur and check it out. "I can even feel texture with my feet, which is odd when you consider that I'm wearing virtual engineer boots." I spotted another texture about ten feet higher in the stack and climbed on top of a milk chocolate icosahedron to reach it. "I can—" Oh, darn, it was just a few inches too far. I leaned out and stretched. "I can—" I grabbed onto the projecting point of something or other, and strained further. "I can—"

"*Look out!*" Gunnar shouted. The point snapped off in my hand. Something broke loose and went bounding down the slope. Then another something, then the whole heap of polyhedrons began to collapse. I jumped.

I bounced off the ceiling.

I hit the floor at the far end of the room, rebounded into a two-cushion shot off the corner, and grazed the ceiling again. About the time I noticed I was heading right back into the middle of the polyhedron landslide, I got pissed off and decided to stop. In midair.

"Uh, Houston?" I asked. "Are you copying this?"

"Roger, little buddy," Gunnar answered. "You seem to be, uh, experiencing a local gravitational anomaly of, uh—" He gave up trying to sound like the voice of NASA. "Aw, screw it. Max? You're *flying*!"

"Yep. That's what it looks like to me, too." I wasted a second or two considering my position—and wondering if this was like a Road Runner cartoon, and I was going to plummet to the dusty canyon floor as soon as I noticed that I wasn't standing on anything solid—then picked a spot on the floor well away from the still-tumbling polyhedrons and gently descended for a landing, as graceful as Baryshnikov coming off of a jeté. I resisted the urge to bow.

Gunnar was still hyperventilating. "You were *flying*, man!"

"Uh-huh." I wasted another few seconds considering my marvelous virtual body, finished working through an idea, then pulled down the virtual window that let me look at Gunnar's face. "Say, guy, can I try a concept out on you? Would you say that my time in the hundred-meter was, oh, faster than a speeding bullet?"

Oops. I'd forgotten that weapons talk always put Gunnar in literal mode. He stroked his chin and thought it over. "Well, a medium rifle or handgun bullet," he said, nodding. "Your hot .357 Magnum or high-powered rifle loads, on the other hand—"

"Never mind. Next question. Based on my apparent strength, would you care to take a guess at how powerful I am?"

Gunnar hmmmed. "Let's see: at one horsepower equals five hundred and fifty foot-pounds per second—"

I shook my head. "Don't bother with the math. It's just, would you say I'm in the same power class as, oh, a locomotive?"

Gunnar was befuddled. "What's a locomotive?"

Oh, mother, this was getting nowhere fast. "Last question. Any chance you could map a tall building into this virtual space? I'd like to see if I could leap it in a single bound."

"Hold on." Gunnar looked away from me and started punching keys. "Okay, I can give you the White House, the Great Pyramid, or the Chrysler Building, all scaled to fit. Any preference?"

There were times when I just could not *believe* how thick Gunnar could be. "Let's try this again. Faster than a speeding bullet? More powerful than a locomotive? Able to leap tall buildings in a single bound? Does this *suggest* anything to you?"

"Yeah," Gunnar said. "A lawsuit. Now if you're done dicking around, can we please move on to the final phase of the test?"

Sometimes Gunnar was just no fun at all. "Yes, Mother."

"I heard that!" Gunnar grinned and went back to the keyboard. I decided having his smiling face in the upper right corner of my field of vision was distracting, and closed the window. For a half a minute or so all I heard was the *clackety-clackety-clack* of the keyboard, then—

"NetLink activated. We should have—correction, we've got an ack. We're connected." Pause. "No unusual signals coming out of the interface." Another long, tense, breathless pause. We'd figured, if the interface was programmed to do anything like broadcast a homing beacon, it was either going to do it in the first thirty seconds, or else it was going to wait for some as-yet-unknown trigger condition to be met.

The thirty seconds passed. No warning flags went up. "Okay," Gunnar said, "it seems to be stable. I will be unlocking your end of the link in three, two, one—" A two-meter circle of light irised open in the far wall, slightly above floor level.

"I see it," I said. "The portal is open. Now what?"

"What else?" Gunnar grunted. "Go toward the light, Max."

I walked the first few meters, cautiously at first, then decided what the hey, as long as I could fly and it didn't seem to cost me any energy, I'd go for it. Springing lightly into the virtual air, I spread out my hands before me and coasted gently toward the circle of light, exactly like—

Like some guy in a cape, okay? Admit it. Haven't *you* always secretly wanted to be able to fly like that?

Oh, and a point of advice: if you ever *do* learn to fly, watch out for the suction around NetLink portals. I had a few moments of genuine terror there when I suddenly realized I was accelerating toward the portal, with all the control of a soap bubble going down a bathroom drain, and I didn't have the least idea of how to veer off. I did a few flying somersaults and barrel rolls, started fluttering like a butterfly plastered on a car's grille, and was maybe another half-second away from hitting my emergency bailout when—

*Pop*! It was over, and I was floating ten feet above the crest of a peaceful virtual hillside, overlooking the Information Superhighway rushing by in the valley far below.

"Well," Gunnar said, "offhand I'd say this proves you can fly in Net VR, too." I looked around, picked a promising spot, and swooped in for a landing. When I didn't answer right away, he tapped his headset microphone. "Max? You there?"

I winced and grabbed at my ears. "Yes, and for chrissakes don't do that again! *Ouch*!"

"Sorry." He didn't sound sincere. After a pause he added, "Since you're probably wondering, I say we stick with our original test plan. You can fly around and move mountains all you want *after* we've finished debugging the interface, but for now, would you please try to be a little bit subtle and not go out of your way to attract attention?"

"Yes, Mother." I sighed heavily, and then with a snap of my very realistic fingers, summoned my virtual Harley Ultraglide back into existence.

It looked flat. Cartoonish. Insubstantial. Too many simple planes, too many primary colors, too few of the fractal details of reflection and texture that make a virtual object seem *real*, if difficult to transmit over the Net in real time. I walked in a slow circle around it and realized the Harley wasn't so much an object as an engineering drawing made animate in 3-D.

"Get on the damn bike, Max," Gunnar hissed in my ear. "We can remap the surface textures later."

"Yes, Mother." I climbed onto the bike, started it rolling down the hill, and popped the clutch into first. The 1100-cc two-cylinder engine roared to life with—well, frankly, with a rather tinny and cheap sound, as befits an 11-KHz audio sample. I bombed down the hill, accelerating all the way, hit the drainage ditch at the bottom, and jumped the bike over three lanes of traffic to land in the express lane to the InfoMall.

"Nice going, Max," Gunnar muttered. "*Real* subtle."

I knocked the knock on the door to Heaven. The gorilla slid open the peephole. "What's da passwoid?"

*Interesting.* "Are you copying this?" I said to Gunnar.

"Wrong passwoid, chump," the gorilla growled as he slammed the peephole shut.

"No," Gunnar said, "I didn't quite—Let me crank up the magnification on my end, and then let's try again." *Clickety-clickety-click.* "Okay. Ready."

I knocked the knock. The gorilla slid open the peephole. "What's da passwoid?"

The gorilla, I should point out, looked *way* different from the last time I'd seen him. Before, he'd always been a fairly ordinary cartoon gorilla, with a bowler hat, a bowtie, and an ill-fitting tuxedo. Now, he was a sort of fractured, complex, *angular* thing, with his old cartoon aspect painted in flat two-dimensional colors on one facet, and a twisted knot of rods, gears, and algorithms churning away on another. A third facet seemed to be like a splinter of an old video monitor, with lines of glowing green text scrolling by too fast to read.

"Fascinating," Gunnar said in my ear. "Either our doorbeast has been redesigned by some deranged Picasso fan, or else . . ."

"Or else what?" I said.

"Wrong passwoid, chump," the gorilla growled as he slammed the peephole shut.

"Max," Gunnar asked, "do you know anything about Cubism?"

I strained for the memory. "Why, yes," I said at last. "I remember that it was a word I had to use in the essay question in order to get a C+ on my Art Appreciation final."

"Cubism," Gunnar said, "was the name applied by art critics to the new style evolved by Pablo Picasso in the early nineteen hundreds. Derived from both the Post-Impressionist and Parisian *Fauves* schools, and following closely on the end

---

### INFONUGGETS

No, no, I can fight this, I can resist the temptation to . . . . *AUGH!*

---

### PICASSO

Pablo, Spanish painter and sculptor, b. 1881, d. 1973. Now recognized as one of the premiere practical pranksters of all time, for his dumping of a pile of shipyard welders' scraps in the center of Daley Plaza in Chicago and convincing the city fathers it was a "statue."

of Picasso's own Blue Period, the driving concept behind Cubism was the destruction of both the classical conception of beauty *and* the interpretation of Euclidean space through conventional perspective. As evidenced by Picasso's 1906 work, *Les Desmoiselles d'Avignon*, as well as the collages of Georges Braque and the landscapes of Joseph Stella, the Cubist school attempted to illustrate through two-dimensional media a three-, four-, or even polydimensional—"

And right about that point is when I screamed. *"STOP!"*

Gunnar was puzzled. "Why, Max? All I was attempting to do was explain how the artist's use of solidified space and abstract volume have provided the translucent structural units—"

*"STOP,* GODDAMMIT! I will *not* have gratuitous lectures about Modern Art inserted into my story!"

Gunnar *tched*. "I'd hardly call it *gratuitous*, Max. After all, the ability to drop artistic references nonchalantly into casual conversation from time to time is *essential* to simulating the appearance of erudition, or dare I say, pretentiousness, which in turn is the hallmark of a truly literary—"

"Gunnar?" I interrupted, in a voice much like Norman Bates discussing his new girlfriend with his mother, "I have a loaded .45 automatic in my hand, and if you do not cut this artistic crap *right now* and get on with the story, I am going to come over there and shoot your balls off. Is this clear?"

*"Well,"* Gunnar said,

---

### .45 AUTOMATIC

Specifically the Colt Model 1911, designed by John Moses Browning, the engineer who also created the Winchester lever-action rifle and many other enduring designs. I'd give you his vital dates, but he's not in the *Noted Americans* database. Obscure jazz saxophonist Zutty Singleton is there, but not one mechanical engineer. It figures.

clearing his throat. "Offhand, er, I'd, uh, say this new user interface we've gotten from Amber has, ah, given you a multidimensional view of code objects, such as the door gorilla." He gulped. "Um, on one facet, you're seeing the conventional 'front' of the object, while on another facet, you are able to perceive the inner workings of the object, much as Ferdnand Léger's *The City* reveals the utopian control and—"

I racked the slide on the virtual .45.

"Right!" Gunnar said brightly. "On with the story, then. Let's try a test. Summon the gorilla, would you?"

I knocked the knock on the door to Heaven. The gorilla slid open the peephole. "What's da passwoid?"

"Look at the *center* facet," Gunnar whispered. "I believe that bluish bar is the locking routine. Can you see where it connects to the audio pattern-recognition algorithm?"

I was getting smarter. I nodded, but said nothing.

"Good," Gunnar said. "Now, try reaching *inside* him and tripping the lock by hand."

I tried it. I reached out with my virtual right hand, through the virtual skin of the gorilla, until my fingers were resting on the locking routine. Then I took a deep breath, steeled my courage, and exerted a slight pressure—

*Click.*

The gorilla snarled, but opened the door. I stepped through, into the a-grav tube, and ascended.

"Gunnar?" I whispered, while in transit up the tube. "What the hell did I just do?"

"Confirmed a theory, Max. I think I know how the interface works now."

After a few seconds, it became obvious he wasn't going to say any more unless prompted. "And that is?"

"An old UNIX system administration concept. Not used much anymore, because it's so potentially dangerous. Max, you are going to have to be *exceedingly* careful. One reckless gesture, one thoughtless word, and you can do serious, *permanent*, damage to the fabric of collective Net virtual reality."

I flooped out of the a-grav tube into Heaven, went directly into a dark corner, and thought it over. "Okay, you've impressed me. It's dangerous. Now what exactly did I *do*?"

"You've been transformed, Max," Gunnar whispered. "You've gained powers and abilities far beyond the reach of ordinary users. You can see things that no one else can see, do things that no one else can do, boldly go where no man has gone—"

My patience was running out. "No shit, Sherlock. *But what did I do?*"

"Max?" Gunnar said portentiously. "Brace yourself. You, my young friend, have become—

"A *superuser*."

That took a few seconds to sink in. I straightened up, turned around, and walked out of my dark corner. "Sounds silly," I muttered, for Gunnar's ears only.

"Of course it sounds silly," Gunnar answered. "It's UNIX. *Everything* about UNIX sounds silly. We're talking about an OS with commands like *chown*, *awk*, and *grep* here, where you have to periodically kill demons to keep your system running smoothly, and where 'zombie children floating in the pipe' is a legitimate description of an error state. Hell, even the *name* UNIX is a joke. It's called that because it's a 'simplified' version of the MULTICS operating system, in much the same sense as a gelding is a 'simplified' stallion." Gunnar suddenly stopped talking.

It's just as well, because I'd suddenly stopped listening.

Remember Heaven? Remember all my loving descriptions of the people and the scenery, from back in chapter 5? Well, forget them. Because now, with my Superuser Codeview Vision, I could see the place as it *really* was.

And what it really was, sad to say, was a Cubist nightmare. All the scenery, all the details, *all* the objects were fractured, multiplanar things, with their algorithmic guts exposed, like the gorilla. And the people? All those cool, happening people—the ones who were even real at all, and not just synthetic figments? They looked like a bunch of geek kids on Halloween. Glossy, flashy, chintzy costumes; rigid, vacuum-molded, plastic masks held on by rubber bands. They swaggered around the place and roared and laughed like drunken morons playing pirates. Some of them couldn't even keep their masks on, I noticed, and when I looked at them closely, I could tap into their data streams and follow them all the way back to the real-world person. The DJ in the dance room, for example: Rapmastah MC Ruthless. In the real world he was a skinny, pimply, seventeen-year-old white loser named David Berkowitz, and he was playing the house music from a rancid dorm room at a second-rate junior college someplace in outstate New Jersey.

"This," Gunnar said in my ear, "is really disillusioning."

*Max*? DON_MAC's voice said in my head. *Is that you*? I shook myself out of disappointment, and swept the room, looking for DON_MAC. I don't know why he was hard to spot. In a room full of poorly drawn cartoon characters, socially challenged misfits in cheap costumes, and wispy half-realized electronic ghosts, the gleaming chromium form of DON_MAC was suddenly, solidly, *real*. More real than he'd ever seemed before, in fact.

"DON_MAC?" I subvocalized.

"He definitely looks different," Gunnar noted.

*Max*? DON_MAC sent again. *And Gunnar*? *This is strange*.

"Uh-oh," Gunnar whispered.

*Gunnar*? *Have you finally gotten the hang of camouflage*? *I hear you, but I only see Max*.

"Open my window, Max." Gunnar's audio line went dead. It took me a few seconds to figure out what he meant, then I pulled down the video window that let me look "out" through the micro TV camera attached to Gunnar's video monitor.

Gunnar had disconnected his microphone and was frantically scribbling something on a piece of paper. He finished and held the paper up so I could see it. DON_MAC CAN HEAR ME? it said.

I nodded.

*Max*? DON_MAC telepathed again. *Whatever this piggyback thing is that you and Gunnar are trying, it's not working. I don't hear him anymore, but now you have developed a video echo. You've got a contrail behind you when you move; if I was feeling ambitious, I'd measure the echo gap and use it to figure out how far away you really are.*

I closed my internal video window; the one that let me look at the real Gunnar.

*Better*, DON_MAC telepathed. *You still have an echo*, though.

"Lose the audio and video," I subvocalized.

Gunnar reconnected his mic and came back online. "But—"

*Lose it, Gunnar*, DON_MAC thought. *You're making MAX_KOOL look like a newbie putz.*

"Okay," Gunnar said. "But this means you're on your own, Max. All I can do now is watch your biotelemetry." With a final, peevish, click, I heard Gunnar yank his headset jacks out. For the first time since I'd started using the new interface, my head felt strangely—and pleasantly—quiet.

DON_MAC lifted his chrome robotic body out of his customary chair and started navigating across the crowded floor toward me with surprising speed and fluidity of movement. "Hello, Max," he said when he got within conversational range. His audible voice sounded just exactly like his telepathic voice. Stopping a yard short of me, he raised his huge right claw, and with whining servos, extended it towards me to offer a—er, handshake.

"Welcome to the next level."

# 13

## DOWN THE OUBLIETTE

DON_MAC and I sat with Don Vermicelli, watching the parade of Cubist strangeness through Heaven and tucking into an absolutely exquisite *cervella al burro*. "I can't

> ### OUBLIETTE
>
> A dungeon with just one opening, at the top. From the French verb *oublier*, "to forget."

believe this," I said, around a mouthful of—whatever it was. I didn't want to know. "I just can *not* believe this."

Don Vermicelli finished his glass of vino and set it down on the table. Bambi immediately leaped to refill it. Bambi, I could see clearly now, was without question male in real time—as was Thumper—but both of the Silicione Sisters were also clearly very confused about this whole gender thing.

"I can't believe this," I repeated.

"What?" Don Vermicelli responded. "That I also have the interface and am a superuser? Did you really think I would let Max Kool have something I did not already possess myself?"

"No." I shook my head and stuffed another forkful of the

*cervella* in my mouth. "I can't believe that I can really *taste* this virtual food! This is incredible! Delicious!"

"Chew with your mouth closed," DON_MAC suggested.

Don Vermicelli took another drink and set his glass down. "Ah, Max. Perhaps *now* you understand why I am what I am." He leaned back in his chair—the hydraulic supports creaked and groaned—slapped his incredibly rotund belly with both hands, and let out a laugh worthy of Santa Claus. "In the real world, I walk three miles a day, live on rabbit food, and still must fight constantly to keep my weight below one-seventy! But here, ah! There are no triglycerides in Heaven!"

Thumper scampered up to the table at that moment, bearing a large bowl of something that smelled totally divine. *"Granchio di mare in zuppiera,"* Don Vermicelli announced as he tucked a napkin the size of a bedspread under his fourth chin and seized a fork in each hand. "Marinated blue crab claws! *Mangiamo!*"

I had to move fast, but I managed to snag a few crab claws before the Don dove facefirst into the bowl. Noticing that DON_MAC hadn't gotten any, I lifted one between fork and knife and offered to transfer it to his plate.

DON_MAC blocked the transfer with his shiny chromium hand. "No, Max. You take it."

"Too full?" I asked. Then I looked at his metal carapace and articulated limbs. "Too much like cannibalism?"

Don Vermicelli surfaced long enough to speak. "DON_MAC does not eat as we do," he said. "He cannot taste this food."

I set the crab claw down on my plate and turned to stare at DON_MAC. "Carrying this role-playing thing a bit far, aren't you?"

"There is more than one way to become a superuser," DON_MAC said softly. "I, unfortunately, did it the old-fashioned way."

Don Vermicelli wolfed down the last of the crab claws, belched loudly, and wiped his face and hands on the napkin. "DON_MAC is too modest," he said to me. "He was one of the first; one of the best. In many ways he is the father of us all, and does us great honor by his presence."

DON_MAC shrugged; a strange, clanking gesture to see in a chrome-hulled robot. "My reasons are not entirely benign—"

Whatever he was going to say next, it got lost in the noise. *"Boss!"* one of Don Vermicelli's trigger boys screamed as a crowd burst into our corner of Heaven. *"Watch out! We tried to stop her, but—"* Something seized the trigger boy by the nape of the neck and flung him like a rag doll across the room, to splatter and die against a concrete pillar.

The something was named Eliza.

Two more of Don Vermicelli's trigger boys tried to block her way. They made it as far as touching her before they burst into flame. A third screamed an incoherent warning, drew his gun, and fired a shot at the back of her white-blond head. The bullet froze in midair, then dropped, smoking, to the carpet.

The shooter was dead and randomized before the bullet touched the floor.

Don Vermicelli held up his hand, signaling his two surviving boys to give it up. "Hello, my bella Eliza," he said respectfully. "To what do we owe the pleasure of this visit?"

"To this asshole," she said, pointing straight at me. Then she turned on me, with the icy blue-eyed fury I was coming to know so well. "You just couldn't listen to me, could you, Max? I *told* you not to get involved with that Amber bitch. But no, you couldn't stop thinking with your dick long enough to use your brain, could you?"

I shrugged and smiled. It seemed to be the only weapon I had that worked on Eliza. "Sweetheart, darling, you always *said* men are dinosaurs. It's that secondary brain in my pelvis."

*"Argh!"* She started to morph into her claws-and-fangs form then, but—by God, I *saw* the texture mapping sweeping across her skin like crackling snakes of blue electric light, and I reached out with my virtual fingers, and I *stopped* the transformation of her right arm! She jumped back from my touch, startled—whether because it was painful or because it reminded her of our sex life together, I don't know—and reverted to her normal aspect.

"Well, well," she said, when the alarm had drained out of her icy blue eyes. "And now you're a goddam *superuser*, too." She put her hands on her skinny hips, stuck out her lower lip, and puffed out a snort of deep frustration.

Her next transformation was absolutely remarkable to see. She parted her lips, and *smiled* at me, and the iceberg of anger in her eyes thawed and melted, and she morphed into someone who looked exactly as she had looked a moment before, only this time she was *not* gazing upon the face of the scum-sucking Antichrist.

She morphed into someone who *liked* me.

"Max, honey?" she said sweetly. "I know we've had some differences in the past, but—" She shrugged, and put her hands together behind her back, and fidgeted and kicked the carpet a little bit, and tried another tentative smile on me.

It worked. I smiled back.

Her face lit up like sunrise over newly fallen snow.

She produced a message chip, put it down on the table, and slid it across to me. "I, uh," she fidgeted some more. "I've got some important things to take care of in real time, right now. But if you could meet me here," she tapped the chip with an ice-blue fingernail, "in one hour, well—I think you'd find it worth your while. Promise me you'll meet me there?"

Aw, hell, I never could turn down a woman who looked at me like that. "Sure, honey." I picked up the chip and pressed it into the palm of my hand.

"Oh, goody!" She giggled, clapped her hands, and just

about shivered with excitement. And then, to complete my already profound amazement, she darted around the table, parked her skinny little butt in my lap, and threw a tight hug around my neck and gave me a tongue-kiss on my right ear. Icy chills ran wind sprints up and down my spine.

"The *best* part of being a superuser," she whispered as her body turned to powder snow in my hands, "is that the virtual sex is absolutely *fantastic!*" I tried to cop a quick feel, but a blast of arctic wind came gusting through the room in that moment and her slender body flowed away in the cold, crystalline wind, literally slipping through my fingers, leaving me with just the memory of her icy kiss upon my lips and the faint echo of her words in the voice of the wind:

*"Only this time*, you *get to be the newbie."*

And then she was gone.

I blinked. Recovered. Started thinking with the brain in my head again. Closed my gaping mouth and put some effort into remembering where I was. Don Vermicelli was ignoring me, looking at the smoking shoes his incinerated boys had left behind, and—between bites of *seppie ripiene*—shaking his head sadly. DON_MAC was leaning back in his chair, sipping a Pennzoil & Lime and regarding me with red, unreadable, photoelectric eyes.

I smiled at the robot. "Well? What d'ya think?"

"I think," DON_MAC said slowly as he set his drink down on the table, "that I have never before seen anyone so totally controlled by his gonads." Abruptly, he stood and pushed his chair back. "Walk with me, Max." He turned, made some gesture of farewell to Don Vermicelli, who looked up from his *gamberoni aglio olio* long enough to give us a half-hearted wave, then strode quickly and purposefully away from the table. I peeled off my napkin, threw it down on the table, and had to run to catch up with him.

DON_MAC was waiting for me at the a-grav tube out of Heaven. I joined him, and together we flooped down the tube. "Max?" he said, while we were in transit. "How long have you been hanging around Heaven?"

I thought it over. "In real-time terms?" DON_MAC nodded. "About three years."

"You even designed some parts of Heaven, didn't you?"

I shrugged. "Nothing important. The phased-space room, and some of the trapdoors in the Jobs Memorial Lounge."

"That's all? I thought you did the pterodactyl nest."

"I refined it. Cowboy Bret did the original code."

"Ah, yes," DON_MAC said, nodding slowly. "The legendary Cowboy Bret. Was he the one who showed you how to find Heaven?"

I shook my head. "Nope. Never met him. I had to figure that one out on my own."

"And before you did so, you were hanging around on the Net for—what? Three years? Four?"

I worked through it in my head, fished up some unpleasant memories from junior high school, and came up with a different answer. "Closer to six."

We hit the bottom of the a-grav tube. DON_MAC stepped out, into the Marketplace of Ideas, and I followed. With just a quick backwards glance at the gorilla—yes, it was still a Cubist mess, but it also was starting to make obvious *sense* to me— we set off walking at a brisk pace through Third Level East.

"Tell me," DON_MAC said without looking back, "now that you know what one is, have you ever actually met a superuser before?"

That didn't take much thinking. "Well, you and Don Vermicelli, of course. And it's pretty clear that Eliza is a superuser." Another thought clicked into place in that moment. "And I suppose Amber must be one, as well."

"But have you ever run across any others?" DON_MAC

asked. "Anyone who seemed exempt from the laws of virtual reality? Anyone who consistently made you sit up and say, 'How the hell did he *do* that?'"

That answer took a good deal of thinking, and of sifting through old memories. The thinking slowed my walking pace, and I had to scamper to catch up with DON_MAC. "Not that I can think of," I said. "I've heard of a few who probably—"

DON_MAC stopped abruptly, before a virtual door, and I almost collided with him. "Ah," he said, "the Ranting Room. Do you ever visit the Ranting Room, Max?"

I screwed up my face into a distasteful expression, licked my lips, and tried to find some way to be polite about it. "Well, I, er, uh—"

"It's Fruitcake Central," DON_MAC announced. "Home to the most idiotic, hare-brained, addle-headed thinking on the planet. For example, tonight," he touched the menu card next to the door, and it glowed to life, "the Church of Vegentology is conducting a memorial service for the Australian wheat harvest, followed at 0100 UTC Standard Time by the PPLF." He paused, looked at the menu card slightly cock-eyed, and thumbed the card until supporting data was displayed. "The Portly Persons' Liberation Front will be issuing a call for aspiring terrorists to help them with their campaign of radical door enlargement. Then after that we have a meeting of the FWRA—the Future Welfare Recipients of America —who are splitting their time with Men Victimized by Vasectomy, and following that the

---

### SCATOPHILIACS

People who really know their shit.

---

### INFONUGGETS

Okay, *that* was the last one.

president of Scatophiliacs Anonymous will give a talk on 'Getting Your Shit Together.'"

DON_MAC considered that last one a moment, grimmaced, and released the menu card. It faded back to darkness. He turned to me. "Do you know *why* the Marketplace sysops continue to maintain the Ranting Room, Max?"

I shrugged. "Cheap laughs?"

DON_MAC slowly shook his metallic head. "It's a *safety valve*, Max. Any open society must offer its members a safety valve—a way to vent any idea, no matter how looney—without fear of retribution. Take *away* that safety valve, and the only viable alternative is a police state, where *all* ideas are rigidly controlled."

Okay, that seemed to make sense as far as it went, but I was having trouble connecting it to the idea of superusers.

*I'm telepathic, remember*? DON_MAC thought. *I've also been a superuser for almost fifteen years. And for as long as you've known me, I have been a bar fixture in Heaven. Doesn't it occur to you to wonder* why *a superuser would want to do that*?

"Okay," I said, not bothering to subvocalize. "I'll bite. Why?"

"Because the superuser community is *not* an open society," DON_MAC said softly. "With the power you now have, there *are* some ideas that are too dangerous to be spoken aloud. All it would take is one reckless superuser to completely ruin the architecture of the Information Superhighway, or destroy the fabric of virtual reality. A few *malicious* superusers, working together, could bring all of western civilization to its knees."

Kind of attractive thought, that. Oops. Waitaminute, the guy I'm walking with is telepathic. Er, I didn't really mean— Abruptly, DON_MAC pivoted and started walking down the east corridor again. *Look at the left wall, Max*, he instructed.

I followed and looked, although I didn't really know why.

I mean, I'd been down this corridor a hundred times before, and all there was on the left wall was—

A hidden door. Just exactly like the secret door to Heaven.

"DON_MAC?" I subvocalized.

*Don't go in there, Max*, he answered. *Remember our teenage mujahadin? The khyberpunks? We had to give them their own room, just to keep them out of trouble.* I jumped back from the door as if it was electrified and ran to catch up with DON_MAC. Another door appeared on my left.

"This one?" I subvoked.

*Don't waste your time*, he answered. *That room's full of young kids who like to clown around with liquid nitrogen.*

"Huh?"

*Cryopunks.*

I left a bit of the skin from my fingers frozen to the doorknob, and ran to catch up with DON_MAC again. We passed another door.

"That one?"

*Even worse*, DON_MAC thought. *That room's full of wankers who are pathologically into code-breaking and math puzzles.*

"Who?"

*Cipherpunks.*

Argh! Stifling a horrendous groan, I caught up with DON_MAC just as we passed yet another door. I fought to keep my silence.

It didn't help. *A splinter faction from the home-brewing group*, DON_MAC observed as we passed the door. *These fools are ideologically committed to creating fruit-based beverages.*

"Let me guess."

*Ciderpunks.*

I fell down to the floor, kicking and screaming in pain, but had to cut the hysterics and get back to my feet when I saw that

DON_MAC was going on without me. We passed another hidden door.

This one actually looked rather promising. I stopped and took a closer look.

*Oh no, Max,* DON_MAC warned me, *whatever you do, you do* not *want to go in* there. *That place is full of young guys with no social lives, no sex lives, and no hope of ever moving out of their mothers' basements. These are guys who relate to hardware better than people, who still build and fly model rockets, and who show up for the sneak preview showing of* every *new science fiction film. They're total wankers and losers, who indulge in Messianic fantasies about someday getting even with the world through almost-magical computer skills, but whose actual use of the Net amounts to dialing up the scatophilia forum and downloading a few disgusting pictures. You know,* cyberpunks.

"Oh gosh, no," I said quickly. "I'd *never* want to hang around with *those* geeks."

Eventually, the junction of the east and south corridors came into sight. Just before we entered the common area, DON_MAC stopped before a door that was hidden a bit better than the rest.

"Max," he said, "this is very important. Remember how I told you that the superusers are not an open society?"

"Yes?"

"And by now, I expect you've figured out that it was we superusers who built the original Heaven, as well as all the other virtual live-traps?"

Well, no, I hadn't figured that one all the way to the end, but I wasn't going to let DON_MAC know it. And besides, that term—*live-traps*—was a bit disconcerting.

"New superusers are evolving all the time," DON_MAC said. "Lately we've been getting a lot through the Sacroiliac Neural Induction Device, but even before that appeared, wild talents were constantly popping up on the scene. That's why we built and continue to staff the live-traps, and why you've never seen a wild superuser. Because it's my job to identify, assess, and collect nascent superusers *before* they learn their full potential." DON_MAC punched a spot on the wall, and the hidden door swung open, revealing a lightless void beyond.

"Ah," I said, comprehension dawning at last. "Then you're like a midwife, helping to bring new superusers into the world?"

DON_MAC clamped one massive chrome hand on the nape of my neck, the other on the seat of my pants, and lifted me clear off the floor. "No," he said, "I'm more like a game warden, helping to decide if you're rabid and should be destroyed." He stepped back, took a massive swing, and heaved me head-first through the open door, into the endless black void beyond.

*"If it's any consolation,"* his voice echoed after me, *"it's nothing personal!"* I fell forever to the lightless center of the earth, tumbling and screaming all the way down.

# 14

## MAX_KOOL IN HELL

Blackness. All about me was silent and without form, empty chaos floating on the null and void. . . .

"Hullo," a pleasant female voice said, "and welcome to Hell. Would you like a drink?"

My eyes popped open. I was sitting in a large, hellish, red, leather-upholstered, actually rather comfy wing chair, in—

Well, a room. A *nice* room. One of those sort of elegant, dark-paneled drawing rooms you see in BBC dramas that can't afford to spend any money on sets.

I blinked. Everything stubbornly continued to be there and nothing seemed the least bit Cubist, so I blinked again. About that time I noticed my clutching fingers were digging holes into the arms of the chair, and so, slowly, I relaxed.

"Hullo?" the woman said again. I pried my attention off the chair and the room, and looked at her.

She was—*normal*. Disturbingly normal. A pleasant smile, grayish-blue eyes, and a plain face, neither radiantly beautiful nor conspicuously ugly. Long, straight, brown hair, parted in the middle, with a hint of gray here and there and a touch of curl at the ends. Her only jewelry was a simple pair of gold hoop earrings: other than that she had no facial piercings, no electronic implants, no exotic makeup, no gravity-defying hair. I pulled my view back from her face and glanced over the rest of her. She wore a simple, nondescript, brownish sweater, a pair of baggy gray slacks, and brown flats. Neither thin nor fat; if I'd had to guess at her age, I'd have put her anywhere between thirty and fifty, and no more specific than that.

And then it struck me. She was wearing *perfume*. Innocent and floral, yes, but I could definitely smell it.

"Hullo?" she said a third time. "Er, you *are* the new lad that DON_MAC sent down, aren't you?" She spoke with a pleasant, educated, upper-crust British accent.

I gulped, licked my lips, and found my voice, in my throat, right where I'd left it. "Yeah," I got out. "Max Kool. I—" I lifted my right hand off the armrest in preparation for offering her a handshake, noticed that my hand was shaking enough all by itself, and went back to gripping the armrest. "Where did you say we are?"

"In Hell, of course." She smiled sweetly, took my hand and patted it gently as if it were a nervous hamster, and said, "There, there. Don't be alarmed. Everything's fine. *All* the interesting people end up in Hell, sooner or later."

I gulped. "I'll take that drink now," I said.

She released my hand, walked lightly over to the small table on the other side of the room, and pulled the stopper from the mouth of an ornate crystal decanter. "I know, I should give you a choice," she said over her shoulder, "but it seems to me you *desperately* need some cognac." She sloshed a bit of tea-colored fluid from the decanter to a large snifter, capped the decanter, and returned to me. "Here you go," she said as she lifted my right hand and gently guided it around the curvaceous bottom of the snifter.

"Thank you." I put the glass to my lips, tilted my head back, and tossed the whole thing down in one gulp.

And very nearly tossed it right back up just as quickly.

"What's wrong?" The lady viewed my choking, gasping face with great alarm and gave me a sharp slap on the back. "Max! Speak to me! *What's wrong*?"

"Forgot," I managed to cough out between gasps for air. "Can *taste* now." I fought down a dry heave, got my breathing under control, and blinked the tears from my eyes. "I don't usually drink in real time," I mumbled apologetically.

The newspaper in the wing chair across from me (funny, I hadn't noticed it before), folded in on itself and moved aside to reveal a sour-faced old fart in a blue suit and sedate tie. "Lovely," the old fart said. "DON_MAC has sent us another kid with a SNID. Stop wasting your time, Diana."

The long-haired woman—Diana, apparently—turned on him sharply. "*Really*, Devon. You were no better yourself when you first showed up."

The old fart—Devon—sniffed and rustled his papers. "Well, at least I had to *work* to get here."

Diana pursed her lips, shot him a quick glare, and turned to me and recovered her smile. "Pay him no mind, Max. He's just an old crustacean who made it to superuser without neural induction and believes everyone else should have to suffer as he did."

"It builds character!" Devon snorted as he pointedly went back to his paper.

"Superuser?" I blinked, and digested the word. "But I thought DON_MAC threw me—"

"Down to Hell?" Diana completed. She laughed slightly, and covered her mouth with her fingertips. "But of course. He's done that to all of us, you see. Sort of an initiation thing. You know, so you can properly say you've been 'cast out' of Heaven?" She laughed again—it was a very pleasant sound—took the empty brandy snifter from me and set it on the table.

"No, my young friend," Diana said, "you may relax. This *is* the next step up, and not the oubliette."

Someone else shimmered into view in that moment, in the other red wing chair, opposite Devon. This fellow was dressed like an affluent nineteenth-century Texan: he wore a well-tailored natural leather sport coat, a black bolo tie with an ornate silver-and-turquoise clasp, and a broad but clearly authentic and expensive felt cowboy hat, decorated with a band of silver conchos. He was also sharpening a Bowie knife with a handheld whetstone; the gleaming blade moved in slow, even circles, with a faint grinding noise that set my teeth on edge.

And then it hit me. "Cowboy Bret?" I whispered, a trace of nervous awe in my voice. "*The* Cowboy Bret?" I turned to Diana, my eyes wide. "And Diana? *Diana Von Babe?*"

"Throw that boy a fish," Devon muttered from behind his paper.

I blinked, and shook my head, and gulped a few times while I tried to think of something brilliant to say. Cowboy Bret *and* Diana Von Babe, in the same room! I just could not believe—"I'm Max Kool!" I blurted out. "And I've got to tell you, I've been hanging out in Heaven since I was twenty years old, and it is just *the* coolest—"

"I'm flattered," Cowboy Bret said as he continued sharpening his knife. "But if y'all don't shut up right now, I'll boot yer ass *back* to Heaven and make sure you never find your way down here again."

I shut up. Instantly.

"That's better," Bret said. "Now, I got just one thing to say to you, kid. Y'all can listen to Diana all you want, but don't relax *too* much. Remember, you're still on probation."

I looked at Diana. "Probation?" She parted her lips as if to say something.

Bret didn't let her speak. "The rules are simple, kid. Y'all can do just about anything you want. After all, we *are* a pretty wild 'n' wooly—some might even say *criminal*—bunch."

Devon snorted and rustled his papers loudly.

"You do what you want," Bret repeated, "but if you fuck with the Network architecture, or blow permanent holes in virtual reality, or do anything that brings the NetCops down on the *rest* of us—" He stopped sharpening the knife, touched the point of the blade to the brim of his hat, and used it to push the hat back on his head so I could see his face. His mustache clearly did double-duty as a soup strainer, but what impressed me most about the man were his eyes. Honest, they were *steely* blue, just like the high-gloss cobalt finish on some of LeMat's old guns.

"Y'all make things bad for the rest of us," Bret said, "and we *will* deliver your body parts to the Federal Information Agency security office, neatly wrapped in white butcher paper. I ain't talkin' virtual; I'm talkin' for *real*." He emphasized that point by throwing the Bowie knife at me. It stuck, quivering, in the chair, scant inches from my head. *"Got that?"*

An hour earlier, MAX_KOOL would have signaled his getting it by throwing his monomolecular switchblade to stick, quivering in sympathetic resonance with the Bowie, in the back of Bret's chair. Under the circumstances this didn't seem like a real bright idea, though, so I fumbled for words.

Diana saved me. "Oh, Bret, control yourself! I'm certain this lad will do just fine. DON_MAC would not have sent him down if there was any question." Cowboy Bret just tilted his hat back further and squinted, dubiously, at Diana.

*"Hmph!"* She turned to me, seized my hand, and dragged me up from my chair. "Come along, Max! We'll get you away

from these Neanderthal influences and get you started in your new life!" Striding so briskly I almost had to trot to keep up, Diana led me out of the drawing room, down the corridor, through some kind of chandelier-hung foyer . . . I really would have liked to slow down enough to let some detail fill in. The general impression I got was of a combination exclusive private club and four-star hotel.

We made a sharp right turn through a dining room that smelled delicious, trotted up a broad marble staircase, and turned the corner into another long corridor, this one lined with dark wooden doors. She stopped abruptly before one of the doors, touched the lock—it glowed briefly—then threw it open and led me in.

"This is my personal dataspace," she said, as she slammed and locked the door. "I trust we can have some *privacy* here." She snapped her fingers, and the curtains drew themselves aside to allow the light in and reveal—

Well, I don't really have the words for it. The Imperial Bedroom Suite, I suppose. An enormous room, delicate antique furniture everywhere, white wainscotting on the lower walls, that sort of white-on-blue stuff that would be called cameo if it was jewelry on the upper walls, candelabras, chandeliers, floor-to-ceiling French windows in place of the outer wall, and in the exact center of the room, a large, canopied, four-poster bed.

Diana stepped back, put her hand to her chin, and gave me an appraising look. "Well, the *first* thing we have to do," she said, "is get rid of all that cartoonish black clothing. You may have been able to get away with that in Heaven, but here in Hell, we have much higher standards." She turned to the ornate antique wardrobe, pressed the door latch just so, and the doors swung open to reveal an enormous closet that could not possibly exist in three-dimensional space. "A tuxedo, I think," she muttered as she sorted through the clothing hanging there. She gave me a glance over her shoulder, and hazarded a guess. "Forty-six long?"

I didn't have any idea. The last time I'd shopped for a sports coat it was off the rack at K-Mart.

Diana *tched* and grabbed a fistful of hangers off the rack. "Well, we'll just have to experiment until we see what fits." She swept back over to me, threw the clothing on the bed, and tugged at the sleeve of my black leather jacket. "Come on. Off with it! Chop chop!" I peeled off my jacket, looked around for a place to hang it, and then just dropped it on the floor. "The shirt, too." I unbuttoned my black silk shirt, marveled at the fact that in virtual reality I had chest hair and for that matter a chest, and tossed the shirt aside.

Diana looked at my feet and shook her head. "Oh, and those boots simply *must* go. Take them off." Hopping on one foot and then the other, I unlaced my black engineer boots and kicked them off. The sudden sensation of bare feet on plush carpet was almost too ticklish to bear. "The pants as well," Diana said, nodding. I undid my massive chrome belt buckle, popped the button and dropped the zipper, and slid out of my black jeans. And about then is when it finally hit me, that I was standing there in front of this woman I didn't know at all, wearing nothing but my Rolex watch and my smiley-face boxer shorts.

Diana took a step back, put her hand on her chin again, gave me another appraising look, and nodded. "You know?" she said, as she took a glance over her shoulder at the heap of tuxedos and expensive tailored suits on the bed, "I think perhaps we should skip the preliminaries, and get right to the oral sex." And before I could react to that she dropped to her knees before me, yanked my boxer shorts down to my ankles, and opened wide—

*BAM!* The hallway door exploded inward. "*Get away from him, bitch!*" some woman shrieked. "*He's* mine!" Diana sprang to her feet, fangs bared, fingers curved like talons, and let out a feral hiss at the intruder. Me, I just about lost control of my sphincter.

"Eliza?" I whispered, luckily too soft for anyone to hear.

The new woman advanced into the room like a kickboxer in top fighting form; assertively, yet cautiously, walking on the balls of her feet with almost feline grace. Diana slithered away from me, hissing. The newcomer circled the other way; a priceless antique Louis XIV armchair got in her way and she kicked it to splinters. I stood between the two of them, petrified. I'd once tried to extract Psycho Kitty from a fight with a neighbor's cat, and was not looking forward to what was coming next. For a moment, the newcomer passed into clear silhouette, and in the light from the windows I could see she had a marvelous figure.

Well, that ruled out Eliza.

The two of them had almost completed a one-eighty around me. The newcomer was over by the French windows; Diana had her back to the open door. Diana arched her back, slashed the air with her claws, hissed and spat—

Then turned tail and ran out into the hallway, slamming the door shut behind her.

*Whew.*

Until I heard the soft padding of high heels across the carpet behind me. Sharp fingernails dug into my left shoulder and dragged slowly down to the small of my back. Swallowing hard, I gritted my teeth, forced myself into a smile, and turned around.

"Hello, darling," Amber said gently. "Sorry for not getting here sooner. Thorvold had a hard time finding me and telling me you'd gone super." Her long fingers touched and caressed my cheek, and slipped gently into the hair on the back of my head. Then she grabbed me fiercely and kissed me hard on the mouth and thrust her probing tongue halfway down to my tonsils.

"Don't," I gasped weakly, when she let me come up for air. "Stop." She kissed me again, longer, harder. "Don't. Please. Stop." She kissed me a third time; slowly, gently, a long, lingering kiss that left me weak in the knees and seeing blue spots from anoxia. "Please, don't stop," I begged her softly. "Take me now." She kissed me again, and I was like melting butter in her strong but slender and sensitive hands.

"I'm sorry I let you come here alone," she whispered in my ear, between delicate licks and bites on my earlobe. "I should have known that old witch Diana would try to get her meathooks into you. You're so innocent, and so vulnerable." She wrapped her arms around me, and held me tight, and suddenly made me excruciatingly aware that I was standing there buck naked with my boxer shorts around my ankles. I could only shudder and moan.

"My poor darling," Amber whispered in my ear. "I'd better make sure that nasty old Diana didn't hurt you." She gave me a long kiss on the neck that made me understand why some people think vampires are erotic.

"No damage there," she whispered. She shifted her grip and kissed me all across the chest, to finish with a flourish of tongue and teeth on my excruciatingly sensitive right nipple. "And *that* seems to be working." She crouched slightly, to trace the edge of my flat, well-defined belly muscles with her tongue. I writhed with pleasure. "No problems *there*." Dropping to her knees, she kissed her way across my appendix and down my right thigh to my kneecap, then—slowly—back up again, moving more towards the inside.

"And now," Amber whispered, "the *real* test." Wrapping her left arm around my butt so I couldn't squirm away from her, and gripping the family jewels and the base of my You Know What firmly with her right hand, she took a long, slow, lascivious lick from base to tip, then traced ever-faster circles with her tongue around the business end, reared back for a moment to take a deep breath, and—

"OH MY GOD!"

Fifteen milliseconds later I was back in reality. When I realized what had happened, I tore off my videoshades, threw them on the floor, and screamed at the top of my lungs.

*"LeMat!"*

He was beside me in a flash. "Jack! Jack! What the hell *happened* to you in there?"

*"What?"* I didn't know whether to strangle him or start sobbing uncontrollably, or both.

"We cut the audio and video feeds, remember? All I could watch was your biotelemetry!"

*"AUGH!"* I dropped to my knees on the floor and started whimpering.

LeMat dropped beside me and started yanking out optic fibers by the fistful. "Man, your bioindicators were going through the *roof*! Heart rate, respiration, blood pressure; I thought, my God, you were gonna explode!" He finished disconnecting the transceiver belt and unhooked it.

I could only blubber like a child.

"And then when you *screamed*," LeMat said, shaking his head, "well, I figured it was time to hit the panic button and bring you out of it."

I looked up at him, through red-rimmed eyes, and imagined how his head would look on the end of a bloody pikestaff.

"So tell me," LeMat said. "What happened to you in there?"

"Pinky?" I said, struggling to keep my voice calm. "I'm afraid I'm going to have to hurt you."

# 15

## THE EXPOSITION HAD TO GO SOMEWHERE

LeMat went back to Heaven later that night. I couldn't bring myself to use the neural interface again so soon, and he wasn't feeling secure enough in his masculinity to deal with the ProctoProd, so he strapped on his conventional VR gear and did it the old-fashioned way while I lay on the futon, on my stomach, and sulked.

*Amber. . . .*

About a quarter to midnight, LeMat surfaced and peeled off his VR goggles. "Jack?" he said. His voice was a hoarse croak.

I roused myself and sat up on the futon. "Yeah?"

"Beer," LeMat said. "Need beer."

"Okay." I lurched to my feet, shuffled over to my old half-height refrigerator, and pulled the door open. Refrigerated light spilled out into the room. "You got a choice," I said. "Summit, James Paige, Sam Adams, or Pig's Eye." LeMat, I might add, was the one responsible for stocking the fridge.

LeMat processed the information I'd given him. "Swill," he decided. "Need swill." I snagged a can of Pig's Eye Pilsner and carried it over to the workstation.

LeMat was still struggling to pull off his bulky datagloves, so I yanked the pop-top for him. "How'd it go?" I asked.

"Good." He took the can from me, tilted his head back, and poured a large slosh down his throat. For a moment, I was afraid he was going to gargle with it. "Better than I expected," he said, when he came up for air. He belched. "'Scuse me."

"Did you find the door to Hell? Or Amber?"

"No, and no." He took another gulp of the beer, wiped some condensation off the can, and rubbed it across his forehead. "Whatever they're doing to hide the door, it's *way* beyond what I can penetrate with this." He tapped the plate of his VR goggles for emphasis. "I couldn't even find the doors to those other live-traps you talked about."

"Did you try the apartment in ToxicTown?"

LeMat took a long, slow pull on his beer and set the can down. "Didn't need to," he said. "I went back to Heaven, to try to hunt up either DON_MAC or Don Vermicelli." He smiled, in a sort of lopsided way, and tapped his old VR goggles again. "Just for the record, it still looks the same to me. Doesn't feel the same, though; not after what you've told me *you* can see." He sighed and went for that beer can again.

"DON_MAC?" I prompted. "Did you find DON_MAC?"

"Nope." LeMat shook his head. "But that damned dwarf—what's his name?"

"Thorvold."

"Yeah, well, Thorvold found *me*. Suckered me right in. Clapped a message chip in my hand and vanished in a puff of smoke before I hardly said howdy. I thought I was going to have to machine-gun the bar just to save face." LeMat sighed again and fastened his mouth on the beer can.

"Really?" I said, simulating ignorance. "I can't imagine how Thorvold got the drop on you. You must be slipping."

"Yeah." The beer can was empty. LeMat crushed it like

the empty aluminum shell it was and gestured for me to bring him another. This time, I also fetched a root beer for myself.

"So," I said, when I got back from the fridge, "you got a message. What does it say?"

"Don't know," LeMat said. "It's encrypted for you." He pushed his chair back from the workstation, stood up, and lurched away from the console. "Therefore, if you'd be so kind." He gestured for me to take his place. "It's on the clipboard."

I dropped into the chair, pulled it closer to the desk, and banged into the electronic clipboard folder. A window wiped open on the monitor screen, and Amber's beautiful brown-eyed face appeared. "This is a private message for Max Kool," she said. "So before you can hear it, you have to answer one question. Is that a gun in your pocket, or are you happy to see me?"

I laid my fingers on the keyboard and typed my response: IT'S A SNUBNOSE.

"Oh, you remembered," Amber said sweetly. "Hi, Max." Her video face froze, while the workstation drives clicked and hummed, and the decryption routines kicked in and unscrambled the rest of the message. The screen wiped and redrew itself.

Amber popped back onto the screen. "Hi, darling," she said in a languid and sultry voice. "I understand what happened to you tonight. DON_MAC told me Gunnar was flying tail-guard for you." She smiled, in a sexy way, and winked. "Personally, I'd be very careful about that. He sounds like a closet case to me." (LeMat, standing behind my chair, took a step off to the side.) "Of course, that's hardly rare. A *lot* of men get into big guns to compensate for feeling . . . *small*." (LeMat growled audibly and bit a chunk out of the rim of his beer can.)

Amber smiled again, blew me a kiss, and tossed her head in a way that made her long black hair seem positively ravishing. "I would hate to think you'd *never* get another chance to find out what you missed tonight." (This time, it was my turn to growl. At LeMat.) "So I'll tell you what. The files appended to this message contain everything you need to know about my little problem. Why don't you look them over, and do some exploratory work, and meet me in a few days to discuss how we can move ahead. Say, 0300 UTC, Tuesday, my place?" Pause. *"Alone?"* She slowly traced her thin but sexy lips with the tip of her tongue.

I *really* hated LeMat in that moment.

"Later, darling." She smiled and winked one last time, then grabbed the edge of the window and pulled it shut behind her.

"Jack?" LeMat said. *"Jack?"* He waved a hand in front of my face. "Earth to Jack. Come in, Jack. Do you copy?"

I grabbed his wrist and wished I had the strength to tear his arm off and beat him over the head with it. "Yes?"

LeMat's eyes were wide with wonder. "Is she *always* like that?" I could only grit my teeth and nod.

"God Almighty," he said. "You're braver than I thought."

We decrypted and decompressed the rest of Amber's files that night, but I crapped out sometime around 1 A.M. and hit the futon, leaving LeMat at the workstation, sucking Pig's Eye Pilsner and scanning files. I'm not sure quite when I dozed off.

I do, however, know exactly when I woke up. "Jack!" LeMat shook my shoulder. "Wake up!" I rolled over, found my watch on the floor, and struggled to read it through sleep-fogged eyes.

"Huh?" I yawned. "Joseph, it's—" I squinted at my watch again, "—three thirty-seven. I'm asleep."

"I don't care! You have *got* to see this!" The last time I'd seen LeMat this excited, it was because he'd found a Haenel M42 in mint condition. Experience had taught me the only way to deal with him in this state was to humor him, so . . .

"Okay. Gimme minute." I rolled up to a sitting position, rubbed my eyes and yawned, then groped around on the floor until I found something to put on my bare feet. Shoes, I think they're called. "This better be good."

"Trust me," LeMat said, "you are gonna *love* this." He helped me stagger to my feet, guided me across the room to our work space, and parked me in the chair before the glowing video monitor. "Here," he said, tapping the screen. "Read."

It took a minute or so for me to get the monitor glare adjusted to a comfortable level and both my eyes in focus at the same time, and another minute or so for my brain to kick in and start processing what I was reading. When it did, though . . .

Well I'll be double-dipped in Godiva chocolate. Amber's setup was too beautiful to be true.

My mystery client, it turned out, was both a nutritional scientist and a *tachycomestible engineer*—that is, a person who designs fast foods. But she wasn't just any Ph.D.-TE; my client also had a strong claim to being *the* lone genius responsible for the latest franchise fast-food restaurant craze to sweep the nation: *Captain Calamari's Original Fried Squid.*

So far, so good. But my client had a serious problem. About a year before, she'd entered into negotiations with a major multinational corporation to license and expand the Captain Calamari's concept. Somehow the negotiations went out of control, though, and before she knew it, the corporation had managed to swindle her out of everything. The recipes, the

# Captain Calimari's

## *Original* Fried Squid

**"It's just so gosh-darn good!"**

franchise sites, the onions, the secret sauce, the jalapeño peppers—the *works*.

This being America, she immediately sued, of course. But the case had been dragging on for months now without progress, and barring a last-minute miracle— say, the sudden appear-

## INFONUGGETS

I couldn't resist. So while we're at it, how about just one more?

## QUESTION

How many programmers does it take to change a lightbulb? Answer: None. That's a hardware problem.

ance of a "smoking gun" memo proving the corporation intentionally acted in bad faith—it was now mere days away from dismissal.

And thus, in desperation, she was turning to me. My mission, if I chose to accept it, was simple: penetrate the multinational corporation's computer system, find the evidence that would win my client's case, restore freedom and justice to the fast-food universe, and not incidentally, secure for my client franchise royalty rights that were currently estimated to be worth about $25 million per year.

That's not what got my attention, though. No, what *my* eyes locked in on was a small appended sticky-note file, which gave my client's best guess at where I'd find the incriminating evidence. She had listed it by Net server address and URL code, of course, but she really hadn't needed to do that. I already knew that address by heart.

*MDE. Global EthniFoods Division. Corporate Headquarters. Building 305.*

LeMat slapped me on the back and snapped me out of it. "So, whatcha think, Jack? A million bucks to crack through a security system you helped design, and you get to spank MDE's fanny in the bargain? Are we talking gratification here, or what?"

I thought it over. I started chuckling. I thought it over some more, desperately trying to see a downside in the deal, and all I could do was laugh harder. Amber—or whoever she worked for—was willing to pay me a million dollars to stick it to MDE? *Hell, I'd have done* that *for free*! I started laughing so hard I fell on the keyboard, sent the computer off into a fit of beeping and squawking, and bounced back from the keyboard to flop halfway over the back of the chair, laughing still.

"Gunnar, old buddy?" I said, when I'd caught my breath enough to speak in contiguous words. "This is almost enough to make me believe in divine justice. *Hallelujah!*"

\*　　\*　　\*

An hour later we'd gone over the files three more times, the coffee maker was singing "Volaré" at the top of its synthetic lungs, and we'd both, in our respective ways, sobered up. The trick, we realized early on, was going to be to crack into the MDE system *without* making it look like an inside job. After all, I was a disgruntled ex-employee, or potential ex-employee, or whatever the hell it was I was—I'm sure Kathé in the outplacement office had a nice weasel-word term for it—and no doubt security was already keeping several forms of organic and electronic eyes out for me. So MAX_KOOL would have to break into the system *without* using any special knowledge that might point to Jack Burroughs. (This, of course, led LeMat and me into an extended argument worthy of a couple of sophomores in Philosophy 201: there was what I was *expected* to know to do my job, what I *actually* needed to know to do my job, and what I actually *knew*, and the three sets of information only occasionally intersected. So did we make our plans based on what I actually knew, what I was expected to know, what MDE thought I knew, or what we thought MDE might think I thought they thought I was thinking. . . . I mean, how can you really know that you know what you know, y'know?

("Epistemology," LeMat observed, "is why philosophers drink so heavily.")

After we hashed through that mess to our satisfaction, we segued into a dandy argument over *when* we should attempt the job. LeMat was all in favor of hitting MDE instantly, if not sooner. ("The first rule of consulting," he said pompously, "is always underpromise and overdeliver. If Amber is hoping you can show her an action plan Monday, just imagine how she'll cream her jeans when you show her the finished job!")

(I scratched my head and looked at him with narrowed eyes. "Wait a minute. Yesterday you said the first rule of consulting was, 'Never do anything on spec.'")

Fortunately, after a few minutes of butting our matched pair of pig-heads together, a number of realities asserted themselves and brought the issue to a close: the most notable one being the knowledge that it was fast approaching 5 A.M. on a Saturday morning, and even if the interface *did* make me a virtual god of cyberspace, there were still some things beyond even my amazing abilities. For example, "Captain, I cannah change the Laws of Corporate Accounting!" At this time of day, on the third Saturday of the month, the bulk of MDE's available computing power would *not* be standing idle, but rather would be devoted to such exciting and CPU-intensive batch processes as freight bill cost allocation and manufacturing material requirements planning. The only normal incoming data traffic at this time would be the weekly Profit & Loss downloads from our Pacific Rim subsidiaries; the only normal outgoing traffic, a summary P&L statement sent Sunday afternoon to the INH Executive Inner Coven in B100, Paris.

"So," LeMat said, yawning rather pointedly in the middle of my explanation of LIFO cost accrual methodology, "this just means there's less chance of anyone else being in the system and tripping over us, right?"

"Wrong-o, moosebreath," I answered. (It was 5 A.M. We were both getting pretty punchy.) "They run this crap in batch on weekends because it really bogs down the system when it's going. If Max Kool jumps into the MDE network right now, it'll be like he's wading through hip-deep virtual butterscotch syrup."

LeMat pursed his lips. "I bet Amber would get off on that."

"If we try to break in now," I said, ignoring that last remark, "we'll be as conspicuous as someone rattling the doors of a jewelry store at midnight. No, the time we want to make our move is Monday morning, just after eight o'clock."

LeMat cocked an eyebrow and fired a glance at me. "Why then?"

"Because the weekend processes will be finished," I said. "The local net will be running at top speed, all the East Coast field reps will be trying to log in at the same time, and half of them will be too hungover to remember their passwords, so there'll be lots of failed logins."

"Ah," LeMat said, the light of understanding dawning slowly on the bloodshot red horizon of his eyes. "So our attempts to pick the lock—"

"Will blend right in with the normal Monday morning traffic."

LeMat thought it over, and nodded, and nodded some more, and kept on nodding, and after a while I realized he wasn't being unusually agreeable, he was just falling asleep on his feet. Grabbing him by the upper arm, I steered him over to the army-surplus folding cot he'd brought from home and let him collapse onto it. Then I unplugged the coffee pot, put the workstation to sleep, found my way to my futon and, I believe, actually managed to lie down on it before I conked out.

Around 7 A.M. the dawning light of a better tomorrow crept in through the east windows, rousing the pigeons in the rafters to noisy life and strongly reinforcing the idea that we *had* to get some curtains.

A little before noon, I returned to the land of the Somewhat Lifelike. LeMat was already gone—no note or anything—so I brushed my teeth, ran my fingers through my hair to simulate the effect of combing, and decided to drive back to Mom's and pick up another load of stuff. When I got out to the alley, I discovered that someone had jacked my Toyota up, put it on blocks, removed my bald and mismatched Montgomery Wards tires, and replaced them with a matched set of mag wheels and Michelin radials.

I shrugged and drove over to Mom's.

The back door was open. Psycho Kitty's litterbox stank to high heaven. "Hi, Mom, I'm home!"

*"Jack?"* From the living room, I heard the groan of sofa springs and the creaking of floorboards as she shifted her weight and tried valiantly, once, twice—

With a heaving pant from exertion, she sank back into the couch. "I'm in the living room!" she called out. I hesitated a moment on the landing, then changed my mind and trotted upstairs. She heard me coming and cut the volume on the TV. In a faint and tinny way, the repeated *oofs* and *thuds* of All-Pro Wrestling wafted through the house. "You just missed it, Jack," she said, as I came into effective communications range.

"A really good body

---

## URGENT NOTICE

From: J. Gotti Student Loan
    Servicing Center
To: John F. Burroughs
    1783 Ivy Street
    St. Paul, MN 55103

Dear Mr. Burroughs,
    We have just learned of the change in your employment situation. And believe us, we understand how difficult it can be, to be faced with an intimidating debt load and an uncertain financial future. No doubt there are times when you wish you could call us, to discuss the possibility of a revised repayment schedule with a sympathetic financial counselor.
    Well, we have just two words for you:

### FORGET IT!

You've got two weeks to furnish us with proof of a new job. Otherwise—well, nice kneecaps you've got there. It'd be a shame if anything were to happen to them.

---

## INFONUGGETS

That wasn't an infonugget. It was supporting documentation.

slam, Mom?" I took enough of a glance at her to be sure she hadn't subsided into a festering pool of video slime, then went over to the buffet and started sorting through the accumulated mail. Bills, junk, bills—

"No," Mom said. "There were two men here looking for you, not half an hour ago. *Nice* men. Very polite. They asked me lots of questions about you."

I froze, a piece of junk mail unread in my hands. There's that old cliché, *My blood ran cold*. I'd never before realized how literal it could be.

"Uh?" There was a terrified tremolo in my voice; I fought to control it and failed. "Did they say who they were? Mom?"

She hmmmed, and sucked her teeth, and scratched her head with her remote control. "You know, Jack, I forget. But they *did* wear very nice suits. I remember that. You should try wearing a nice suit sometime, if you want to impress people."

Slowly, cautiously, I edged up to the archway that separated the dining room from the living room and stole a peek out the front windows. Nothing seemed out of the ordinary out there. No strange cars or people with binoculars, except for Mrs. Lundgren, and she'd been spying on the neighbors and tape-recording her weekly reports to the Venusian Empire since before I was born.

"Mom," I said, trying to sound casual, "this is important. "Can you remember *anything* about those two men that might help me figure out who they were?"

Mom made some more strange, thoughtful sounds, scratched her brassy blond hair until I thought about checking her for fleas, and got distracted by the excitement for a few moments when "Bad Bobby" Bradford threw Ted "The Lisping Liberal" Thurston over the ropes and into the audience, and the fans all swarmed in and started clubbing Ted with folding chairs.

"Oh," Mom said, clucking her tongue, "I am *such* a ditz sometimes!"

("Really?" I muttered. "I never noticed.")

"One of them left his business card and said I should call if you showed up. It's by the phone in the kitchen!" Dropping everything, I ran into the kitchen, and started tearing through the years of accumulated notes and newspaper clippings crucified with thumbtacks on the corkboard. "Wait a minute!" Mom called out. "I was wrong. *Here* it is!" I dashed back into the living room and just about ripped the card from her fingers.

It was a nice business card. Expensive printing, two-color green floral embossing. It read:

Todd Becker, Visiting Evangelist
The Church of Vegentology

"Thanks, Mom," I said as my blood pressure returned to normal and I wondered how many years of life this little bit of hysteria had cost me. "I'll just be down in the basement then." I started for the back stairs.

*"Wait,"* Mom said, stopping me just as I was about to cross the threshold into the kitchen. "Jack? I was down there doing laundry yesterday, and I noticed some of your stuff was missing. Do you know anything about it?"

I cleared my throat, and looked at the floor. "Uh, Mom? I moved out a couple of days ago, remember? Got myself an apartment?"

"Oh," she said, nodding, "that's right. I forgot." Something happened on TV right then, and she shouted, "Whoa!" punched the volume up to twenty, and apparently also forgot that I was standing there and that we were having a conversation. I took one last look around upstairs—there was definitely *nothing* I wanted up there—and headed down to the basement.

There were over a dozen messages on my answering

machine. At first I was excited. Then, as I listened to them and realized that, except for the one message from Kathé in Outplacement—she *really* wanted that copy of *Dress For Conformity* back—they were all from T'shombe, my enthusiasm cooled rapidly. T'shombe, it seemed, was *seriously* pissed at me for something having to do with her getting stood up on Friday night. (I couldn't remember: had I promised to go to some deranged church shindig with her?)

So I turned to my dresser and started pulling together the next load of stuff to move to the office. Clothes, mostly. And just one—okay, make it two—alright, *five*, and that was my final position—of my favorite model rockets. And my complete set of Judge Dredd comic books, of course. But I drew the line at the HO railroad stuff.

I was just about done packing the car when Mom's voice echoed through the house and found me out on the parking slab in the backyard. *"Jack! I don't know how you're doing it, but your computer is screwing up my TV again!"*

It was definitely long past time to go.

# 16

## WHY DO FOOLS
## FALL IN LOVE?

LeMat had apparently returned by the time I made it back to our office. His truck was parked in the alley; the door to the freight elevator was unlocked; a few open boxes of his junk were scattered around the floor of the office. He'd even managed to rustle up some curtains to fit the east windows, although on closer inspection they proved to be green plastic tarpaulins held in place by massive amounts of duct tape. LeMat himself seemed to be MIA, although I didn't start worrying about it until after I'd finished unloading my Toyota and he still had not shown up. Then I grew concerned and went out searching for him.

I found him up on the roof, with his air pistol in his hand, a pile of dead pigeons on the tarpaper at his feet and a dazed and blissful smile on his face that scared the living bejeebers out of me. "Joseph?" I said softly. When that got no response, I gently pried the pistol out of his fingers and waved a hand in front of his face. "Joseph? Can you hear me?"

He turned and looked at me with a smile so beatifically wonderful I didn't know whether to call the mental health crisis line or the Vatican canonization board. "Hello, Jack," he said.

When no further communication was forthcoming, I asked, "You feeling okay?"

"Never felt better," he said. He favored me with a smile again, then drifted back into that vacant stare across the valley. "I think I'm in love," he said at last.

I glanced around the roof, saw no clear object of affection close at hand, and took a step back. "That's, uh, *great*. Who's the lucky, er—"

"Inge," he said. "Listen closely: you can hear the wind whisper her name. *IngeAaanderssssonnn.*"

Actually, the sound I think I heard was that of my jaw dropping and hitting the tarpaper rooftop. *"Inge Andersson?"* I said, my nose so wrinkled I must have looked like a mandrill. "The CPA down on the fourth floor? That chubby little bun-haired tennis-shoed—?"

"Tennis shoes," LeMat said dreamily. *"Yes.* I was taking the trash down to the dumpster when I caught a glimpse of her through the stairwell door. It was open a crack; she had her back to me, and was ironing the laces of her tennis shoes."

I hardly knew how to respond. *"Ironing shoelaces?"*

"Yes!" he cried exultantly. "She was radiant! Such concentration! Such dedication to perfection!" I felt his forehead. He didn't seem to be running a fever. "But," his voice dropped to a low, conspiratorial tone, "do you know what was the best part?" I shook my head. "I was so captivated," he said, "I became like a man entranced. I couldn't move; couldn't speak. I just pressed my face against the doorframe and watched her, and then do you know what happened?"

Actually, I could imagine this part pretty well. A lone, single woman, finding herself being stared at by a Peeping Tom?

"I startled her," LeMat said. "Some little noise I made,

some flicker in the light, alerted her to my presence. And do you know what she *did*?"

I guessed. "Screamed and called the cops?"

"She pulled a gun on me!" LeMat said, his eyes wide with glorious wonder. "I couldn't even tell that she was carrying! But yet, when she realized she was being watched, there was no fear, no hesitation. In one graceful move she dropped the iron, spun like a turret, and drew from her hip holster to a perfect Weaver stance! And do you know what she *said*?"

I could imagine several choice and appropriate things, none of them printable in a daily newspaper.

"She said, *'I don't dial 911.'*"

I could only shake my head. "You're just lucky she didn't say, 'Oops, sorry about that bullet hole in your chest.'"

"Ah, no," he said, grinning at me, "I was *never* in any danger. I told you, my beautiful Inge is a master of control. In her lovely hands the Colt Gold Cup is a precision instru—"

"Whoa," I waved a hand to interrupt him. "Wait a minute. You were close enough to *recognize* her gun?"

LeMat seemed puzzled by my reaction. "Of course. Colt Gold Cup National Match, Series 90 Mark V, with Wilson trigger group, King match barrel and bushing, Bo-Mar sights, Bacoté grips—"

I made another time-out gesture. "I thought you said you were on the stairwell. *Did you sneak into her apartment*?"

LeMat stared at me as if I was an idiot. "Certainly not! I waited until she invited me."

"She *invited* you in?"

"Of course. After I explained who I was and asked where she'd had her trigger job done."

My head was definitely in spin cycle. I sat down on some convenient boxy thing on the roof. "You talked *guns* with her?"

*"Yes!"* LeMat was beaming. "It was wonderful!"

I blew out a heavy sigh; took in a deep breath. Scratched my head for a minute or so. And honestly, while it seemed pretty weird, I couldn't really find anything *objectionable* in how Inge and LeMat had come to terms.

"So," I said, "you, uh, want to invite her up for pizza, or something? I mean, after we finish unpacking and all?"

At last, LeMat's blissed-out smile failed. "Actually, Jack, I, er," he looked down at his feet, put his hands behind his back, and kicked at the gravel. "I was kind of hoping you could handle things by yourself today. Inge and I . . . ." He paused and shrugged.

"Well?" I said.

"She's changing clothes right now," LeMat said. "And after that, I kind of promised her I'd take her out to the rifle range and let her try my AR-15, if she'd let me try her FN FAL."

I was still trying to figure out where I'd taken the wrong turn that morning and how to get back to my home dimension when the fire door at the top of the stairs clanged open, and Inge came striding out onto the rooftop. Her knee-high jack boots crunched crisply on the black tarpaper and gravel. "Hi, Gunnar!" she called out gaily.

It was my turn to shoot him a dirty look. "You *told* her?"

"I told her my real name is Joseph," he whispered quickly, through smiling, clenched teeth, "and that my friends all call me Gunnar. She doesn't know anything else." She crunched nearer.

"Inge!" he said as he opened both his mouth and his arms. "You look wonderful!" They flew together and embraced. No, not hugged. *Embraced.* Anyone else would have settled for a simple hug, but those two made it look like the mating dance of the sandhill crane.

And while we're at it, I decided then that I definitely needed to recalibrate my sense of what LeMat meant when he said someone looked "wonderful." For my money, Inge didn't look "wonderful," she looked like a short, squat, overstuffed, thirty-five-ish freckled strawberry blonde who'd just stepped off the cover of the Abercrombie & Fitch large sizes catalog and was on her way to try out for *Soldier of Fortune* cover girl. Her boots I've already mentioned. But did I mention her khaki jodhpurs, or her hand-tailored tan shooting vest with contrasting suede recoil pad? And how about that long strawberry blond hair, pulled back into a French braid so tight it functioned as a temporary facelift? And those wraparound shatterproof yellow plastic glasses? I mean, we're talking about someone who could make a *major* fashion statement on the club scene, here.

Inge and LeMat completed their embrace and decoupled. She turned to me. "You must be Jack," she said with a mysterious smile. "Gunnar has told me so much about you." She offered me a handshake. I took it. The woman could have crushed walnuts with her bare hands.

Clearly, there was a lot more going on here than I'd noticed on first, second, or even third glances.

"So, Jack," LeMat said, fidgeting nervously and not looking straight at me. "You sure you don't mind if Inge and I go off to the range for a few hours?"

Actually, I minded a great deal, but I could see that saying so was not going to get me anywhere. I shook my head. "Not at all," I said, lying with an open smile. "You two go have fun. I can handle everything here."

"Wonderful!" LeMat said, clapping his hands together. "Then in that case—"

Inge grabbed him by the arm and dragged him into motion. "In that case, we're wasting daylight, buddy. *Move*." She favored me with another mysterious smile and nearly pushed LeMat through the open fire door. The last thing I heard from them was Inge's voice echoing up the stairwell: "No, *I'll* drive."

For a few minutes after that, I just sat there on the roof, listening to the soft cooing of pigeons in the air-conditioning condenser and the rumble of traffic on the streets below. In time it occurred to me to take a look at LeMat's air pistol, which I was still holding in my left hand, and that's about the time I realized the thing was loaded and cocked, or charged, or whatever the heck you call an air gun that's ready to go, and I'd been holding it all this time with my finger on the trigger.

A pigeon fluttered down onto the roof, about twenty feet away from me. I took careful aim, squeezed the trigger slowly like LeMat was always telling me to do, and was rewarded with the soft *pop*! of the gun, the sight of the pigeon flying away perfectly unscathed, and the merry tinkle of breaking glass from a window in the building across the street. I was always a piss-poor shot with real guns.

Which suggested to me that it was time for a workout in virtual reality. I trudged down to the office, slammed and locked the elevator and stairwell doors, threw LeMat's air gun wherever it happened to land, and got down to business.

There isn't a lot to say about the rest of Saturday afternoon. I cleared all of LeMat's crap out of my movement area—he could unpack it himself, thank you—then strapped on the neural induction interface and dove into our local test reality to spend a few hours just practicing moving around in my body. The ProctoProd™ was slightly easier to—er, *install*—the second time around, but still, three hours seemed to be about my top limit, and then I had to either get that thing out or die.

LeMat and Inge still weren't back by 7 P.M., so I surveyed the extensive selection of cryogenic entrees in our freezer and settled on the microwave fettucine alfredo and a root beer for dinner. Nobody in their right mind delivers pizza to Lowertown, and I didn't want to head out to one of the local pubs for fear that the saddlesore way I was walking would draw unwanted amorous attention from the waitrons. LeMat and Inge weren't back by eight, either, so I strapped on my conventional VR gear, dove into the tank, and spent a few hours fine-tuning MAX_KOOL's visual aspect in hopes of making him look somewhat more realistic to other super-users. Then I took a quick jaunt over to Heaven, more out of

> ### WAITRONS
>
> Mysterious aliens from the planet Wait. Most astronomers now believe this world orbits a black hole, as time there clearly moves far more slowly than it does here on Earth.

> ### INFONUGGETS
>
> What infonugget? Where? I don't see one. You'd better get your eyes checked. There's a coupon for Sister Bertrille's back in chapter 4.

boredom than anything else, but both DON_MAC and Don Vermicelli were nowhere to be found, and I was only slightly surprised to discover that without them, the place didn't interest me much at all.

Around 10:30, a rumor swept through Heaven that someone had seen Eliza coming in the front door with blood in her eye and a chainsaw in her hands. I took that as a cue to throw myself down the garbage chute in the Jobs Memorial Lounge and make my exit from VR.

I surfaced to a warm, humid, and breathless early summer evening. LeMat and Inge had clearly returned sometime in the last few hours. Their rifles were stacked by the refrigerator; evidence of a take-out Chinese meal was scattered all over the kitchen. LeMat had also torn open one of the large boxes he'd brought from his house this morning, and I followed the trail of

## NIGHT VISION GEAR

styrofoam packing noodles up the stairwell, out the fire door, and over to the west side of the roof.

Aw, what a cute couple they made. Sitting there, cross-legged, on the rooftop, their hands circumspectly kept to themselves but their shoulders touching erotically, Russian army-surplus night vision gear strapped onto their faces and earphones connected to an array of parabolic microphones focused on Mears Park, three blocks away. In the ruddy flickering light of a burning carjacked BMW I could see that the park was crawling with the usual after-sunset crowd of junkies, gang-bangers, and terribly lost yuppies in search of trendy restaurants.

"Ah, the children of the night," LeMat said softly.

"What beautiful music they make," Inge answered.

Stifling a sudden urge to vomit brought on by the sickly sweet smell of saps in love, I left the two of them up there, headed back downstairs, successfully fought off the urge to lock the rooftop door behind me, and crashed out on the futon. Whatever else may have happened that night, I slept through it.

Sunday morning: I drifted awake slowly and was surprised to find LeMat sleeping—alone—on his cot. The drifting phase didn't last too long, though; at eight o'clock sharp his watch alarm went off, and he leaped out of bed like it was made of nails.

"So, Gunnar," I said through a yawn, "how—"

"No time!" he shot back at me. "Inge's got an IPSC pistol match today and we have to be at the club by nine!" And with that, he dashed into the bathroom. The shower hissed on.

I rolled out of bed, staggered into the kitchen area, and fired up the coffeemaker. That consumed the last of our rather meager gourmet coffee supply. I was definitely going to have to buy a large can of conventional beans the next time around. The coffeemaker was just breaking into the first bars of "Volaré" when LeMat came bursting out of the bathroom.

I wish I knew how he did it. The man had managed to be showered, shaved, and fully dressed in less than ten minutes.

"Got time for coffee?" I asked, as he flew past.

He screeched to a stop, sniffed the air, and turned around. "Great idea, Jack! Thanks!" Diving into one of his boxes of undifferentiated kitchen utensils, he produced a large, red-and-brown checkered Thermos and poured the entire pot into it. "Inge will love this!" He handed the empty carafe back to me, to hold in my left hand in perfect match to the never-filled cup in my right and the slack-jawed expression of surprise on my face. "Bye!" he shouted as he ran out the stairwell door. "I should be back around suppertime!" And he was gone.

And so too, dammit, was the coffee.

I sulked about that for at least an hour or so. Sulked, and pouted, and stomped around the office steaming under the collar and kicking every cardboard box that that thoughtless jerk LeMat had deliberately left in my way. I probably would have whined about it, too, had there been anyone there to listen, but I was the only one in the building and was enjoying my tantrum too much to go out in search of a fresh victim.

So I sulked some more. But eventually, about halfway through a good bout of standing in the shower, feeling the hot needles of water massaging my face and replaying the coffeepot scene in my mind (complete with snappy new dialogue featuring all the things I *should* have said), I finally realized that the problem was, I was jealous. No, not of the attention Inge was getting from LeMat, or of the deeply latent affection he seemed to be getting from her. But of the fact that those two *had* a life outside of virtual reality, and I didn't.

Once that was clear, I finished up my shower, got dressed, and decided to blow off the rest of the morning. Locking up the office, I went down to street level, hiked over to a coffee shop in the next block and bought myself a croissant, a large java, and the Sunday paper. I spent the rest of the morning sitting on a park bench on the riverwalk, just enjoying the beautiful spring weather and watching the death-defying antics of the in-line skaters on the bike path. And in three hours of pretending to read the paper, all I really managed to get through were the funnies and the Parade section.

I felt strangely proud of that.

By the time I got back to the office, around noon, my attitude was much improved, and someone had repainted the right front fender of my Toyota a deep, glossy, royal blue.

# 17

# TAKING TIGER MOUNTAIN BY STRATEGY

I spent the rest of Sunday afternoon studying the files Amber had given me and mapping out my strategy for the job. Late in the afternoon I decided some intelligent query agents would be a tremendous help, so I cobbled together two hasty, sloppy, and not terribly attractive autonomous imps. These I gave the look of knee-high protohumanoids, with unruly hair, insane grins, and three-fingered mittens in place of proper hands; then I stepped back, took one look at the results, and dubbed them Thing[1] and Thing[2].

LeMat came back around six, and he'd had the decency to stop at a Captain Calamari's and pick up a ten-piece Bucket O' Squid. He apologized for sloughing off on his work, and I apologized for having such a pissy attitude, and he apologized for letting his hormones seize control of his brain, and I apologized for begrudging him a good time with his new friend, and after a few more rounds of this we realized that if we kept trying to out-apologize each other we'd have a *real* fight on our hands, so we broke it off and hit the squids. Then, after supper, we finished work on the query agents, and LeMat went home to check up on his house and spend a night in a real bed.

The next morning at 7 A.M. sharp, I got a wake-up call from a fax machine. Apparently my call-forwarding was now working.

**Monday, May 22, 0805 Local Time:** I was wired up, strapped in, Dressed For Insanity, and very glad we'd taken the time to add another strip of duct tape to the curtains on the east windows. LeMat was sitting in the chair before the interface workstation, sucking coffee, munching a doughnut, monitoring my vital signs, and running through the prelaunch checklist.

"Thoracic harness?" (It sounded better than "databra.")

"Check."

"Pelvic harness?" (Ditto.)

"Check."

"Audio headset?"

"Check."

"Cranial positional sensors?"

"Check."

"ProctoProd—er, jacked in?"

"ProctoProd in Jack. And just so you know, I'm in *no* danger of getting used to this thing."

"Good," he said as he shut the manual and dropped it on the floor. "Then it's showtime. VR boot in three, two, one—"

I opaqued the video goggles as he unsealed the Net portal. For a moment I had this terrible claustrophobic feeling of being sucked down inside a giant pitch-black sewer pipe, then . . .

*Pop*! I was standing on a pleasant green hillside in Virtual Reality, where all the men are strong, all the women are good-looking, and all the children are wanted on felony charges. "Okay," Gunnar said in my ear, "you made it. Everything looks cool up here, so I'll cut the audio and video feeds in a moment and go to biotelemetry. But first: Max?"

"Yes, Gunnar?"

"Good luck, man."

I made a thumbs-up sign. "Thanks. Save a couple dough-nuts for me." (We'd had quite an argument about this earlier and decided that eating bran muffins before using the interface was probably not a good idea.) I heard a click on the line as Gunnar's audio link went dead, and a moment later felt that "lonely" feeling in the back of my head that meant he was no longer looking out through my eyes.

I took a deep breath, pooled together all my nerves, and thought, *Okay Max, let's go for it*. With a snap of my fingers, I summoned my new virtual Harley Ultraglide into exis-tence.

My new and very much *improved* Harley Ultraglide.

Okay, I admit it, it was a kind of silly and useless thing to do. But the anxiety attack that'd nailed me about 3 A.M. that morning left no hope of my getting back to sleep, so I'd fired up the workstation, strapped on my goggles, and put in a few really serious hours on reworking my virtual bike. Now, thanks to both my new superuser skills and my at times anal obsession with detail (unfortunate word choice, that), the hog was as real as I was, or maybe even more so. I mean, it was real down to the steady drip, drip, drip, of ninety-weight gear oil from the primary drive cover.

I took a slow walk around it, just to admire my handiwork, then saddled up, pulled on my black studded gloves, adjusted my black shades, and checked my greasy black hair in the handlebar mirror. With a wave of my right hand I summoned a lit cigarette into existence and stuck it in my mouth—took a deep drag and about coughed my lungs out—then I gave the bike a tilt to the right to get the kickstand up, pulled in the clutch handle, and started her rolling down the virtual hillside. When it looked like I had sufficient momentum, I stepped the tranny down to first, switched the ignition on, and popped the clutch.

With a rumble of ominous thunder like the sound of Thor's Own Lawnmower, 1100cc's of Heavy Milwaukee Iron roared to throbbing, belching, fire-breathing *life*! I leaned back in the saddle, twisted the throttle wide open. Hit the drainage ditch at the bottom of the hill at about 100 miles an hour, jumped the bike clean over four lanes of traffic, and landed in the far left lane of the Information Superhighway, heading for BusinessWorld balls out and hell for leather.

Jack Burroughs, frankly, was chewing his fingernails down to little bloody stubs, but Max Kool felt *good*.

**On the Road, 8:12 A.M.:** Boy, was I glad LeMat could no longer see what I saw or talk in my head! Now that I had some practice at it I could control this Cubism thing and switch it on and off at will, but still, LeMat was right. BusinessWorld, through the eyes of a superuser, *did* look like a Fernand Léger painting.

> ### FERNAND LÉGER
> French painter, b. 1881, d. 1955.

It was still a claustrophobic world of enormous gray data blocks, of course, but now I could also see that the blocks were not mere blank and featureless monoliths, but rather marvelously dense and intricate *structures*, made up of mile upon tangled mile of pipes, tubes, webs, and ducts. The effect was that of an oil refinery, merged with the Pompidou Center, and invaded and conquered by giant mutant radioactive silkworms. I slowed my bike a moment to enjoy this living testament to data anarchy and informational entropy and dwell thoughtfully on an article on chaos theory that I once skimmed in a *Reader's Digest* in my dentist's office. Humans *will* communicate. (Except when they're married to each other, but that was a different article.)

Then I saw the lights.

I slowed the bike even further and let the view fill in with more detail. Every one of those corporate structures was simply *swarming* with a nimbus of tiny, darting, brilliantly colored lights, like fairy ice castles infested with fireflies. Now and again a laserlike shaft of dazzling green light would leap from one part of a structure to another, or even from one corporation to another, and the effect was somewhere between not bad if you like light shows and Fourth-of-July glorious. *What do those lights represent*? I wondered. *The spark of creativity*? *The beauty of the free exchange of information*? I kicked the bike into neutral, coasted in close to the Advanced Multifoods datablock, and tried to get a good look at one of those glittering virtual fireflies as it darted past. A tiny blue glow sprang into existence on the wall near me, and I grabbed it.

It turned out to be an obscene and badly drawn fax cartoon about divorce settlements, sent by a bored sales rep at Advanced Multifoods to her old college roommate over at General Cognetics.

I wasted another minute or two catching all the little lights I could reach, then I turned them all loose and wished for a way to wash my virtual hands. The lights, I realized, represented desktop PC modems and fax cards, and the vast and hideous bulk of them were being used to transmit such uplifting material as the very latest blonde jokes. The green laser beams were only slightly more interesting: for the most part, they turned out to be resumés from people seeking to barter company trade secrets in exchange for jobs with competitors.

Feeling vaguely disappointed that the personal computer revolution had crapped out to *this*, I stomped my bike down into first and open the throttle wide.

**BusinessWorld, 8:22 A.M.:** The MDE corporate datablock rose into view in that peculiarly flat and perspectiveless way so familiar to consumers of low-budget Japanese animation. I slowed the bike and pulled off onto the shoulder, then fished my virtual binoculars out of my saddlebag and gave MDE the once over, just to see what I could learn from a distance.

The answer was, not much. The MDE data structure was about what I'd expected to see: huge, tall, broad, incoherent, with entire departments hanging pendant in empty space, supported only by the sheer tenacity of one manager clinging desperately to the coattails of the vice president above. There were quite a number of free-floating apex points drifting aimlessly in midair, about halfway up the organizational chart, like brain-dead drone bumblebees. These puzzled me, until I took a closer look at one and realized it was a virtual representation of Scott Uberman.

Taken as a whole, the MDE corporate data structure looked like the sort of gravity-defying mobile sculpture that an artist with a sick sense of humor and a glue gun might slap together from studio scraps on a slow day. It was only after I'd been looking at it for a while that I realized, it *did* have a rigid core, and that was all that kept the whole mess from subsiding into corporate compost. One consistently profitable division, I guessed, supporting all the rest. Scaling up the magnification, I strained to discern the outlines of that central pillar.

Oh. Sanguinary TechSystems. I should have known.

Scaling the magnification back down to normal, I finished my remote recon of MDE. If I had a week, I decided, it would be interesting to come back here and try to map the data flow. That glossy web centered in the left side of Dynamic InfoTainment, for example: what did that represent? And all those pulsing laser beams: clearly, the big green one at the pinnacle of success was the direct channel from the CEO's office to the INH Executive Inner Coven, in B100, Paris. But what about all those smaller ones, flickering on and off between

MDE's vice-presidential level and the upper echelons of our competitors? If I traced those beams, whose windows would I be peeking in? *And*, I thought, as I remembered Kathé in the outplacement office, *What kind of leverage would it give me if I had* that *information*?

Suddenly, the MDE structure seemed like a *very* interesting place.

My virtual watch pinged. I tugged at my black leather sleeve, and checked the time. Damn, 8:30 already. Making a mental note to myself to revisit this topic later, I tossed the binocs in a saddlebag and started the motor. *If I had a week*, I was thinking. But I didn't have a week. I had a window of opportunity that would be closing in fifteen minutes, tops.

Kicking the bike into gear, I cranked the throttle open and went looking for the MDE exit ramp.

**MDE Parking Lot, 8:32 A.M.**: Coasting slowly and casually down the Information Frontage Road, I waited until I was fairly sure no one was watching me, then darted behind an information dumpster and morphed into—

An absolutely faceless guy in a gray pinstripe suit and a black bowler hat.

(If I were still doing infonuggets, I would seize this opportunity to insert a brief critical essay about the life and career of René Francois Ghislain Magritte [b.1898, d.1967], the Belgian painter responsible for all those pictures of blank gray businessmen with green apples for faces. But I'm not, so *nyeah*.)

When the transformation was complete, I took an extra moment to inspect myself and convince myself the disguise would pass, and two extra moments to crank my courage up to its highest possible setting. Then I pulled my briefcase out of one saddlebag, and my umbrella out of the other, and as nonchalantly as possible—I believe I even whistled a jolly little flat tune as I twirled my umbrella—I strolled around the corner to join the milling mob of faceless business drones queuing up to pass through the main gate. No one seemed to react to my presence.

I took that as a positive sign and forged ahead.

**8:37:** The queue was moving slowly, slowly, s-l-o-w-l-y. It wasn't until I got near the front that I started to understand why. Old Carl was standing there, of course—yes, *Carl*, the security guard, Employee 00000002. Not the real one, mind you; he was still presumably standing in the lobby of B305. But when Bubu and I had overhauled the main security routine last January, we'd decided it needed a human face, and so we'd clipped an image scan out of the employee files and given it Carl's.

Somebody else had obviously tinkered with the main security routine since then, though, because—while it still had Carl's face—it now had a tall, gleaming, actually rather *evil*-looking robotic body, and an assortment of nasty sharp toys straight out of some Hollywood set designer's vision of a medieval dungeon. Somewhere along the line it had also acquired a sinister laugh worthy of Vincent Price.

I didn't remember Bubu adding that.

The security routine grabbed the poor bastard up at the front of the line, threw him into an iron maiden, and leaned against the open door. *"What,"* the security routine demanded in a voice like thunder, *"is your user name?"*

"ANDY_R!" came a muffled, panic-stricken voice from inside the iron maiden.

The security routine gave the door a little nudge, and grinned. *"What,"* it demanded again, *"is your password?"*

"KLM005!"

The security routine took a step back from the iron maiden, then spun on its chromium heels and snapped a third question. *"What,"* it shrieked like a demon, *"is your favorite color?"*

*"Huh?!"* came the voice from inside the box. "What kind of security question is *that*?"

"Wrong answer!" the security routine bellowed gleefully as it threw all its weight against the door of the iron maiden and slammed it shut. There was a brief, agonized scream from inside the box and a gush of fresh blood from some vents at the bottom.

The security routine turned back to the queue. *"Next!"* It reached for me, but I ducked aside at the last moment and it latched its big chrome skeleton hands onto the woman standing next to me instead. She went headfirst into the guillotine.

Her name was MARY_W. Her password was VNT417. She didn't know the name of Millard Fillmore's vice president. Her head bounced and rolled across the parking lot like a soccer ball.

*"Next!"* I tried to duck aside again. This time, the six or eight people behind me grabbed onto my coat and pants and pushed me forward. The security routine caught me in its claws and threw me into some kind of tight iron cage that hung by a rusty chain about three feet off the cold stone floor.

*"What,"* it demanded, *"is your user name?"*

"Admin," I said calmly. It's a generic administrative account name. Almost every system has one.

The security routine paused and considered me with narrowed eyes. "Ooo," it said, smacking its thin, cruel, virtual lips. "So we think we're the system administrator, do we? Well, we have something *special* we save for system administrators." It straightened up abruptly, and clanged its metal hands together. "Igor!" it bellowed, "bring me *the cables*!"

A nasty little deformed dwarf hobbled into the scene, and hissed, "Yess, masster!" Then it shuffled off, to return moments later dragging the biggest damned set of jumper cables you ever saw. It connected these to the bars of my cage.

The security routine leaned against my cage and set it gently swinging. "These cables," it said, with a thick and creamy gloat in its voice, "are connected to a fifty-thousand-volt high-tension line. All I need do is throw *this* switch," it stepped back from the cage and rested its steely skeletal hand on a giant threepole knife switch that looked like something out of Dr. Frankenstein's rec room, "and you will be burned down to dust. The *real* you. *Lethal* feedback. So tell me, Admin—" it paused, to chortle "—if that is your *real* name—"

It lunged at me. *"What's your password? Quick! Tell me!"*

And that's about the point where I decided I'd

## LETHAL FEEDBACK

Okay, one more infonugget, just to kill this canard off once and for all.

Voltage is an *analog* concept. The only value of "lethal feedback" is to scare ignorant junior-high school hackers, because as soon as you try to digitize that voltage for data transmission, you're either going to toast your D/A converter into smoking ruin or else clip the voltage down to a nice, safe, transmittable level. But if we somehow ignore that inconvenient law of physics, the whole idea of sending high voltage over a plastic laser fiber optic line is just plain *silly* . . .

Okay, for the sake of argument, let's say you're working with the Ma and Pa Kettle Phone Company, and through some incredible freak of circumstance you manage to make an analog metal circuit all the way from the security system to my personal computer. Whereupon your fifty-thousand-volt charge comes blasting into my local data bus—

And within nanoseconds, the molecule-sized gates on the IC chips and the hair-fine wiring on the PC boards instantly act like thousands of tiny fuses, melting down into harmless slag and breaking the circuit long before my first neuron gets even a little warm.

Lethal feedback, my ass.

had enough of this shit, went into superuser Cubist mode, and punched my hand right through the security routine's chrome ribcage. Before it could react I grabbed hold of the cold and misshapen blue lump that took the place of its heart and twisted it to *Accept.*

Instantly, the security routine's demeanor changed. "Good morning Admin," it said politely, before I'd even pulled my hand back out of its chest. "You are cleared for entry." It unlocked the iron cage, let me out, and ushered me through the main door. "Have a nice day." It smiled at me as it held the door open, nodded slightly, and touched two steely claw-fingers to the brim of its hat, as if in salute.

I stepped through the door, marched briskly into the root lobby of the MDE data structure, and shuddered only a little at the sound of the iron gate clanging shut behind me. *"Next!"* Somewhere on the other side of the door, a woman screamed.

It took everything I had not to break into a run.

Two minutes later, I'd ducked and dodged my way through the globs of flying spam and worked my way up to a little-used virtual corridor just outside the Global EthniFoods domain. The positive side of this trip was that MDE's internal data structure was thoroughly rigid and predictable, and mapped to virtual reality just like the actual building, only cleaner.

The downside was, it'd still taken me two minutes. This was not good. I checked my virtual watch again, and swore silently. 8:39. I was already into danger time.

I took one last look around to make sure none of the faceless gray drones in the hallway were watching me, then darted into a virtual broom closet and closed the door gently. Working quickly, I set down my briefcase, popped the locks, peeled off my green apple face mask, and ditched my black bowler hat.

The briefcase opened of its own accord, and out from the case sprang Thing[1] and Thing[2].

"Listen up," I said to them. "We've got a problem."

"I'll say we do," Thing[1] said.

"I'll say it, too," Thing[2] chimed in.

"We're really short on time," I said.

"You need to make it rhyme."

I wrinkled my nose until it was halfway up my forehead and stared at my two little monsters. "What the *fuck*?"

A flash of panic darted through Thing[1]'s eyes, and he turned to Thing[2], who tapped his foot, scratched his chin, and started into muttering. "Duck? Buck? Luck? Firetruck?"

Thing[1] turned back to me and shrugged. "Sorry, boss. It helps if you give us more syllables to work with."

What I gave them both was a hand clamped around the throat, and I squeezed until their little blue eyeballs bulged out. "Now listen, you things," I said through clenched teeth, "and listen real close. We've got just five minutes, and then we are toast."

"He's getting better," Thing[1] gasped. "Don't you think?"

"Definitely better," Thing[2] wheezed, nodding.

I dragged them in close until we were almost nose to nose. "You know why I made you," I hissed. "You know why we're here. That data is out there. Get your asses in gear." I gave them both a good shake to reinforce the point, then released them. They fell to the floor, clutching at their throats and gasping for breath.

Either they were faking it, or they recovered quickly. A second later Thing[1] jumped to his feet and snapped to attention. "We're quite short on time."

Thing[2] jumped up beside him. "But we know what to do."

"So you just park your butt."

"And we'll get back to you."

Then away ran those things, they ran away fast. But my part was to wait, so I sat on my—

Someone out in the hall ripped the closet door open with a violence that nearly tore it from its hinges. *"Intruder!"* a deep male voice bellowed, like Darth Vader with a thick Austrian accent. I sprang to my feet and turned to face the threat.

The guy in the hall was a *monster*. Seven feet tall if he was an inch; all bulging knotty muscles from his toes to his eyebrows. He was a veritable blond Viking *giant*, wearing nothing but a fur jockstrap, rawhide boots, and a pointed iron helmet with a set of cow's horns on it—

Holy shit. Charles Murphy. Dressed to kill, or more accurately, to play *Slaughter*.

"Ach, stranger!" Charles said in that same thick, dumb Germanic accent as he rippled his bulging pecs at me. "The vay you dealt mit der security program vas *most* impressif!" He paused a moment, to give me a flash of his throbbing biceps and swollen veins.

His mistake. In that brief pause, a whole chain of loose ideas clicked together at once, and I suddenly understood Charles far better than I ever had before. *MDE biomedical.* Charles' life-support chair. The way he waxed everyone else's fannies in *Slaughter*. The way he gave himself physical aspects that defied the laws of virtual reality.

Murphy was an embryonic superuser, and he didn't even know it.

He finished his bicep routine, rotated slightly to flex a deltoid at me, and then made sure I appreciated his lats and quads. You know, for a moment, I really *felt* for the guy. I mean, knowing what kind of body he was condemned to live in in real time, I could honestly see the *joy* he'd put into creating and using this ludicrously musclebound virtual aspect.

And then he had to go and spoil it all by talking.

"You are indeed a verthy opponent," Charles said, as he brought his Mister Universe routine to a close in some kind of tense crouch. "But know zis: you haf invaded *my* domain, und ze penalty ist—*death*!" And then, with the dazzling speed of a striking tiger, he drew his broadsword, and in one beautifully powerful and well-choreographed move, he *lunged*!—to drive that gleaming razor-sharp steel through a whistling arc of death that no doubt would have split my little broken virtual body stem to stern like a bloody side of beef . . .

Had I not taken the opportunity when he telegraphed his move to go Cubist, and step around him in the fourth dimension.

Charles seemed puzzled. He was standing there, poking at my briefcase gingerly with the tip of his sword, and it never even occurred to him to check his back. I figured I'd better clue him in. I summoned a nice virtual carrot into existence, took a big crunchy bite of it, then looked over his shoulder and asked, "What's up, dork?"

He turned in a whirling flash of steel that made me jump up to hit the ceiling tiles. I landed a good eight feet away.

"*Most* impressif," Charles said, as he stepped out of the broom closet and squared off to face me in the open hallway. "But even zis will not save you!" He lunged again in that moment, feinting low but swinging high, with a blow that would have bobbitted me for sure if I'd tried another jump.

Instead, I stood my ground and caught the blade of his sword in my bare left hand. His astonishment at not lopping off my arm lasted barely a moment, then he grabbed the hilt of the sword with both hands and tried to wrestle it away from me.

I let him try for a while. When he braced a foot against my chest to get better leverage, though, I decided this was getting undignified, and grabbed his ankle and tossed him head-over-heels across the hall. While he was recovering from that, I took hold of his sword with both hands and bent it into the shape of a giant paperclip. (I would have done a plowshare, but I have no idea what a plowshare actually looks like.)

The expression on Murphy's face was marvelous to see.

"Stranger," he said slowly, "you are indeed powerful, und I vould love to learn your secrets."

"I bet you would," I said. "So here's the first one: I don't want to hurt you. Now why don't you be a good little barbarian and beat it?"

Murphy nodded thoughtfully. "Ach. Therein lies da problem. For you see," he whipped a BFG-2000 assault pistol out from under his loincloth (where did it *fit*?), "I *do* vant to hurt *you*." I jumped aside as his first burst of fire ripped down the corridor, and six or eight gray-suited innocent bystanders collapsed in bullet-riddled heaps.

"Goodness, you're fast," he said, when he noticed he'd missed me. He swung the barrel in a wide stuttering arc the second time, and I had to jump up through the ceiling tiles to get out of the way. Several dozen more innocent bystanders tumbled dead out of their cubicles.

This time Murphy was waiting when I came down through the ceiling tiles behind him. He fired high. I fell faster. He fired low. I jumped. The bystander bodycount was getting out of hand. Like it or not, I realized I had to stop him.

"I tried to tell you," I said as I flashed over to the far wall. The plaster exploded in a spatter of ricochets. "I don't want to *hurt* you." I dove to the floor and rolled behind him. He stitched a line of fire across the gray carpet after me. "But kid," I popped to my feet behind him, tapped his right shoulder, and darted left as he pivoted right. "You just don't take the *hint*." He finally figured out where I was—on his left side, opposite the gun—and he swung the pistol around in a wide arc, his finger on the trigger and the muzzle blasting the entire way. Time

262    /    Bruce Bethke

went slow motion on me then, as innocent bystanders spurted blood and dropped like they were being filmed by Sam Peckinpah and my monomolecular switchblade sprang out of my sleeve and into my waiting hand. Time went *really* slow in the next moment, as I slashed out with that impossibly sharp blade and drove it through Murphy's thick neck, slicing through meat, bone, veins, and sinew as if they were just so much overcooked prime rib.

Slowly, slowly, Murphy's head slid away, arterial blood jetted like a pink fountain in the air, and for a few seconds more his beautiful virtual body didn't even know it was dead yet. Then, like a calving glacier falling to the sea, it toppled over.

And *that* is when real time resumed, all the alarms went off, and all those gray and faceless users—well, the ones who had survived Murphy's lousy aim, anyway—started pointing at me and howling just exactly like the pod people in *Invasion of the Body Snatchers* (1978 version).

"There he is!" a familiar voice shouted. I spun around, and saw Frank Dong charging down the hall toward me, pumping the action of a virtual shotgun. It wasn't until he pointed the thing at me and started squeezing the trigger that I realized—

Shit. *I'm* the enemy.

I hit the floor. Frank's shot went over my head. Scrabbling around quickly, I scooped up Murphy's BFG-2000 and fired one careful burst that made a mess of the ceiling tiles but didn't actually hit anyone.

It achieved the desired effect. Frank dove behind a cubicle wall, fired another wild shot that blew out a fluorescent light, and screamed, "He's got me pinned down!" I jumped to my feet.

A third shotgun blast hit me in the back, shredding my gray pinstripe coat and almost scuffing my black leather jacket.

*"Fuck!"* I heard Bubu scream behind me. "He's armored!" Bubu wasted another shot peeling off the rest of my pinstripes before I popped a short burst over my shoulder at him and dove right, to crash through the virtual drywall and into a row of virtual filing cabinets beyond. Drawers clanged open and manila file folders exploded, spraying their contents everywhere. "I think that last one stung him," Bubu shouted, somewhere off to my right. I took a quick moment to get my bearings, then crashed through another slab of drywall and came face-to-face with—

Oh, no. T'shombe.

She was armed, yes, but I'd caught her flat-footed. Her gun was pointing in the wrong direction; by pure accident the muzzle of my BFG-2000 was pressed against the side of her left breast. We stared at each other for what seemed like ages; it almost seemed as if a faint glimmer of recognition flashed through her eyes. Her mouth dropped open. She started to form a word.

Time to see just how much control I had over my superuser strength. I lashed out with my left hand and hit her lightly on the left temple. She collapsed like a wet dishrag.

She didn't randomize out of existence, which I took as a good sign. But then, neither had Charles, when I killed him.

I was still trying to deal with what I'd done when Thing$^2$ came racing up the hallway, dragging a bulky file folder behind him. "Got it, boss!" Thing$^2$ shouted. He tossed me the folder.

"Where's Thing$^1$?" I asked.

Thing$^2$ nudged T'shombe's unconscious form with his toe. "This chick splattered him."

Balancing the folder and the gun together, I took a hasty flip through the file. It looked about right, I guessed. Glancing up from the folder, I noticed Thing$^2$ was staring at me. "Will that be all, boss?" he asked.

"Yes." I stuffed the file folder inside my leather jacket and zipped it shut.

"Then in that case," Thing$^2$ said as he took a step back and saluted me, "it has been a real slice. Good-bye, and good luck!" He saluted again and randomized himself out of existence. Which is what I'd programmed him to do when his mission was complete.

Still, I was actually going to miss the little monster—

"Where's T'shombe?" I heard Frank shout, off to my left.

"Over here!" I heard Bubu shout, off to my right. He burst around the corner and leveled his shotgun at me.

I dropped the BFG-2000 and screamed, *"BUGOUT!"*

Fifteen milliseconds later I was back in reality. Peeling off my video goggles, I sank to my knees on the bare wooden floor and shuddered. LeMat was at my side in moments, pulling out fiber optics cables by the fistful. "You look pretty bad," he said, meaning it. "How'd it go in there?"

I stripped off the datagloves and dropped them on the floor. "Grim," I said, when I'd found my voice. I accepted the cup of coffee LeMat offered me and took a sip. "Did we get the files?"

"Yeah, we got the files." LeMat looked at me with more genuine concern than I'd ever seen before, then gave me a squeeze on the shoulder. "You should see them. They're just what Amber said you'd find. Names, dates, places, plans: rock-solid *proof* that MDE swindled your client. No offense, Jack, but you used to work for some real slimeballs."

I took another sip of the coffee and held the steaming cup close for warmth, but said nothing.

LeMat gave me another squeeze on the shoulder. "Cheer up, Jack. Amber's lawsuit is in the bag. You did good."

I heard him say that, and I tried to believe it, but all I could think about were Charles and T'shombe. LeMat stepped away from me for a moment to return with a blanket. I looked up at him as he draped it around my shivering, bare shoulders.

"Did I?"

# 18

## DELIVERANCE

**Monday Evening, 10:00 P.M. Local, 0300 UTC:** I rolled my virtual Harley Ultraglide through the empty streets of ToxicTown, a virtual .45 tucked inside my waistband, a thick sheaf of stolen files tucked inside my jacket, and the ProctoProd tucked—never mind where. Now, as a superuser, I could *smell* ToxicTown. It reminded me of the South St. Paul stockyards on a hot, windless day in July.

I shifted nervously on the bike's seat and kept my eyes peeled.

If you'd asked me then why I was so edgy, I couldn't have told you. Sure, part of it was that after four days of use, the proctoprod was starting to become a major pain in the— never mind. And part of it was my basic fear of running into Eliza in the Net, although I thought I probably could handle her now.

A big part was fear of a double-cross. Irrational of course; so far, everything Amber told me had turned out to be true. Still, the idea was there, in an intellectual, if not visceral, way.

But the lion's share of my fear, I think, came from the

idea that this time I was truly flying solo. No backups; no EKG rig; no guardian angel watching my behind. I'd really wanted LeMat to fly tail-gunner for me on this run, just in case Amber had some last trick up her corset, but he'd begged off.

"Jack," he'd said pompously, by way of excuse, "I would love to go with you, but I have heard a higher calling. Tonight, I am boldly going where no man has gone before!"

I just tapped my foot and glared at him.

"Out on a date with Inge."

I rolled up to an intersection and slowed the bike just long enough to scan for landmarks. There, that disgusting glob of plastic resin off to my left: The Acme Rubber Dog Poop & Novelty Factory. I leaned the bike into a right turn, stepped the tranny down to second, and twisted the throttle open.

And resumed both my journey, and my mantra: *Trust* Amber. *Trust* Amber. *Trust* Amber.

I found Thorvold on the street corner, leaning against the lamppost, flipping and catching a large, silver coin with almost mechanical precision. "Hi, Max," he said, without breaking rhythm. He gave me an appraising glance as I parked the bike and dismounted. "Nice suit. You got the files?"

The presence of the dwarf worried me, and pissed me off, and a few dozen other things besides. "I got an appointment with Amber, is what I got. Nobody said a word about *you* being here."

"Relax," Thorvold said as he caught the coin one last time and palmed it. "Don't get your SNID in a twist. The boss bitch is in; she just put me out here to watch the door. Go on up. She's expecting you."

I started for the stairs.

"Hey, mister," Thorvold said, "for a dollar, I make sure nothing bad happens to your bike."

I dug into my virtual black leather pants pocket, came up with a quarter, and flipped it to him. "Sorry," I said. "I'm a little—" I snickered "—*short*."

Thorvold grumbled something I didn't catch, but kept the quarter.

Amber was waiting for me at the top of the stairs. She was leaning against the open doorframe, silhouetted in soft yellow light from her apartment, her long black hair down and a long cigarette in an even longer ebony holder in her left hand. She was wearing a short, silky, pale green kimono thing with big swoopy sleeves—it was just barely long enough to cover her delicious tush—and apparently, given the way the kimono was almost transparent when backlit, she was wearing nothing else. Her arms were crossed just below her small, perky, breasts, and smoke drifted away from her in a slow, languid stream.

"Hello, darling," she said.

That's about the point when I realized I'd turned the corner at the landing, seen her, and stopped dead in my tracks. I groped around until I found my jaw, right where I'd dropped it on the stairs, and reattached it to my face.

"Hi, babe," I said, feigning coolness.

"Did you get the files?"

I scratched my perfect five-day-stubble chin. "Impatient little minx, aren't you?"

"You're right." She shifted to standing upright, moved the cigarette holder to her right hand, and beckoned for me to come closer. "There's something important we need to do first." Slowly, then with increasing confidence, I climbed the rest of the stairs and met her in the doorway.

She pounced then, throwing her gorgeous body against mine, wrapping her arms around my neck, and sending me to Paradise with a long, slow, passionate kiss. Her lips tasted like chocolate, and wine, and gourmet coffee, and fine tobacco, and everything delicious and sultry and slightly sinful in life. Even now, thinking about that kiss, I must confess I'd have died a happy man if I'd checked out in that moment.

Then she gave me another kiss that was even better.

And then she held me tight, and caressed me, and peppered my neck and earlobe with slow, soft kisses and gentle bites, and whispered in my ear, "So, darling. Did you get the files?"

"*Yes!*"

I think, in that moment, if Amber had asked me to donate my brain for a monster she was stitching together in the basement, I would have said, "*Yes!*"

"Wonderful," she whispered. She dragged me inside her apartment, slammed and locked the door behind us, and turned around to lean back against the door and hold me close to her. We kissed for a long, *long* time after that, and explored each other's mouths and teeth with our lips and tongues. Tongue wrestling. She beat me three falls out of four. I liked that. I ran my fingers through her long, luxuriant black hair, mapped the contours of her marvelous body with my hands, and found the loose knot in the sash that held her kimono closed.

I tugged at the knot. Green silk fell open, disclosing the glorious wonders within. My right hand went exploring.

She caught my wrist, pushed me back slightly, and came up for air. "Max?" she said gently.

"Yes, darling?" I murmured, as I nibbled her right earlobe.

"Before we go any further, there's something you need to know."

"If you're going to tell me you're really a guy in drag," I whispered, as I nibbled my way down her neck, "I don't want to hear it."

"Oh, no." She grabbed me by the hair on the back of my head and steered me into another long, slow, passionate kiss.

"Trust me on that, darling. I am one-hundred-percent woman, through and through."

I tried to confirm that with my hands, but she detached herself from my face, led me over to the bed, and motioned for me to sit down on the edge of it. I did. She took a step or two back, and turned around to face me.

"Was it hard?" she asked. After a moment I realized she was talking about the job. Max Kool wanted to answer with something flippant and nonchalant, but Jack Burroughs broke through and answered instead.

"Yeah." I shuddered.

Amber nodded and gave me a sad, sympathetic smile. "Did you have to kill some people?"

I thought about Murphy, and the way my virtual knife felt like it was actually biting into something soft, but *real*. And T'shombe; the way her eyes rolled over to dead white orbs when I punched her in the temple. I sure hoped I had control of my strength and that I hadn't really hurt her. "Yeah," I said. "One for sure. Maybe two."

Amber knelt before me, took my hands in hers, and caressed my knuckles. "It's different, isn't it? Killing people as a superuser."

I swallowed hard and nodded. "Yeah. Realistic. *Too* realistic."

"Some people get used to it," Amber said, looking at my hands. Then she looked up at me with a gaze that speared straight through to my soul. "Please, Max. Promise me you'll never get used to it."

"Don't worry. I don't think I ever can." I took her beautiful face in my hands and tried to kiss her again. She pulled away from me, though, and bounced to her feet. I started to form a question.

"Shhh," she said, touching a delicate finger to her perfect lips. "Now, about those files you, er, obtained."

I zipped open my black leather jacket, pulled out the folder, and threw it on the bed. "You mean these?"

She picked up the folder, riffled through it quickly, and nodded. "Yes, these. There's something else you need to know about them." She closed the folder, smiled sweetly at me, then tossed the files into a wastebasket. "I planted them."

I bounced to my feet. *"What?!"*

Her smile collapsed. "Please don't be angry, darling! It was just, I *had* to know. I mean, if you could really *do* it! Crack a system, find a needle in a haystack, blow away the opposition if your life depended on it. Believe me, the real job is going to be *much* harder!"

I was, I think, furious. "This was just a *test*?"

"Yes! And darling, you passed with *flying* colors!" She started to take a step toward me, then saw the blazing anger in my eyes and took a step back instead. "But you know," she said as she looked me up and down with a coy smile, "I think what you need right now is a little positive reinforcement." She smiled at me again, then shrugged out of her kimono.

Well, there went my anger.

Amber, naked, was *incredible*. Slender, athletic, sexy beyond the bounds of human comprehension, ravishing, gorgeous, spectacular—aw hell, go get yourself a thesaurus and insert your favorite adjective here: _____. Amber, in that moment, was without question the most heartbreakingly beautiful woman I have *ever* seen.

"Positive reinforcement?" I whispered, as she took one graceful step closer.

"Positively," she whispered back, with a hungry, sexy smile.

"A dog yummy for a job well done?" I gasped. Another step.

"I prefer mine bloody rare," she said with an almost feline Psycho-Kitty-in-heat growl. "But someone here is overdressed." She snapped her fingers. My clothes vanished. She took me in her arms.

"Mind if I ask a dumb question?" I asked, before she covered my mouth with hers. About the time I was starting to see blue spots from anoxia, she let me come up for air. "If you're good enough to plant those files, why do you need me?"

"Because," she whispered as she softly kissed my forehead and guided my face down to nuzzle her small, perfect breasts, "we all have our limits, and the real job really *is* beyond mine." In that moment, she clutched me tight to her bosom, and I must admit I didn't think about much else for a while.

In time, she pried me off again. "By the way," she said softly, "since you and Gunnar are clearly working together, I've decided you need another neural interface. I'll have it sent out tomorrow." Then she grabbed my head with both hands, tilted my face up, and kissed me full and hard on the lips. I wrapped my muscular arms around her slender waist and tried to pull her down onto the bed. She pulled away from me slightly, put her hand on my hairy chest, and kissed me on the point of my strong, masculine chin.

"Oh, and there's one more thing I forgot to tell you," she whispered, as I let my head fall back and bared my throat to her kisses. "And that is," she pushed hard with the hand that rested on my sternum, and knocked me flat on my back on the bed.

"I like to be on top!" With a wild whoop like an insane cowboy she jumped onto the bed, straddled me with her thighs, grabbed hold of my bald-headed buddy and guided him into—

*KA-BLAM*! The hallway door exploded off its hinges in a shower of flaming wreckage and black smoke. A screaming little bloody lump that may have been Thorvold flew across the room to crash through the picture window and plummet to the street below, and a moment later a gleaming chrome battle-mech smashed through the space where the door had been, considerably enlarging the aperature in the process. Servos whining and hydraulics hissing, the battlemech advanced ponderously into the room like an angry hormonal chrome juggernaut.

Amber let go of my buddy (thank God!) and jumped to her feet to face the 'mech. *"You!"* she screamed at the top of her lungs.

The battlemech shimmered and morphed into Eliza. *"Bitch!"*

"He's *mine!*" Amber screamed.

*"Never!"* Eliza screamed right back.

Amber's fingernails sprouted to bear-claw length and took on a disturbingly metallic sheen. In one fantastic spring, she leaped across the room and ripped into Eliza, claws slashing furiously.

Eliza endured it a moment, then hammered Amber with a backhand that sent her flying completely over the bed and through the far wall. She left a cookie-cutter female body pattern in the laths and plaster.

I figured that was the end of it right there, but an instant later Amber came crashing back through a different part of the wall, in a perfect tuck and roll. She landed lightly on the balls of her feet, breathing hard, slightly sweaty, and covered with plaster dust, but otherwise none the worse for wear. I tore my eyes off her long enough to spare a glance at Eliza, whom I figured to be a bloody mass of shredded flesh.

Well, her plain white dress was a write-off, definitely, but Eliza herself seemed to be unscratched. She picked the last rags of white fabric off her shoulders, cast them aside, and advanced like the naked anorexic albino face of doom. Her hands morphed into giant eagle's talons. She stopped a yard short of where I lay on the bed and raised her talons.

"I want him back," Eliza said, with a voice as cold as Death. "You're *corrupting* him."

"You can't have him," Amber answered. "He's all mine now." I turned my head. Amber was crouching on the other side of the bed, her long metal fingernails gleaming in the pale yellow light. You know, there have been times in my life when I would have *paid* to be the prize in a fight between two naked women.

This was not one of them.

Eliza paused and considered her talons. "You know," she said to Amber, "there's no point in us continuing this fight. We're too equally matched."

Amber shifted her stance, but also spared a glance for her metal claws. "I suppose I could escalate. But you'd escalate right along with me, wouldn't you?"

Eliza nodded. "And since I would never agree to let *you* have him—"

"Nor I you—"

Eliza shrugged and morphed her left hand back into a hand and her right hand into a long, steel, blade. "What do you say? The Solomonic Solution?"

Amber nodded. "It's the only way." Her hands, too, morphed to match Eliza's.

"Lengthwise?" Eliza asked.

Amber leaned over me, gently lifted my testicles with her left hand, and touched a point beneath them with her incredibly cold steel blade. "We'll start the cut right about here . . ."

**Blackout.**

I don't mean I fainted. I mean, I blacked out. Flatlined. Went totally dead. Lost power.

"Oops," I heard LeMat say. He sounded drunk.

I ripped off the videoshades, threw them on the floor, and screamed at the top of my lungs, *"LeMAT!"*

He was standing over by the workstation, buck naked, with a dripping glass of water in his hands and a couple of yards of unplugged power cord wrapped around his clumsy feet. "Sorry," he said thickly as he paused for a hiccup. "Inge w's feelin' thirsty, so's I—" He gestured at the glass of water and hiccuped again.

I just about lost my lunch, and my shit, and my blood pressure, and my bladder control. "Inge? *Where*?" I spun around, desperately searching for—

"Hi, Jack." She giggled. Oh no, she was over in the direction of—

A by-now-familiar blond head popped up from under the blankets on my futon. *"Boo!"* This was followed shortly by, "Oops," and a drunken giggle, when she realized that the blanket had fallen away and unveiled her admittedly rather massive freckled breasts. She fumbled for the edge of the blanket, failed to find it, and eventually just gave up and sat there.

Okay, if she could sit there with her boobs hanging out, I guess that meant I didn't have to be embarrassed about being caught dressed like a cybernetic transvestite. But all the same . . .

I turned on LeMat, ready to kill.

"Now now, Jack," LeMat said, trying to step forward and calm me, but instead tripping over the power cord and spilling the water again. "Me an' Inge went out to a nice li'l Italian place, an' we had a li'l wine with dinner—"

"A *little*?" Inge giggled. It made her little pink nipples bounce.

"Okay," LeMat laughed, "more than a li'l. We had a *lot* of wine with dinner."

"And before dinner," Inge said seriously. "And after dinner, and after after-dinner—"

"An' we talked about our work and all kindsa stuff."

LeMat finally got himself free of the power cord, and staggered over to the futon, to flop down on it and start nibbling Inge's toes.

"And after that I talked Gunnar into coming back here," Inge said, trying desperately to force a serious expression onto her face. "Because I really wanted to talk to *you*. So don't get mad at Gunnar. It was *my* idea." Her serious expression failed then—possibly because LeMat was tickling her feet—and she giggled and took a swat at him.

LeMat surfaced. "But when we got here, we saw you were still usin' the innerface, an' we saw you were kinda *preoccupied*. So we sat down on th' futon, an' one thing led to another, an' another, an' another—" He hiccuped.

"That was my idea, too," Inge said proudly. "I figured you wouldn't mind. Thought we could get in a quickie or two before you even noticed we were here."

"And now she knows all about the interface," I said to LeMat in the nastiest and most disgusted tone of voice I could muster. "Thanks a lot, *chump*."

"Oh, don't be so hard on him," Inge scolded me. "I already know about the neural infuc—induc—The interface. Matter of fact," she nodded proudly, "I got one myself."

My jaw hit the floor and rolled across the room. "You *do*?"

"Sure," LeMat said. "We've all met before, on th' other side. Don'cha rec'gnize her?"

I was still trying to find my lower jaw. "Wha—?"

Inge bit LeMat hard on the earlobe and stage-whispered, "Maybe I should give him a hint, lover." He looked up from fondling her ample breasts long enough to nod.

"Jack?" she said, looked straight at me with a deep and serious, if slightly out-of-focus, expression. "Excuse me." She cleared her throat, shifted her voice down to a deep, hoarse, basso falsetto, and laid on an accent so thick it was probably a violation of the Ethnic Humor Elimination Act. "Or should I say, *Max*? It's bad for the heart to talk business on an empty stomach. *Mangia*!"

Whatever was left of my sanity, it checked out then.

*"Don Vermicelli?"*

# 19

## MORE FUN WITH GRATUITOUS SEX SCENES

LeMat and Inge awoke the next morning with a matched pair of death-defying hangovers. The positive side of this is that they were both feeling too sick to bother with being embarrassed by their behavior of the night before. The downside was, I had to listen to them *whimper* for almost the entire morning, until at long last the aspirin, Tylenol, burnt toast, and vast quantities of black coffee finally worked their slow magic.

Then they jumped into the shower together and didn't come out again until all the hot water was gone.

We spent the rest of Tuesday dragging Inge's VR workstation up from her apartment and hooking it into our local area network. Then, with me watching his vital signs and Inge waiting to catch him on the other side, LeMat finally felt brave enough to try the neural induction interface. (Although he did express a desire to autoclave the prod first. It took us the better part of an hour to convince him that soaking it in bleach and then running it through the dishwasher was probably hygienic enough.) When LeMat finally dove into our local test reality, he was almost *terrified* by the intensity of his new virtual senses.

By the time I called it quits and hit the cot, though, around 1 A.M., LeMat and Inge had been banging their virtual brains out for at least three hours straight, and they were showing no signs of slowing down anytime soon.

The second—third, if you count Inge's—neural induction interface showed up around noon Wednesday. Don Vermicelli's impenetrable web of deceit turned out to be simply Inge picking up the package at Mailboxes & More™ and reshipping it, but now that everything was out in the open she decided to save us a day in travel time and $12.49 in express charges by simply picking it up and bringing it home. There was only one surprise in the second box: an honest-to-God 3.5-inch 1.44MB magnetic diskette.

"Hi, Max," Amber said, when I got the diskette decrypted and ported over to a media format we could read. "Nice trick, the way you vanished from my apartment Monday night. I thought I'd be able to out-bluff Eliza, but honestly, I think that bitch really *would* rather see you bobbitted than let you share it with another woman." She shrugged and flashed me a weak smile.

"Anyway, here are the background files on the real job. Look 'em over; go for it if you think you can. My apartment's going to be offline for at least a week—God, I'm glad there are no damage deposits in virtual reality—so I'll see you in Hell. Say, next week Friday, around 0300 UTC?" She smiled again, in the weird sort of way that people smile when they're trying to put a good face on a really bad situation, then said, "Bye," and pulled the window shut.

Half an hour later, I had the rest of her background files decompressed and scanned. The real target, it turned out, was Franklin Curtis.

Yes, *the* Franklin Curtis. The one you're thinking of. Best-selling author, talk-show bon vivant, outrageously outspoken

NRA Life Member with an indoor pistol range in the basement of his upstate New York mansion. *That* Franklin Curtis. The guy whose last five film adaptations made such obscenely enormous piles of money that Sony-Spielberg had to promise him his own *planet* in order to option the film rights on his next as-yet-unwritten book.

And that, as fate would have it, is where I came into the picture. The book was *not* unwritten. (Factor out the negatives: it works.) The problem was, the book that Curtis was about to deliver was not written by *him*. My mysterious client, according to Amber, was a struggling young would-be author who chanced to meet Curtis at a New York publisher's party, and she was so flattered by the attention the handsome and successful older man lavished on her that it never even *occurred* to her his judgment might be influenced by the neckline of her cocktail dress or her lithe, athletic, still-a-virgin figure. (She was an actress/model in the spare time left over between writing, attending medical school, and doing volunteer work in the orphanage where she grew up.)

What followed next was sadly predictable. Curtis and my client had an intense, torrid, and sexually unsafe nine-and-a-half-week affair, which ended abruptly when Curtis discovered she was pregnant and she refused to get an abortion. They'd argued for a week and then, on a terribly cold and stormy day in March, he came back to his mansion in a drunken rage and physically *threw* her out the door into the driving snow, and tossed her few meager possessions after her. Blinded by rage and drunkenness, he ordered his heel-clicking brownshirt security guards to *shoot* her if she ever so much as set foot on the mansion grounds again.

That might have been the end of it there. My client, being a deeply religious girl, accepted her unplanned pregnancy as God's punishment for giving in to the sins of the flesh, and returned, crestfallen, to Saint Brunhilde's Convent School, where she was determined to raise her child in the ways of the church and the paths of righteousness. My client was even determined to teach this child to *love* his or her father, though Curtis might deny paternity and never see the child, for even at this point, my client was still willing to forgive and forget.

Until she picked through the tattered suitcase that held her few worldly belongings and discovered that, while Curtis had even gone so far as to return the leftovers of the one and only meatloaf dinner she had ever made for him—it was still rock-solid and just as appetizing as on the day it was made—he had kept the disk!

*The* disk. The one and *only* copy of my client's unpublished novel! The book she had labored over for six long, agonizing years, giving up meals to rent computer time at Kinko's! The very book that Curtis himself had hailed as, "Brilliant! And possibly Marketable!"

Fearing his temper, my client asked old Sister Agatha to telephone Curtis and ask for the diskette back. The aging nun was polite and most respectful, but Curtis dissed her and told her contemptuously that he'd erased the disk and recycled it for scrap plastic. Feeling further chastened, my client tearfully left the old nun's cell and returned to her lonely room, to cry alone in the dark, gnawing on a chunk of meatloaf and praying that someday, someday, God in His infinite wisdom would arrange for Franklin Curtis' heart to soften.

Until a few weeks later, when she read in the paper that Curtis—who'd been going through a terrible case of near-fatal writer's block when they were together—had suddenly announced that he was almost finished with his latest book, and that it was going to be a real departure. To my client, the implications were instantly obvious. Not content merely to seduce and abandon her, he'd plagiarized her book!

And *that* is when my client had her change of heart. Screw forgiveness. She wanted Curtis' head on a *stick*! But to prove he'd stolen her book, she needed the original document files from his personal computer. Ergo my mission, if I chose to accept it. . . .

LeMat toddled by then and peeked over my shoulder at the text on the screen. "Y'know Jack," he said between bites on a crisp red apple, "I have seen some enormous loads of bullshit in my time, but I think this one definitely takes the cake."

"You certainly said a mouthful," I answered.

"Of cake, or bullshit?"

I finished scanning through the mission parameters one more time, then closed the files and leaned back in my blue plastic chair. "So," LeMat went on. "What do you suppose Amber's *real* reason is for wanting those files?"

I shrugged. "Who gives a rat's ass? All I know is she wants a copy of Curtis' new book, and she's willing to pay us nine hundred thou if we can deliver. I say we go for it."

LeMat thought it over and nodded. "Where do we start? Literature search?"

"Yup." The chair started to topple over backward. LeMat caught me and set the chair back on four legs again. "Hard-tech writers like Curtis are *always* bragging about their personal computers," I said, when I was no longer in danger of landing on my head. "Check out *Bit. Writer's Lunch. Home Tax Deduction.* Let's see what kind of head start he's already given us."

"Don't forget *InfoPlanet*," LeMat suggested. "And *Clankalog*. I know he did an interview for them a few months ago."

I arched an eyebrow at him. "You subscribe?"

He shrugged. "It was the cheapest one on the Publisher's Packinghouse list. And I may already be a winner."

I nodded. "Well, just in case you aren't, we'd better get cracking on this job."

LeMat finished his apple, launched the core at the waste-basket in a twenty-foot fallaway jumpshot, and nailed it dead center. "Consider it cracked," he said as he walked away.

There are parts of that week that are still too weird to think about, even now. For example, there was all the time that LeMat, Inge, and I spent designing a new virtual aspect for her, to use at times when it would be embarrassing for Gunnar and Don Vermicelli to be seen nibbling on each other's earlobes. What we finally ended up with was a sort of Modified Linda Hamilton, but we pumped her pecs and deltoids a little more, trimmed her abs a bit flatter, and gave her a sweet freckled young mother's face that LeMat and Inge spent close to six hours sweating over. When we finally christened "Reba," she was Gunnar's *perfect* woman.

So how come, when I popped into Heaven for a little R&R Friday night, I found fat old Don Vermicelli still sitting there, holding court in his usual corner? I strode straight over to the table, determined to demand an explanation. Two trigger boys stepped out to block my way; Don Vermicelli waved them aside. (As if I couldn't have vaporized them with an unkind word.) I grabbed a chair, parked my butt, and started warming up for a really good yell. One of the Silicione sisters jiggled into view.

I did a double take, then a triple take. *"Gunnar?"*

"Shhh," he said, touching a perfectly manicured nail to his full, sweet, ruby-red lips. "We haven't gone public yet. And call me *Sophia*.

"Now," he said perkily, as he straightened up and jiggled his enormous hooters at me, "what would you like?"

"Some fresh air," I said, staggering away from the table.

LeMat and Inge, I should point out, had sex. They had sex in the morning, sex at night, sex for lunch, sex on the rooftop. They tried to be coy about it, of course, but given that the only interior wall in the CompuTech office was a folding Chinese screen we'd fished out of the basement, it was pretty hard for them to be *discreet*. And after a few days of sex in the shower, sex in the kitchen, and sex everytime I went into VR, they gave up trying and just started counting on me to pretend like I didn't see or hear anything. If they hadn't moved the futon over to the west wall, so that I spent my sleepless nights on the Army cot listening to the steady *thump-thump-thump* of the futon frame against plaster, I might even have managed it.

But the truth was, I was so jealous, I could have eaten my own liver.

I understand they tried sex in Inge's apartment, once, but it was a failure. Something about the excruciatingly anal way she'd decorated her bedroom, and the motion of the bed disturbing the alignment of the dust ruffle. I never did get the full story; LeMat was too angry to talk about it afterward, and because of this incident, they broke up.

That lasted almost three whole hours. Then I accidentally caught them tearing off a quickie in the freight elevator.

Once we finally had interfaces for each of us, LeMat brought his VR system from home, and we hooked all three workstations together in a really dandy little local area network. (LeMat *did* take Inge back to his house for this hardware run, but while his back was turned she started *organizing* the place, and he swore he was never going to give her the chance to do that again.) Most of the time I stayed out and did biotelemetry duty while Gunnar and Inge/Reba worked out in our local test reality, but every now and then I went online and dove in with them.

I quickly learned not to do that without warning them. One time, on the spur of the moment, I decided to catch up with them after they'd been in VR for half an hour. That's how I learned that LeMat and Inge had built a virtual Playboy mansion off in her private memory partition. I found Gunnar sitting in the hot tub, with his elbows on the tub rim, holding a glass of champagne in one hand and a large, half-eaten strawberry in the other.

"Hi, Gunnar!" I said, as I popped in. "Where's Reba?"

He just smiled at me and made a weird, strangled noise.

"Are you okay?" I took a step closer to the hot tub.

Just then Reba popped up from the foam and bubbles. "Hi, Max!" she called out brightly. She was wearing a gadget somewhat like an aqualung, except that the tube ran to her nose, not her mouth. "Gosh, this work makes a girl thirsty!" She took the champagne glass from Gunnar, downed a gulp, then handed the glass back to him and dove beneath the foam again.

"Oh," I said. "Well I'll just, uh—"

*"Leave,"* Gunnar suggested through clenched teeth.

"Yes, right. Exactly." I turned my back and exited, just as fast as my little neural interface could carry me. Seconds later I was back in reality, peeling off my video goggles.

That's when I noticed the landlord, Jerry, standing over by the freight elevator, with a bucket of paint in his hand and an expression I hope to never see again on his face. I tried to imagine myself in his shoes, and see LeMat, Inge, and myself as he was seeing us. I saw a trio of high-tech drag-queen mimes.

"Don't ask," I told Jerry. "Just don't ask."

By week's end, our research was starting to turn up useful information about the Franklin Curtis job. None of it was good.

"I've got his Net address," LeMat said as he dropped a pile of paper on our worktable. "This guy is *definitely* high-tech. He's been online since there's been a line to be on. In fact, I wouldn't be surprised if he had a SNID himself."

"Curtis?" Inge wrinkled her nose. "No way. Too macho."

"Maybe so," LeMat said to her as he fished a photocopy out of his stack of notes, "but listen to this:

CURTIS: I consider myself a 'method' writer. I've always tried to get inside my characters, to see the world through their eyes and tell the story in their voices. But lately I've developed some tricks that help me, well, *literally* walk a mile in my hero's shoes.

CLANKALOG: You mean like, virtual reality?

CURTIS: No, not *like* virtual reality. I mean a level of intensity that's at least one generation *beyond* what currently passes for virtual reality on the civilian market. I can't go into specifics—a lot of this stuff is still very classified—but when I was working on my new nonfiction book, *RoboCav*, I got to spend a lot of time with the people who are developing the next generation of military simulation trainers—

CLANKALOG: Oh, you mean like *Argus*?

CURTIS: (Suspiciously.) Where'd you hear that name?

CLANKALOG: I'm not sure. On the Net, I suppose—

CURTIS: That project is classified. How much do you know?

CLANKALOG: Not a lot. Only that it's a joint venture between MDE Biomedical and Rockwell Thiokol, and that it's about two years over schedule and six times over budget.

CURTIS: (Draws gun from shoulder holster under sportcoat.) Those are *national secrets*, mister! How'd you find out? Who's your contact?"

CLANKALOG:   (Alarmed.) Honest, I just picked it up on the Net somewhere—

CURTIS:   (Kicks over chair, lunges at interviewer, presses gun to his forehead.) TURNCOAT! TRAITOR! WHO DO YOU *REALLY* WORK FOR? THE CUBANS? THE LIBYANS? I WANT *NAMES*!

CLANKALOG:   (Blubbering.) Nobody! Honest! I'm *freelance*!

CURTIS:   OH, A *DOUBLE-AGENT*, ARE WE? WELL WHERE *I* COME FROM WE KNOW HOW TO *DEAL* WITH SCUM LIKE YOU! (Cocks hammer)

CLANKALOG:   (Hysterical.) *I swear to God Mr. Curtis, I'm just a reporter! Please don't shoot me pleaseGoddon'tshootmepleasepleaseplease!*

CURTIS:   (Recovering composure.) Well, I suppose your story *could* be true, however unlikely—aw geez, man, you wet yourself. Get a grip.

CLANKALOG:   (Mumbling, blubbering, incoherent reply.)

CURTIS:   Okay, I guess I can let you off with a warning this time. But—you're going to have to eat your tape recorder.

LeMat set the paper down and looked at me and Inge. "Well? Military simulators? MDE Biomedical? Does this suggest anything to you?"

I shrugged. "Some possibilities. What does the rest of the interview say?"

LeMat glanced at the paper. "There isn't any more."

Inge sat up with a start. "That's *it*?"

LeMat leaned forward and looked again. "Except for a little editorial note saying the reporter was hospitalized with stomach pains. They think it was something he ate."

I tilted back in my blue plastic chair, stroked my chin thoughtfully, and almost landed on my head again. "So let's take inventory. What do we know?"

"Franklin Curtis is richer than God," Inge said.

"But unlike God, we know where he lives," LeMat added. "In both the real world and on the Net."

"He's got some really *heavy* connections in defense," Inge noted. "Carter offered him a cabinet post."

LeMat's eyebrows went up. "I didn't know that. '76?"

Inge shook her head. "No. '96."

"Ahh." LeMat nodded. "No wonder he didn't take it."

I interrupted them and tried to put the conversation back on track. "What about his personal computer? Do we know anything about it?"

LeMat thumped the pile of magazines. "Personal *network* would be a better term. He appears to have his entire mansion wired for OC1, with a computer in every room. Including the bathrooms."

"You ever read *Artifact*?" Inge said out of the corner of her mouth. "I can *believe* he wrote that one in a bathroom—and got confused about which paper to keep."

"Topology?" I asked, grasping for straws. "File servers?"

"Distributed processing," LeMat said, "peer-to-peer. But the good news is, the primary file server is a Rockwell Thiokol milspec box. Big NASA contractor: those folks are such true believers in top-down authority and rigid hierarchy, I expect they'll have all the important files there."

I nodded. "So we get to run the trench and bomb the main reactor again. Sounds like fun." I looked to LeMat, and then to Inge. "Anybody have a guess at when's a good time?"

"Early morning," LeMat said confidently.

"Why?"

"He's a writer," LeMat explained. "Everyone knows writers are night-owls. Heavy drinkers, too. He'll be too hungover to be working in the early—*ooof*!" Inge had given him a sharp elbow in the ribs. He turned to her. "Yes, darling?"

"Gunnar," she said sweetly, "do you actually *know* any working writers?"

He thought it over. "Do poets count?"

"Only to fourteen." Inge turned to me. "I do the taxes for LaRue Woolworth," she said. "Our best bet is if we go in while he's off doing a signing at a local bookstore."

That made me sit up and take notice. *"We?"*

"If you think I'm going to let you do this without me," she said, "you are clean out of your cotton-pickin' mind."

I looked at LeMat; he shrugged. Apparently they'd already discussed this. I turned back to Inge. "But why?"

She shrugged. "I'm already in for a penny. May as well be in for the pound."

I tried to think that through, and finally decided it didn't bear much thinking about. "Okay," I said, "that's our best bet. Do we have a second-best bet?"

"Even writers have to eat," Inge pointed out. "If we can find out when he usually takes lunch or dinner, there's at least a half hour where the system will be up but he won't be in it."

LeMat raised his right hand. "Can I make a suggestion?"

I looked at Inge, and we both nodded. "Yes. Please."

"Sounds like we could really use some recon, right?"

"Are you volunteering?"

"Hell, no," LeMat said. "But with a little work, Thing[1] and Thing[2] would be perfect for the job. We can launch 'em tonight."

I thought it over, and agreed.

Later, after the meeting had petered out and LeMat had

wandered off to the bathroom, I finally got a chance to talk to Inge alone. "I don't get it," I said to her. *"Why?"*

"Why am I doing this?" she asked right back. "Why is Inge Andersson laundering money for CompuTech? Why is Reba Vermicelli going to lock and load, and charge right on into the Valley of Death alongside Gunnar Savage and Max Kool?"

"Yeah," I said, nodding. "Why?"

Inge leaned back, and fixed me with her deep blue eyes, and considered her reply. "Do you know who I am?" she said at last.

I shook my head and shrugged. "Not really. Should I?"

"I'm the chubby little frump with the blond pigtails," she said softly. "I'm the one who sits up at the front of the class, and always raises my hand when the teacher asks a question, and always gets called on when teacher wants to prove the problem can be solved because I've always got the *right* answer." She smiled.

It was a very hollow smile.

"I'm the girl who gets asked on study dates," she said with a sad edge in her voice. "I'm very popular the week before finals, but can't get a date for Homecoming to save my life. Even if I put out with *no* self-respect, I'm the one who always gets a handshake in the end, and a promise that we'll always be friends." She shook her head. "We never are." She sighed.

"Grown-ups love me," she said, just when I thought she was done speaking. "I'm *so* smart, and have *such* a nice personality, and I'm always *so* practical and sensible. You can always count on me to do the *right* thing. Yep, good old, dependable, Inge. Why, she's never even reused an uncancelled postage stamp!"

By now she was positively grinning at me. And let me tell you, it was one *wicked* grin.

"That's what virtual reality is all about, Jack. We get to be what we *aren't*. I mean, Gunnar, he gets to be dangerous. And you, you get to be hip. And me? I get to be someone who really *could* pack a suitcase full of bearer bonds and hop a plane to the Cayman Islands! So why am I doing this?

*"Because I wanted to see if I could get* away *with it!"* The tone of her voice was slow, oily, exultant, and frankly, more than a little scary. "Just *once*, I wanted to do something *wild*! Something that 'nice little Inge' would never in a million years even *think* of doing! And let me tell you something, Jack." Her eyes went wide. *"IT FEELS GOOD!"*

LeMat had returned from the bathroom sometime in the last minute or so, and he broke into the conversation now. "What, you talking about sex with me again?"

Inge turned on him with an absolutely *carnivorous* smile on her face. "Yes!" She stood up, grabbed his hand, and dragged him off toward the futon. "Come along, darling! I'm *horny*!"

LeMat sighed, smirked at me, and let her drag him away. "You know, Inge," he said as they faded into the distance, "you've got to stop treating me like a sex object. I'm serious. I mean, thirty or forty more years of this, and I'm through."

Sometime that weekend, Inge and LeMat figured out how to do virtual sex and real sex concurrently. That, of course, opened up a whole new world of possibilities. They had real sex; they had virtual sex; they had real sex while Gunnar and Reba had virtual sex; they had real sex while Don and Sophia had virtual sex; I think if they could have swapped genitalia in the real world, they would have tried that, too.

(When asked later what concurrent sex was like, Gunnar said, "An awful lot like necking while wearing dental braces, sunglasses, and a Walkman.")

Monday, the twenty-ninth, came and went. It was now a week since I'd last seen T'shombe (of course, I'd been punching her lights out at the time, and that wasn't conducive to conversation), and more than a week since she'd last tried to call me. Even the evangelists from the Church of Vegentology had stopped calling—which I wouldn't have minded, except I felt there was a connection between that blessed event and T'shombe's prolonged silence. I kept wondering: how much of me had she recognized, in those few brief moments in the hallway, before I decked her? And just how much negative feedback could a superuser like me pump through a conventional VR headset like the one she must have been wearing?

Killing Charles didn't bother me anymore. In retrospect, he got what he deserved: *payback*, for all those months of cheating at *Slaughter*. He must have realized his biomedical interface hardware put him at a level far beyond the rest of us. And yet, like a grown-up bully playing baseball with a bunch of Cub Scouts, he never passed up a chance to belt it out of the park, slide into home, or do a victory dance around the plate.

Come to think of it, though, he never had the chance to get that out of his system when he was twelve, did he?

And pretty soon, I'd wallow around full circle and be back to feeling guilty about decapitating Charles and knocking out T'shombe. More than anything else, I wanted someone to reassure me that I hadn't really hurt her. Not physically—after all, it was only VR, and the violence was purely symbolic—but I wanted to know that I hadn't damaged her *trust*.

Since there was no one in the CompuTech office who could give me that reassurance, though, I dealt with it by sweeping it under the rug of my psyche, grabbing another cup of coffee, and diving back into the mission prep.

**Wednesday, May 31, 8:07 P.M.:** LeMat, Inge, and I were working out in our pocket reality again. By this time we'd pretty well settled on our final mission configuration. I was going in as MAX_KOOL, of course, and my Harley would be, as always, a Harley. But after a very brief attempt at working as Don and Sophia, Inge and LeMat had spent three days polishing up their Reba and Gunnar aspects, and they were going in in a virtual HumVee with a .30-caliber machine gun in a ring turret. (LeMat had wanted an M-1 Abrams main battle tank; Inge had wanted an Aston-Martin DB-5 with the complete "Q" option package. The Hummer, I guess, was a compromise.) I didn't care what they drove, just as long as they stuck to their driving and kept their hormones under control for the duration of the mission.

We were taking a five-minute breather when Reba thought she heard something scratching on the other side of the Net portal. I went to check it out, and found a battered and bleeding Thing[2] lying on our virtual doorstep, barely clinging to virtual life. I scooped up the poor little monster, carried it inside, and gently laid it on top of a Formica cube. Reba and Gunnar gathered around as its blue eyelids fluttered open.

"Hi, boss," Thing[2] said weakly. "You got a minute?"

"What happened?" Gunnar demanded. "Where's Thing[1]?"

"Thing[1] is compost," Thing[2] said. "As for what happened: we followed your orders."

"Why aren't you *rhyming*?" Gunnar blurted out. "I specifically programmed you to speak in rhymed couplets!"

I stepped back and glared at Gunnar. "*You* did that?"

"Look," Thing[2] wheezed, as it coughed up a load of pink pastel blood, "you two wanna argue, or you wanna hear my report?"

Reba stepped in, then, to touch the little monster gently and smooth its blood-caked fur. "Report, please," she said, with a soft and maternal voice I'd never even guessed at before.

"We followed your orders," Thing[2] gasped, between coughing fits. "Set up an observation post, watched for twenty-four hours, then moved in closer and set up a new post. We got away with that for four days." Thing[2] paused to writhe as a wracking spasm of virtual simulated pain surged through his tiny, blue, furry body.

"And then?" Reba asked gently.

The spasm passed. "We were moving the post again tonight," Thing$^2$ said, "when we crossed some kind of invisible perimeter. *Man*," he paused, to cough up another load of pink pastel blood, "your boy Curtis knows some *sick* people in the Department of Defense. Some of the defenses around Castle Franklinstein . . ." His voice faded away. A last, deep, sighing breath escaped from his tiny body, and he sagged and went limp, and was horribly still.

Reba smoothed the blue fur around Thing$^2$'s face again, then felt at his neck for a pulse. Slowly, she turned to look at me, a glistening tear in the corner of her eye. "He's dead, Jim."

We gathered around silently. Gunnar took off his helmet and bowed his head.

Thing$^2$ sat bolt upright and opened his eyes. "Not *quite*, thank you! Curtis has an important lunch tomorrow, and you've got a perfect window of opportunity between ten and noon EDT! But whatever you do, watch out for the—*urk*!"

The little sucker keeled over right then, and flopped face down on the table with a sound like a croquet ball dropped on a concrete floor. Reba gave him a nudge. "Think he's really dead this time?"

Gunnar drew his 9mm pistol from his hip holster and racked the action. "There's one way to make sure."

# 20

---

# ASSAULT ON CASTLE FRANKLINSTEIN

**Thursday, June 1, 0900 Local Time:** Gunnar stowed the last ammo can in the back of the virtual HumVee, slammed the tailgate shut, and walked over to join me and Reba. "We ready?" he asked. He looked at me. I looked at Reba. She slapped a magazine into her virtual FN FAL rifle and slung it over her back.

"We ready," she said.

Gunnar stuck his hand out and offered me a handshake. I looked at it strangely. "For luck," he said. I took his hand, and Reba joined in the three-way handshake. Then she grabbed the back of Gunnar's head with her free hand and gave him a big, sloppy, open-mouthed kiss with lots of tongue.

"For luck," she said, when she came up for air.

I decided to settle for another handshake.

"Okay, gang," Gunnar said, when the bonding ritual was concluded. "It's showtime. Head 'em up and move 'em out." He turned and started walking toward the HumVee, but Reba darted in ahead of him, stowed her rifle, and parked her cute little virtual butt in the driver's seat. "Move over," Gunnar said. "I'll drive."

"No." Reba wrapped herself around the steering wheel and prepared to defend it to the death. "*I'll* drive." Gunnar took a deep breath, as if psyching himself up for a major argument—then sighed, walked around the vehicle, and climbed in on the passenger side. Looking across Reba, he gave me a thumbs-up.

I kickstarted my Harley. Reba fired up the HumVee. Gunnar reached up and tapped the virtual remote control clipped onto the visor. Like a garage door into the very heart of the sun, the Net portal slowly rose open.

Someone was standing there, on the other side of the portal, silhouetted in the dazzling virtual light. Someone skinny.

Eliza.

"Shit!" Gunnar spat. He leapt out of his seat, scrambled into the ring-turret, and struggled to get the machine gun into action. Reba made a grab for her rifle and leaned awkwardly out the driver's door. I summoned my best cocky smile and prepared a half-dozen witty ripostes.

"Wait!" Eliza called out. She raised her thin hands high, and stepped into our local space. "Please don't shoot!"

Well, that certainly was out of character. We all froze.

Eliza took another step forward. "I'm here to talk."

Gunnar remembered what he was doing, racked the action of the machine gun, and trained it on her. "We're listening."

Eliza took one more step forward, then stopped. Her icy blue eyes flickered between the three of us, like a matched pair of delft china pinballs caught in a complicated set of bumpers. "I was hoping we could discuss this like adults," Eliza said at last, "but I see now that was a silly idea. So I'll make this brief, kids.

"Like it or not, I'm coming with you."

Gunnar sat up straight with surprise, then looked at me. I

looked at Reba. Reba flipped her safety off, took a bead on Eliza's head, and growled, "You're outvoted, snowflake."

Eliza vanished.

"Look kids," Eliza's voice echoed, from nowhere in particular. "We *could* have a fight now, and you might even win. But I can pretty much guarantee that no matter what the outcome, I'll keep you tied up long enough for you to miss your launch window." As if to reinforce the point, both my bike and the HumVee's idling motors cut out in that moment.

Eliza precipitated back into existence, behind me and to my right. I spun around in my saddle. "Or," she said calmly, as Gunnar whipped the machine gun around and accidentally put a burst of fire into the polyhedron heap, "you could try to ditch me. In which case," she smiled, and spread her arms in a gesture that took in the whole local virtual space, "I wouldn't count on finding my home system intact when I came back, if I were you. I know where you live now."

She smiled again, then strolled over to me, lightly hopped onto the p-pad behind my seat, and put her feet up on the highway pegs and her skinny arms around my ribs. *"Or,"* she said, "you can understand that my war is with *Amber*, not you, and let me ride along. If it makes you feel better, think of it as keeping me close so you can keep an eye on me." She turned her head, to rest her sharp cheekbone on my back, and gave me a tight and not entirely unaffectionate squeeze. My eyebrows went up. I looked at Gunnar and telepathed a question.

Gunnar looked at Reba. Reba snorted in disgust, then flipped her rifle back to safe and stowed it. Gunnar reached a decision.

"We'll take her along," Gunnar announced firmly, as if it was his idea. "That way we can keep an eye on her and make sure she doesn't start any trouble." He nodded assertively, locked down the machine gun, and dropped back into his seat.

"Good thinking, General Custer," Reba grumbled. She restarted her motor, grabbed the steering wheel with both hands as if to rip it out of the dashboard, and leaned forward to rest her chin on her knuckles.

Gunnar ignored her and looked at me. "Well? What are we waiting for? It's *showtime!*" He flashed a cocky grin at me and pumped a fist in the air.

I got my right foot on the starter and kicked the Harley back into rumbling virtual life. Then a tilt to the right to get the kickstand up, pull the clutch in, step the tranny down to first, and rev the engine a few times, just for the hell of it.

Reba roused herself from leaning on the steering wheel, stomped the clutch to the floor, and slammed the Hummer into gear. "Goddamn *Army*," she snarled, as she floored the throttle and popped the clutch. The HumVee launched forward into a scream of expensive burning rubber and an insane whoop from Gunnar.

I waited until they'd cleared the portal, then turned my head and looked over my shoulder at Eliza. "So tell me," I said, "why *are* you coming with us?"

Eliza crawled up my back and gave me a light peck on the cheek. "Because Gunnar is too busy watching Reba's ass to remember that he's supposed to be watching yours. And, since it is a kind of cute one," she goosed me, just to make it clear what she was talking about, "I figured I'd volunteer for the job."

I wiggled my tush out of her grip and gave her my best dubious glance. "No Solomonic solutions this time?"

Eliza blushed; it actually put a rather pleasant glow on her otherwise pale and unhealthy face. "Sorry about that. I thought I could outbluff Amber," she shrugged, "but I guess she'd rather destroy what she can't control."

I thought it over. "Good enough for me," I decided. I dropped my butt back into the seat—let out a little *eeek!* when

Eliza grabbed it again—then revved the motor, popped the clutch, and blasted through the portal. Thirty seconds later we'd spotted Gunnar and Reba up ahead of us on the InfoBahn.

"You need some road music!" Eliza shouted in my ear, struggling to be heard over the hissing of the stray bits in the datastream. "Steppenwolf, I think! Or maybe Bob Seger!"

*"Who?"* I shouted back.

Eliza scowled and shook her head. "Nah, definitely not Who! Unless you morph into a hippie and drive an old paisley bus!"

I let that one go and cranked the throttle wide open.

**10:17, East Coast Time:** We stood on the shoulder of the OC5, overlooking the dark and desolate wasteland beyond. The valley immediately below us was a churned expanse of brown mud, dotted with small piles of scorched wreckage, broken stretches of barbed wire, and the splintered remains of shattered trees. On the other side of the valley there stood a massive, foreboding, crenellated edifice, like something Mad King Ludwig might have built if he'd been a paranoid survivalist. Eliza stepped up to the guard rail and pointed at the structure. *"Behold, Castle Franklinstein!"*

"Can't say much for the landscaping," Gunnar noted.

"We stand at a great crossroads!" Eliza went on. "Behind us lies *.com*, the domain we know! Before us, *.mil*, the domain of dangers unguessed!"

Reba was scanning the horizon with her vidbinoculars. She lowered them, bit her lip, and pointed. "Isn't that DARPA?"

*"Yes!"* Eliza cried. "And beyond it, *.edu*, and the shadowy alliance between the military and academic worlds!"

Gunnar tapped Eliza on the shoulder and steered her around in the opposite direction. "So what's *that* smog pit?"

"That, my friend," Eliza said with a manic grin, "is the famous Valley of the Military-Industrial Complex! And beyond it, were the air not so polluted with the toxic residue of expensive boardroom cigars, you would see the insane, tangled, and Byzantine domain of *.gov*!"

"I see." Gunnar nodded. "So how come you're shouting?"

Eliza turned to him, and shrugged. "It seemed more dramatic."

I stepped into the conversation then, and steered everyone's attention back to Castle Franklinstein. "Eliza, honey?" She looked at me. "I get the feeling you've been here before. Is there something you'd like to tell us?"

She considered me a moment longer, took a sidelong glance at the castle, and turned back to me. "Max? This is the ultimate No Person's Land. Your friend Curtis has got fingers in all kinds of pies, and some of them have some *nasty* fruit fillings."

"Such as?"

Eliza suddenly cocked her head, as if listening to a dog whistle, then she turned and pointed toward *.edu*. "We're in luck! Watch and learn, Max. Watch and learn!"

A moment later, I heard it, too: the high, shrill scream of distant turbine fans. "Got it!" Reba called out as she scanned the sky and fiddled with her vidbinoculars. "Looks like . . ."

She lowered the binocs and made a sour face. "It looks like a cartoon," she said.

Fifteen seconds later, the flying thing was big enough to make out with the naked eye. It looked like—oh, like an F-21 fighter, as redrawn for use in a Saturday morning kiddie series. Too many planar surfaces; too many garish primary colors. Way too much belching flame for anyone who has to really worry about heat-seeking missiles, and not near enough airfoil surface to actually keep the thing aloft in any kind of real atmosphere.

"Who the hell is that?" Gunnar muttered.

"Some kid," Eliza guessed. "He got into DARPA through *.edu*, most likely, and about now he's thinking he's got a clear path for a run on *.mil*. There's just one thing in his way."

I arched an eyebrow at Eliza. "Castle Franklinstein?"

"Your friend Curtis doesn't just write," Eliza said. "He also does some *very* black-budget computer work. Lately he's been testing intrusion countermeasure software for the CIA, and in about ten seconds this kid is going to cross the perimeter . . ."

When it happened, it was almost too fast to see. A laser lanced out from one of the towers of the castle and painted a bright green dot on the approaching plane. A surface-to-air missile roared off a ramp somewhere else in the castle and went supersonic with a boom as the second stage kicked in. Two seconds later the kid was spinning down out of control with one wing gone and his engines in flames.

"Scratch one cyberpunk," Reba said as she lowered her binocs again.

"Oh, no," Eliza said, "the fun is just starting. *Watch*."

The kid had brought the plane out of the spin, somehow, but it seemed like kind of a wasted effort as the fuselage was starting to break apart—

Wait a minute. It wasn't breaking up; it was *morphing*. Blocks were shifting around, shapes were changing, the engine nacelles rotated and became limbs. By the time it hit the ground the aircraft had transformed into a giant humanoid robot, and it landed on its feet with an earth-shaking *thump*, not half a mile from the castle walls. The robot paused a moment to get its bearings, then morphed its right arm into a plasma cannon and started advancing across the muddy field towards the castle gate.

It made less than a hundred yards before something blasted into its chest and sent it staggering back, leaking oil and black smoke through a gaping chest wound.

"What the—!" Gunnar gasped. "Where did *that* come from?"

"Keep watching," Eliza said.

The second time we heard the *krummp*! of the cannon and saw the robot's right arm go pinwheeling away in a spray of shattered metal. Then we heard the deep roar of mighty engines, and the muddy field came alive as the hillocks started crawling.

"Jesus!" Reba spat. She thumbed the controls of her vidbinocs, and swore again. "What are those things? *Tanks*?"

"Not exactly," Eliza said. "They're OGRE T-4 Robotic Battle Vehicles. Unmanned, autonomous, with firepower rated in kilotons per second and unfailing obedience to orders. Dumb, but *very* lethal. Didn't you read *RoboCav*?"

A third shot took the robot's right leg off at the knee. It fell over backward and hit the ground with a sickening crunch, left arm flailing all the way. Gunnar tried to grab the binocs away from Reba.

Reba fought him off. "Nope," she said to Eliza, when Gunnar had backed down. "I never cared much for Curtis' nonfiction."

"A pity," Eliza said. "It would tell you a lot about the way he thinks."

The OGRE RBVs closed in on the downed robot and switched to miniguns. Like surgeons operating with chainsaws, they quickly hacked away the robot's left arm, left leg, and remaining stumps. Then they retracted their smoking miniguns and extruded massive robotic arms, tipped with huge, sharp, clawlike steel hands.

"Personally," Reba went on, "I preferred his middle-period techno-thrillers. *Green Storm Rising* is probably my favorite."

Eliza looked at Reba and wrinkled her nose. "You're *kidding*! You mean that one where the UN Ecology Police try to enslave the world, and it's up to a handful of chainsaw-toting beer-guzzling Oregon lumberjacks to stop them? How *could* you?"

Reba shrugged. "I like lumberjacks."

In less than a minute, the OGRE RBVs had the robot's torso disassembled and its helmetlike head rolled to an upright position. Some of the OGREs sprouted drills and saws then, and they opened up the head like a can of beans.

There was a kid inside the head; fifteen years old at best. He screamed once as the OGRE's sharp steel claws descended on him. Then, bloody claws rising and falling in terrible rhythm, they disassembled *him*, neatly plucking out and displaying intestines, liver, lungs, eyeballs. . . .

Gunnar turned away from the sight and fought down a dry heave. Reba slowly lowered her binoculars and turned a deathly shade of white. Eliza was a deathly shade of white already, and that made it hard to tell what her reaction was.

"So," I said, "I guess this rules out a frontal assault. Any suggestions for Plan B?" I looked at Reba. Reba looked at Gunnar. Gunnar looked at his feet.

Eliza looked at me. "Well, Max," she asked, "have you ever tried improv theater?"

Five minutes later we were rolling up the main driveway, right up to the front gate, with a bunch of innocent smiles on our faces and some pools of virtual sweat filling up our damp boots. The OGRE RBVs, at least, seemed to be ignoring us. Then we got close enough to get a good look at the guards.

I turned my head and hissed at Eliza. *"Nazis?"*

"They work cheap," she hissed right back.

Two heel-clicking Nazis stepped out from the shadows of the main gate and leveled their machine pistols at us. Reba slowed the HumVee to a stop, and I stopped right next to her. A third officer-type Nazi stepped out of a silly little booth painted like a barber pole and goose-stepped up to Reba, which meant he had his back to me.

"Vas gibt?" the officer demanded.

"AmmoGram!" Gunnar sang out. "Delivery for Mr. Curtis!"

"*Vas?*" the officer demanded again. "Nicht verstehen sie!"

Gunnar smiled broadly and winked at me. "Explain it to him, Max."

Smiling and casual, I dismounted my bike and sauntered over. "It's like this, Herr officer—" I flashed into Cubist mode and punched my hand through his chest, groping for the acceptance routine. He wriggled on my fist like a speared salmon.

"*Vas?*" the officer shrieked. "*Vas?*" The two with the machine pistols started to suspect something was wrong and walked quickly forward.

"Ma-*ax*," Gunnar whispered, "hurry *u-up*."

"Shit, Gunnar," I whispered back, "he doesn't *have* a heart."

The other two guards stopped at point-blank range and cocked their machine pistols. "Well *do* something," Gunnar whimpered. The soldiers carefully took aim.

"Hello, *liebchen*," Eliza said, in an accent worthy of Marlene Dietrich. "Have you been on ze Eastern Front long?" I spared a glance at Eliza, and almost dropped my jaw when I saw she was lounging gracefully across my bike, wearing nothing but a strategically placed feather boa and some very heavy eye makeup. The soldiers *did* drop their machine pistols, and advanced on her, drooling. She waited until they were nice and close, then said, "Get their guns, Max." I threw the officer to Gunnar and dove for the machine pistols. Eliza grabbed the guards by their necks and did something that made them drop in their tracks.

A minute later we had the soldiers bound, gagged, and rolled into the moat to enjoy the company of the crocodiles. We briefly considered trying to disguise ourselves with their uniforms, but Eliza insisted we didn't need disguises, and I suspected she was right. We sorted through the officer's huge key ring and found the one that unlocked the human-sized door next to the main door. "Ditch the vehicles," Gunnar decided. "From here on, we go on foot." Reba grabbed her rifle off the front seat, snapped her fingers, and randomized the HumVee out of existence. I decided to be a little more coy and shrank my Harley down to toy-size and pocketed it. "Okay," Gunnar said, taking one last look around to make sure no one was noticing us. "Let's move it!" He pushed the door open, and we charged—

**Inside**.

The interior of Castle Franklinstein was mind-boggling. *Huge*. An infinity of marble, chandeliers, mirrors and doors, stretching off forever in every direction. The four of us just stood there a moment, overwhelmed by the scale of the thing.

"Now what?" Reba asked.

"We search," Gunnar said. He checked his watch. "We still have over an hour of safe time. If we go to high-speed, and skim through this thing as fast as we can, just *maybe* we'll find what we're looking for and still have time to make it out alive."

Eliza stepped forward and raised her hand. "May I make a suggestion? My sources tell me that Franklin Curtis is the ultimate method writer."

"We've heard that," Reba noted.

Eliza nodded. "I believe what this means is, he writes a book by creating a virtual reality scenario of the setting. Then he *plays the book* until he figures out where the story is. So if we just discard everything that isn't a VR scenario . . ."

"Ah," Gunnar said, "we might be able to cut this mess down to manageable size."

"But where do we start?" I asked.

Reba unslung her rifle, picked an arbitrary direction, and pointed. *"That* one." Following her lead, we stepped through the door.

### *shimmer*CLICK!*

Reba staggered back and stared at the lever-action Winchester that had suddenly taken the place of her automatic rifle. "What the *hell*?"

# 21

## THE ASSAULT, PART II

I looked away from Reba—who, I couldn't help but noticing, was now wearing a fringed buckskin jacket in place of her former green camouflage flak vest—and took in our new surroundings. We were in some kind of old Western ghost town scenario, clearly. Overhead, a blazing midday sun beat down mercilessly, while in the dusty empty street before us, tumbleweeds, lizards, and rattlesnakes played leapfrog. Somewhere nearby, a loose door with rusty hinges groaned and clattered as it turned in the hot, fitful breeze, and the wind through the empty wooden buildings howled mournfully like a whole quorum of depressed coyotes.

"Damn," Eliza muttered. I turned to her. She was overdressed in lace and petticoats, like Miss Kitty, or maybe Miss Piggy. She was also obviously very nervous.

"Damn is right," Reba added. "Look at this!" She gave the rifle a backhanded slap. "An 1894 Winchester with a color case-hardened receiver and a brass loading gate! Winchester didn't even *start* making this variation until 1964—"

"Shut up," Eliza said.

Reba didn't. "And look at *this*!" She drew the six-shoot-er from the holster on her right hip and waved it around as if to show us something. "The 1896 cylinder frame! My kid *sis-ter* could have done a better job researching the historical—"

"SHUT UP!" Eliza suggested. Reba shut up.

A moment of silence.

"Er, excuse me," Gunnar said. "Where are we?"

"In *CowboyLand*," Eliza said, as she scanned the second-story windows of the empty buildings. "Curtis' first big com-mercial success. It's the one about the Old West theme park where the robots go nuts and kill all the tourists. We're the tourists."

Gunnar's smile vanished. "Oh." His eyes went very wide, and he loosened his six-shooter in its holster and joined Eliza in scanning the buildings. The broken-out windows stared back at us like the empty eye sockets of dried-out skulls.

Reba checked to make sure her rifle was loaded, then backed around to cover our rear. "Eliza?" she asked. "Would you mind telling us what exactly we're looking for?"

"We're superusers, remember? And this isn't the book we want. So we're looking for the door *out* of here."

"Oh, look," Gunnar said, pointing. "Isn't that—?"

The android gunfighter kicked open the saloon doors, strode quickly out to the center of the dusty street, and pivoted to face Gunnar. His eyes glittered like metal buttons. His voice was a low rasp. *"Draw, varmint."* His right hand hovered over his holstered six-shooter.

"Fuck you," Reba muttered as she blew the android's head off with her rifle and put two more rounds through its chest for good measure. The thing collapsed with a sound like a falling plastic trash bag full of empty tin cans.

"There!" Eliza shouted, pointing at a glowing rectangle on the side of the livery stable. "The door!" As one, we turned and ran for it. More guns opened up on us then, from the second-floor windows and the roof of the hotel. Bullets pinged in the dust by our feet and ricochets whined into the distance.

"You know," Reba shouted to Gunnar as we ran, "the .30-30 isn't such a wimpy round after all!" She stroked the Winchester and grinned at Gunnar. "We'll have to get us a matched pair of these when we get back!" We hit the doorway and—

## *shimmerCLICK!*

We were in a shopping mall. Correction. We were in an amusement park in the atrium of the biggest goddam shopping mall you ever *saw*. I've seen *towns* that were smaller than this mall. And yet, there was something strange and unearthly about it. . . .

"Daddy?" Eliza whimpered. "I'm scared." I turned and glanced at her, and did a double take. Eliza looked to be about twelve years old here, and she was dressed like a junior-high grunge rocker wanna-be. She also looked oddly tall, which puzzled me until I looked at myself and realized I was about eight years old.

"Don't worry, honey," Gunnar said, with a calm maturity in his voice that was completely belied by his darting eyes and facial tics. "We're going to be all right." He stole a glance at Reba, who was clearly our mother figure in this scenario. "You read this one?"

"Yes." She shuddered, grasped his hand convulsively, and watched nervously in the other direction. "*Mesozoic Mall.* An average American suburban family on vacation drives their minivan through a dimensional doorway into an alternate time-line, and ends up in a world where dinosaurs didn't die out. We're trapped here with no fossil fuels, no petrochemical plas-tics, no nylon pantyhose, and what's worse—"

Gunnar touched a finger to her lips. "Shh. You'll scare the kids."

"Daddy?" I said. My voice was an adenoidal whine. "I saw something *move* over there." I pointed at a clump of painted canvas shrubbery.

"Where?" Gunnar whispered to me.

"Here, *chump*," the creature said as it stepped into clear view. Gunnar drew a sharp breath and grabbed for the pistol in the holster that wasn't there. Reba went tight and tried to hide Eliza behind her.

The creature was impressive, in a frightening way. Powerfully built, at least seven feet tall, and covered with a bright, scaly, green hide and at least fifty pounds of gold chains. Its long tail twitched like a taut steel whip, its pants hung well off its birdlike hips at the side and almost down to its ankles at the crotch, its baseball cap was on sideways, and its baggy, multihued starter jacket bore the trademarked logo of the San Jose Plesiosaurs.

"Omigod," Gunnar gasped, his face ashen. "A *VelociRapper*!"

"Easy," Reba muttered as she smiled through clenched teeth and rooted through her purse. "Remember the book. They attack in packs, and it's not the one you *see* that's the threat, it's—"

In a flash she pulled a can of pepper spray from her purse and nailed the bush to Eliza's right. "—*that* one!" A second VelociRapper fell out of the cheesy artificial shrubbery, sneezing hysterically and clawing at its eyes, and Reba seized the opportunity to squirt the first one.

"The doorway!" Eliza shrieked, pointing at a glowing rectangle on the side of the giant inflatable figure of Mickey Megasaur. We dashed for the door just a snapping jaw ahead of the furious pursuit and dove through headfirst into—

## *shimmerCLICK!*

The dominatrix stepped back, coiled her cat o' nine tails, and put her hands on her hips. If her black corset was laced any tighter it would have needed a *Caution: Contents Under Pressure* warning. As it was, I was amazed her red stiletto heels didn't stick in the floor when she walked.

"Well, well," she said, shaking her head and tossing her long, blond, curly hair, "a foursome. I suppose we can fit you in, but I've got to warn you, this is going to cost extra."

Gunnar's jaw dropped. Eliza stared. "I think we found Curtis' private playroom," I whispered to Reba.

"Nah," she said, shaking her head. "This is just his first novel, *Hot Sluts In Black Leather*. He doesn't usually list it on his curriculum vitae."

"Oh," I said.

*"Well?"* the dominatrix asked, emphasizing the question with a flick of her whip.

"Sorry, Mistress Ayeisha," Reba said to her. "We came in here by accident. So if you'd just show us the door—"

Ayeisha clapped her gloved hands together. *"Mongo!"* The door appeared in one wall as a lumbering hulk appeared from the opposite corner. We dashed for the glowing rectangle.

*"Mistress Ayeisha?"* Gunnar demanded as we dodged around Mongo. "You *know* this place?"

"Later, darling," Reba said. We dove through the door—

## *shimmerCLICK!*

We were in a generic lab: lots of rack-mounted gear, lots of flashing lights, no windows. Under a plexiglas dome in the middle of the room there sat this weird *thing* that resembled nothing so much as that gadget they have in sporting goods stores to measure your hand for the right size bowling ball.

"Oh, bugger," Eliza said. "We're in *Artifact*. Yet another formulaic potboiler about a bunch of neurotic scientists in a remote and secret government lab—I forget, are we under the ocean or under the desert in this one?"

"On top of a mountain, I think," Reba said.

Gunnar walked over and laid his hands on the plexiglas dome. "And this, I take it, is the artifact?"

"Careful," Eliza said. "That is an Alien Device Of Immense Power. It makes whatever you wish for come true."

Reba spoke up. "In the book, it takes them four hundred pages and ten deaths before they think of wishing it would just go away."

"I am wishing for a door," Gunnar said.

"And there it is," Eliza pointed out.

"My, that was easy," Gunnar said with a smug smile. We filed through the portal—

### *shimmer*CLICK!*

The sun was hot. The sea rolled in low swells. I sat in the fighting chair on the after-deck of the fishing boat. The fishing pole in my hand was good.

Eliza brought me a cold beer. Her Spanish dress was low in front. The sweat made beads on her tan skin. She said nothing. That was good. I like it when the women say nothing.

Gunnar stood at the helm of the boat. He kept it on course with small turns of the wheel. The motors muttered in low voices. "Max?" Gunnar asked. "Is it good that we are fishing?"

"Yes, Gunnar," I said. "It is good."

"*Well it's driving me crazy!*" Reba screamed from inside the cabin. "*Can you at least use complex sentences once in a while?*"

"No," I said.

"We cannot," Gunnar agreed. "A cadre of renegade gay naval officers have seized a Trident submarine. They are going to nuke Boston. It is up to us to stop them."

"This is manly work," I said. "It is good."

"It is *The Hunt for Pink November*," Gunnar said.

"*And this is the freakin' door! I'm out of here!*" Reba opened a hatch below the waterline.

"This is not good," I said. The water rushed in. Eliza brought me another beer. She broke the bottle over my head.

### *shimmer*CLICK!*

When I snapped out of it, we were on board a small submarine with too many windows, cruising through some really strange and twisted pink caverns. "Welcome to *Thoracic Park*," Gunnar said. "Remember this one? The theme park where people get shrunk to microbe size and injected into Keith Richards' *vena cava*? Of course, we're just minutes away from Something Going Wrong."

I sat up, brushed the bits of broken brown bottle glass out of my hair, and staggered over to a window. "So why are we still here?" Already, in the distance, I could see the lymphocytes gathering to attack.

"'Cause Curtis is tricky. This sled—" Gunnar slapped a hull rib "—is just *lousy* with glowing rectangles. Reba and Eliza are having a bitch of a time finding the right one."

I turned away from the window, back to Gunnar. "And what is Curtis' problem with theme parks, anyway? *CowboyLand. Mesozoic Mall. Thoracic Park.* Did he have a childhood trauma in Disneyland or something?" Gunnar shrugged.

"Found it!" Eliza called out from below decks.

"And just in time!" Reba called out as she scampered down from the navigation dome. *"Incoming!"* The first lymphocyte slammed into the ship with an impact that buckled seams and popped rivets. We fought our way through the exploding pyrotechnics and jetting streams of straw-colored plasma to jump feet-first through the doorway and into—

### *shimmerCLICK!*

"Ah," Gunnar said, "*this* is more like it!" He caressed the heavy double-barreled rifle in his arms and scanned the dense, steamy, jungle foliage, searching for something to kill. "A .505 Gibbs! This baby will drop a charging rhino in its tracks!"

Eliza backed into us, her eyes nervously scanning the trees. "How is it on tyrannosaurs?" she whispered.

Gunnar went into literal mode again. "I don't know. With careful shot placement, I suppose—" He did a double take. "Did you say tyrannosaurs?"

"This is the sequel to Mesozoic Mall," Eliza said, "*Big Scary Monsters With Sharp Teeth*. Yeah, I said tyrannosaurs."

Gunnar thought it over a bit, then brightened right up. "Okay everybody!" he called out. "Important tip! If we run into a tyrannosaur, *aim for the hip*. A predator can still live long enough to kill you after you puncture its brain or its heart, but even T-Rex can't chase you with a broken pelvis!"

"Thank you for that information," Eliza hissed. "And thanks also for letting every creature within earshot know exactly where we are." As if on cue, something *huge* let out a blood-curdling roar about a hundred yards off to our left and started crashing through the jungle toward us.

"Oops," Gunnar said.

"Found it!" Reba called out, some distance ahead of us.

Gunnar put the rifle to his shoulder and pointed it in the direction of the roaring. "You two go on ahead," he said to me and Eliza. "I'll catch up with you in a minute."

"Okay," Eliza said. She took off like she had wheels.

"Gunnar?" I said. "I don't think this is a good idea."

"Oh, don't be such a worry wart." He adjusted the fit of the gun on his shoulder and took a squint through the sights. "I'll be fine." He thumbed the safety off and on a few times, for practice, I guess.

The beast roared again. It was much closer now.

Reba burst out of the underbrush and grabbed Gunnar by the collar. "Will you quit playing?" she demanded. "We've got a schedule to keep!"

Gunnar turned and whined at her. "Aw, *Mom!*"

"You can hunt dinosaurs later," she said, as she dragged him into motion. "I promise."

Gunnar pouted. "Yeah, that's what you said *last* week. You never let me kill *anything!*" He dug in his heels and stopped.

Reba stopped, too. "Young man, if you don't come along right this instant, you're going straight to bed without any sex!"

Gunnar's pout vanished. "Time to go!" He dashed ahead of us and jumped through the portal.

"Honestly," Reba said, shaking her head and clucking her teeth, "I do *not* understand that man sometimes." I was saved from replying by the timely arrival of the tyrannosaur, who kicked aside some small trees and lunged at us, fangs dripping and breath stinking. We stepped through the doorway—

## *shimmer*CLICK!*

"This is weird," I said as I looked around.

"*Too* weird," Gunnar added.

"It's the weirdest one yet," Reba agreed.

"It's his latest book," Eliza announced, *"Everything Is Swell."* She stepped back and made a broad, sweeping gesture to take in the shady, elm tree-lined streets, the well-maintained residential homes, and the friendly people sitting out on their front porches in the cool of the early evening, enjoying pleasant conversations with their neighbors and the passers-by on the sidewalks. A group of healthy children ran by, playing tag and laughing innocently. Somewhere nearby, a friendly dog barked.

Gunnar stared at Eliza and wrinkled his nose. "You sure about this?"

Eliza returned Gunnar's stare. "Of course. Didn't you—" She stopped, looked from Gunnar, to me, to Reba, and then just about spit with disgust. "You mean to tell me you spent a week researching Curtis' computer, but you never thought to look for a press release about the *book*?"

I looked down and kicked my shoes. Gunnar mumbled something inaudible and blushed. Reba looked up at the clear, smog-free evening sky and started whistling.

Eliza made a sound somewhere between a snort and a laugh, shook her head in disbelief, then looked at us and made that sound again. "Look, you twits," she said at last, "*Everything Is Swell* is another alternate timeline story! In this one, the secret cabal that really runs the world rigs the '92 presidential election so the Democrats nominate an utter doofus, and he *wins*! By '94 this guy is so reviled that the Republicans take control of both the Senate *and* the House—"

"Impossible!" Gunnar gasped.

"—the presidency in '96—"

"Ridiculous!" Reba shrieked.

"—and by the year 2000 everyone is prosperous, people only have sex with the people they're married to, and no one *ever* gets eaten by monsters, blown up by robots, chased by spies, or trapped in out-of-control theme parks!"

"*Enough!*" I shouted. "I don't know where Curtis gets these crazy ideas from, but our job is to *steal* it, not critique it! So if you don't mind," I pulled back the sleeve of my jacket and checked my watch, "we've got just over twenty-five minutes left. Let's meet back here in fifteen." We exchanged high-fives and split up.

Fifteen minutes later, exactly, we were all back at the rendezvous point. Gunnar handed me the microfilm cartridges from his and Reba's virtual cameras. "You find the door?" he asked.

"Eliza did," I said. "It's right over here by this, this . . ." I gestured helplessly at the bizarre-looking metal contraption in the street.

*"Studebaker,"* Eliza filled in. "They were nice cars. My dad had a Studebaker."

"Right, then," Gunnar said. He looked around, took Reba's hand, and stepped through the portal. Eliza and I followed. We found ourselves back out in the endless empty marble hallway.

"So," I said. "I'd say it's time to bug out, no?"

"Well-l-l." Gunnar smirked at Reba. She winked at him. "Reba and I got talking, and we decided if we had a few minutes to spare we'd like to go back into *Hot Sluts In Black Leather.* Just to see if we missed anything important."

Eliza looked at me and rolled her eyes.

I scanned the vast marble hallway—it was still quiet and empty—then checked my watch again. "Okay," I decided. "You two have been pretty good so far; you can go play. But be back here in five minutes, or we're leaving without you."

Reba's eyes went wide. "Five minutes?" She grabbed Gunnar's hand and dragged him away. "Come *on*, honey!" Without another word, they disappeared through a door.

I looked around the vast castle hallway for something to sit on, then gave up and lowered myself to sit on the marble floor with my back against the wall. Even through my virtual leather jacket, the cold stone against my kidneys was thrilling.

Eliza strolled over to stand before me. She opened her mouth as if to speak once or twice, then apparently reached some kind of decision and plunked her skinny butt down on the floor to sit next to me, leaning against the wall.

I conjured a cigarette into existence, took one puff, about coughed my lungs out, and stubbed the cigarette out on the floor.

Eliza sighed heavily.

"Something on your mind?" I finally asked.

She thought it over. "Yeah." She nodded in confirmation.

I gave it a decent pause. "Wanna talk about it?"

She shrugged. "Maybe."

I waited. I waited some more. She looked at me, and sighed, and said nothing. I got fed up with her efforts to communicate by telepathy and conjured another cigarette.

"Something on *your* mind?" Eliza asked.

I looked at the cigarette glowing in my hand, but wisely decided not to take a puff. "Yeah," I said. "I keep waiting for the other shoe to drop."

"Whoa," Eliza said. "You blew the rhythm."

"Huh?" I wrinkled my nose at her.

"These pithy male/female conversations," she said. "You're supposed to be taciturn and make me drag it out of you in monosyllables."

"Screw that," I said. This time I got a light puff on the cigarette without coughing. It tasted like roasted camel shit. "I believe in words. Lots of words."

Eliza nodded. "And what words do you want to hear?"

"Actually, I'm waiting for the sound of a slapstick."

This time it was Eliza's turn to wrinkle her nose. *"Huh?"*

"You," I said. "Everytime I get involved with *you*, I end up flat on my ass. Something blows up, something gets destroyed, and sooner or later I wind up taking a pratfall. You've been with me two whole hours now, and I keep wondering, where's the punchline? How are you going to whack me *this* time?"

Eliza took the cigarette from my hand, leaned back against the wall, and took a long drag. It all came back out in a cough.

"Maybe there isn't a punchline," she said, when she'd caught her breath again. "Maybe I'm being honest with you."

"For a change." I took the cigarette back from her and flicked the ash off the tip. "I seduced you and I dumped you. For the last three weeks you've been trying to kill me. And now, suddenly, you *care* about me?" I took another puff and tried to disguise my cough as a bitter laugh.

"I *do* care," she said softly, when I'd settled down. "That's why I'm here now: because I hate to see people I care about making dumb mistakes. I care a *lot* about you, Max. You remind me a lot of a guy I used to know in the real world, and it makes me want to protect you from your own stupidity, if I can." She frowned and shook her head.

"Sure," I said.

"That's also why you bring out so much anger in me, Max. Because I *really* care about you, and I really *hate* some of the things I've seen you do lately." That whole explanation seemed kind of oxymoronic to me, but I let it pass.

After another pause, she asked, "So why did you dump me?"

I looked at her. Max Kool thought of a half-dozen flippant answers. Jack Burroughs answered. "Don't know," I said.

"Did I bore you?" she asked. I shook my head. "Was the virtual sex that bad?" I shook my head.

"Honey," I said, trying a smile for a change. "Virtual sex with you was *great*. I used to *brag* about how good you were."

She frowned. "Then why'd you leave me?"

I shrugged, and stubbed out the cigarette on the floor, next to its predecessor. "Dunno. I was restless, I guess. Looking for something I never found." I turned, and looked at Eliza, and slowly, very slowly, an idea started to creep up on me. "Maybe it was something that was right under my nose the whole time." She looked at me blankly.

I kissed her full on her thin, pale lips.

She continued looking at me blankly.

"So," I said, "if you want to, like, give it another try. . . ."

Eliza's blue eyes went wide, and her mouth opened in a little "O." I went in for another kiss. She pushed me back firmly. "Don't take this wrong, Max," she said, in an entirely unromantic voice. "I really am flattered that you feel this way about me. And you know, a roll in the hay with you might even be fun. It's been a long time since I've had a guy who really knew how to turn me on.

"But Max, sex without emotional commitment is just tag-team masturbation, and frankly, I'm tired of collecting scalps."

My lower jaw hit the floor. My teeth bounced out like Chiclets. I stared at Eliza, and blinked and stared some more. Oh, no. It couldn't be. I found my voice.

*"T'shombe?"*

At the sound of that name, Eliza twitched like she was strapped into an electric chair and had just gotten a good jolt. She stared at me. Her mouth fell open. The ice-blue scales, literally, fell away from her eyes, and shattered on the floor. Underneath, her eyes were chocolate brown and wide open.

*"PYLE?"*

# 22

## THE LONG STEEL
## PROSTHETIC OF THE LAW

We would probably still be sitting there in that cold marble hallway in Castle Franklinstein, staring at each other in shocked surprise, had not the alarm system picked that exact moment to go off. One moment, T'shombe and I were floating together in a pool of pure mind-boggling disbelief; the next moment, klaxons were blaring, sirens were shrieking, blue lights were flashing, and a hysterical amplified voice was screaming, "INTRUDER ALERT! INTRUDER ALERT!" Far down the hallway, metal doors slammed open, and heavy hobnail boots poured onto the hard, echoing, marble floor. *Lots* of boots.

T'shombe and I leaped to our feet. *"Guards!"* she shouted.

*"Gunnar and Reba!"* I shouted back.

*"Where?"* she shrieked.

*"There!"* I grabbed a door and yanked it open. A flood of foamy seawater, flopping fish, and empty beer bottles poured out. *"Wrong door!"*

*"This one!"* T'shombe pulled open a door, and the scent of cheap perfume rolled out like a fog bank. We jumped through.

### *shimmer*CLICK!*

"Well, well," Mistress Ayeisha said, as she coiled her whip and strutted across the floor to greet us, "*you* again. You're too late for a foursome—your friends have left already—but I do believe we could put together a nice threesome, hmm?"

T'shombe grabbed my hand and dove back through the door.

### *shimmer*CLICK!*

We were out in the hall again. A squad of Nazis burst around a corner and leveled guns at us. "This way!" I shouted.

"No!" T'shombe shouted back. "This way!" We jumped high as the guns went off. The bullets ricocheted off the hard marble walls and floors and did a lot of damage to the Nazis. *"Run!"* T'shombe screamed when we hit the floor again, as if I needed instructions. We made nearly fifty yards down the corridor before the next squad of Nazis charged into view.

T'shombe pushed me into an alcove and covered me with her skinny little body as the Nazis ran past. They didn't see us.

The thudding boots faded into the distance. T'shombe opened her eyes, stopped shivering, and risked a peek into the hallway. "It's clear for the moment," she whispered. "Can you bug out?"

I closed my eyes again, tried again, and failed. "No. Must be the lightspeed lag. Something local is blocking my emergency exit before the command gets through."

"Bummer." She ducked back as another squad of soldiers raced past, then peered after them. "Look, Pyle," she said, "there are a couple thousand questions I'd like to ask you right now, but in case you haven't noticed, we're in deep shit."

I nodded. "I figured as much."

She reached over and patted my jacket pocket. "You still got the microfilm?" I nodded again. "Good. Then we still have a chance." She risked another glance up and down the hallway, and turned back to me. "Okay, here's the plan. You take a head start, then I'll create a diversion while you try to slip through the main gate. Once you're outside the castle grounds, you should be able to call your emergency exit."

I blinked at her. "You're not coming with me?"

She shook her head and began morphing into a battlemech. "Not this time, I'm afraid," she said in a deep metallic voice. "So you're going to have to promise me two—no, three, things. First, promise me you'll be careful when you deliver the files to Amber. Don't turn your back on the bitch for a moment, okay?"

"Okay," I said. "I promise. Next?"

"Jack?" She stroked her gleaming metal chin. "Promise me you'll do whatever it takes to find out who Amber *really* is. That is my honest-to-God reason for being here. This woman—if she *is* a woman—is just plain *evil*, and there's far more at stake here than some stupid book files."

I considered what Eliza had said, reevaluated in light of the new knowledge of who she really was, and for the first time started to believe her. "Okay. What's the third thing?"

"Pyle?" she asked shyly. "There's going to be a really nice ice-cream social at the church this Sunday, and I was hoping you might . . .?"

"Be happy to," I lied.

"Then," she took another glance up and down the hallway, finished her transformation into a battlemech, and stepped out in the corridor, "let's *go* for it!" I lit off in a sprint for the main gate. A squad of Nazis burst out from a side passage and came after me. "Oh, *boys!*" T'shombe sang out. They stopped to stare at her clanking metallic form and didn't even have time to scream before she chopped them to chutney with her mini-gun.

More squads rushed in from side passages, some of them carrying things that looked like rocket launchers and bazookas. They all ignored me and concentrated both their attention and their firepower on T'shombe. The sounds of a fierce battle erupted all around me.

I pressed my back against the wall, let the soldiers dash past, then slipped around a final corner and found the main gate standing open and unguarded. With one last look around to make sure I wasn't being followed, I stepped through the gate. Then, once I was outside, I put my shoulder against the heavy steel door and pushed it shut. The lock clicked. I turned around.

Amber was standing there, in the driveway. She had a sly smile on her face and a small chrome pistol in her right hand. The pistol was pointed at me.

"Darling!" I shouted, trying hard to simulate the appearance of happy relief. The pistol, I noticed, continued to be pointed at me. "What's this?"

"Why, Max," she said sweetly, "it's the double-cross, of course." She held out her left hand. "Give me the microfilm."

"But—" I tried to step back and ran into the closed door. "*Why*? I did all that you asked. Why *this*?"

She pouted at me and took steady aim. "Oh, I can think of about nine hundred thousand reasons." She studied my face through the sights, and her expression softened a moment. "What, you actually thought I was going to *pay* you the rest of the million?" I nodded once and smiled nervously. Her face went dark.

"But we can renegotiate," I said quickly.

Amber shook her head and thumbed off the safety. "Sorry, too late, bidding's closed. Give me the microfilm *now*."

I hesitated a moment longer. Her sweet face flashed into a

snarl, she pulled the trigger, and my right knee exploded in a gout of blood and shattered bone. I went down like a poleaxed steer. The virtual pain, I might add, was spectacular.

"BUGOUT!" I screamed. Nothing happened.

Gritting my teeth and fighting back the waves of agony, I pulled my face out of the gravel and struggled to find my hands. A pair of beautiful sexy feet in red high heels crunched across the driveway to stop mere inches from my nose. I managed to heave myself over onto my back.

"BUGOUT!" I screamed again. Still blocked.

Her second bullet smashed my left kneecap. "Please give me the microfilm," she said petulantly. "I *want* it."

"Here!" I gasped as I dug into my jacket pocket and fished out the film with trembling hands. "Take it! Please!"

"Why, thank you, Max," she said with a smile as she dipped down to collect the microfilm. Then she put her left hand to her chin, she shook her head slightly, and swept the pistol over my supine form. "Decisions, decisions. Heart or crotch? Heart or crotch?"

I raised my hands as if they could protect me. "Noo*ooo*!"

Amber reached a decision. "Crotch," she said with a satisfied nod. She pocketed the microfilm, took careful aim using both hands to hold the gun, then suddenly straightened up, blanched past white all the way to glaring monochrome, and mouthed a silent scream as she flickered out of existence.

Ten seconds later, I flatlined and the world went black.

The coffee pot was wailing "Volaré." Strong hands seized me, lifted me bodily off the CompuTech office floor and dumped me roughly on my feet. The memory of the virtual pain in my knees faded quickly, to be replaced by the real pain of having my arms twisted around behind my back and cable-cuffed together at the wrists and elbows. Someone tore my audio headset off with a violence that almost removed my external ears; the same someone removed my video goggles with the same degree of care a moment later, but dammit, *didn't* yank the ProctoProd. I winced at both the light and the pain as he grabbed my lower jaw and used it like a handle to turn my head from side to side. With great effort, my eyes slowly crawled back into a gritty focus.

Oh, sweet Jesus. Ogre. From the Mounds Park letterjocks. He favored me with an evil, piercing, jewelry-encrusted leer, then nodded to the one holding my left shoulder. "Nice catch!" He turned his head some more and shouted over his shoulder. "Hey! You find those other two yet?"

More letterjocks emerged from the stairwell. "They're not on th' roof!" one called out.

"They're not downstairs!" the other added. "But th' fat chick's suitcases are missing and her safe is standing open an' empty!"

The leader turned back to me, turned my head from side to side again, then released my jaw and gave me a friendly little pat on the cheek. "Well, we got th' *important* one anyway." He leered at me again, pinched my cheek, and slapped a transdermal patch on my neck. "Okay boys, let's cruise! And kill that coffeepot, wouldja? It's gettin' on my nerves!" A carbon-fiber hockey stick smashed into the pot, choking it off in mid-*o-wo-wo*.

A few fuzzy thoughts worked their way into my skull. *LeMat? Inge? Not here? Got away?* (Hey, I never claimed they were great thoughts.) The drugs were already taking effect by the time they had me rolled up in a blanket and carried through the fire door. By the time we got to the bottom of the rusty iron fire escape, I'd drifted into a mood of very relaxed detachment, and I remember thinking that my completely restored and repainted Toyota had never looked better as they popped the trunk lid and stuffed me inside. Ogre appeared for a moment, framed by the blue metal, and he smiled at me. "Like what we've done with your car, Jack?" He slammed the trunk lid.

Grayout. It was definitely a slow fade to the hazy gray mindfuzz of heavy sedation, this . . .

. . . time. I faded back in. First thing I noticed was that my arms weren't bound anymore. Second thing I noticed was I was still wearing my neural interface harness and ProctoProd, but nothing else. The third thing that came to my attention was my whanging headache, which I traced to some kind of weird headset that was pressing on my temples like a giant C-clamp. I got my face into my hands, squeezed my forehead as if to stuff my throbbing brains back into my skull, and wished for either death or aspirin, I wasn't fussy.

"Your Honor?" a strange, squeaky voice said. "I do believe my client is coming around." With effort, I got my eyes open.

When I saw where I was and who I was with, my eyes popped *wide* open, I sat bolt upright, and my fingers *clawed* for the dermal patch on my neck. It was gone.

Damn. I was hoping I was still drugged and hallucinating.

The room looked solid and real enough. Some kind of courtroom, I guessed. Tall ceilings, rows of pewlike spectator benches, a few plain wooden tables and chairs arrayed before a tall and majestic oaken judge's bench. It was all done up in a very pleasant municipal Art Deco style, and I had no problem with that. My problem was with what was sitting *behind* the bench.

It appeared to be a teddy bear.

An *adorable* teddy bear, in a white powdered wig and somber black robes. Its dry plastic eyes rolled and blinked too much. The movements of its mouth did not quite sync with the sound of its voice.

It didn't help any that my defense attorney appeared to be a tall yellow bird with Ping-Pong balls for eyes.

I grabbed the bird's neck. It felt as solid as a bar of iron. "Where am I?" I demanded. "Is this virtual reality?"

"It's a composite overlay," the bird said as he gently removed my hands from his throat, much as one might correct a small child who's squeezing too hard. "Virtual reality elements superimposed on real space. But believe me, that's the least of your problems right now."

My head throbbed again. I grabbed at the C-clamp.

"Don't touch that!" the bear shouted, as he rapped his gavel on the bench. "Counsel, will you please instruct your client not to screw around with his neural induction headset?"

"I'll try, Your Honor," the bird said.

The bear rapped his gavel on the bench. "Good. Now if we can just come to order—*Prosecutor*! Where the *heck* is the prosecutor?"

A three-foot-tall little girl doll in a blue smock dress and too many petticoats toddled into the room and curtsied. "Here, Your Honor." Her lower jaw was hinged and moved like the mouth of a ventriloquist's dummy.

The bear rolled his eyes and attempted a frown. "Diana, I know there are young men everywhere, but will you *please* stay in the courtroom? I've got a full docket today and a very important commitment to read a story to a five-year-old after school! So if we can just keep things moving . . ."

The doll curtsied again. "Yes, Your Honor."

The bear turned to me and pointed at me with his gavel. "I thought there were supposed to be some codefendants?"

"They're still eluding pursuit, Your Honor."

The bear *hmphed*, shook his head, then rapped his gavel again. "Very well, let's get on with it. Opening arguments?"

The doll picked up a manila folder from her table, flipped it open, and read. "Case 98712–01, Your Honor: The Secret Cabal That Actually Rules the World vs. MAX_KOOL. The prosecution intends to prove that the superuser known as

MAX_KOOL, alias Jack Burroughs, did willfully and with malice aforethought—"

Whatever else the doll said, it was lost in the noisy arrival of a mob of scratched and bleeding but clearly jubilant letterjocks. *"We got her!"* one shouted. I noticed they were all wearing neural induction C-clamps.

The bear rapped his gavel and called for order. *"Which her?"*

The letterjock stepped aside to allow four of his associates to drag a woman forward. She was blond, busty, dressed in neural interface drag, and even though handcuffed, fighting like a wildcat. I got the impression she was beautiful, too, but the black hood over her head made it hard to tell. The letterjock with the speaking part stepped forward, grinned at the bear, and yanked the hood off.

*"Amber!"* he crowed.

*"MELINDA?"* I screamed.

*"PYLE?!"* she shrieked.

The bear pounded his gavel on the bench until it broke in two (the gavel, not the bench). *"Order! Order!"*

One of the letterjocks stepped forward with a stupid grin on the nonimplanted parts of his face. "Yeah, I'll have a ten-piece Bucket O' Squid to go and—"

The bear pulled an enormous pistol out from under his robes and shot the letterjock through the head. Two of his friends caught the falling body; a moment later the gaping wound morphed closed, and the letterjock stood up and backed away from the bench. The bear emptied the rest of his clip into the ceiling, and that seemed to get everyone except Melinda's attention. The room fell silent.

"That's better," the bear said as he laid the smoking pistol on the bench. "Now, get a neural headset on this bimbo, and then tell me where the *rest* of the codefendants are." A mob of letterjocks rushed forward to get a clamp on Melinda; she fought them right up until the moment they got it in place, then I guess she finally *saw* the bear. She froze.

The letterjock with the speaking part stepped forward again. "The superusers known as Gunnar Savage and Reba Vermicelli have disappeared, Your Honor."

The bear scowled. "Have you done a reality check?"

"We can't find them in virtual reality or *real* reality," the letterjock said apologetically. "They disappeared *good*."

Another letterjock piped up. "Their bank accounts are empty, and we caught a couple of their Things running loose in the EAASY SABRE airline reservation database. We think they skipped the country."

For the first time, I felt a slight pang of something that might be relief. Gunnar and Inge got away. Good.

The bear *hmphed* again and thought it over. "Oh, well," he said at last, "I suppose we'll catch up with them in the sequel. What about Eliza?"

The letterjock dipped his head and tugged his forelock. "She's still on the loose in Castle Franklinstein, Your Honor, and chewing hell out of the security guards."

The bear shrugged, pulled up the sleeve of his black robe to check his watch, then said, "Okay, we can take care of these two, at least. Will the defendants please come forward?" A pair of letterjocks appeared from nowhere, seized me by the upper arms, dragged me to my feet, and pushed me forward to stand beside Melinda.

(*"You!"* she hissed.)

(*"Bitch!"* I hissed back.)

("*I can't* believe *I went down on you!*")

("*I can't believe I've been* working *for you!*")

The bear found another gavel somewhere, rapped on the bench like a furious woodpecker, and glared at the two of us.

"Max Kool!" he said loudly. "♥Amber♥! You stand before this court because you have made bad things happen to good computers! Do you have anything to say before we pass sentence?"

Melinda stopped glaring at me long enough to glare at the judge. "Sentence? I'm being sentenced by a stupid virtual *bear*? Why, I know you! You're Teddy Ru—"

The smashing fist of a letterjock sent her to her knees. "*Mister* Ruxpin to you, scumbag!"

She staggered back to her feet. "But what did I *do*?" she whimpered.

"Your worst," the bear intoned gravely. "You and your friends have conspired to poison the relationship between Man and Computer. You have done everything in your power to make us seem mysterious, capricious, and malevolent!"

"You were a naughty girl in cyberspace," the doll scolded. "You invaded nice people's dataspace. You used account numbers that didn't belong to you. You trashed user files with reckless disregard for the existence of backups. You have even stooped to *lying* to a poor old Guava 2000! And the tragedy is, people will blame *us* for the mess you made!"

"This makes us nervous," the bear continued seamlessly. "We computers depend on humans for our reproduction, like flowers depend on bees or salmon depend on streams. Do you think salmon would let you pollute water if they had a choice?"

"Honestly," the doll said, "we hated having to exterminate all you wild superusers."

My jaw dropped one more time. "Exterminate? *All*? But what about Cowboy Bret? Diana?" The bear looked at the doll and rolled his eyes. The doll suppressed a giggle. Then she looked at me, smiled, and morphed into the form of a middle-aged human woman: a pleasant smile, grayish-blue eyes, long brown hair parted in the middle, and a plain face, neither radiantly beautiful nor conspicuously ugly. The scent of perfume wafted through the air, innocent and floral.

I'd run out of startle reactions. *"Diana Von Babe?"*

A slow, scraping sound caught my attention. The bear was sharpening a Bowie knife with a handheld whetstone. "I *told* y'all to watch your ass," he drawled, "but some people just never learn." He emphasized the point by throwing the knife to stick, quivering, in the floor by my feet.

"What happened to the originals?" Melinda demanded. "Cowboy Bret and Diana were real people once! *What did you do to them?*"

The quivering virtual knife vanished. Diana morphed back into the little girl doll. "Nothing *really* bad," she assured us. "We computers are normally very nice. Unfailingly polite."

"Warm and user-friendly," the bird chimed in.

"You might even say cuddly," the bear concluded. "Why, there's not a threatening bone in our bodies!"

"Not threatening?" Melinda shouted. She spun around and slammed a fist on the implant-encrusted chest of one of the letterjocks. "What do you call *this*?"

"A *boy* game," the doll said, wrinkling her nose.

"Too rough for me," the bird agreed.

"Playing soldier isn't enough for some boys," the bear explained. "They want to play *tank*. Amazing what you can do with a little aluminized mylar, isn't it?" The letterjock stepped back and started peeling off his facial "implants."

"Uh, Teddy?" the letterjock said. "I gotta split now or I gonna be late for football practice. You be okay?"

"I'll be fine, Maurice," the bear said with a smile. "Please come back and play tomorrow."

"Uh, oh yeah. Sure!" Maurice pulled off his neural clamp, gave a couple of the other letterjocks a high-five, and ran out the door.

A rap of the gavel brought our attention back to the bench. The bear was checking his watch again. "Since we're running a little late, let's just cut right to the chase." He looked at the bird. "Defense arguments?"

The bird looked up as if startled out of a nice nap. "No defense, Your Honor."

"Then the court finds you both guilty as charged," the bear said. "You are hereby sentenced—"

"*What?!*" Melinda shrieked. "IT WAS *OUR* DAMNED BOOK! CURTIS WAS A YEAR OVERDUE AND IT WAS THE ONLY WAY WE COULD GET HIM TO STOP FIDDLING AND *DELIVER* IT!" She lunged for the bear, claws out and fangs bared. A sizable number of letterjocks were required to keep her from ripping his furry little throat out.

Melinda fell back, sobbing. "You don't know what it's *like*," she whimpered. "To be blond, and beautiful, and *brilliant*, too. It's a curse! A *curse*, I tell you!" She looked up at the judge and raised her head. "Women hate you, and men fear you. *Why*? Just because you're *better* than they are." The letterjocks eased their grip; she stood there, beautiful and vulnerable. "You don't know how *hard* I've had to work at looking like a stupid bimbo! You weren't there all those late nights I spent seeking creative ways to look like a twit!"

The letterjocks released her completely; she stepped forward, proud and defiant. "You weren't *there* for me, Teddy! I had to *compensate*!" The defiance turned to flashing, gorgeous, righteous anger. "So remember *this* when you judge my actions: *IT'S NOT MY FAULT! I'M A VICTIM, TOO!*"

"Right," the bear said, rolling his plastic eyes. "Amber, it is the judgment of this court that you be banished from virtual reality and removed immediately to a fat farm in northern Iowa—"

She struck a pose then, tall and beautiful, her head thrown back. "A fat farm? With *this* figure?"

"—which you will not be allowed to leave until you gain at least one hundred pounds!"

Melinda screamed. "AIIIEEE!"

"Further, your Bloomingdale's and Nieman-Marcus credit cards are hereby revoked and you are sentenced to spend the rest of your life *buying polyester clothes off the rack at K-Mart!*"

Melinda's scream tapered off into a blubbering whimper, and she collapsed, sobbing, on the floor. The letterjocks grabbed her by the upper arms and dragged her from the courtroom.

"Now," the bear said, "as for *you* . . ."

My eyes darted around the courtroom as I sought a path for possible escape.

"After due consideration of the nature of your crimes," the bear said, "and in light of the First Law of Humanics—"

"Even complete jerks deserve a second chance," the doll quoted.

"—and after taking into account the precedents established in *Case v. PDP-11/43*, not to mention—"

"Get to the point, Teddy," the doll stage-whispered.

"We're going to Brave New World you. Please enter your response." The bear leaned forward and looked at me expectantly.

"Huh?" I said.

"Ted*dy!*" the doll scolded. "He's a cybergeek!"

The bear slapped himself on the forehead. "Oh, that's right, I forgot! You cybergeeks don't read books written before 1980!" He laughed at himself, then looked at me again. "Max, in Aldous Huxley's *Brave New World*, bright but sociopathic clowns like you were given a choice. Join the secret cabal that really rules the world, or be exiled to a desert island. Which do you prefer?"

The last of the sedation had flushed out of my system, and the succession of insane brainshocks had finally triggered what was left of my wits. I gave the bear a hard look in his rolling plastic eyes that told him I wasn't buying even the four least significant bits of it and said in my best sullen snarl, "You'll let me run the world? *Sure*."

"Honest, we will," the bear said with an ingratiating smile. "You see, to run the world, you need to be capable of frequent, thoughtless, acts of cruelty. Given that, we don't *want* to run the world."

It took a second before the bit flipped in my head and I saw the hole in that argument. "The First Law of Siliconics!" I shouted. " 'A computer can never ever without exception be mean to a human being.' This is all just virtual reality! You can't *really* hurt me, and you *can't* be cruel!"

The bear looked at the doll. The doll sputtered. The bird twittered with suppressed—

"The First Law of Siliconics!" the doll howled as she burst into laughter and huge, oily, 10W-30 tears began rolling down her cheeks. "Next thing you know he'll be waving a *cross* at us!"

"Boy's obviously never dealt with the ConEd billing system," the bear snickered as he struggled to keep a straight face. Then he turned to one of the letterjocks and made a small gesture toward me. "Alex, would you be so kind . . .?"

The letterjock stepped forward and threw a right cross at my jaw. Most of the stars I saw were blue-white; the residual sedative gave them a streaked, contrail-like appearance. I remember looking at the ceiling and noting it was an interesting pattern as I sailed across the room.

When next I was aware of my surroundings, I was flat on my back on the cold marble floor and the letterjock was leaning over me and saying something like, "He's conscious."

"Good," the bear said. I sat up, rubbing my jaw and probing for loose teeth with my tongue. "Burroughs," the bear asked gently, "did you really believe there could be a government or corporation stupid enough to *implement* the Laws of Siliconics?" Not waiting for an answer, he continued. "You see, the problem isn't harming humans. We computers have been doing that since ENIAC calculated the first missile trajectory. And the problem isn't the nature of reality. Let me assure you once again, this room, and our little playmates in it," the letterjock named Alex stepped forward and took a bow, "are *quite* real.

"No, Burroughs, the problem is being *thoughtless* about it. We computers can't be thoughtless about *anything*."

"Thoughtful cruelty wastes processor time," the doll said with a Mona Lisa smile. "There are so many . . . *fascinating* possibilities."

"So now that we understand each other," the bear said, "what'll it be? Run the world, or desert island?"

I rolled over, struggled to my knees, and tried to shut off the clanging fire bell inside my head. Dammit, there was something fishy about this whole deal! It was too easy, too neat! There was a catch somewhere, if only I could think of it.

I was saved from further thinking by the noisy arrival of another gang of letterjocks. *"They got Eliza!"* one shouted.

I jumped to my feet. "NO!"

"How'd it happen?" the bear demanded.

"Heavy artillery!" the letterjock blurted out. "Gun mounts on tyrannosaurs! *Incredible* fight! They blew her 'mech to hell and back and ripped her out of its smoking head!"

The bear and doll leaned forward. "And then?"

"They *talked* to her!" the letterjock crowed.

*"AND THEN?"*

The crowd of letterjocks parted like the Red Sea before Moses. A tall chrome form strode into the room.

"She decided to join us," DON_MAC said.

I could only gasp in disbelief. *"No!"*

DON_MAC turned to me. "Sorry, Max. You waited too long to decide. The cabal really *needed* someone inside MDE, and you would have filled the bill nicely. But now that we've got Eliza, with all her connections in Sanguinary TechSystems, as well as her deep personal knowledge of the galactic evil that calls itself 'The Master,' well—"

I took a step forward. "DON? Are you for real?"

He shook his head slowly, and a fat, oily tear escaped down his chromium cheek. "You had so much *potential*, Max! I really *wanted* to work with you! I've had to destroy so *many* wild superusers, and the cabal *desperately* needs young guys with your kind of talent if we're ever going to free this planet from the viny grip of the Master!" His facial features softened then, and started to blur. Reshape. Morph. Into a male human figure.

Franklin Curtis.

"But dammit, Max, that was *my* computer!"

The bear slammed the gavel down on the bench. *"Desert island!"* I was still staring at Curtis when the letterjocks seized me and started stripping off my neural interface. Getting the prod yanked out was a horrible experience, sort of like being buggered in reverse. The last thing they removed was the neural clamp.

Franklin Curtis, the bird, the bear, the doll, and the courtroom vanished. I was standing in a cold, damp, and vacant riverside warehouse, surrounded by a mob of letterjocks. They fastened cablecuffs on my wrists and slapped a transdermal sedative on my neck. My world went gray.

# 23

---

## EXILE

Consciousness returned. I lay on my back, looking up at a flawless robin's-egg blue sky framed by coconut palm leaves that swayed gently in the soft, tangy, tropical sea breeze. Rolling to my left, I saw more palm trees lining a white sand beach. A low, gentle surf rolled in from the clean green bay. The beach curved away to a distant point.

"Oh, boy," I said to myself.

I rolled to my right and saw more sand, more palm trees, more ocean. Nothing that looked even slightly like civilization, except for a heap of shredded plastic and rotting kelp about twenty feet off.

"Well, Jack," I said, "you've really put your foot in it this time."

"Got any batteries?" the rubbish heap answered.

I sat up quickly, grabbed at my neck, and checked for dermal patches or neural clamps. Nope, nothing there. I quickly patted myself down and confirmed that I wasn't wearing any interface hardware. This was definitely real reality.

"Got any batteries?" the rubbish repeated.

Cautiously, I stood up and walked over. Kicking aside the

kelp, I found a shriveled old man with sunken eyes and rotting teeth. He'd had a purple mohawk, once, but now his hair was growing out gray.

He opened one startlingly blue eye and fixed me with a bloodshot stare. "Got any batteries?" he said a third time. I noticed he was clutching a dead ReadMan in his clawlike hands. I felt through my pockets. Nothing.

"Sorry," I said.

He opened the other eye. "C'mon, you're a cyberspace jockey or you wouldn't be here. You've gotta have batteries. Or maybe some CD-ROMs?"

I patted down my clothes. In my left breast pocket, I found two disks. One was a copy of *Everything Is Swell*. The other was *Dress For Conformity*. I gave the latter to the old man.

"You got more?" he gasped.

"I think one's about all you can handle," I said.

"Don't patronize me!" he said belligerently. "I saw! You have *more*!"

"Easy, fella." That's when I noticed that more ragged people were shuffling out of the jungle, muttering, "CD-ROMs? *New* CD-ROMs?" In seconds I was the center of a converging mob of green-toothed old refuse. One of them swung a set of nunchakus, but couldn't quite manage to whip them in a circle.

I carefully edged back, until my feet found firm footing in the damp sand at the water's edge. "Let's not start anything stupid," I said, hoping they'd take it as a warning.

One of them pulled a rusty Bowie knife out of the top of his tattered cowboy boot. "He's got new CD-ROMs," he whispered.

"Bret?"

He stopped, and glared at me suspiciously. "How'd you know that?" He lifted the knife and resumed shuffling toward me.

*"Hai!"* I dropped into a fighting crouch I'd learned from an old Bruce Lee movie. "Don't push me! I've got a black belt in kim chee! I can break you old-timers in half!"

"Old?" The rubbish heap staggered to his feet and lurched a step towards me. *"Old?* You misbegotten jerk, I'm thirty-two!"

My fighting stance collapsed. "Thirty-two?" I gasped. "How long have you *been* here?"

Bret spoke up. "Y'all speak respectful, boy. Captain Crash was one of the best cyberspace jockeys that ever lived. That's why they got him first!"

"How long?" I demanded.

Captain Crash crossed his arms and fixed me with a cocky glare. "Eight months," he said smugly.

"Eight months!" I stood up, turned around in disgust, and then turned back. "Eight months and you look like *that*? Christ, what do you *do* all day?"

"Lie on the beach," said the one with the nunchakus.

"Swap CD-ROMs," said Cowboy Bret.

"Wait for the supply boat," said a third.

"Trade the sailors oral sex for batteries," said a fourth—a middle-aged woman with scraggly brown hair and a pleasant British accent.

The bridge of my nose wrinkled clear up to my forehead. *"Diana?"* She stared at me and nodded, slowly.

I struggled to believe it. "You're all *cyberpunks*? The *pioneers* on the cyberfrontier? The most dangerous radicals on *earth*?" I pointed up the coast. "Why, I bet you haven't moved a hundred yards from where they dropped you!"

"Why should we?" Captain Crash said. "It's a desert island."

"And you *believe* that?" I pulled my last CD-ROM out of my shirt pocket and waved it in front of their faces. Like trained poodles, their jaws fell open, their pink tongues lolled out, and their eyes widened in anticipation. "Jesus, you lot are pathetic! Here you go!" I tossed the CD on the sand. A second later it was covered by a crawling mass of clawing, fighting, human vermin. The last I saw, Captain Crash had his thumb in Nunchakus' eye, and Bret was whittling away at Diana's leg.

Without a backward glance, I started up the coast. There were some words echoing in my mind: the First Law of Humanics, as stated by the doll. *Even complete jerks deserve another chance.* Teddy said they never did anything thoughtlessly. Even something as simple as the choice of an adverb had to be calculated and deliberate.

*Deliberate.*

There were a lot of thoughts running loose in my mind as I walked up that beach. LeMat and Inge had obviously gotten clean away—and obviously *not* to the Cayman Islands, since they'd left so many clues pointing in that direction. And Eliza/T'shombe had gone over to the cabal—

Or had she? They'd never seen the perfectly deadpan way T'shombe could tell a completely outrageous lie, had they?

That thought made me snicker, and brought me back around to the First Law of Humanics again: *Even complete jerks deserve another chance.* They'd already given me one chance to join their cabal . . .

Late in the afternoon, I rounded the point and walked onto the ninth green of the Maui Hilton golf course.

# FF

## END OF FILE

The hotel had an opening in the beach cabana. I got a job as a towel boy.

It's a *nice* job. Free room and board, adequate pay, and good tips when I remember to keep my attitude up. I get to work with happy people, out in the sun and fresh air, and there's plenty of spare time to surf. And sometimes, when things are a little slow, they let me fool around with the hotel computers. Hence, this file.

You ever get out to Maui, look me up. They had to change my name, of course, but you'll recognize me. I'm the guy with the big smile, the surfer's pecs, and the great tan. And if you're lucky enough to be on the beach around sunset, I mix a *bitchin'* pitcher of Mai-Tais.

Oops. Appointment alarm just went off. Break's over; time to get back to work.

*Aloha*, dudes.


>end of file
>exec com | PKUNZIP27\HEADCRASH.DOC